AN AMISH HOPE

OTHER NOVELS BY THE AUTHORS

BETH WISEMAN

THE AMISH SECRETS NOVELS

Her Brother's Keeper

Love Bears All Things

Home All Along

THE DAUGHTERS OF THE PROMISE NOVELS

Plain Perfect

Plain Pursuit

Plain Promise

Plain Paradise

Plain Proposal

Plain Peace

THE LAND OF CANAAN NOVELS

Seek Me with All Your Heart

The Wonder of Your Love

His Love Endures Forever

OTHER NOVELS

Need You Now

The House that Love Built

The Promise

An Amish Year

Amish Celebrations (Available July 2018)

STORIES

A Choice to Forgive included in *An Amish Christmas*

Ruth Reid

The Mercies Novels
Abiding Mercy

Arms of Mercy

The Amish Wonders Novels
A Miracle of Hope

A Woodland Miracle

A Dream of Miracles

The Heaven on Earth Novels
The Promise of an Angel

Brush of Angel's Wings

An Angel by Her Side

AN AMISH HOPE

THREE STORIES

Beth Wiseman

Ruth Reid

Kathleen Fuller

 **ZONDERVAN**®

ZONDERVAN

An Amish Hope

Copyright © 2018 by Elizabeth Wiseman Mackey, Ruth Reid, Kathleen Fuller

This title is also available as a Zondervan e-book.

Requests for information should be addressed to:
Zondervan, *3900 Sparks Dr. SE, Grand Rapids, Michigan 49546*

Mass Market ISBN: 978-0-7852-1758-9

Wiseman, Beth, 1962–
An Amish Hope / Beth Wiseman, Ruth Reid, Kathleen Fuller.
pages cm
    2013025298

Scripture quotations are taken from THE NEW KING JAMES VERSION ©
1982 by Thomas Nelson, Inc. Used by permission. All rights reserved. And
from the Holy Bible, New International Version®, NIV®. Copyright © 1973,
1978, 1984, 2011, by Biblica, Inc.® Used by permission of Zondervan. All
rights reserved worldwide. www.zondervan.com

Any Internet addresses (websites, blogs, etc.) and telephone numbers in
this book are offered as a resource. They are not intended in any way to be
or imply an endorsement by Zondervan, nor does Zondervan vouch for the
content of these sites and numbers for the life of this book.

Publisher's Note: This novel is a work of fiction. Names, characters, places,
and incidents are either products of the author's imagination or used
fictitiously. All characters are fictional, and any similarity to people living
or dead is purely coincidental.

Printed in the United States of America

18 19 20 21 22 / QG / 5 4 3 2 1

CONTENTS

Glossary

ab im kopp: off in the head, crazy
ach: oh
aenti: aunt
appeditlich: delicious
Ausbund: Amish hymnal
ausleger: undertaker
baremlich: terrible
bauch: stomach
bauchduch: napkin
boppli, bopplin: baby, babies
bruder: brother
buwe: boys
daadi, grossdaadi: grandfather
daag: day
daed: dad
danki: thanks
Das Loblied: Amish hymn of praise, sung in every
    Amish worship service
Demut: humility
Derr Herr: God
dippy eggs: eggs cooked over easy
Derr Herr: God
Dochder: daughter
du bischt wilkumm: you're welcome

dumm: dumb

dummkopf: dummy

dummkopp: dunce

dummkEnglisch or Englischer: a non-Amish person

familye: family

fraa or frau: wife

Frehlicher Grischtdaag: Merry Christmas

freind: friend

freinden: friends

fremm: strange

froh: happy

gebet: prayer

gegisch: silly

geh: go

gern gschehne: you're welcome

gern schöna: so willingly done

glay hotsli: little heart (endearment)

grank: sick

grossmammi/grossmutter: grandmother

grossvader/grossyatter: grandfather

guder mariye: good morning

gut: good

guten nacht: good night

gut-n-owed: good evening

gutguckich: good-looking

gut: good

hallo: hello

halt: stop

haus: house

hatt: hard

herr: mister

hiya: hello

hochmut: pride

Ich liebe dich: I love you

in lieb: in love

kaffi/kaffee: coffee

kalt: cold

kapp: prayer covering or cap

kichlin: cookies

kind, kinder, kinner: children or grandchildren

kinn: child

kumm: come

lieb: love

liebschen: dearest

maedel or maed: girl or girls

mamm: mom

mammi: grandmother

mann: man

mei: my

mudder: mother

naerfich: nervous

narrisch: crazy

nau: now

nee: no

net: not

nix: nothing

onkel: uncle

Ordnung: the written and unwritten rules of the
     Amish; the understood behavior by which the
     Amish are expected to live, passed down from
     generation to generation. Most Amish know the
     rules by heart.

Pennsylvania Deitsch: Pennsylvania German, the language most commonly used by the Amish

perfekt: perfect

recht: right

redd-up: clean up

rumschpringe: running-around period when a teenager turns sixteen years old

schee: pretty

schtupp: family room

schul: school

schweschder: sister

schwester/schwestern: sister/sisters

sehr: very

sehr gut: very good

Sei se gut: please

Seltsam: weird

Sohn: son

The Budget: a weekly newspaper serving Amish and Mennonite communities everywhere

Was iss letz?: What's wrong?

wedder: weather

welcum: welcome

Wie bischt?: How are you?

Wie geht's: How do you do? or Good day!

willkumm: welcome

wunderbaar: wonderful

ya: yes

yer: your

yummasetti: a classic Amish hot dish made with spaghetti, cheese, and hamburger

A Choice to Forgive

Beth Wiseman

CHAPTER 1

Lydia opened the front door, expecting her friend Sarah or one of the children's friends. Instead, a ghost stood in her doorway, a vision from her past—*Englisch* in appearance, Amish in her recollection of him. A man long buried in her heart and in her mind, he couldn't possibly be real. But his chest heaved in and out, and his breath clouded the air in front of him, proof that he was no apparition. He was real. *He* was Daniel Smucker.

Up till this moment, Lydia was having a routine day, busying herself with baking and household chores. On this Thursday afternoon she was enjoying some solitude while her children visited her sister Miriam for a couple of hours. Chilly November winds whipped around the farmhouse, hinting of a hard winter to come, but a cozy fire warmed the inside of the hundred-year-old structure. Aromas of freshly baked pies and cookies wafted through the house—shoofly pie and oatmeal raisin cookies—just like her mother used to bake when Lydia was a child.

Lydia smoothed the wrinkles in her black apron, tucked strands of dark-brown hair beneath her white prayer covering, and headed to the front door, thankful to God for all that she'd been blessed with. Three beautiful children, a lovely home, and a church community that encouraged her to be the best Amish woman she could be, especially since the death of her husband two years ago.

Elam's fatal heart attack shocked everyone, especially since there was no family history of heart problems. After he died, Lydia had struggled to get out of bed each morning, but with the help of the Old Order district, she and the children were doing much better.

Today she was trying to keep her thoughts in a happy place, one filled with hope for the future, the promise of good times with friends and family during the upcoming holiday season, and a blessed Christmas to celebrate the birth of their Savior.

Then she opened the door, and this man's presence threatened to steal all that she'd been working toward.

"Hello, Lydia."

He stood tall before her in black breeches and a black coat buttoned to his neck. His half smile was enough to produce the boyish dimples she remembered from their youth. His sandy-brown hair, now tinged with gray at the temples, reminded her how much time had passed since she had seen him—eighteen years.

His voice was deeper than she remembered. But his slate blue eyes were unmistakably the eyes of her first true love, tender and kind, gentle and protective, reflective of a man she'd known as a nineteen-year-old girl. And now he stood shivering on her doorstep, clearly waiting for an invitation to come in out of the cold.

But Lydia couldn't speak. She couldn't move. And she didn't want to ask this man into her home—this man who had once promised to marry her, then disappeared from her community and her life in the middle of the night. And on Christmas Eve, no less.

But that was a long time ago, and she'd gone on to marry his brother. Thank goodness Elam had been there to comfort her after Daniel's desertion. Elam, the man she was meant to be with, whom she'd married and shared fifteen wonderful years with.

"Do you think I could come in for a minute?" Daniel finally asked, teeth chattering. "My ears are frozen." His smile broadened.

Lydia swallowed hard and took a deep breath. She was trembling, but not from the frigid air blowing in from behind him. Had he come to ask for forgiveness after all these years? Curiosity compelled her to motion him through the threshold.

As he brushed past her, he began to unbutton his coat and then hung it from a peg on the coatrack near the door—the coatrack *Elam* built. She scowled as she reached for the garment to move it, but stopped herself when she realized there was nowhere else to hang it up. Her arm fell slowly back to her side, and she watched Daniel walk toward the fireplace as he scanned the room—a room filled with memories of the life she'd lived with Elam.

Daniel warmed his palms above the flames for a moment and then focused on her husband's collection of books on the mantel. He gingerly ran his finger along each one, studying the titles. Lydia cringed. *Those are Elam's things.*

"You've made a fine home, Lydia." He pulled his attention from the books and turned to face her.

His striped *Englisch* shirt reminded her that his Amish roots were long gone.

"You are more beautiful than I remember."

Lydia couldn't recall the last time she'd thought about Daniel, but suddenly old wounds were gaping open. "What are you doing here, Daniel?"

He walked toward her as if he might extend his arms for a hug. She backed away and walked to the other side of the room.

He raked his hand through his shaggy hair, hair not fit for an Amish man. He wasn't Amish, she reminded herself, and hadn't been for many years. What length he chose to wear his hair was of no concern to her.

"I just thought you should know that I have talked to my family, and also to Bishop Ebersol. I'll be baptized back into the community two Sundays from now."

Lydia's heart was thudding against her chest. Had she heard him correctly?

"I'm back for good," he went on. "I'll be making my home at the old Kauffman farm up the road, eventually. Right now, I'm staying with my parents." He smiled again.

"*Ach*, I see." She nodded, then turned away from him and took a few steps. She folded her arms across her chest and tried to steady the quiver that ran from her toes to the tip of her head. "What made you decide to come back?"

She heard his footsteps close the space between them, and as he hovered behind her, she recognized his scent. Oddly, it was as though he still used the same body soap, toothpaste, and whatever else made him smell the way he did. She breathed him in, closed her eyes, and imagined his arms wrapped snuggly around her waist, his lips nuzzling her neck, the way he'd done so many times back behind the barn following the Sunday singings.

Lydia silently chastised herself for having such thoughts. She blinked away any signs of distress and turned to face him.

Daniel shrugged. "It's time. My family is here. My roots. I want to live out the rest of my life here."

He sounded like an old man on a course with death, not a man of a mere thirty-eight years.

"But you can't just go be *Englisch* for eighteen years, come back, and expect to just—to just be welcomed back into the community. You've been shunned, for goodness' sake." She shook her head. "I don't understand."

"You know as well as I do that if I seek forgiveness from the bishop—which I have—and commit myself to the *Ordnung*, then I can be rebaptized into the community. And that is what I choose to do."

This can't be happening, Lydia thought, as she soaked in what he was telling her.

"I'm hoping you'll forgive me too," he said softly, with pleading eyes.

Lydia knew that forgiveness freed the soul of an unwelcome burden, and she'd forgiven Daniel many years ago. So what were these resentful feelings spewing to the surface now?

"If God can forgive me, if the bishop can forgive me . . . maybe you can too."

"I forgave you a long time ago, Daniel." *Even though you left me one night without a word.*

Daniel breathed a sigh of relief. "I'm so glad to hear that. I know that leaving a note wasn't the best way to handle things."

It was a terrible way to handle things. Lydia recalled

Daniel's hand-scribbled missive. He'd left a similar letter for his parents, telling them all that he could no longer adhere to the strict guidelines of the Old Order district and that he would be heading out into the *Englisch* world.

She quickly reminded herself what a wonderful life she'd had with Elam for fifteen years, a life she wouldn't have known if she had married Daniel. Nor would she have Anna Marie, now sixteen; Jacob, who'd just turned twelve; or nine-year-old John. "I suppose everything turned out as it should."

Daniel's brows drew together in an agonized expression, but he didn't say anything.

Lydia studied him for a moment, wondering exactly how much his being here would affect her and her family. Quite a bit, she decided. And she knew that to harbor any bad will toward Daniel was not only wrong in the eyes of God, but it would also hurt her more than anyone else. She would need to pray hard to keep any bitterness away.

"I just thought you would want to hear the news from me," Daniel finally said.

Lydia nodded, then walked toward the door, hoping he would follow.

Daniel reached for his coat on the rack. He looked like he had more to say, but Lydia didn't want to hear any more. His presence was enough of an upset for now. As she reached toward the doorknob, the door bolted open, almost hitting her in the head. She jumped back and bumped right into Daniel, whose hands landed on her hips. She slid sideways and out of his grasp instantly.

"*Aenti* Miriam sent this lemon pie," Anna Marie said. She handed Lydia a pie as Jacob and John bounced in behind her.

John closed the door behind him, and all three of her children stood barely inside the doorway, waiting for an introduction. And Lydia realized that Daniel's return was going to complicate her life in more ways than one. Her children had a right to know their uncle, but did Daniel really deserve to know her children? He hadn't even shown up for Elam's funeral. His only brother. But her children were waiting, and so was Daniel.

"Children, this is Daniel, your *daed*'s *bruder*."

Lydia watched as Anna Marie, Jacob, and John in turn extended a hand to Daniel, who smiled with each introduction. Lydia wondered if maybe she was dreaming all of this. A disturbing dream, one she hoped to wake up from any minute.

"Very nice to meet you all," Daniel said.

"Your *Onkel* Daniel will be making his home here in Paradise, at the old Kauffman place," Lydia said. Not even a half mile down the road. "Right now, he is staying with your *mammi* and *daadi*." Lydia steadied her voice and tried to appear casual in the presence of her children. "He is being rebaptized into the faith."

Lydia's sons nodded, then excused themselves. But Anna Marie eyed Daniel with suspicion. "You are dressed *Englisch*," she said.

Daniel shifted his weight. "Uh, yes, I am. I haven't been in town long, but I'll be stocking up on the traditional clothes."

Anna Marie narrowed her eyes into a scrutinizing gaze. "Where've you been?" She paused, but before Daniel could answer, she added, "Why weren't you at *mei daed*'s funeral?"

Good question, Lydia thought, as she waited to hear Daniel's answer. Elam had told the children that their uncle chose a life with the *Englisch,* and that he was shunned for doing so after baptism. But he never told them that their mother almost married his older brother before she married him.

Daniel rubbed his forehead, and Lydia could see the regret in his expression. "It's a long story," he said.

Anna Marie, a spirited girl in the midst of her *rumschpringe*, questioned everything around her. Daniel's return was no exception. "I have time," she said. She edged one brow upward and lifted her chin a tad.

Lydia cupped her hand over her own mouth to hide the grin on her face. Anna Marie reminded her so much of herself at that age. She glanced at Daniel, who seemed rattled by the inquisition.

"I'm sure I'll be seeing lots of you. We can talk later," he said to Anna Marie. His eyes shifted to Lydia.

Lydia pulled from his gaze, and his words echoed in her mind. *I'll be seeing lots of you.*

She and the children had remained close to Elam's parents and his two sisters and their families. Of course, his family would be including Daniel in all of their activities from now on, which would indeed mean that Lydia and her children would see him often. It wouldn't be fair to the rest of the family to keep away just because Daniel was in the picture now. Lena and Gideon had been wonderful to their grandchildren, and to Lydia, since Elam's death. So had the rest of the family. But they all had to realize how strange this was going to be for her.

"Fine." Anna Marie responded flatly to Daniel's offer to talk later. "*Mamm*, I'm going to go finish sewing Jacob's shirt upstairs." She studied Daniel hard for a moment. "Nice to meet you." And she headed up the stairs.

"They're beautiful children," Daniel said when Anna Marie was out of earshot. His tone was laced with regret.

"*Ya*, they are." Lydia pulled on the doorknob and swung the door wide, allowing the chilling wind to coast inward. She had no parting words.

Daniel pulled his coat from the rack and slipped it on. When the last button was secure, he looked down at her, towering over her five-foot-five frame. "I know this is a shock for you," he said.

"It's fine." She tried to sound convincing, unaffected. There was a time when Daniel knew her better than anyone. She wondered if he could see past her words now and into her heart, where everything was anything but fine.

He walked out the door, then turned to face her.

Lydia started to close the door, but Daniel put his hand out, blocking her effort. "Lydia . . ."

Her cheeks stung from the wind, but she waited for him to speak.

"I've come home to start a new life." He paused, fused his eyes with hers. "Thank you for forgiving me."

Lydia forced a smile, then pushed the door closed. She stood still and faced the door, not moving, as an angry tear rolled down her cheek.

Had she really forgiven him?

CHAPTER 2

Nothing about Daniel's life had felt right since the day he left Lydia. But leaving Lancaster County was the right thing to do all those years ago, no matter how much the separation had pained him and hurt those he loved. If Elam were still alive, Daniel would have never returned home, despite his longing for family. His love for both his brother and Lydia had overshadowed his own desires.

He regretted not receiving his mother's letter in time to make it to Elam's funeral, but he'd moved too many times for his forwarded mail to catch up with him. By the time he'd gotten word, the funeral had long since passed. He recalled his sobs of regret, his feelings of despair at the news, and his confusion as to what Elam would want him to do. But it took another two years before he was ready to come home. Hopefully, he could be a friend to Lydia and a good uncle to the children. To speculate about more after so many years seemed far-fetched and out of reach at the moment.

Daniel parked the rental car in the designated parking area at Avis. It was strange to think this was the last time he would drive an automobile for the rest of his life. Change was on the horizon, and he continued to hope and pray that he was making decisions that were right in the eyes of God.

His parents openly wept when Daniel told them the truth about the night he left the community—that Christmas Eve so long ago. Their forgiveness partially plugged the hole that had been in Daniel's heart since then. But if things were going to be right for all of them, Lydia would need to know the whole story too—a secret that Daniel had carried for eighteen years, and one that Elam took to his grave. Daniel worried whether his confession was a betrayal of his brother. He could only pray that now Elam would want him to step forward with the truth.

Lydia's olive skin still glowed, just as he remembered. The dusty rose of her cheeks and full pink lips lent a natural beauty to her delicate face, a face that reflected the perfect combination of strength and femininity. Her dark-brown hair, barely visible from beneath her *kapp*, hadn't speckled with gray over the years like his own, and her deep brown eyes still reflected her every emotion. She still moved with grace and poise. And she still rubbed her first finger and thumb together when she was nervous, something she'd done more than once today.

But did Lydia have enough forgiveness in her heart, not only to forgive him, but also to forgive her own husband—a man no longer in a position to explain his choices? Could she forgive two brothers who had betrayed her one Christmas Eve so long ago?

Daniel climbed out of the car and closed the door.

I hope so.

· · ·

Lydia heard a knock at the door shortly after Daniel left.

Please don't be Daniel again.

She was relieved to see Sarah Fisher, but one glance at her friend's face told her that Sarah had heard the news of Daniel's return. Sarah scooted past Lydia into the den. Lydia followed her in and closed the door behind them.

"Have you heard?" Sarah asked, breathless.

Lydia gulped and fought the tears welling on her eyelids. "*Ya.* He was here."

Sarah put both hands to her mouth. "Oh no. Are you all right?"

"*Ya.* It was a shock though." Lydia shook her head, then stared hard into her friend's eyes. "It was so long ago, Sarah. But after seeing him, it feels like just yesterday that he left. How can the pain bubble up after all these years?" She swiped at her eyes and hung her head.

Sarah walked to one of the wooden rockers near the fireplace and sat down. Although fifteen years Lydia's junior, she and Lydia were close friends, and Lydia knew Sarah would sympathize with her distress. Lydia took a seat in the other chair.

"You were *in lieb* with him once," Sarah said soothingly. "It's only natural to have these feelings."

Lydia yielded to the tears as heaviness settled in her chest. "I will have to see him all the time. His parents are the children's grandparents. He'll be at church services, family gatherings, social get-togethers—" She searched Sarah's eyes for answers. "It will be awkward."

Sarah seemed to be choosing her words carefully. She reached over and touched Lydia's arm. "*Mei* friend, is there any chance that you and Daniel—"

"No! I could never have a life with Daniel. I don't even know him anymore. He lived his life in the *Englisch* world, the world he chose." Tears ran down her face, and her voice choked in her throat. "Besides, I loved Elam with all my heart. We had three beautiful children together. We had a *gut* life. I would never, never . . ." She shook her head, determined to stay true to her words.

Sarah patted her arm. "But you did love Daniel very much once."

"*Ya*, I did. But he left me, Sarah. We had so many plans, and to this day I can't understand his choice." She paused. "I don't want to have any bad feelings toward him. I forgave him a long time ago." *I did. I know I did.* Lydia looked up and stared into her friend's hazel eyes, sympathetic and kind. "I loved *Elam*, Sarah."

"Of course you did."

Sarah understood about love and loss, and Lydia suddenly regretted dumping all this on her young friend. She attempted to pull herself together. "What about you, Sarah? How are you doing?"

Lydia knew that the approaching holidays would be a hard time for Sarah. Her friend had lost a baby last Christmas Eve, and Lydia knew the miscarriage still lingered painfully in Sarah's heart.

"I'm all right," Sarah said. She tried to smile.

Lydia knew Sarah better than that, but before she could say more, she heard footsteps coming down the stairs. She quickly gathered the edge of her apron and blotted her tear-streaked face. "I don't want the children to know of this."

Sarah nodded.

"What's wrong?" Anna Marie asked when she entered the den.

"Nothing." Lydia tried to sound casual. "Just chatting with Sarah."

Anna Marie narrowed her eyes in her mother's direction. "You've been crying. What is it, *Mamm*?"

"I'm fine, Anna Marie. Did you finish your sewing?" She held her head high, looked at her daughter.

"*Ya*, I finished." Anna Marie cupped her hands on her hips and blew out a sigh of exasperation. "Why? Do you need me to do something else?"

Lydia cringed at the sound of Anna Marie's tone—and she needn't show such disrespect in front of Sarah. She sent her daughter a warning with her eyes and said, "We need to put labels on the jams and jellies later, and bind more cookbooks. I also have some soaps packaged to sell. Pauline Sampler said she has sold everything we've brought to her store."

"That's *wunderbaar*," Sarah chimed in.

"A true blessing." Lydia walked across the room to a small table, where her loosely bound cookbooks were piled. She picked one up. "We've sold enough of these to pay for all of our winter supplies this year. The *Englischers* seem to love them."

Anna Marie stomped across the den toward the kitchen. "I'll go put the labels on, but I don't know why Jacob and John can't help more. Plus I'm tired of putting cookbooks together." She twisted her head around. "And I know you are not telling me something. You treat me like a child."

"We do not talk that way in this *haus*, Anna Marie," Lydia said as her daughter rounded the corner.

Sarah stood up. "I should probably go," she said. "I still need to stop by the market. I just wanted to check on you."

Lydia walked alongside her. "Ever since Anna Marie began her *rumschpringe*, she is testy with me."

Her friend smiled. "It's her age."

"I reckon," Lydia conceded.

She hoped and prayed that Anna Marie wouldn't do half of the things she'd done during her own running-around period. The thought instantly brought her back to Daniel, and recollections of the time they spent together in their teenage years. Then the reality of his return punched at her gut, and she grabbed her side.

Sarah leaned in for a hug. "Everything will be fine, Lydia. You will see."

Lydia returned the embrace, unsure how her friend could possibly think things would ever be fine again.

· · ·

Later that same afternoon, Daniel's father was in the front yard when Daniel pulled up in his new buggy, led by Sugar, a fine horse he'd purchased from Levi Lapp. It was surprising how quickly it all came back to him—gentle flicks of the reins and the subtle gestures necessary to guide the animal.

"He's a fine horse," Gideon Smucker said. He looped his thumbs through his suspenders and pushed his straw hat back to have a better look. "How does he handle?"

"*Gut*. I had no troubles." Another surprise—how easily his Pennsylvania *Deitsch* was coming back to him as well. Daniel could tell that it pleased his father to hear him speak the dialect.

"And I see you are back in plain clothing and got yourself a proper haircut," his father added. He eyed Daniel's black pants, dark blue shirt, and straw hat, then nodded his approval. But his face quickly grew serious, and he stroked his gray beard. "Did you talk to Lydia?"

"Just briefly." Daniel paused, secured his new horse, and then walked alongside his father toward the house. "She was surprised to see me, to say the least."

"*Ya*. I reckon she was."

He pulled the door open for his father. As Gideon Smucker shuffled across the wooden floor in the den and headed toward the kitchen, Daniel breathed in the smells of his childhood home, flooding his mind with precious memories—and awful pangs of regret.

He continued through the den behind his father. The years that had passed were evident in the older man's stance. His shoulders curled forward, forcing him to bend over slightly at the waist as he walked.

The house was almost exactly as it had been when Daniel left—two rocking chairs to the right side of the fireplace, a dark green couch against the far wall, and the rug in the middle of the floor, now much more weathered and lacking the vibrant colors Daniel remembered. He'd played a lot of card games on that rug with his sisters. When he first saw Bethany and Eve upon his return three days ago, he'd been so proud of the fine women they'd become. They were just kids when he left—Bethany ten and Eve twelve. Now each woman had two children of her own. More regret plagued Daniel's heart for all that he had missed.

He pressed his lips closed and breathed in the familiar smell of fresh bread baking, then headed to the kitchen.

"Smells mighty *gut*," his father said to his mother as he took a seat in one of the wooden chairs surrounding the table—a long, wooden structure that could seat ten comfortably.

Daniel stood in the kitchen. A stranger in what used to be his home. But when his mother turned around and smiled in his direction, it calmed Daniel, just the way her smile had when he was a child.

"Sit down, Daniel," she said warmly. "I'll serve you up some butter bread. Got plenty of jams there on the table too. Supper won't be ready for a bit. Havin' meat loaf." She paused, fused her green eyes with Daniel's. "Is it still your favorite, no?"

Daniel recognized the same regret in her voice that he himself felt. "It is still my favorite," he assured her. He sat down in a chair across from his father, but he couldn't seem to pull his eyes from his mother. Her warm smile was exactly the same, but most everything else about her face was different. Deep lines webbed from the corners of her eyes, and similar creases stretched across her forehead. Daniel wondered how many of those wrinkles had his name on them. Like his father, Lena Smucker was much thinner than he remembered, and frail.

Daniel was lost in regret for what he'd done to his parents. The event itself. And then the lie. But he reassured himself that his choice at the time had been best for all of them.

As if reading his mind, his father said, "You said you spoke with Lydia. Did you tell her the truth about why you left?"

"No. Not yet." It had been hard enough to tell his parents and the bishop.

"The sooner you do that, the better. You owe her an explanation." His father shook his head. "It was so wrong what you boys did—the both of ya. I'll never understand—"

"Gideon, please . . ." *Mamm* spun around and faced the two men, a wooden spoon dangling from her hand, dripping brown sauce onto the floor. "Let's please don't do this now. Please." Her voice begged Pop to let the conversation drop.

Gideon's mouth thinned with displeasure, but he stayed silent.

Daniel knew that his father's response to his confession could have been much worse. His anger seemed padded with gratitude that Daniel was home now.

Bishop Ebersol, too, had accepted the news much better than Daniel expected. But Daniel knew who his harshest critic would be. Lydia. Daniel and Elam made decisions one Christmas Eve that changed the way all three of them would live their lives, with no consideration of Lydia's thoughts on the matter. And for that, she might never be able to forgive either of them.

. . .

Three days later, Lydia went to bed early after spending a quiet Sunday with her children. Thankfully, she hadn't seen Daniel since Thursday, but she couldn't shake the memories that continued to flood her mind, which kept her tossing and turning until much too late. She'd barely been asleep an hour when she bolted from her bed at eleven o'clock. Mother's instinct. Something was wrong. She scurried into her robe, pushed back tangled tresses, and blinked her eyes into focus as best she could in the dark.

She grabbed the flashlight she kept on her nightstand and made her way down the hall. She quietly pushed open the door to John and Jacob's room and pointed the light toward them, enough to see that they were both sleeping soundly. After breathing a sigh of relief, she closed the door and took a few steps to Anna Marie's door on the opposite side of the hallway. She stood still for a moment and recalled all the times she'd sneaked out of the house during her *rumschpringe*— most of those times to meet Daniel.

She rubbed her left temple and tried to push away the visions of him, but Daniel's presence in her home—in her and Elam's home—kept replaying like a bad dream, the kind you can't wake up from. She squeezed her eyes closed and took a deep breath, blowing it out slowly.

Please, God, let her be in there. Times were much different now than during her running-around period. The *Englisch* world was a far more dangerous place.

Lydia's heart pounded. She hesitated for a moment, then pushed the wooden door wide and shined the flashlight.

Anna Marie wasn't there.

After searching the entire house, and even outside, she finally went back into John and Jacob's room. She knelt down beside her older son.

"Jacob. Jacob, wake up." She shined the light on his quilt, away from his eyes, but illuminating his blond locks.

"*Mamm*? What is it?" He rubbed his eyes with one hand and pushed the flashlight away with the other. "It's too bright."

"Jacob, I can't find your sister. She's not in her room."

Jacob sighed. "*Ya*, she does that sometimes." He attempted to roll onto his side.

Lydia poked him on the shoulder. "She does what? Tell me, Jacob."

"She sneaks down the stairs and leaves," John said from across the room.

Lydia bolted up and turned the light toward John, who immediately shielded his eyes. His own blond hair spiked upward. Only Anna Marie had inherited her mother's dark hair.

"What?" Lydia looked back and forth between the boys. "What do you mean?"

Was it possible that both her sons were aware of this treason going on right under her own roof? Why didn't they tell on their sister? Lydia could recall a time not too long ago when both younger boys wouldn't miss an opportunity to snitch on their older sister—most recently, when Anna Marie had purchased a portable phone at the store in town. Her daughter had prepaid minutes and spent hours on the device before Lydia found out. The boys told on their sister when she wouldn't let them use the phone.

"Why haven't you told me about this?" she demanded. She flashed the light from one boy to the other.

Young John shrugged, but Jacob spoke up. "She said

we'd be havin' our *rumschpringe* some day, and if we told on her, she'd tell on us."

Lydia stomped her foot. "Neither of you made a *gut* bargain, since Anna Marie will likely be gone and married before either of you have your *rumschpringe*! Shame on you both for keeping this from me. Anna Marie could be in danger, or—"

"I reckon she's with Amos Zook." Jacob sat up and rubbed his eyes again. "She done took a fancy to him months ago."

Amos had driven Anna Marie home from Sunday singings on several occasions, but Lydia didn't think they were officially courting. They seemed like an unlikely couple to Lydia. Her daughter was very outspoken and social, always right in the middle of any youth activities, especially volleyball after the Sunday singings. Amos stayed more to himself and could often be found on the sidelines. He seemed a very nice boy, but a bit timid.

Again her mind raced back eighteen years—to how unmatched everyone thought she and Daniel were. Lydia had been spirited, like Anna Marie, but mostly followed the rules. Daniel was softspoken until he felt an injustice had occurred, and then he reacted in a way that often got him into trouble.

She recalled a time in the eighth grade, when Daniel thought the teacher had treated a student unfairly in class, reprimanding the boy unnecessarily in front of the other students. Daniel voiced his feelings to the teacher—in front of the entire class. He told Lydia later that his behavior earned him a paddling from his father when he got home, but he said he had no regrets.

When they were a little older, Daniel even approached the bishop when a member of the community was shunned for installing a small amount of electricity in his barn, claiming it was necessary for his business. The man was a carpenter, but because of arthritis in one hand, he could no longer operate some of his non-powered tools—devices not available in gas-powered or battery-operated versions. He refused to disconnect the power, and the bishop had been unsympathetic and upheld the shunning. Daniel voiced his opinion about that too.

Lydia shook her head, trying to clear the images from her mind.

She sat down on the side of Jacob's bed and looked hard at her son. "You best tell me where your sister is, if you know."

Jacob avoided her threatening stare and scratched his chin.

"Jacob!" Lydia snapped.

Her son rolled his eyes. "She's going to be real mad at me."

When did her children start being so disrespectful? Jacob would have never rolled his eyes if Elam were in the room.

"You best stop rolling those eyes at me," she demanded. "*I* will be mad at you if you don't tell me where Anna Marie is."

Jacob twisted his mouth from side to side, then said, "The old oak tree."

"How do you know this?"

Jacob shrugged.

"I will deal with you later, more than likely out by the woodshed!"

Elam had spanked all the children from time to time, out by the woodshed, but Lydia could never bring herself to discipline them in that way. Maybe she should. Maybe if she had, Anna Marie wouldn't be at the old oak tree—with Amos Zook.

A muscle quivered in Jacob's jaw, and his hurt shone in his sleepy eyes. Lydia knew her comment was fueled by fear. She reminded herself that Jacob was barely twelve, a long way from being a man, but too old for her to make idle threats. She pushed back his hair, then leaned down and kissed him on the cheek.

"I'm sorry I snapped at you, Jacob. I'm just worried about Anna Marie."

Jacob responded with a lazy half smile. "I know, *Mamm*."

Lydia patted his knee and then stood up. She pointed her finger back and forth between her boys. "Don't you boys ever do this." She blew them both a kiss. "Watch your brother," she said, and walked out the bedroom door.

Lydia went to change out of her nightclothes. She couldn't believe that the teenagers were still going to the old oak tree off Leaman Road. So many times she'd met Daniel there. . . .

She hoped that the innocent encounters at the old oak tree hadn't escalated into something else over the years.

But times were different. And Lydia's heart was heavy with worry.

CHAPTER 3

Daniel couldn't sleep, and it was no wonder. Ever since he'd seen Lydia again, his mind twisted with longing, regret, and feelings that he'd suppressed for almost two decades. And yet, when he'd laid eyes on his first love a few days ago, it was as if no time had passed at all.

But the years *had* passed, and they weren't the same people anymore. Lydia wouldn't approve of the life he'd led in the outside world. Daniel himself didn't approve of the choices he'd made.

He turned onto his side and buried his face in the white pillowcase, appreciating the fresh smell of line-dried linens. A small gas heater warmed his childhood bedroom, and the aroma of meat loaf and baked bread hung in the room like a reminder of all he'd missed. How different his life would have been had he not left this idyllic place.

Instead, he'd moved in with Lonnie, an *Englisch* buddy he'd met during his *rumschpringe*. Lonnie gave Daniel a place to stay until he could get his own apartment, but Lonnie also introduced him to a world he hadn't known anything about prior to him leaving the Old Order district—a world filled with alcohol, drugs, parties, and women. Even though he'd never felt comfortable there, Daniel had allowed himself to live that life for much too long. Almost six years. He took odd jobs to get by, mostly carpentry work since that was all he really knew. But with each step he took further into the *Englisch* world, he felt more and more detached from all he'd never known. Most important, from God.

Then he'd met Jenny, a beautiful woman who'd been raised Catholic. Jenny had a strong faith, and his friendship with her was a turning point for Daniel. He said good-bye to a way of life in which he'd merely been existing. He dated Jenny and ultimately reestablished a relationship with God. He thought about Lydia often during that time, comparing the two women. Perhaps that's why he'd never asked Jenny to marry him. For almost two years he found a sampling of what he remembered from his youth, a certain calm that settles over a man when he is living the way the Lord wants him to live. He went to work every day, spent time with Jenny in the evenings and on weekends, and even attended church with her.

But when Jenny was killed by a drunk driver, Daniel in his grief wasted no time returning to his old ways. His relationship with God suffered, and accepting anything as his will became a challenge. How could his Father have put him on this path of self-destruction, when all Daniel had ever wanted was to do the right thing by God and by others? For the next seven years he moved from place to place, working at jobs that barely afforded him enough to live on. With each year that had passed, it was harder and harder to remember the peace he'd known when he was young.

But then Daniel met Margaret. When he was as down on his luck as a man could be, seventy-year-old Margaret took him in and showed him another way to live. Daniel felt a connection to this wise woman that he could only explain as divine intervention.

He started out doing handyman work in exchange for room and board, but eventually he became to Margaret like the son she'd never had. They'd often drink hot tea late in the evening, and Daniel would tell her all about his childhood. Margaret listened intently, never pushing Daniel to confide more than he was ready to share. But eventually he told her everything, even what had happened that fateful Christmas Eve. When Margaret passed peacefully in her sleep four years later, Daniel was in a new spiritual place, and it was time. Time to go home.

He tossed and turned again. He closed his eyes to pray, but his communication was interrupted when he heard horse hooves, faint at first, then louder.

He glanced at the clock on his bedside table. A quarter to midnight. He threw the covers back, stepped onto the cool wooden planks, and then crept across the floor, purposely stretching his legs wide to avoid two slats in the floor that creaked loudly enough to wake his parents—something he'd found out in his youth.

His pants were thrown across the bed instead of hung on the rack or stowed in the dirty clothes bin. His mother would be appalled by his sloppy housekeeping.

He pulled on the dark trousers, then grabbed a crisp white shirt from the rack and buttoned it on his way down the stairs.

By the time he reached the door, the visitor was already on the porch. Lydia. And she was frantic.

"What's wrong?" he asked, opening the screen for her. She just stood there.

"I need your *daed*. He's the only person Anna Marie listens to these days." Lydia cupped her cheeks with both hands. "I hate to wake him and Lena. I should just go myself." She turned to leave, then swung back around. "But I'm so afraid . . . and if anyone can get through to her, it's Gideon."

Daniel wasn't sure what to do. Lydia couldn't even stand still, twisting about, shaking her head. He felt guilty for thinking how beautiful she was even in her desperate state and with her daughter in some sort of trouble.

"What are you afraid of? Do you know where she went?" Daniel glanced down and realized his appearance. Shirttail hanging, barefoot, slept-on hair.

Lydia finally brushed past him and into the den, shivering. Her black cape and bonnet were not enough protection from the night air. "I'm going to go wake him," she said, stepping around Daniel.

"Wait." He gently grabbed her arm. "Don't wake Pop. I'll go with you to look for Anna Marie."

Lydia pulled out of his hold. Anger swept across her face, and her hands landed on her hips. "I don't need to *look* for her. I know where she is." Then her face softened a tad. "I—I just don't know what to do when I get there. It will be awkward, and I—"

"Where is she?"

Lydia looked down for moment. When her eyes finally lifted to meet his, a blush engulfed her cheeks, and she gazed into Daniel's eyes. "She's at the old oak tree—with a boy."

Daniel stifled a grin. "Kids still go there?"

"*Ya*." She pried her eyes from his. "And you know what they do there."

Daniel didn't know Lydia as a mother, only as a young woman with dreams—dreams she had fulfilled with someone else. He didn't recognize this maternal Lydia, whose eyes shone with worry. "They kiss," he said softly as his eyes homed in on Lydia's lips.

Then her eyes met with his in such a way that Daniel knew Lydia, too, was recalling the tenderness they'd shared, innocent kisses beneath moonlit nights, stars twinkling overhead. It was no surprise that young love still flourished underneath the protective limbs of the old oak tree.

"Times are different now," she whispered. "Elam and I..."

She paused, and now it was Daniel who couldn't look her in the eye. They'd had a life together, Elam and Lydia. Three children. To hear her refer to them as a couple was difficult.

"Elam and I," she went on, "tried our best to protect the children from outside influences, but with Anna Marie in her *rumschpringe* and all—I'm just worried. Times aren't the same as when we were..."

"Under the old oak tree?"

"*Ya*," she said softly.

Daniel stepped forward and reached for the words. "Lydia, I'm sure that you and Elam raised Anna Marie properly, and given that, I'm sure you have nothing to worry about. Why don't you let me go with you to get her?"

"No," she said, straightening to attention.

"Pop sure looked tired when he went to bed. Sure you want to wake him?" It was a stretch. His father hadn't looked all that tired, but suddenly Daniel was desperate to go with her, to be a part of her life.

Lydia took a deep breath. "No, I really don't want to wake him, but he has been so *gut* with Anna Marie since Elam died. She listens to her grandfather, and mostly she just gets angry with me. Besides, what would I say to her and Amos?" She scrunched her face into a scowl, then rapidly shook her head back and forth. "Anna Marie shouldn't be in such a place."

"The old oak is a beautiful place." But Daniel could see in Lydia's face that somehow what seemed fine for her so many years ago did not seem okay for her daughter. "I'm sure Anna Marie is using good judgment, Lydia. Let me put my shoes on and grab a jacket. I'll go with you."

Her forehead creased, and she pressed her lips firmly together. "All right," she finally said.

Daniel hurried up the stairs, quietly as he could. In his room, he fished around in the dark for his shoes and then remembered the flashlight on his nightstand. He shined the light around the room until he located his black tennis shoes in the far corner, then pulled a pair of black socks from the chest of drawers. He sat down on the bed, stretched the socks over his cold feet, and slipped his shoes on, his stomach rolling with anticipation.

He tiptoed to the bathroom, swooshed mouthwash, and spit, wishing he had more time to groom himself properly. But she was waiting.

Daniel walked briskly down the stairs, shining the light as he walked. When he hit the floor in the den, he stopped abruptly, his heart thudding against his chest. *Where is she?*

Her scent tarried in the room, but he knew before he even reached the window that she was gone. He gazed out into the night just in time to hear a faint whistle, the pounding of hooves against the dirt, and to see her buggy begin its descent down the dirt driveway.

Daniel flung open the door and hurried onto the porch. He opened his mouth to yell out to her, but remembered his parents asleep upstairs.

"Lydia," he whispered instead, as he watched her disappear into the darkness.

CHAPTER 4

Lydia maneuvered her buggy across Lincoln Highway, propelled by the kind of determination that only a fearful mother could understand. Her glove-clad hands trembled as she neared Leaman Road, and she fought to keep a steady hold on the reins. As the lights from the highway grew dim behind her, Lydia pushed forward into the darkness of the cold night, wondering why her daughter and Amos would be so silly as to choose the old oak tree in this frigid weather.

But, of course, she knew why.

Lydia recalled the massive trunk and the sprawling branches that stretched upward, then draped to the ground. She remembered the way the moonlight charmed its way between the forked offshoots, gently illuminating those seeking to bask in the magic of the moment. Lydia could almost feel the misty dew dusting her cheeks, clouding the air around her—around her and Daniel—and the tenderness of his lips against hers. She should never have gone to get Gideon, knowing there was a chance she'd run into Daniel.

She pulled back on the reins, slowed the buggy, and pulled to the side of the road, trying to remember what it was like to be sixteen and in love, and how she would have felt if one of her parents had ever approached her when she was under the old oak tree with Daniel. Lydia leaned out the window, making sure she was completely off the road, and clicked off the lights on the buggy.

She had shared tender moments of first love with Daniel underneath that tree. Did she really want to ruin that for Anna Marie by charging in there like a hysterical shrew, demanding Anna Marie hightail it home, and destroy what Lydia knew deep in her heart was an innocent encounter between a boy and a girl enjoying the thrill of sneaking out during their *rumschpringe*?

She'd raised Anna Marie well, and despite the recent distance between them, she knew her daughter would make wise choices. Perhaps she should trust her, let her enjoy this special moment, and then make it clear to her tomorrow that sneaking out was unacceptable. Even more improper on a Sunday.

Lydia smiled, thinking how her parents would have never taken that approach. Her mother would have sent her father to drag her home, and she would have been humiliated beyond recovery. *Thank goodness we never got caught.*

She wrapped the thick, brown blanket tightly around her, hoping Amos had been smart enough to at least bring a blanket, the way Daniel always had. Lydia sat in the buggy and recalled the events of the day, still not confident enough to ride away and leave the two teenagers. In the distance she could see the spanning might of the old oak against blue-gray skies.

Part of her still wanted to storm forward and drag

Anna Marie home—the motherly part of her. But the woman inside of Lydia beckoned her to let the girl be, just for tonight. Recollections invaded Lydia's mind, sending her back to a place and time with Daniel. For a few moments she lost herself in the past, a place she seldom chose to visit.

Then pangs of guilt stabbed at her insides, and she reminded herself that she'd married another, and that such memories should be squelched in honor of Elam. Daniel had betrayed her, and she had married his brother—a wonderful man who had picked up the pieces of her broken life and patched her back together. Over time, Elam's patchwork grew stronger and became a thick barrier of resistance against the memories she harbored of Daniel. And she'd fallen in love with Elam.

Why did Daniel have to come back? After all these years, she'd never considered the possibility that he might return. The way he looked at her today, the sound of his voice, his touch—it rattled her. She could feel her heart starting to spider with tiny cracks, threatening to tear down the protective armor where memories of Daniel had lain dormant for all these years.

Her thoughts were interrupted by a faraway rustling, and Lydia watched as Amos's buggy began the trek from the tree to Leaman Road. She considered trying to turn around and get back on the road ahead of them, get home, crawl into bed, and talk with Anna Marie in the morning, but instead she stayed where she was.

It was several minutes later when the headlights from Amos's buggy drew closer, and she shielded her eyes from the light in front of her. As they passed by her,

Amos did not look her way, nor did Anna Marie. But they knew she was there, and that's all that mattered.

Lydia doubted Anna Marie would be sneaking out again, at least for a while. And no one had been embarrassed or humiliated, and her daughter would be home soon enough. She knew the Zooks well. Amos was a good boy, and he would be a fine choice for courting Anna Marie. Although tomorrow Lydia would need to sit down and establish some boundaries for her daughter.

Lydia twisted her neck around and waited until Anna Marie and Amos had safely crossed Lincoln Highway, then she motioned her horse into action. But she didn't turn the buggy around. Instead, she headed toward the old oak tree.

. . .

Daniel made his way down Leaman Road, unsure what he'd walk into but determined to be there for Lydia if she needed him. Maybe in some tiny way he could start to make up for his own past by helping her with her children in the absence of Elam.

But as he neared the old oak tree, wondrous recollections of his time there with Lydia paraded through his mind, mixing with a sense of anguish over the life he'd missed out on. He reminded himself, the choices were his to make.

He turned onto the worn path created by generations who had sought privacy beneath the tree, where he had first told Lydia that he loved her. As he traveled down the winding trail, it felt like he was entering a time warp, a magical place where the past stayed the past and you never had to leave.

Daniel pulled up beside the only buggy parked near the tree. Since all the buggies looked almost exactly the same, he wasn't sure who he would find. Maybe Lydia had changed her mind about coming out here, and Daniel was about to intrude on Anna Marie and her beau, which certainly was not his place. He stepped out of the buggy, closed the door, and knew that whoever was beneath the branches was certainly aware of his presence.

With slow, intentional steps he moved forward, tucked his head to pass under a low branch, then straightened within the magical dome. He filled his nostrils with the familiarity of the air around him, a sweet, dewy fragrance that he'd never smelled anywhere else. Lydia used to say that no one left the old oak without falling in love.

He blinked his eyes several times, adjusted to the darkness, and briefly wondered if he was dreaming. But there she was—his Lydia—standing alone, delicate rays of moonlight brushing her cheeks, her eyes twinkling mysteriously, and Daniel wondered if there was enough magic in the night to re-create what they'd shared so long ago.

"Is everything all right?" he asked. She had the strangest look on her face, and he couldn't help but wonder if her thoughts mirrored his. "When I came downstairs, you'd left, and I just wanted to make sure you were okay."

She didn't respond, but took two steps toward him.

"Lydia?" he said after a few moments. She took another step toward him, her eyes hazy with emotion.

"Do you remember the first time we came here?" she asked.

Of course he did. He remembered every single time he'd been with her anywhere. "As if it happened yesterday," he said, hoping his eyes would convey the importance of his statement.

"You promised to love me forever," she said as her lips curved slightly upward.

But her brown eyes narrowed, confusing him. She leaned close to him and looked up, putting her lips within a few inches of his chin. He could feel her breath, and she smiled again. But something about the smile caused Daniel to feel uneasy.

"You lied," she added simply. Then she backed away from him, but she never took her eyes from his.

You lied. You lied. You lied. The words echoed in Daniel's head, reverberating against the part of his brain that was trying to decipher whether or not he really had lied. He'd always planned to love her forever.

"I didn't lie," he said with boyish defensiveness. "I wanted to love you forever, but . . ."

She shook her head feverishly. "It really doesn't matter," she said, and then shot him the same confusing smile. "I found my true love. If you hadn't left, Elam and I would never have married and had three wonderful children." She arched her brows proudly.

Daniel hung his head for a moment, then raised his eyes to hers. "I guess you're right." He couldn't deny the truth in what she said. Maybe his leaving was meant to be.

He filled his lungs with the atmosphere around

them, losing hope that there was enough magic to let them pick up where they'd left off so many years ago. *Please, God, let me do right by her*, he silently prayed.

"Of course I'm right!" she finally said.

Then why was she raising her voice in such a way? Daniel took a couple of steps toward her. "Lydia," he whispered. As he grew closer, he could see tears in her eyes. He took a chance and stretched his arms forward. "Lydia," he said again.

But she backed away.

"Leave me alone, Daniel." She swiped at one eye and held her chin high. "It's true that you are my children's uncle. I will respect that. For the children, and for Lena and Gideon. But I would prefer to keep company with you only when—when it's necessary."

All he could muster was "I'm sorry." Then he realized that the whole purpose of the mission had gotten lost somewhere. "What about Anna Marie? Is she all right?"

"*Ya.*" Lydia didn't elaborate, and her eyes were still fused with his.

Did she have more to say? Was she waiting on him to say something else?

"That's *gut*," he said finally.

Maybe now was the time. Maybe he should tell her the truth now, tell her why he'd left Lancaster County that Christmas Eve. But would it even matter? She said she'd forgiven him, but it sure didn't sound like it right now.

As he considered his options, Lydia walked toward him once again, and this time she cut him off at the knees.

"I never loved you the way I loved Elam," she said coolly and with the same smile on her face as before. Then she turned away, bent low, and slid beneath the branches.

Daniel listened to her rush across the grass and climb into her buggy. His feet stayed planted with the roots of the tree beneath him.

Hooves met with dirt, and with each *clippity-clop*, Lydia grew farther and farther away. Until it was quiet, eerily quiet, beneath the old oak tree.

CHAPTER 5

Lydia spooned dippy eggs onto Jacob and John's plates the next morning, so the boys could eat and get started on their morning chores. Evidently, Anna Marie had overslept. She knew breakfast was served promptly at five, and Lydia assumed her daughter was exhausted from her little trip last night. No excuse. There's a household to run and much to do in preparation for Thanksgiving in less than two weeks.

Lydia had hosted Thanksgiving since the first year she and Elam were married. Both her side of the family and Elam's would gather at her home again this year. She pulled the biscuits from the oven, put them on the table, and realized that there was no way to exclude Daniel from the festivities.

"Where's Anna Marie?" Jacob asked with a mouthful of eggs, trying to stifle a grin.

"I'm sure your sister is tired this morning." Lydia shot Jacob a look signifying that no more discussion was needed.

"Anna Marie's in trouble," John added with a twinkle in his bright blue eyes.

Lydia put her hands on her hips. "No one said

anything about trouble. You mind your manners and eat your breakfast." She glanced toward Jacob. "Both of you. Those cows are ready for milking, and I have a very long list of things we need to do to get ready for Thanksgiving."

Lydia refilled John's glass with milk, then turned when she heard footsteps descending the stairs.

"Sorry I'm late." Anna Marie slid onto the wooden bench across from her brothers and bowed her head in silent prayer.

"*Ya*, and we know why." Jacob chuckled.

Anna Marie raised her head and cut her eyes in Jacob's direction. "You better be quiet."

"Stop it," Lydia said sternly. She served Anna Marie some eggs and then turned to Jacob and John. "Finish your breakfast. Quietly. You both have chores to tend to."

All the children ate silently, and Lydia contemplated the conversation she would have with Anna Marie after the boys left for school. There was a fine line between parenting Anna Marie and pushing her away, but Lydia knew she couldn't tolerate sneaking out of the house, no matter how sympathetic she was about her daughter's budding romance.

It was hard for Lydia to believe that Jacob would be sixteen in four years and also entering his *rumschpringe*. Thankfully, nine-year-old John had even longer to go before Lydia would have to watch her baby boy venture out to learn about the *Englisch* world.

She walked to the kitchen counter, placed her palms on the edge, and took a deep breath, wishing Daniel's face would stop creeping into her thoughts. It was a distraction that caused her a variety of emotions, none of which she wanted to feel. This morning, it was mostly guilt. It was as if her heart had been dipped in truth serum and was sending confessions to her brain about a love that had never died.

But I loved Elam.

"I'm done. I'll go start the washing." Anna Marie pushed her plate away. "Hopefully we have enough gasoline left to power the wringer."

Lydia nodded, but was mentally calculating. Today was Monday, wash day. No worship service yesterday, which meant they would attend church this coming Sunday, as was always the case—every other Sunday. Lydia cringed, realizing that Lena and Gideon were scheduled to host worship in their home this next weekend. She was sure Daniel would be attending, no matter who hosted, but it would seem even more intimate being at his childhood home.

The first time Lydia ever ate supper at Lena and Gideon's house, she was Daniel's guest, with no way to know that she would end up spending fifteen years alongside his brother at that very same table.

She recalled the first time Daniel asked her to a Sunday singing, when she was sixteen and just entering her *rumschpringe*. They were both working at the annual mud sale at the fire station in Penryn. The event was mostly run by Amish men and women. Plows, farm equipment, and large items were auctioned in the field next to the firehouse. Inside, the women auctioned quilts and household wares.

On that particular day, the auction had held up to its

name. Heavy rain had doused the ground, and everyone's shoes were covered in mud. Lydia left the indoor auction to go find her father. Instead, she'd bumped into Daniel and Gideon. Her father-in-law to-be was bidding on a plow out in the open field. When Daniel saw her, he sloshed toward her in mud up to his ankles, smiling as he maneuvered his way through the crowd.

He'd already been in his running-around period for a year, and Lydia recalled the smoothness of his voice on that day. "Wanna get out of here?" he'd asked.

She'd nodded. No words were really necessary. She'd seen the way Daniel stared at her during worship service. They sneaked away from the mud sale, walked down the paved street that ran in front of the fire station, and then cut down a gravel street that wound through the meadows, speckled with mostly *Englisch* farms. Lydia was sure they walked five miles that day. She had blisters when they returned to the auction site. They'd talked and talked, about anything and everything. She knew on that day that she would marry Daniel Smucker.

She sighed. Thanksgiving, then Daniel's baptism, worship every other Sunday, family visits, social gatherings . . . There was no way around it, Daniel was sure to become a permanent part of their lives. She'd need to harness any feelings that attempted to creep to the surface and focus on the things she had been tending to prior to his arrival—raising her children and running her household in a way that would make Elam proud.

And with that thought, she finished packing Jacob's and John's lunches.

"*Mamm*, we're out of gasoline for the washer." Anna

Marie walked back into the kitchen, toting the red gasoline container they kept in the shed. "I'm going to take the buggy to *Mammi* and *Daadi*'s house to get some."

Lydia nodded. Her father-in-law always had plenty of gasoline on hand, and he always enjoyed a visit from one of the children.

Daniel. He would be there, of course. Lydia clamped her eyes tight, again fighting the visions of him.

"Anna Marie," she said before her daughter reached the front door.

"*Ya?*"

"We need to have a talk when you get back."

"I know, *Mamm*," Anna Marie said. "Thanks to my brothers, no doubt." She smiled slightly and then turned to leave.

Maybe it was Anna Marie's tone—calm, understanding, all-knowing—but Lydia had a sudden realization. Her baby was growing up.

• • •

Daniel had just finished helping his father milk the cows when he heard a buggy pulling up.

"That'd be Anna Marie," Gideon said to his son. "It's Monday. I reckon she's out of gas for the washing machine." He chuckled. "I think she does that on purpose as an excuse to come visit and avoid some of her chores. She's become such a regular on Mondays, your *mamm* usually bakes somethin' special for the girl to snack on when she gets here."

Daniel watched Anna Marie step out of the buggy.

She looked a lot like her mother. Similar in height and frame, dark hair, deep brown eyes with a brightness and wonder all their own.

"I'm out of gas," Anna Marie called to her grandfather in such a way that Daniel knew immediately his father had been right—she ran out on purpose.

"Ain't that a surprise." Gideon grinned. He tipped his straw hat with his finger, walked toward the girl, and retrieved the empty can. "Get on into the house now and see what your *mammi*'s got cooked for ya."

Daniel started to follow his father across the yard, but Gideon turned and said, "Go spend some time with your niece. Get to know the girl." He pointed toward the farmhouse.

Daniel complied, but to himself he said, *I'm not so sure Anna Marie wants to get to know me.*

"I'm headed to town," his mother said when Daniel walked into the kitchen. "Daniel, sit down and have yourself a muffin with Anna Marie." She pointed to a chair across the table.

If Daniel didn't know better, he'd think that his parents had set up this whole scenario. He pulled out the chair and sat down.

When his mother left the room, Anna Marie eyed him with the same skepticism as before.

"Great muffins," he mumbled after he took a large bite and swallowed.

Anna Marie finished chewing and narrowed her eyes. "Why don't you have a *fraa* and *kinner*?"

Daniel shrugged. This was not a conversation he wanted to have with Lydia's daughter. "Just don't."

"Haven't you ever been *in lieb*?" Anna Marie's eyes began to sparkle, reflective of someone who was in love herself.

"*Ya*, I have been in love," he said.

"With who? Why didn't you marry her? Was she *Englisch*?"

Daniel cocked his head to one side. "You sure ask a lot of questions."

"I'm *in lieb*," she said breezily.

Daniel stifled a grin. "Really?" He reached for another muffin.

"*Ya*. We're going to be married next November." Anna Marie propped her elbows on the table and rested her chin in her hands.

Daniel wondered if Lydia had heard this exciting news. "And what does your *mamm* think about this?"

Anna Marie's expression soured. "She doesn't know yet." Her brows furrowed. "And please don't tell her."

Daniel shook his head. "No, I won't. That's your place." He paused. "Why the secrecy?"

"*Ach*, it's no secret. Amos just proposed last night, and I haven't had a chance to tell yet."

Her face lit up, much like Lydia's did when she was really happy—from what he remembered.

Daniel couldn't help but smile, knowing Amos had proposed under the old oak tree. He recalled his proposal to Lydia. While it wasn't under the oak tree, like their first kiss, it had been equally as romantic—a picnic on a spring day, wildflowers in full bloom, and enough love to sustain the two of them forever. At least, that had been the plan.

He and Lydia sat on the paisley quilt with the picnic lunch his mother had prepared, the bubbling creek only a few feet away. Blue skies and a gentle breeze, the best chicken salad he could remember eating, and Lydia—her eyes gazing into his.

Daniel returned to the present to find Anna Marie scoffing at him. "Are you listening?" she asked.

"Uh, sure." Daniel left the creek and the past and tried to focus on what his niece was saying, wondering how much he'd missed.

"Why, then?" Anna Marie leaned slightly forward and widened her questioning eyes.

"Why what?"

Anna Marie sighed. "I didn't think you were listening. I asked you if you knew why *mei mamm* was crying after you left. Did you say something to upset her?"

Daniel pulled his eyes from hers and hung his head. "I certainly didn't mean to." He looked up to see Anna Marie growing less fond of him with each passing second, her eyes clawing at him like talons. Lydia's daughter was not going to be easy to win over. He wondered why the girl had already formed such a harsh opinion of him.

"I'm sorry I missed your *daed*'s funeral," he said. "I used to move around a lot, and my forwarded mail didn't make it to me in time." Daniel sighed, his heart filled with anguish. "I regret that more than you know."

But Anna Marie's expression didn't soften. She narrowed her eyes and pressed her lips together. Daniel reached for another muffin and tried to avoid her icy glare.

"What are you *really* doing here?" she finally asked.

Daniel took a bite of muffin, swallowed, and chose

his words carefully. "I've spent enough time in the *Englisch* world to know that this is where I want to be. I miss my family."

"It took you eighteen years to realize that?"

Daniel leaned his head to one side and glared at her, wondering if the girl was always this disrespectful. "*Ya*," he said sternly. "It did."

Anna Marie rose from her chair, and it was then that Daniel noticed her right hand curled into a fist. She slowly opened her hand, and Daniel hoped she wasn't holding what he thought she was. *Couldn't be.*

She showed him her open hand. "Is this why you're back?"

Daniel took a deep breath and reached for the worn piece of blue paper crumpled atop her flattened palm. His heart raced as he unfolded the note. There hadn't been much time, and he recalled how he had hurriedly scribbled the words. Seeing it again ripped open wounds that had never fully healed.

> Dear Lydia,
>
>   I will love you until the day I die, but I can't stay here. The Englisch world is calling to me, and I can't live within the confines of our Old Order district. I hope that someday you can forgive me.
>
> Forever yours,
Daniel

"Where did you get this?" Daniel asked. *And why does Lydia still have it after all these years?* He wondered if he should be hopeful about this.

Anna Marie leaned down on both palms and looked Daniel in the eyes. "I hope that you have truly come back for the reasons you stated, that you miss your family and realize that you belong in the Amish community. Because if you have any hopes of rekindling a romance with *mei mamm*, you will be greatly disappointed. She loved my *daed* with all her heart and soul. He was her forever love. Not you."

And then she left without looking back.

Daniel stared at the note and wished that there was some way to change history, go back in time. He thought about how a split-second decision had changed the course of his life, and how he would forever live with its consequences.

CHAPTER 6

Lydia walked across the yard to join Anna Marie at the clothesline.

"This is the last load," her daughter said as she pinned up a pair of black socks.

Lydia scooped up a brown towel, grabbed two pins, and shivered. "Mighty cold out here."

"Not as cold as this morning when I took the buggy to *Daadi*'s *haus*. I plumb near froze."

Lydia twisted her mouth from side to side and debated how to approach the subject of Anna Marie's late-night outing. "I reckon it was even colder under the old oak tree last night," she said.

Anna Marie finished hanging another pair of black socks, then turned to face her mother. "Please don't be mad, *Mamm*. Not today. I promise I won't sneak out again." She grabbed both of Lydia's hands in hers and squeezed. "Amos asked me to marry him last night!"

"What? But I didn't even know the two of you were officially courting. Don't you think that's a bit quick?" But Lydia couldn't help but smile. Anna Marie was glowing, and she recognized the look.

"But I love him so much, *Mamm*. You know we've

been going to the Sunday singings, and we spend all of our free time together. We want to get married next November!"

Relief washed over Lydia. They weren't going to have to plan a wedding within the next month or two, and both Anna Marie and Amos would benefit from a year of courting, giving their relationship more time to mature. They would still only be seventeen when they married.

Lydia hugged Anna Marie and kissed her on the cheek. "It's *gut* to see you so happy." She pulled back and pointed a finger at her daughter. "But no more sneaking out of the house at night, Anna Marie. It worries me so. If your *daed* was here—"

"I won't, *Mamm*."

They were silent for a few moments as they pinned clothes to the line. Chilling winds blew through Lydia's black cape, and she could see Anna Marie shivering.

"One more towel," Lydia said. She clipped it to the line, then grabbed Anna Marie's hand. "Let's go sit by the fire."

"I talked with *Onkel* Daniel when I was at *Mammi* and *Daadi*'s," Anna Marie said when they walked inside.

Lydia closed the front door behind them and headed toward the fireplace. "I see." She tried to sound casual, but just the mention of Daniel's name caused her stomach to knot.

Anna Marie joined her mother in front of the hearth and warmed her palms. "I don't like him," she said as she scrunched her face in a most unbecoming way.

Lydia quickly turned toward her. "It's not proper to

say such things." She wasn't sure what upset her more—the fact that Anna Marie would make such a comment, or the fact that it was directed at Daniel.

"Yes, ma'am."

"Let's get to putting these cookbooks together." Lydia walked to the table by the window where stacks of criss-crossed recipes were waiting to be organized and bound.

Anna Marie sat down at the table across from her. "Do you like him?" she asked. She lined the piles up in front of her and began to slip one page behind the other.

"Who?"

"*Onkel* Daniel."

Lydia took a deep breath and blew it out slowly. "He is your *daed*'s *bruder*. Of course I like him." She paused and then said, "Although, I don't really know him." The words stung with truth.

Anna Marie stopped working and twisted a strand of loose hair that slipped from the confines of her prayer covering. "Did you know him when you were young?" Her daughter's bottom lip quivered, and Lydia wondered what exactly Anna Marie and Daniel had talked about. Lydia clicked the pages on the table, smoothed the edges, and started inserting the binder into the square holes on the left margin.

"Of course I knew him. We all grew up together." Lydia sat up a little taller. Anna Marie was working again and handed her another stack ready to bind. "Why do you ask?"

Anna Marie shrugged. "He just seems very different from *Daed*."

"He spent many years in the *Englisch* world. I'm sure

he'll come back around to our ways, since he's planning to be re-baptized the Sunday after Thanksgiving." Lydia knew that Daniel's shunning would be cast aside following his baptism, but she also knew that in *her* heart the shunning would continue.

"I bet he hurt a lot of people when he just up and left," Anna Marie said. "Especially—especially *Mammi* and *Daadi*."

"*Ya*. It was hard for them." Lydia didn't want to talk about this anymore. "What do you think about this cover your *aenti* Miriam came up with? I like the wood-burning stove she drew and all the little details. Look at the smoke swirling up from the pot." She held the book up and faced it toward Anna Marie.

"I like it." Anna Marie looked up and smiled briefly.

"You finish up here," Lydia said. "I reckon I'll go brew us some hot cocoa. Your brothers will be home from school soon, and I'm sure they'd enjoy something warm in their tummies after a cold walk home."

Anna Marie nodded, but Lydia could tell her thoughts were somewhere else.

. . .

Daniel helped his father ready the house for Sunday worship. The sun was barely over the horizon when they carried the last of the benches from the barn into the house. His mother had been busy preparing food since before Daniel woke up, and the smell of freshly baked bread permeated the farmhouse.

"This should do it," Gideon said when the last bench

was in place. "What else, Lena?" he hollered into the kitchen.

"That's all. I think we're ready." His mother walked into the den and touched Daniel's arm. "*Wunderbaar gut* to have you home for worship service."

Daniel smiled. His mother's joy warmed his soul, but regret still plagued his heart. Margaret had helped him learn to forgive himself through prayer, but true peace would come when he knew that Lydia's words of forgiveness were sincere. He hadn't seen any of her family all week, not since Anna Marie had sprung the note on him. He wondered if his niece said anything to Lydia about the letter. He suspected not.

Daniel felt the sting of the girl's words. *She loved my father with all her heart and soul. He was her forever love. Not you.*

As it should be, Daniel thought. But it didn't lessen the pain. He suddenly wondered if coming back here had been a mistake. Would it be simply a constant reminder of all he'd missed?

He could hear buggies pulling up outside and faint voices. He walked onto the front porch to greet visitors, many of whom he hadn't seen since he left the district. But when Lydia stepped from her buggy, smiled, and hugged his mother, Daniel closed his eyes and sighed.

"Hello, Daniel," she said politely when she walked up the porch steps. Then she turned to her sons. "Remember your *onkel* Daniel, boys?" She seemed intentionally formal.

Each son shook Daniel's hand. Anna Marie walked in behind the rest of them and crinkled her nose.

"Hello, Anna Marie." He tipped his straw hat in her direction.

She raised her chin a bit. "Hello." Then she scooted past him and into the kitchen.

· · ·

Daniel's back started to ache about an hour into the service. It was going to take some time to adjust to the backless benches again, particularly during the three-hour church services.

As was customary, the men and boys sat on one side of the room, the women and girls on the other. From where Daniel was sitting, he couldn't see Lydia, but he could see Anna Marie, who took every opportunity to fire him a look that screamed, *You stay away from my mother.*

Sunday worship hadn't changed one bit in eighteen years, and Daniel was glad he could still understand the service, spoken mostly in German. The temperature had dipped into the thirties, leaving it much too cold to eat outside. The men and boys sought seats throughout the downstairs, where tables had been placed. Women and young girls bustled around, serving meadow tea and placing applesauce, jams, and jellies on the tables. Daniel had missed the sweet tea leaves that grew wild in the meadows along the creeks in the area.

Lydia brushed past him, carrying two loaves of home-made bread. Their eyes locked, but she quickly looked away. Daniel joined his father at a table on the far side of the den.

He wasn't sure how or when, but he knew he needed to somehow find a quiet moment to speak with Lydia, to let her know that Anna Marie had found the note. It wasn't going to earn him any points, but Daniel felt Lydia needed to know.

It was almost two hours later before the large crowd dis-assembled. Daniel saw Lydia gathering up casserole dishes, and it looked like she was preparing to leave. She had avoided him all afternoon, refusing to even make eye contact again.

"Can I talk to you for a minute?" he whispered to her in the kitchen when no one was around.

She didn't look up, but continued gathering up miscellaneous kitchen items and placing them in a brown paper bag. "Talk," she said.

Daniel was hoping to talk somewhere quiet, away from everyone, but this might be his only chance. He touched her arm, and he could feel her body go stiff.

He found his way to her hand and slipped the note into her palm. "Anna Marie gave this to me."

Lydia kept her head down, unfolded the note, and appeared to be reading it over and over again. For several moments, he watched her trembling hand.

"I didn't tell her anything," he finally said. "I felt like it was your place to explain in your own way."

Her head twisted in his direction, her eyes blazing with anger and tears. "Explain to her? How do I do that, Daniel? What do I tell my daughter? That I loved you but ended up marrying her father when you abandoned me? Is that what I tell her?"

"Lydia—" Daniel touched her arm, but she pulled away.

"Haven't you caused me enough pain for one life-time? Why did you come back here?"

Her eyes pleaded with him for some sort of relief from the pain she was feeling, and Daniel wanted nothing more in the world than to love her and take care of her for the rest of their lives. But seeing her like this, so distraught, hurting . . .

He knew he had made a mistake by coming back.

Lydia swiped at her eyes and waited for an answer.

"I missed this place, my family." He looked at the floor for a moment, and then back at her. "And I missed you. It was never my intention to hurt you a second time, Lydia."

She didn't bother to brush away the tear as it rolled down her cheek and dripped onto the wooden floor.

Daniel took a slow, deep breath, never taking his eyes from hers, and he spoke the words he thought she wanted to hear. "I won't stay, Lydia. I'll leave in the morning."

CHAPTER 7

Lydia stuffed the note down in the bag with her casserole dishes, wooden spoons, and other items she had brought for dinner. Such an important piece of paper among such mundane items, she thought, as she dabbed at her eyes and turned toward Daniel.

"No. Don't go," she told him firmly. His expression lifted, and Lydia knew she needed to clarify her response. "It would be *baremlich* for your parents." She paused and, for the first time all day, gazed into his eyes.

"I'll be fine, Daniel. You and I were a long time ago, but I have to explain this to my daughter now. And I'm not looking forward to that." She shook her head. "I don't know how she found this. It was in my trinket box, in a drawer, underneath a bunch of other things, and—"

"The cedar trinket box I made for you?" He raised his brows.

Lydia let out a heavy sigh. "*Ya.*"

"I remember when I gave that to you."

"Let's don't do this. No traveling down memory lane. You are a part of this family, and as such, we will be together for a number of activities. It is taking me some time to get used to you being back, but we simply must accept what *was* and what *is*."

He leaned forward, a bit too close for her. "Any chance that we can be friends?"

"I already told you, Daniel. I think it's best if we only keep company when necessary." She paused, but kept her eyes fused with his. "I married Elam, and I lived with him for fifteen years. We have three children. I am not the same young girl you—you proposed to so long ago."

"I think you are exactly the same, Lydia."

She chuckled. "Look closer, Daniel." She pointed to her face. "Do you see nineteen in this thirty-seven-year-old face? I think not." She was suddenly embarrassed, and she pulled her eyes from his and looked down.

"No, I don't see nineteen," he said as his face drew closer to hers. "But what I see is more beautiful than I even remember."

His tone was so tender, Lydia feared she might cry again.

"I'm just asking for a chance, Lydia," he said. "I'm the children's uncle, and I'd like to get to know them. And I'd like to get to know you again."

Lydia opened her mouth, but quickly clamped it shut.

"You were happy with Elam, weren't you?"

"Very happy. His death was devastating. I wasn't sure how I would go on without him . . ." She paused. "It's been hard for me and the children."

Pounding footsteps entered the kitchen. "Let's go, *Mamm.* Jacob and John are already in the buggy." Anna Marie stood poised like a snake, with fangs ready to puncture the air from Daniel's lungs.

Lydia picked up her bag and ignored her daughter's attitude. "We will see you on Thursday, Daniel. For Thanksgiving."

She didn't look back, and barely saw him nod as she followed Anna Marie out the back door of the kitchen. Anna Marie did enough head spinning for both of them, glancing over her shoulder several times, cutting her eyes in Daniel's direction.

. . .

"I'm going to go take these cookies I made to Amos," Anna Marie said later that afternoon.

"Not before you and I have a little talk." Lydia pointed to the stairway. "In my room, away from the boys."

"But I told Amos I would—"

"Now. March." Lydia gently tapped her foot and waited for Anna Marie to move toward the stairs.

"I know what this is about," she huffed.

Lydia didn't answer. She was busy trying to plan out some sort of explanation about the note. Ironically, she was hoping to soften Anna Marie's heart toward Daniel.

Anna Marie sat down on her mother's bed, and Lydia stood in front of her. She opened her hand and offered her daughter the note.

Anna Marie shook her head. "I've already read it."

"Anna Marie, I have had just about enough of your attitude. That tone of yours is about to get your mouth washed out with soap. I don't care how old you are." Lydia paced the room as she spoke. "Daniel and I had a courtship before I married your father. The relationship ended, and then I married your father. And that's all there is to that." She stopped and faced Anna Marie, and put her hands on her hips. "And another thing, young lady. What were you doing snooping through my things?"

"I wasn't snooping. I was looking for my black sweater, and I thought it might have been put in your drawer by mistake." She hung her head. "But then I saw the pretty box. I know I shouldn't have opened it, but . . ."

Lydia sat down on the bed next to Anna Marie and patted her on the leg. "All right."

After a few quiet moments, Anna Marie said, "He wants to court you now, doesn't he?"

"What makes you ask that?"

"I can tell by the way he looks at you."

Lydia twisted the ties on her apron and avoided the girl's inquisitive eyes. "That's nonsense," Lydia said after a few moments.

Anna Marie sighed. "*Mamm*, I am *in lieb*," she said smugly. "I recognize that look he gives you."

"*Ach*, Anna Marie, you're not old enough to recognize anything." Lydia shook her head, but then turned to Anna Marie, whose eyes shone with unshed tears. "I'm sorry," she added. "I keep forgetting that you are growing up."

"And getting married next year." Anna Marie held her chin high and folded her hands in her lap.

Lydia thought for a moment. "Anna Marie, I loved your father very much. But before him, it's true that I loved Daniel." She reached over and squeezed one of

Anna Marie's hands. "But that was a long time ago. I'm sure you mistook any looks between us."

"*Gut!*" she said. "Because I don't like him!" And she bolted off the bed.

"Anna Marie!" Lydia hollered before her daughter reached the door. "Daniel is your *onkel*, and I will not have such talk from you. I expect you to treat him with the courtesy and respect that you would anyone else. Do you hear me, young lady?"

Anna Marie slowly turned around and faced Lydia. "Yes, ma'am."

"Now go check on your brothers and see if they've tended to the cows yet this afternoon."

When Anna Marie was out the door, Lydia unfolded the note in her hand and slowly read it again.

. . .

By Thanksgiving Day Lydia was a bundle of nerves, worrying about way more than the Good Lord would approve of.

Was the meal going to come together and would the turkey be juicy enough? Did she forget anything? Would Anna Marie mind her manners with Daniel? And—how was Daniel going to act?

"Jacob, more wood for the fire," Lydia instructed from the kitchen. "And John, I think your *Daadi* John and *Mammi* Mary are pulling in with *Aenti* Miriam. Go see if you can help them carry things into the house."

Jacob and John moved toward the door, and Lydia realized that she'd been barking a lot of orders at them the past couple of days. She'd been so preoccupied with Daniel's return and Thanksgiving preparations, she hadn't spent much time with her sons.

"John. Jacob."

The boys turned around.

"When you get done, I have one more chore for you."

John sighed, and Jacob twisted his mouth to one side. Lydia smiled. "I need testers for my desserts. Is that something you boys might be interested in?"

"Before our meal?" John's eyes grew wide, and a grin stretched across his small face.

"*Ya*, I think so," Lydia said with a nod and wink.

Both boys scampered out the door.

Lydia's mother always brought more than was on her list. Lydia peeked out the window and wasn't surprised to see them coming up the walkway with their arms full. Her two brothers, John Jr. and Melvin, were pulling up with their families. Daniel and Elam's two sisters were also arriving with their spouses and children.

Mary Herschberger entered the kitchen, carrying two casserole dishes covered in foil. "Yams and a fruit salad." She placed the food on the kitchen cabinet, then walked to where Lydia was standing by the stove. "Lydia?"

"*Ya.*"

Her mother wiped her hands on her black apron and pushed her eyeglasses up on her nose, ignoring the strands of gray hair that hung loose from beneath her prayer covering. She glanced around the room, then whispered, "Are you all right, dear?"

"I'm *gut, Mamm.*"

Her mother's forehead creased with concern as she pressed her lips together.

"Really, *Mamm*," Lydia assured her. "I'm fine." Now if she could only convince herself she was all right.

"I know this must be *hatt* for you, having Daniel return."

Lydia loved Thanksgiving Day, and if nothing else, she was going to pretend things were all right. "That was a long time ago, *Mamm*."

Mary frowned a bit. "I know, dear. But I remember the way it was with you and Daniel."

So did Lydia. And those images kept assaulting her thoughts. She kissed her mother on the cheek. "No worries today, *Mamm*. It's Thanksgiving."

Her father was less subtle when he entered the room. "So, I hear Daniel is back." John Herschberger looped his thumbs beneath his suspenders. Lydia quickly glanced around the room to see if anyone else had heard her father's remark. Only Miriam. Her sister scooted past her father, carrying two large bags. She smiled sympathetically in Lydia's direction.

"Shush, John. We all know he's back," Mary whispered as she rolled her eyes at her husband.

"Hi, *Daed*." Lydia hugged her father, then made her way to where Anna Marie was hovering over the sink.

Her daughter was peeling potatoes cheerfully, since Amos was coming for dinner. Lydia had always served the Thanksgiving meal at noon, and the Zook family planned to eat much later in the day.

Lydia glanced at the clock on the wall. Eleven fifteen. Everything was running smoothly.

Next to arrive was Lydia's sister Hannah, with her family, followed by her other sister, Rachel, and her group. Lydia poured the brewed tea from the pot into a pitcher and looked up to see Gideon, Lena, and Daniel standing nearby in the kitchen.

"*Ach*, hello. I didn't see you come in," she said to the three of them. She tried to avoid looking toward Daniel, but her eyes seemed to have a mind of their own.

"Gideon pulled up 'round the back of the house," Lena said. "Which is making it a mite hard to carry in all of my dishes."

"Anna Marie, I'll finish the potatoes," Lydia said. "You go help *Daadi* and *Mammi* bring things in." Lydia took the knife from her hand.

"Let me," Daniel said when Anna Marie was out the door. "I seem to recall that you dislike peeling potatoes." He reached for the knife, but Lydia pulled away and slid the blade down one side of the potato.

"You've been in the *Englisch* world too long. You know that the men folk don't help with meal preparation," she said. "You best go busy yourself in the den."

"Suit yourself," he said. Then he picked up a peeled potato, inspected it, and placed it back in the colander. "You missed a spot."

Lydia looked up to see him wink before he turned and walked toward the den. That type of flirtatious behavior would get him nowhere. Even so, she felt herself blushing. Several men in the community had shown an interest in her over the past couple of years, but she couldn't recall any of them invoking a blush with such a simple gesture. And none of those potential suitors caused her heart rate to speed up the way it did when Daniel was in the room.

She picked up the potato and sliced off the leftover piece of skin. She recalled fussing to her mother every time she was asked to peel potatoes. *Hmm. Daniel remembered that.*

At straight up noon, everyone began to find a seat. Two tables were set up in the den, plus a small table for the young ones. Once everyone was settled, Lydia took a seat at the table in the kitchen. She was glad that Daniel had chosen to sit at a table in the den—but not so glad that he'd selected a seat near her father. Pop thought Lydia should have remarried by now, and she worried what thoughts her dad might be having concerning Daniel's return. Then she noticed Anna Marie by the window, and she realized that Amos hadn't shown up yet.

"I'm sure he'll be here, Anna Marie," Lydia said. "Come sit down so we can offer our blessings."

Anna Marie pried herself from the window and joined her mother at the kitchen table, along with Lena and Gideon and other family members. One seat was left for Amos.

But two hours later—after everyone had stuffed themselves with rhubarb pie, shoofly pie, banana pudding, and a variety of other desserts—Amos still hadn't arrived. Anna Marie had barely touched her food. Lydia knew how much she'd been looking forward to spending her first holiday with a boy, the one she intended to marry . . .

That was a concept still hard for Lydia to believe.

Anna Marie seemed so young to her. Lydia knew that seventeen was an acceptable age for marriage, but it was still considered young by community standards. It saddened her to know that she would only have her daughter under her roof for one more year. Since weddings were always held in November or December, after the fall harvest, there'd be plenty of time to pick a date and prepare.

"Maybe his kin changed the time of their Thanksgiving meal," Lydia whispered to Anna Marie after everyone was gone. Everyone except for Daniel and his parents.

And Daniel didn't seem in a hurry to go anywhere. She scowled in his direction.

But what she saw next softened her mood. Jacob, John, and Daniel were huddled together, laughing and carrying on. Anna Marie might not have taken a fancy to Daniel, but clearly her sons had. Lydia had done her best to be both parents since Elam's death, but boys needed a male role model. They had her father and Gideon, but for the first time, she began to see something positive in Daniel's return to the community. Perhaps he would play catch with the boys or teach them things their father hadn't been able to before he passed.

"Come on with us, Anna Marie," Lena said. She retrieved her cape and bonnet from the rack by the door. "We'll run by the Zooks' place and make sure everything is all right over there."

Anna Marie's face lit up, and she rushed to her grandmother's side.

"You fellas come on too," Gideon said, much to Lydia's horror. "We'll dig out your Pop's old box of games."

Lydia knew how much the boys loved it when Gideon offered to play games with them, games that had belonged to their father when he was a boy.

"Gideon, they best stay home," Lydia blurted out, "with school and all tomorrow."

Jacob and John were already at the door. "Ain't no school the day after Thanksgiving, *Mamm*," John said. He scooted past his grandfather and out the door.

No, no, no. They can't all leave me here alone with Daniel.

But that's exactly what they did. Even Anna Marie didn't come protectively to her defense. She was too anxious to see Amos to worry herself about her mother's crisis.

Daniel was once again warming his hands by the fire. Everyone else was outside and loading into the buggy, except for Lena. It had taken her a little longer than the others to bundle for the weather. After she tied her black bonnet, she leaned over and hugged Lydia.

Then she whispered in her ear, "I love you, Lydia, like my own daughter. Please hear him out. It might make a difference to you." Then she pulled away, smiled, and walked out to the buggy.

It appeared Lydia didn't have a choice in the matter. She closed the door and turned to face Daniel.

He just shrugged, as if to say, *I had nothing to do with it.*

Lydia knew better.

CHAPTER 8

Daniel watched as Lydia lit two lanterns and placed them on opposite sides of the den. After the door closed behind his parents, he was prepared for her to ask him to leave. But to his surprise, she didn't.

"It will be dark soon." She turned to face him. Her blank expression didn't offer any hints as to her thoughts about being coerced into this meeting. But one thing he remembered about her—the woman had an independent way of thinking and doing things. Daniel knew she was not happy at being set up.

He smiled slightly in her direction, afraid to say too much too soon, and waited—waited for her to tell him to get out.

She didn't return the smile, and her voice was monotone when she spoke. "Would you like some *kaffi*?"

"That sounds great. I mean *wunderbaar gut*." Again he smiled, but she just turned and walked toward the kitchen. Daniel followed her. "I'm surprised how much Pennsylvania *Deitsch* I remember."

Lydia poured two cups of coffee into white mugs, and Daniel noticed how she'd retained her youthful figure. Her black apron, tied snug atop her dark green dress, defined the smallness of her waist.

He sat down at one of the wooden chairs at her kitchen table and glanced around the room. Lydia owned more gadgets than his parents, who still did everything the old way. His mother still mashed potatoes with a hand masher and refused to buy a modern gas stove, but Daniel noticed a battery-operated mixer on the counter and a shiny white gas range next to the propane refrigerator in Lydia's kitchen. There was also a weather-alert radio at the end of the counter, also charged by battery.

"I was surprised to see that *mei mamm* still uses a woodstove to cook," he said. Lydia handed him the coffee and took a seat across from him at the kitchen table. He noticed a shift in her expression, from blank to fearful. Her coffee cup was in one hand, but she was grinding her thumb and forefinger fiercely with the other hand. "I would have thought that *Mamm* and *Daed* would have upgraded to something more modern. Something like what you have." He nodded toward Lydia's stove.

"They have talked about purchasing a gas range, but—" She stopped, locked her eyes with his. "But they haven't yet." Her eyes stayed fused with his, and her fingers were on overdrive.

She was so nervous and upset, Daniel wasn't sure this was the right time to tell her what he wanted to say. Perhaps he should just use this time to reconnect with her, hear about her life, her children—and Elam—see how all that went first.

"I told Anna Marie about us, about the note," Lydia finally said after a few moments of silence between them. She pulled her eyes from his and clutched her cup with both hands. She took a long sip, then kept a tight hold on the mug and lifted her eyes back to his. "She doesn't like you very much." She eased into a grin.

"It's nice to see you smile," he said. "And no, I don't seem to be Anna Marie's favorite person at the moment."

"That's understandable, I reckon. Now she knows her father wasn't my first true—" Her cheeks flushed, and she looked away. "She'll come around."

"But will you?" Daniel 's pulse grew rapid as he waited for her to respond. She wasn't kneading her fingers together anymore, but her cheeks were still a rosy shade of pink, and her eyes reflected her unease.

Lydia sat taller and released her firm grip on the coffee cup. She folded her hands in front of her on the table, took a deep breath, and fused her eyes intently with his.

He waited for what seemed like an eternity.

"We will be friends," she said matter-of-factly. "You are the children's *onkel*, and I love Lena and Gideon as if they were my own parents. But . . ." She sat taller and lifted her chin a bit. "There can be no courtship between us."

"I never said anything about *courtship*." He couldn't help but smile at her presumption. Not that he didn't want exactly that.

"Well, I'm just—just making that clear." She paused, but held her head high and went on. "I was thinking earlier, when I saw you with Jacob and John, that perhaps it would be *gut* for you to be in the boys' lives."

"I'd like that," he said.

She was softening a little. During their first

encounter, she'd made it quite clear that there would be no unnecessary socializing.

And he would settle for being her friend, although he didn't think it would ever be enough—for either of them. But one thing loomed over him, something equally as important to him as having her in his life.

"Lydia . . ." he began slowly. "I need to know if you have truly forgiven me in your heart. You said the words, but . . ."

She gazed at him with a faraway look in her eyes. Lydia had always been transparent, and he could tell she was about to tell a lie. An unintentional lie that she might not even recognize as such, but a fib just the same. "Yes, I forgive you."

He considered her response for a moment. "You said that awfully fast." Then added, "And I don't believe you."

"You think I would lie?"

"Not intentionally." Daniel looked her in the eye. "I think you *want* to forgive me, because you know it's what God wants you to do. But I think you are struggling to do so."

"Well, you're wrong," she huffed. "I do forgive you. I reckon you might give yourself a bit too much credit."

"Maybe," he said. Then he leaned his elbows on the table and leaned forward. "But I don't think so. We were in love, Lydia. It was real, and I've never gotten over it. I have missed you every single day, dreamed about you—and I know you felt it too. I think you still do."

She stood from the table. "Get out!"

He stood up and faced her from across the table. "Lydia, wait. I'm sorry. We don't have to talk about that, but there is something I need to tell you. Something about that night, Christmas Eve. Maybe you will understand—"

She rounded the corner of the kitchen into the den, and Daniel followed in time to see her yank the front door open. Flames flickered in the fireplace as a cold rush of wind swept into the room. "Please leave," she said.

"Lydia, just let me explain."

She refused to look in his direction and kept her chin held high. Daniel walked toward her and stood in the doorway as she reached for his coat on the rack by the door. She handed it to him without glancing his way. "Good-bye, Daniel."

"Lydia, please . . . let me tell you about the night I left."

. . .

Lydia closed her eyes and remembered what Lena had said. *Please hear him out. Listen to what Daniel has to say. It might make a difference to you.* She took a moment to silence the voices in her head and concentrated on the only voice that was important. She lowered her head and asked God for his guidance. Then she slowly opened her eyes and faced Daniel to see his eyes brimming with tenderness, begging her to reconsider. She pushed the door closed and motioned him to the couch in the den.

"*Danki*," he said.

Lydia flung his coat on the sofa and sat down in one of the rocking chairs facing it. She wasn't sure if she wanted to hear what Daniel had to say, or if it would make any difference. He'd given up on their love and left her. What more did she need to know? Besides, it was such a long time ago. Although, even all these years later, despite her marriage, the children, and her own belief that she had led the life she was meant to live, the raw hurt had resurfaced.

She wanted to forgive him. To understand. But those untapped emotions were bouncing around in a tight box of fear that gripped her, and she worried the lid might pop off any minute and expose what her heart screamed to her—that she'd always loved Daniel, and still did. And that thought made her feel like she was betraying Elam.

Lydia knew she needed to live righteously in the eyes of God, to forgive those who trespassed against her. *All this worry and guilt is a sin*, she thought. Daniel opened his mouth to talk, and Lydia made up her mind to forgive him and mean it, no matter what he had to say.

His expression seemed full of the life he'd led, in a world she knew nothing about. His brow furrowed, and the pain in his eyes was unmistakable. Whatever he was about to tell her, it was of great importance and discomfort to him.

"Go on, Daniel. I'm listening."

"Lydia, that night, on Christmas Eve—" He shook his head.

What in the world is he going to tell me? She realized she was literally holding her breath, and she forced herself to exhale. "It's all right," she said soothingly, as she would to anyone so tormented. And she hoped it would be—all right.

The sound of footsteps coming up the porch steps diverted their attention. No sooner did they both look in that direction than they heard a loud knock on the door.

Lydia rushed across the den and pulled the door open. "Amos! What are you doing here?"

He struggled to catch his breath. "Hello. I, uh—could I please talk to Anna Marie?"

Lydia scrutinized him for a moment, and then gently touched his elbow and pulled him over the threshold. She closed the door and glanced at her clock on the mantel. "Amos, Anna Marie was expecting you for dinner at noon. When you didn't show up, she left to spend the night with her *mammi* and *daadi*. They said they were going to stop by your house on the way. Is everything all right?"

Amos's eyes jetted toward Daniel.

"This is Elam's brother, Daniel." Lydia nodded in Daniel's direction, but then quickly turned back to Amos, who was still struggling to catch his breath. "I didn't hear a buggy," she said. "Did you run over here? And where is your coat?"

Daniel stood up and approached Amos with an extended hand. "Nice to meet you, Amos."

"Everything is *gut*, no?" Lydia asked again.

"*Ya*. Everything is *gut*."

Lydia eyed him suspiciously and noticed Daniel wearing a similar expression.

"I just need to talk to Anna Marie." Amos sounded desperate. "It's important, and I need to find her, and—" The boy leaned over, put his hands on his knees, and seemed to be gasping for air. When he lifted his head up, his eyes were clouded with tears. "I have to find her," he repeated.

"Amos, what is wrong?" Lydia brought her hand to her chest. "Is someone hurt? Did something happen?"

Amos stood straight again. He glanced back and forth between Lydia and Daniel and seemed unsure whether to talk.

Lydia put her hands on her hips. "Amos Zook, you tell me right now what's the matter."

"I'm in trouble," he finally said. He looked down toward his shoes and shook his head. "I'm in a lot of trouble."

CHAPTER 9

Daniel heard the anguish in Amos's voice. "What kind of trouble?" he asked.

"Yes, Amos, what kind of trouble?" Lydia echoed.

"I—I . . ." Amos shook his head, and his eyes darted back and forth between Daniel and Lydia. "I have to go." He turned to face the door, pulled on the knob, and bolted down the porch stairs into the yard.

Lydia was instantly behind him. "Amos! Amos, wait!"

Daniel joined her on the front porch and watched the boy sprint across the yard.

"What could possibly be so bad?" Lydia asked. "Amos!"

Then something inside of Daniel ignited. "I'll go after him."

He hurried down the steps, into the yard, and then broke into a run. When he reached the street, he stopped to listen. In the darkness he could hear something moving down the road to his right. Daniel ran, thankful for his time at the gym the past few months. He slowly began to close the gap between them. "Amos, stop!" he yelled.

But the boy didn't slow down, and Daniel wasn't

sure how long he could keep up this pace. He pushed himself to run faster, stretching each stride to its fullest length.

Now he was within a few feet of Amos. "Stop!" *Please.*

Thankfully, the boy slowed his run to a light jog. Daniel tried to catch his breath as he drew near Amos, who finally stopped in the middle of the road.

The boy turned to face him. "There's no need to come after me," he said, breathless himself. "I will handle *mei* troubles."

Daniel held his palm forward, signaling that he couldn't quite choke out any words yet.

"Please tell Anna Marie that I love her. I'll always love her," Amos announced with the authority of someone much older than himself. He took a step backward.

"Please don't take off again," Daniel mumbled. He stood up straight and drew in a breath, releasing it slowly.

"Why are you following me? You don't even know me."

"But I know Anna Marie," Daniel said, hoping to entice the boy to talk to him. "And if you love her as much as you say you do, you won't run away from whatever trouble you're in."

"I don't have a choice." Amos pulled off his straw hat and wiped sweat from his brow.

Daniel wondered how the boy had kept it on. He'd lost his own hat early into the chase.

"We always have a choice." A cool trickle of sweat ran down Daniel's spine, beneath his long-sleeved blue shirt. "It's freezing out here. Can we talk back at the house? Just give me a few minutes to talk to you."

Amos instantly shook his head. "I don't want to talk in front of Anna Marie's *mamm*," he said firmly.

"I understand. Maybe we can talk man-to-man on the walk back—*walk*, no running." He smiled, trying to lighten Amos's mood. "What do you have to lose? If you don't like what I have to say, you can take off again." Daniel chuckled. "Believe me, I don't have the energy to chase you."

Amos stewed a moment, then agreed. Slowly the story unfolded.

He and two other boys—*Englisch* boys—had walked into a convenience store to get a soda. One of the boys, Tommy, noticed that the store attendant had gone into the back storage room. Tommy opened the cooler, and instead of a soda, he grabbed two beers and stuffed them inside his coat. The other boy, Greg, also snatched two beers and hid them in his jacket. Amos didn't want to do it, but the others kept nagging at him, so Amos finally hid two beers in his coat too. None of them counted on the camera in the store feeding to the back room, where the man watched them steal the beers.

To make things worse, when the man confronted them, Tommy took off at a run. Greg followed, then Amos—who ran right into the police officer that the attendant had called. The other boys were caught shortly thereafter.

"I've never stolen anything in my life." Amos shook his head. "I broke one of the Ten Commandments."

Tommy's father was the first one to show up and post bond for his son. It took about an hour for Greg's father to arrive. With no way to get in touch with

Amos's family, the judge had allowed Greg's dad to post the bond for Amos as well. And since all three boys were underage, they didn't have to spend the night behind bars.

But Amos was standing right next to the police officer when he left a message on the phone in the Zook barn: "Mr. Zook, I have your son Amos at the jail. He has been charged with theft."

"I can just picture the look on Pop's face when he hears that message. I have shamed my family." Amos hung his head. "And Anna Marie."

Daniel looked at Amos. The boy was three years younger than Daniel had been when he left on Christmas Eve. Even though Amos's problems didn't compare to Daniel's, it was still a heavy burden for an Amish boy. There might be a trip to the woodshed and a harsh reprimand, but in the end, the boy's father would forgive him for his poor choice. It wasn't like Amos had assaulted anyone.

Daniel stopped in the road and pulled on the boy's arm, and they stood facing each other. "Amos, you have to keep this in perspective. You made a mistake. Your father will be disappointed in you, and Anna Marie might be too, but if she loves you as much as she seems to, then she will stick by you. If you run away, sometimes it's too hard to come back."

"But I went to jail on Thanksgiving Day!" Amos blasted. "It's a day for family and fellowship, and I spent it eating a peanut butter and jelly sandwich in a room that had a toilet in the corner." He shook his head. "It was *baremlich*."

Daniel started to say something, but Amos went on.

"And the police officer—he said I have to go to court! I reckon I'm going to have to pay money and—" He paused and shook his head. "I can't talk to *mei daed* about this."

"It takes a real man to face what he did. Amos, don't make a decision right now that could affect the rest of your life." Daniel took a deep breath and pushed the past out of his head. "What is news in the community today will be forgotten in no time. Are you really willing to lose Anna Marie over this? Where would you go?"

"I don't know," Amos said. "I just wanted to see Anna Marie one last time before I left."

They took a few steps. Daniel's teeth were chattering, and he was anxious to get into Lydia's house where there was a fire going, but not too anxious to take the time to help this young boy see things in the right light.

"Before we get back to the house, I have a story to tell you. A story that might help you decide whether leaving is the right thing to do."

. . .

Lydia heard footsteps and faint voices outside. She opened the front door and was relieved to see Amos with Daniel.

"Thank goodness you are all right." Lydia touched Amos's arm and then glanced at Daniel. "Both of you." She quickly looked away when his eyes met hers.

As she pushed the door closed, Daniel and Amos walked to the fireplace.

"I'm going to give Amos a ride home," Daniel said. He continued to warm his hands in front of the fire.

"*Gut*," Lydia said. "It's too cold out there for walking." She eyed Amos with curiosity.

"I need to go home and talk to *mei daed*," he humbly said to Lydia. Then he turned to Daniel, and appreciation swept across his face. "*Danki*, Daniel."

Daniel smiled affectionately at him. "You're welcome, Amos."

Lydia wanted to ask Amos why he was thanking Daniel, what the two had talked about. A little earlier she'd been afraid to hear what Daniel was going to tell her; now disappointment nipped at the fear. While they were gone, she'd tried to prepare herself for anything, dreaming up every possible scenario that could have happened on that long-ago Christmas Eve. *Did he leave because he found another love? Maybe an* Englischer? *Did he have some grand opportunity for success in the* Englisch *world that he couldn't pass up? Did he decide he didn't love me after all?*

Lydia said good-bye and hugged Amos at the front door. After the boy walked outside, Daniel turned back to her.

"I'd still like to have our talk," he said. "Could I come back over after I take Amos home?"

It was still early in the evening, and Lydia didn't think she'd sleep a wink without hearing what he had to say. "*Ya*. I'll brew a fresh pot of *kaffi*."

Daniel slowly lifted his hand to her face and brushed away a strand of hair that had fallen from beneath her prayer covering. His finger lingered on her cheek. "I'll see you soon," he said softly.

"*Ya.*"

She watched him walk to the buggy, mechanically closed the door, and didn't move for a moment. All the fear she'd fought to harness suddenly returned with a vengeance. If his touch invoked this type of reaction, how in the world was she going to be around him on a regular basis without facing her true feelings? That she had always loved Daniel. And still did.

CHAPTER 10

It was almost eight o'clock when Lydia heard horse hooves coming up the driveway. She stood from her chair at the kitchen table where she'd been putting cookbooks together to use up her nervous energy, wiped sweaty palms down the sides of her black apron, and headed to the front door. Her stomach churned as she turned the knob, then waited for Daniel to come across the grass and up the steps. Lydia swung the door wide, stepped aside, and motioned him in.

She usually went to bed at eight thirty. She considered mentioning that in case things didn't go well, but she didn't have to.

"I know it's getting close to your bedtime—and mine too," he said. "I'm getting back on *Mamm* and *Daed*'s schedule, so I promise not to keep you up too late."

"I made fresh *kaffi*," she said. "Warm yourself by the fire, and I'll bring us each a cup."

When Lydia walked back into the den, Daniel was sitting on the couch. She handed him one of the mugs she was carrying and wondered where to sit—at the far end of the sofa, or in one of the rocking chairs. She backed away from him, eased into the rocker, and pushed the chair into motion with her foot while clutching tightly to her coffee cup with both hands.

"Lydia—" Daniel locked eyes with her. "As much as I want you to forgive me for leaving you that Christmas Eve, by telling you what really happened, I run the risk of losing you yet again."

"You don't *have* me," she said.

Lydia could see pain in Daniel's eyes.

"You might be angry with me after I tell you this story, but it's only fair that you know the truth." He paused. "I just hope that Elam would agree with me."

"Elam?" Lydia's eyes widened, and her pulse picked up. "What does Elam have to do with anything that happened that night?"

"Do you remember when Elam came to your house on Christmas Eve and gave you the note I wrote?"

She shot him a look that nearly knocked him over.

"I guess you do." He diverted his eyes and rubbed his hands together. "Anyway. That morning, Elam and I went to pick up your Christmas present, something I'd made for you. I was having it professionally engraved at a shop in town, and—"

"What was it?" The words flew from her lips. She recalled the present she bought for Daniel that year—a fine set of woodworking tools that she had eventually given to Elam.

Daniel's eyes met with hers again. "A cedar chest."

Lydia gasped. "You made me a cedar chest?" A gift like that was certainly allowable in their community, but considered somewhat extravagant in comparison to the small presents that are routinely exchanged at Christmas.

"*Ya*, I did," Daniel said in a low voice.

Lydia remembered telling Daniel on their way home from one of the many Sunday singings how she longed to have a cedar chest to store heirlooms for their future. She'd told him, but she'd never expected him to make her one for Christmas.

But wait a minute. Daniel was picking up her Christmas present that very day . . . ?

"Daniel . . ."

His eyes reconnected with hers. "*Ya*?"

"If you were picking up my Christmas present on Christmas Eve morning, what changed by that afternoon to—" Her voice broke. "To make you decide you didn't love me enough to stay?"

"What? Is that what you think?" He scooted toward the edge of the couch and leaned forward. "I loved you enough," he said with a quiet but desperate firmness. "Enough to leave."

"That makes no sense." She set her cup on the table next to her, crossed her arms, and waited.

"Something happened before Elam and I were able to pick up the cedar chest." Daniel leaned back against the couch. "We decided to get a glass of homemade root beer and a whoopee pie from the Stoltzfus Bakery."

He seemed to be struggling with every word he spoke, which only added to Lydia's apprehension.

"After that we were strolling past the shops on Lincoln Highway, and then we cut through a back alley to go pick up the chest." Daniel clamped his eyes shut. "We heard sounds of a struggle," he finally said. "An *Englisch* boy had a girl pinned down on the ground, and—and he was doing unthinkable things to her. The girl looked about our age, maybe younger. An *Englisch* girl."

He shook his head, and anger swept across his face. "At first Elam and I kept walking. It wasn't our place to get involved, nor was it our way. But then the girl saw us, and she cried out to us for help. I can see her face as though it happened yesterday. She had blonde hair and a pink shirt. I can still remember the fear in her eyes, begging us to help her, as the boy held her down on the gravel."

Lydia cupped her hand to her mouth.

"There were shops that backed up to the alley, and a few houses farther down the way. I kept waiting for someone to come help her, but there was no one around but Elam and me. She kicked at the boy and tried to scream, but he slapped her across the face and told her to shut up." Daniel paused. "And then something in me just snapped."

Lydia had stopped rocking in the chair and sat immobilized with visions of that poor girl, but she didn't understand Daniel's comment. "Snapped?"

"*Ya*, I snapped—I just couldn't take it anymore. I told Elam to stay back. The boy—his name was Chad—swore at me and told me to be on my Amish way, that it was none of my concern. But I kept walking toward him. He was big too. Muscular. And about my height. I told him to let the girl up.

"Finally, I was standing right beside them." Daniel took a deep breath. "I could hear Elam calling my name. I took a step backward, but then that girl's eyes met with mine again, and I moved forward and told the boy to let her go—or else."

Lydia held her breath and tried to imagine Daniel, or anyone from their community, speaking in such a way.

"He let her go, jumped up, and within seconds my face went numb, and I could taste blood. I knew my nose was broken, but I wasn't sure if the blood was coming from my nose or my lip, which was on fire. I landed on my back, and when I was able to stand up and focus, I saw the girl running and screaming, but he went after her, grabbing the back of her collar and throwing her back on the ground.

"I couldn't imagine him hurting that girl any more than he already had. Elam was yelling for us to go home, but instead I marched over to Chad, grabbed him by the shirt, and returned an equally sound blow to his face. Then I hit him again and again, until he went down and stayed down. When I looked up, the girl was gone, and two men were running toward us."

Lydia's mouth hung open. She knew that violence was wrong, but she still admired his chivalry. And in the back of her mind, she wondered, *What did this have to do with his leaving on Christmas Eve?*

"As it turns out," Daniel went on, "Chad told everyone I'd assaulted him while my brother stood and watched, egging me on. It would have been a pretty unbelievable story—two Amish boys involved in such a mess—but Chad looked much worse than I did, and he knew the policeman who showed up. Officer Turner. I remember the way the cop looked at me with such shock, but he handcuffed me just the same and hauled me to jail."

Lydia gasped as more fearful images swirled in her head. "What about the boy, Chad? He went to jail too, no?"

Daniel shook his head. "Not only did Chad know Officer Turner, but his father knew him too. He didn't spend even one minute behind bars. Only me."

"Where was the girl? Couldn't she explain what happened? And what about Elam? He saw everything." Lydia was wondering why Elam never told her this story.

"The girl was long gone, and Chad refused to admit that there was even a girl there. He stuck to his story that two Amish boys approached him in the alley, and that I beat him up." Daniel cringed. "I wasn't proud of my actions, by any means. Chad had a broken nose, like mine, but also two broken ribs. And always in the back of my mind was Pop. I'd shamed my family."

Lydia searched anxiously for the meaning behind his words. What was he trying to say?

"I just couldn't come back, Lydia. I was being charged with assault of another human being, something unheard-of in our community. I spent the night in a cell with four big, burly-looking men, and the jailer that night asked me repeatedly if I wanted to make a phone call. It wasn't until morning when I decided to call someone, an *Englisch* man I'd met a couple of months earlier; he was someone I trusted not to tell anyone. But it was Christmas Day. I had to wait until the day after Christmas for him to post bail and get me out. It was a *baremlich* two days."

Lydia finally understood. "You left our way of life— and me—because you couldn't face your father?"

"I know it sounds cowardly, Lydia, but I didn't want to shame my family like that. It seemed like I was always getting a lecture from Pop about not being able to hold my tongue, and this was much worse. But not a day went by that I didn't think about you and miss you."

She fought the tremble in her voice. "Did you not think to pen me a letter to explain all of this after you left?" Lydia brought her hand to her mouth as another realization hit her, one equally as bad, if not worse. "Elam knew all this." She rose from the chair and began to pace the room.

"Lydia, let me explain." Daniel stood up and walked toward her.

She held both arms straight out in front of her.

"He befriended me. I cried on Elam's shoulder." A tear rolled down her cheek. "And all the while, he knew! He knew what happened. Elam let me wonder why you would leave me, repeatedly telling me that you just wanted to live in the *Englisch* world. How could he do that to me when he knew how much I was hurting?" Her eyes blazed. "Did the two of you keep in touch?"

Daniel stood before her, his own eyes clouding with emotion. "For a while. Until—until he began to court you."

He took a step toward her, and she backed up.

"I knew Elam was in love with you, and I knew he'd be a *gut* father to your children. I, on the other hand, had a court date to face, and I ended up being convicted of assault and spending six months in jail, so there was no coming back. I wanted you to have the life you deserved. I knew Elam could give you that."

"The life I deserved?" Lydia backed up farther until she bumped against the wall. She flattened her palms against the whitewash wall, steadied herself, and then brought one hand to her chest. "You and Elam got together and planned my future? Instead of telling me where you were and giving me a choice, you both just kept quiet, while my heart was breaking?"

All her wounds reopened. Her beloved Elam. How could he have lied to her? She'd been in such anguish, and he could have put an end to it. Instead he chose to pursue her for himself.

"I'm telling you all this, Lydia, for several reasons. First, it's the truth. Second, I want you to know that I never left because I didn't love you enough. And I knew Elam would treat you as you deserved to be treated. I, however, was a criminal."

"When did you write the note?" She choked out the words.

"Later that afternoon, when I realized I wouldn't be home for Christmas Eve supper or Christmas Day. I sent a note to you and one to my parents."

"Elam wouldn't do this," she said. "I don't believe any of it!"

But deep inside, she knew it was the truth. If there had ever been a chance of her forgiving Daniel, it was gone. Now she would struggle with how to forgive her husband for his role in this convenient lie.

"Why did you come back?" Lydia felt like she'd been hit in the stomach. "Not only did you leave me all those years ago, but now you tell me this news of my husband, that he lied to me so that I would be his. All the while, my heart was breaking for you. It is unforgivable. All of it."

Daniel reached for her, but she pulled away. "Lydia, I

don't want mistruths hanging over us. I have confessed my sins before God, and now I declare them to you."

Lydia clamped her lips together in an attempt to squelch her sobs. She wished Elam was here to explain all of this to her . . . to say that he would never withhold information about Daniel just to win a place in her heart for himself. *Please, God . . .*

When Daniel wrapped his arms around her, she buried her head in his chest and sobbed. He could have been anyone—anyone willing to hold her up. But he was Daniel, and to stay in his arms would cause her nothing but heartache. No matter how much she had loved him, staying righteous in God's eyes was now compounded by her inability to forgive not only Daniel, but her husband as well.

She pulled away from him and pointed toward the door.

CHAPTER 11

Lydia placed a poinsettia plant on either side of the fireplace, and the flowery red blooms invoked bittersweet memories. Elam had loved Christmastime. She placed colorfully wrapped presents in various places throughout the den, adding an air of celebration to the room. But inwardly she was having trouble finding the spirit of the season. She'd been praying for a reprieve from the grief that festered inside her, but it continued to gnaw away at her from the inside out. Amid all her troubles, she knew that forgiveness was the only thing that would free her soul to find the peace she so desperately longed for.

"*Mamm*, when are we leaving for *Onkel* Daniel's baptism?"

Lydia arched a questioning brow at Anna Marie's casual acceptance of her uncle, whom she'd been less than fond of so recently. "Soon," she said.

She hadn't seen Daniel since Thanksgiving, and three days later, her stomach still rolled every time she thought about what Daniel and Elam had done. But there was no way out of attending the baptism, which would be at Daniel's new home at the old Kauffman place. Lena and Gideon told her that he'd moved in the day after Thanksgiving. She said Daniel had spent his time in the *Englisch* world doing odd jobs, mostly carpentry. And according to her sister Miriam, who'd stopped by Daniel's house to deliver eggs on behalf of their parents, he was doing an amazing job restoring the place.

Lydia rounded up Jacob and John, motioned to Anna Marie that it was time to go, and they loaded in the buggy to head to Daniel's baptism.

• • •

Lydia watched as the deacon ladled water from a bucket into the bishop's hand. Daniel sat with one hand over his face, to represent his submission and humility to the church. The bishop sprinkled Daniel's head three times, in the name of the Father, Son, and Holy Ghost, and then blessed him with a holy kiss.

It was such a sacred occasion, and despite the circumstances, Lydia was glad that Daniel received the sacrament of baptism after cleansing himself through prayer and confession, and that he had not accepted such a blessing without first being truthful with her, his parents, and the bishop.

But she couldn't seem to corral her emotions into one central part of her brain, where she might be able to process the information in a new way. Her thoughts were all over the place and filled with what-ifs. And it was that questioning of God's will that kept her up at night. If the events of that night had played out any differently, she wouldn't have Anna Marie, Jacob, or John, and she wouldn't have shared fifteen joy-filled years with Elam.

Every time she prayed for the strength of heart and mind to forgive both men, her heart wrapped itself in a self-preserving cocoon. She knew that for God to do his work, she would have to let down her barriers and allow herself to feel the pain, so his glory could help her move forward.

After Daniel's baptism, the women prepared chicken and wafers for dinner in the kitchen, while the men found seats at one of the many tables set up throughout Daniel's house. Lydia had brought a tomato pie to the event. Elam's favorite. As usual, there was a vast variety of offerings, more than enough to feed the one hundred in attendance: three ham loaves, four meat loaves, succotash, cabbage casserole, several types of potatoes, and at least two dozen desserts. Chow-chow, jams, jellies, and ten loaves of homemade bread lined the countertop.

Lydia glanced at the clock on the hutch in the kitchen. Straight up noon, and she could feel her stomach growling.

She had to admit, Daniel had already done wonders with the old Kauffman place. After four generations raised families in the home, the house was retired two years ago, after the last generation was unable to have children and passed on. A niece, who already owned a home in the community, inherited the place, and the farmhouse had been in need of much repair.

Lydia breathed in the smell of freshly painted white-washed walls and noticed new cabinets throughout the kitchen. Crisp green blinds were drawn halfway up on the windows, and festive garlands were draped across the windowsills, with tiny red bows attached. She poured brewed tea into a pitcher and handed it to Anna Marie, instructing her daughter to add sugar and begin serving the men.

Lydia picked up a bowl of pickled red beets and carried it into the den. Daniel was sitting with his father, the bishop, and two elders on the left side of the room. She veered to her right, where her own father was sitting, and put the bowl on the table.

Daniel's den was warm and cozy with a blazing fire in the hearth, and Lydia noticed the beautiful mantel above the fireplace—simple, with no ornate carvings, but bold and eye-catching. She wondered if Daniel was responsible for the fine carpentry. He'd always had a knack for building things. She thought of the cedar chest and wondered, not for the first time, what had become of the forsaken gift.

She took her time walking back to the kitchen, wanting to soak in every detail of Daniel's home as the what-ifs stirred in her thoughts. What might their home have looked like if she had married Daniel? Did they have similar tastes? While most Old Order homes were simply decorated, each one still possessed character and individuality. She saw Christmas presents placed around the house and bright poinsettias on either side of the fireplace, just as they were in her own home. A green, leafy garland spiraled around the railing of the banister that led upstairs, trimmed with holly and with a large bow at the foot of the railing. Her stairway was also decorated with garland and bows, but she couldn't put her finger on why Daniel's trimmings looked better than hers.

She lingered in the den for a moment and pretended to be checking tea glasses for refills, but her eyes kept involuntarily shifting to the flight of stairs that ascended to Daniel's bedroom.

Does he keep a box of tissues by the bed? A pitcher of water? A flashlight? Does he read at night before he goes to sleep? What color is the quilt on his bed? Which side of the bed does he sleep on?

The questions pounded obsessively in her head. She glanced in his direction, and his blue eyes rose and clung to hers. She jumped when someone touched her arm.

"Are you all right, dear?" Lena asked.

"*Ya.*" Lydia faced Lena, but she could feel Daniel's eyes still on her.

"Daniel said that he told you of his trouble on Christmas Eve. I reckon that must have been difficult to hear." Lena's kind eyes shone with tenderness and sympathy.

"*Ya,*" she said again. "But it didn't make me feel differently about things, Lena, like you said it might. I feel worse. I feel like Elam betrayed me too, and he isn't even here to defend himself."

Lena nodded. "I understand. Both boys behaved badly. Daniel should have come to us instead of running away. We would have felt shame, but we would have gotten through it and had our son in the community." Lena's brows drew together in an agonized expression. "Elam did not act in a *gut* way either. He also should have told the truth. But my dear, sweet Lydia"—Lena's voiced sharpened—"it is not our place to question God's will, nor to pass judgment on others." She paused. "I remind myself of this when *mei* own hurt rises to the surface."

Lena was a wise woman, and Lydia had always been close to her. "I know you're right, Lena." She glanced back toward Daniel, who was busy stuffing a spoonful of food into his mouth and listening intently to something his father was saying. "I'm just trying to find my way through all of this."

Women scurried around them as they stood off to one corner, whispering.

Lena smiled. "You already know the way, my child. Now you must travel the path of least resistance and welcome forgiveness into your heart. Let God heal what pains you."

"*Mamm*, we need more butter bread," Anna Marie said as she brushed by Lydia and Lena.

Lena gave Lydia a quick pat on the arm. "I have bread warming in the oven. I'll go get it." She started to leave, then stopped. "Lydia, I am chilled to the bone, and I'm not about to shuffle around here in my long cape. Upstairs is a closet at the end of the hallway. I saw a sweater in there while I was helping Daniel clean the place up last week. Must have been left behind by one of the Kauffmans. Would you be a dear and get it for me?" She winked at Lydia and headed to the kitchen.

. . .

Daniel watched Lydia going up the stairs. The thought of her that close to his bedroom sent tidal waves of longing and desire pulsing through his very being. He grew restless as he searched for an excuse to go upstairs. As Lydia disappeared out of sight, he pulled his eyes from the stairway and met his father's speculative gaze. Gideon's brows furrowed in Daniel's direction, and he feared a reprimand from his father for ogling Lydia in such a way.

But then Gideon's left brow edged upward mischievously. "Daniel, I reckon I've eaten more of this *gut* food than I should have, and it's left me with a bit of a bellyache. Could you fetch me something from your medicine cabinet?"

"Right away, Pop." Daniel's fork clanged against his plate as he hurriedly pushed back his chair. He saw the hint of a smile on his father's face, which Gideon quickly masked as he reached for a piece of butter bread.

Daniel tried to keep his anticipation in check as he walked up the stairs. He hadn't been alone with Lydia since Thanksgiving, the night she cried in his arms. Her hurt had speared through his own heart, leaving him with regret and despair.

He wondered why she had gone upstairs and where she might be. There was a bathroom downstairs for guests. He glanced through the open door on his left, and then a few steps farther, through another open door on his right. Lydia wasn't in either of the extra bedrooms, which meant she was either in the bathroom farther down the hall or in his bedroom at the end of the corridor. His pulse quickened when he passed by the bathroom and she wasn't in there.

He slowly stepped around the corner to his bedroom, and there she was—sitting on his bed, running her hand gracefully across the dark-blue quilt atop his bed. Rays of sunshine shone through the window and danced on the wooden floor. She didn't look up, but the old stairs and wooden slats down the hallway had crackled beneath his feet, announcing his coming.

"Which side of the bed do you sleep on?" she asked. Her hand continued to stroke the counterpane in a way that tantalized Daniel's senses.

"The side you're sitting on," he said with a shaky voice.

"Hmm—" She raised her eyes to his. "It would have never worked. I sleep on this side too." She patted a spot beside her on the bed.

Daniel nervously ran his hand through his freshly bobbed haircut. His sister had given him a proper trim yesterday in preparation for his baptism. "I would have gladly changed sides."

Hope was alive in his heart, and he feared she'd snatch it from him at any second. So he watched her, savored her, sitting on his bed in such a way. He expected her to get up and walk out of the room at any second. But instead, she slowly rose off the bed and began to wander around his room.

"Do you read before you go to sleep?" She turned to face him, and her expression was that of a woman basking in the knowledge of her power over him.

"*Ya*," he answered, his feet rooted to the floor. Her movements were intoxicating to him.

"Hmm—" she said again as she continued walking

lightly around his room. She scanned every single item in the small room as if her life depended on it.

Daniel felt utterly scrutinized.

She picked up the small battery-operated alarm clock that he kept on his bedside table. "I have this same alarm clock in my bedroom," she said. Then she gently put it back in its place and continued around the room.

He hoped her scent would linger in his bedroom long after she was gone.

"Lydia—" He was finally able to push his feet into the room and draw near her, expecting her to back away. "I'm so very sorry about everything."

She didn't move, and her lips curled slightly. "I know you are."

Did he hear her correctly? Was she coming around? His heart danced a jig of victory, and he moved closer to her. "Can we please spend some time together, get to know each other again?"

She allowed herself a long gaze around his room, and then turned back and faced him with deep longing in her eyes, which her words defied. "No," she said, her voice uncompromising, yet with a degree of warmth Daniel found confusing.

Daniel heard footsteps coming up the stairs and down the hallway. He knew that his and Lydia's presence in his bedroom was inappropriate and would be frowned upon by anyone who found them here, but neither of them made a move to leave. They stood facing each other, longing in both their eyes, and neither moved until they heard Anna Marie's voice at the doorway.

CHAPTER 12

Lydia's delusional state of calm left her when she saw Anna Marie in the doorway. She'd assumed it would be Lena or Gideon, and she could have handled either of their reactions. But Anna Marie was another story. She braced herself for a harsh lashing from her daughter as she and Daniel stood side by side in the middle of his bedroom, looking like they'd been caught doing something they surely hadn't.

"Sarah and Miriam are looking for you," Anna Marie said with an air of unexpected composure, and even amusement. "I reckon they need your help serving dessert."

Lydia recalled the way Anna Marie had referred to Daniel as her uncle this morning, with a fondness in her voice. And now she seemed tolerant of Daniel and Lydia being alone in Daniel's bedroom together.

Lydia walked to where her daughter was standing in the doorway, and they both started down the hallway. Daniel followed.

When all three reached the bottom of the stairs, Lena gave Lydia a puzzled look. Lydia widened her eyes, mirroring her mother-in-law's expression.

"The sweater?" Lena asked.

"*Ach!* I forgot." Lydia twirled around to head back up the stairs, but Daniel gently touched her arm.

"I forgot to get something for Pop. I'll grab the sweater for *Mamm* while I'm up there." He stepped past her and took the stairs two at a time. Lena merely shook her head and walked back to the kitchen.

Anna Marie stood before her. Lydia was having trouble reading her daughter's expression.

"Daniel and I went upstairs together—I mean not together," Lydia stumbled. "We went upstairs because we needed to—No, *ach*. What I mean is, we—well, I reckon I was coming for a sweater for *Mammi*, and Daniel was, uh . . ."

"And *Mammi*'s sweater was in Daniel's room, no?" Anna Marie smiled sagely at Lydia.

This was role reversal at its worst. And Lydia had done nothing wrong. Frustration swept over her in a blanket of confused thoughts, and she shrugged and said, "I have to go help Miriam and Sarah." She shook her head and stormed away, embarrassed that she was behaving like someone Anna Marie's age.

When she entered the kitchen, the cleanup process was underway. Several women were lined up at the sink, one washing dishes, another drying, and a third putting the dishes where they belonged in the cabinets. The young girls were hauling the dirty plates in from the other rooms and stacking them in a pile by the sink. It was almost too crowded for Lydia to maneuver through the room, and she wasn't sure where she was needed. Then she spotted Miriam and Sarah in the corner.

"What do you need help with?" Lydia glanced back and forth between her sister and her friend. Miriam wasn't much older than her own daughter. And Sarah was also considerably younger than Lydia. All of a sudden Lydia felt old and even more ridiculous about her behavior in Daniel's bedroom.

"We just wanted to make sure you were all right," Miriam said. She looked toward her shoes for a moment, her glasses slipping down her nose. She gave them a push upward, then raised her eyes back to face Lydia. "We saw Daniel go upstairs behind you."

Lydia hadn't said anything to Miriam about Daniel, but of course her sister knew. Everyone knew. But Lydia was touched by her concern. "I'm fine," Lydia assured her.

Sarah leaned her face closer to Lydia's. "You were up there for quite a while." Sarah arched her brows and grinned.

Lydia opened her mouth to tell Sarah that her presumptions were out of line, but then she recalled her behavior in the bedroom. Even though she hadn't done anything wrong, she knew her conduct was improper. But then she noticed something. *Sarah is grinning.*

It was so nice to see her friend smiling. Each time she'd been around Sarah recently, the sadness was evident in her eyes. The closer it came to the anniversary of her miscarriage, the more she seemed to revert inside herself. Perhaps Lydia's affairs of the heart were a distraction for her friend. Although she didn't feel comfortable discussing it in front of her sister.

"Miriam." They all turned to see Miram and Lydia's mother holding two brown bags. "Can you carry these to the buggy for me? This one is a mite too heavy for your old mother." She lifted the bag on her left hip up and pushed it toward Miriam.

"You're not old, *Mamm*," Miriam said. She took both bags and walked out the door.

Lydia was glad when her mother went back to the other side of the room.

Sarah's eyes were wide with anticipation, and although Lydia wasn't proud of the way she'd acted upstairs, if a few details would brighten Sarah's day, then so be it.

· · ·

Daniel retrieved the sweater for *Mamm* from the hall closet and then grabbed a bottle of Tums from the medicine cabinet in the bathroom for *Daed*. He slipped into his bedroom and breathed in, but all he could smell was the aroma of food permeating up the stairs. He glanced around for any trace that Lydia had been there and saw the indent in his blue comforter where she'd sat. Why had she come to his room? And what might have happened if Anna Marie hadn't interrupted them?

Lydia had said she was not interested in getting reacquainted with him, but Daniel didn't care what she said—her eyes had brimmed with unspoken passion. There was still something between them. After seeing the expression on her face, the thought of reestablishing a relationship with her didn't seem so far-fetched as when he'd first arrived. He just hoped and prayed that she would give him an opportunity to make up for what he'd done and give him a chance to love her forever.

He edged down the stairs, and the last person he wanted to face was standing near the bottom step with her hands on her hips. The crowd was dispersing, and

Daniel slid past Anna Marie, but not without her calling him back. "*Onkel* Daniel?"

It was strange to hear her call him uncle. He cringed and turned cautiously around. "*Ya?*"

"Can I talk to you for a minute?" Her voice didn't have the sharp edge to it that he'd gotten used to from Anna Marie.

"I need to tell everyone good-bye. Can you wait a few minutes?" he asked, halfway hoping she couldn't. He wasn't in the mood for whatever she had to say about catching him and Lydia upstairs together. They weren't children and didn't need a reprimand from a sixteen-year-old.

"*Ya.* I'll wait." Her voice was smooth and unbothered.

He nodded in her direction and then headed into the den to say his good-byes. It was about fifteen minutes later when he found Anna Marie sitting at the bottom of the stairs, apparently having not moved from that spot. The women, including Lydia, were gathered in the kitchen, chatting about the upcoming holidays, and he imagined his father and the few remaining men were in the barn, telling jokes. He walked over to where Anna Marie was sitting, and she stood up.

"What did you want to talk about?" He prepared for the worst.

"I just wanted to say *danki*," she said as she cast her eyes to her feet, which were twisting beneath her. Then she looked back up at him with glassy eyes. "Amos said you convinced him to stay and face his troubles. Otherwise, he might have left, and I would have died of heartbreak." Her voice rose as she spoke, and then she covered her face with her hands.

Daniel stifled a grin. Anna Marie was as dramatic as her mother at that age. "You're welcome," he said.

Anna Marie dropped her arms to her side and sighed. "The story you told him . . ." she began. "I know you changed the names and all, but I reckon I figured it all out." She cast her eyes downward again. "I'm sorry all that happened to you, but I can't be sorry *mei daed* is *mei daed*."

"Of course not," Daniel said quickly. "Everything that happens is God's will. I made my choices that night, and I have to live with them. Your *daed* was a *gut* man and very deserving of your *mamm*'s affections."

"But she loved you first," Anna Marie said. She seemed to be trying to accept the concept that her mother could love someone else before her father.

"I'd like to think so," he said. "We were courting before everything—before everything happened."

Anna Marie tapped her finger to her chin. "You know . . ." Her eyes twinkled with mischief. "Amos is coming over this evening, and we are all going to play games, make cookies, and welcome in the Christmas season properly." She paused with a grin. "You should come."

Daniel thought he might fall over. "Really?"

"*Ya*. Amos will be arriving at five o'clock. And *Mamm* is making a ham with honey drizzled on top." She smiled, and he knew it was a genuine invitation.

Daniel was starting to feel optimistic about the days ahead. If Anna Marie was coming around, it gave him hope that Lydia could too. "I'd love to," he said, then paused. "But we should probably ask your *mamm* about it."

Anna Marie wrinkled her nose. "She'd just say no. Do you really wanna risk it?" She folded her arms across her chest.

Daniel grinned at his new ally. "I guess you're right. I'll see you at five."

. . .

Lydia had chastised herself enough about her behavior in Daniel's bedroom, flirting with him in a way unsuitable for any woman, especially an Amish woman. She was ashamed to face him, and glad that tonight would be a quiet family night filled with baking cookies and playing games. Amos would be spending the evening and having supper with the family, and Lydia planned to put any thoughts about Daniel to rest for the night.

After devotions with her children in the early afternoon, Lydia spent the rest of the day with Jacob and John in the kitchen. At twelve, Jacob liked to pretend that he was too old to lick the beaters when Lydia made desserts. But when he heard the fun that his *mamm* and brother were having in the kitchen, he joined them. John's sweet little face was covered with cookie dough and icing when Jacob entered the kitchen, and her elder son couldn't resist. They laughed, sang songs, and acted silly all afternoon. Anna Marie had spent most of her afternoon in the sewing area upstairs, finishing a new burgundy dress to wear that evening.

By early evening Lydia's heart was as warm as her toasty kitchen, heated by a small woodstove in the corner. She didn't use the old appliance to cook, but it provided a cozy atmosphere on these chilly nights, and she was able to keep her supper casseroles warm on top of it while her potatoes and celery finished cooking on top of the range. She took a peek at her ham in the oven and was pleased to see a golden glaze forming on top. *Perfect.*

"Anna Marie, Amos is at the door," she hollered from the kitchen when she heard a knock on the door. She twisted her neck to see John in the den. "John, could you please put another log on the fire?"

Lydia checked her potatoes, dried her hands on her apron, then turned around to welcome Amos.

"Daniel!" she gasped. "What are you doing here?" She could feel a flush rising in her cheeks.

"I invited him." Anna Marie bounced into the room. "It's all right, no?"

Lydia's eyebrows rose at the same time her jaw dropped. She stood speechless, her eyes jetting back and forth between the two of them. Then someone else knocked at the door.

"Now, that would be Amos," Anna Marie said. She skipped to the door, leaving Lydia alone in the kitchen with Daniel.

"Lydia, I can go if—" Daniel hesitated. "If you really don't want me here."

I really don't want you here. She bit down hard on her lower lip but didn't say anything. As badly as she didn't want him in her home or in her heart, she was torn by conflicting emotions. But then he smiled, and Lydia reconsidered. "You might as well stay." She shrugged. "There's enough for everyone."

"Anna Marie seems to have softened toward me, and

when she asked me to come for supper, I hated to say no." He said the words tentatively. "But if I make you uncomfortable, I'll go."

Ach. His arrogance! She was not going to let him get the best of her. "I'm not uncomfortable at all." She forced her lips into a curved, stiff smile.

"Hello, Daniel," Amos said. "It's *gut* to see you again."

Amos extended his hand to Daniel, and after they'd exchanged pleasantries, Anna Marie suggested the men go into the den and warm themselves by the fire while she helped her mother finish supper. She sounded very grown-up.

Lydia waited until she could hear Amos and Daniel chatting, and then she put her hands on her hips and faced off with her daughter. "What are you doing, inviting Daniel here?" she asked in a whisper.

The bell on the timer rang. Lydia blew out a breath and swirled around to remove the ham from the oven. She placed it on top of the range by the potatoes and celery, then turned back around and waited for Anna Marie to answer.

"He's in love with you," her daughter said smugly.

Lydia felt weak in the knees. "That's ridiculous. He doesn't even know me anymore." She rolled her eyes. "Why would you say such a thing?"

Anna Marie let out a heavy sigh as a smile filled her young face. "I know about these things."

Oh, my dear daughter, you have so much to learn. "I thought you didn't like him. What made you change your mind?"

"It's wrong for me to harbor such ill will. Such

thoughts are not proper in God's eyes," Anna Marie said with conviction.

Lydia sat down at the kitchen table and motioned for Anna Marie to take a seat across from her. She leaned her head back to check on the men in the den and saw that Amos, Daniel, John, and Jacob had busied themselves with a board game in the middle of the floor. Lydia kept her voice low so as not to be heard above their chatter.

"I'm glad to hear you say that, Anna Marie. But I have told you before, there is no courtship between Daniel and me." She paused and narrowed her eyes. "Besides, you made it perfectly clear that you didn't want me to have anything to do with Daniel, outside of his being your *onkel*."

Anna Marie rose from the table, leaned down, and kissed her mother on the cheek. "I've changed my mind."

Lydia sat dumbfounded.

Anna Marie stood tall, touched Lydia on the shoulder, and gazed lovingly into her mother's eyes. She smiled. "Don't worry, *Mamm*. I will tell you everything you need to know about courtship and love." She left to join the others in the den.

Lydia was amused by her daughter's overstated display of maturity, but for some reason Anna Marie's words lingered in her mind. Maybe she did have much to learn about love, since the only two men she had ever loved had betrayed her.

CHAPTER 13

Lydia couldn't sleep. Two hours had passed since Daniel and Amos left, and the children were already in bed. She kept replaying the evening in her mind. So much laughter and talking. The sounds of family.

Jacob and John clearly adored their *onkel* Daniel, and now that Anna Marie had opened her heart to him, Lydia struggled for a reason not to see Daniel when he asked her to join him for supper on Saturday.

Now, lying in her bed—the bed she'd shared with Elam for fifteen years—she wondered if she'd made a mistake by accepting Daniel's invitation. It would seem like a date, although she made it clear to Daniel that it would be two friends catching up on the past eighteen years, and nothing more.

"Elam, how could you have not told me about what Daniel did?" Lydia whispered. She pulled the covers taut around her chin and fought the shiver in the room and in her heart. "You let me cry on your shoulder, and all the while you knew where he was." A tear trickled down her cheek, and she dabbed it with her quilt. For the first time in months, Lydia allowed herself a good, hard cry. She stifled her pitiful moans with her bedcovers and let it all out, in some sort of effort to release all the pain she felt.

When she was done, she felt drained, and the torment was still there—a future with Daniel that tempted her, and a past with Elam that had been built on lies. She closed her eyes, too exhausted to fight sleep.

It was around two o'clock in the morning when she rolled over in the bed to see Elam sleeping beside her. It was completely dark, but somehow Lydia could see his face, illuminated in a way that allowed her to see every feature, every laugh line, and the tiny scar above her eyebrow that he'd had since childhood. She was lucid enough to know she was dreaming, but the sight of him gazing back into her eyes was a moment she wanted to hold on to forever.

Hello, my love, he whispered tenderly. He cupped her cheek in his hand, the way he'd done a thousand times during their marriage. Lydia closed her eyes and basked in the feel of his touch. *I've missed you.*

She was afraid to move, scared to breathe, for fear she'd wake up and he'd be gone.

I know you have questions, Lydia.

She could hear the regret in his tone, but she didn't care about the past right now. His lie suddenly seemed tiny in comparison to the fifteen years they'd shared as husband and wife. She closed her eyes and placed her hand on top of his as he continued to cradle her cheek.

"Elam," she whispered. "I've missed you so much."

I'm sorry, Lydia. I'm sorry I didn't tell you about the night in the alley. Daniel begged me not to, but I should have told you anyway, given you a choice. It's just that—

"It doesn't matter, Elam. It just doesn't matter." She squeezed his hand, again fearing she'd wake up any second.

He smiled at her—so familiar, so real, so perfect—
and filled with memories only a husband and wife
could appreciate. Her wedding day flashed before her,
and then the births of all three of her children.

It might not matter to you at this very moment, Elam
said soothingly, *but in the morning, the decision I made
so long ago will creep into your thoughts again.*

"Are you really here?" she asked. Lydia didn't care
about anything else. "Stay with me, Elam. Don't leave
me again. Please," she begged. Tears began to well in eyes
already swollen from the night before.

There, there. Elam swept a thumb gently across her
face and wiped away a tear that had spilled over. *You know
I can't stay.*

"Then I don't want to wake up." Her body began to
tremble as she cried in desperation.

Elam pulled her into his arms and held her close.
*Of course you do, Lydia. What about our children? Our
daughter needs you now more than ever. She is at a difficult age, and will need much* lieb *and support from you.*
He paused and pulled her closer. *And then there is Daniel.*

Lydia tensed. "I don't want to talk about him."

Elam leaned back and tilted Lydia's chin upward. He
fused his eyes with hers. *God blessed me so by allowing
me to be in the first half of your life. Consider letting
Daniel into your heart for the second half.*

"No." She pulled her eyes from his and buried her
head in the nook of his shoulder. "Stay with me, Elam."

*You must forgive him, Lydia. Only then will you
find the peace you need to move forward.* He paused. *I
carried a heavy weight on my shoulders, Lydia, by not*

telling you the truth while I could. My love for you was all-consuming, and I was afraid that if I told you Daniel was living nearby, that you'd go to him. She felt his chest rise and fall beneath her. *And you would have. But I'm sorry I didn't give you that choice. Please forgive me.*

Lydia knew that she forgave him the minute she saw him lying next to her. They'd shared a wonderful life, and what she had learned seemed less important now. "I do forgive you, Elam."

Forgive Daniel too, Lydia. He's hurting.

"No." She could feel him slipping away. "No, Elam," she cried. "Please don't go."

I love you, Lydia. I'll always love you.

And then she woke up.

. . .

Daniel was completely out of practice with dating. He'd done very little of it over the course of his life. He'd found out early on that there wasn't going to be anyone to replace the love he felt for Lydia, so he'd more or less given up trying, especially after Jenny died. Jenny was very special, and he'd loved her, but it was never the kind of love he felt for Lydia.

From the little bit he knew about courting, flowers were always a nice gesture. Lydia had made it quite clear that this was no date, but both of them knew otherwise. He chose a traditional bouquet of red roses, sprinkled with baby's breath and greenery.

He knocked on the door with the nervousness of a teenaged boy.

Anna Marie swung the door wide. "Flowers are always a *gut* idea," she whispered. "*Mamm* is in the kitchen."

Daniel walked into the den. He'd worn his best blue shirt and black pants, along with a black felt hat and long black coat. Lydia entered the room in a dark green dress and black apron, looking as beautiful as always, but something was different. The glow of her smile warmed him from across the room, and her eyes glistened with a peacefulness she didn't seem to have before. It had been almost a week since Daniel had last seen her.

"Hello." She sounded nervous as well, but there was a hint of excitement in her voice.

Daniel handed her the roses. "I hope you like roses. I remember that you like orchids, but the boutique in Paradise didn't have any, and—anyway, I—I hope you like these." He was having trouble keeping his voice steady, and it was bordering on embarrassing. "Not that this is a date or anything," he added.

"The flowers are lovely."

Lydia's entire demeanor had changed since he saw her on Sunday after his baptism. Perhaps she'd found true forgiveness in her heart after all.

"Let me go put these in some water." She walked to the kitchen while Anna Marie kept him company.

"Where will you be taking *Mamm*?" Anna Marie asked. She had a concerned expression on her face.

"I thought I'd take her to Paradiso. Does she like Italian food?" He honestly couldn't remember.

Anna Marie smiled with approval. "It's a quaint place, and *Mamm* will be pleased."

"I'm ready," Lydia said. She grabbed her cape and bonnet from the rack by the door.

"Make sure your brothers handle their chores this evening, Anna Marie. And remember to put price tags on the jellies to take to market." She finished tying the strings of her bonnet. "And Sarah will be by to pick up some cookbooks to deliver for me when she goes to Bird-in-Hand this week."

"It'll be fine, *Mamm*." Anna Marie folded her hands together in front her. Her eyes gleamed. "You two just go and have a *gut* time."

Daniel and Lydia's eyes met in mutual amusement at Anna Marie's grown-up comment. Lydia nodded at her daughter. Daniel didn't feel like Anna Marie was too far off base. He did feel like a kid out on his very first date.

Once they were in Daniel's buggy, he pulled the thick, brown blanket from the backseat and draped it around Lydia. He'd love for her to be sharing the blanket with him, but maybe on the way home.

"*Danki*." She turned to face him. Her eyes were filled with childlike enthusiasm that shone bright in the pale light of the moon. Yes. Something had definitely changed, and Daniel couldn't have been more pleased. He'd been praying hard that Lydia would give him another chance.

When they got to the restaurant, Daniel offered Lydia his hand to step down from the buggy. They fended off stares from the *Englisch* tourists when they walked in. It was easy to differentiate the locals from the visitors. The *Englisch* from this area didn't give the Amish a second glance. Daniel recalled how much the stares bothered him when he was growing up. But now he was with

Lydia, and he wanted to scream to the world that he was home where he belonged. *So stare all you want.*

They'd barely finished their chicken parmesan when the waitress asked if they would be ordering dessert.

"Just *kaffi* for me," Lydia said.

Daniel nodded. "Two, please."

For the first time since he'd been back, his conversations with Lydia flowed effortlessly. He wasn't proud of the life he'd lived some of the time, but as he filled Lydia in about his past, she never judged him. Several times, when he felt particularly ashamed, her eyes had shone with more kindness and tenderness than he could remember from their youth, or deserved now. Lydia had always been kindhearted and loving, but this was different, and Daniel wondered if it was due to motherhood or if she had just matured into someone far grander than he could have imagined.

"Now you," Daniel said as they sipped their coffee. "I know you married Elam. And of course, you have three children. Tell me everything."

Daniel would be lying if he didn't admit that it stung a little to see her smile when she spoke about her life with Elam.

"It was a *gut* life with Elam," she said.

Her eyes drifted from his for a moment, and she shifted her weight in the chair. When her gaze returned to his, she seemed hesitant to continue. But Daniel nodded for her to go on.

"Elam was fortunate enough to be able to make a *gut* living working the fields. We always had a fine harvest. Since you left," she went on, "even more farmers are supplementing their income by holding jobs outside of our community. Many work in construction or building furniture. I don't know anyone who wouldn't prefer not to do this, but growing families, lack of land, the economy—well, it's just forced us out into the *Englisch* world more than we would like."

"What about you? I know you have your cookbooks and that you sell jams and jellies at market. But what else occupies your time?"

"*Ach!* You know the answer to that." A gentle laugh rippled through the air, and right before his eyes, she transformed into the bubbly nineteen-year-old love he'd left behind. "Up at four thirty. Breakfast at five. Then there are the cows to be milked, which Jacob and John take of, and Anna Marie and I tend to laundry, sewing, baking. . . ."

She was still talking, but Daniel was only halfway listening. He was lost in the moment—her smile, the sound of her voice, her laughter, and sheer joy about the life she'd lived so far.

After Daniel paid the bill, they left. Once on the road, it seemed much colder in the buggy, so Daniel turned on a small battery-operated heater he'd brought from home and turned the fan in Lydia's direction. She bundled herself in the blanket and thanked him. Daniel's teeth were chattering wildly, and his body shook from the cold. He recalled the way they used to sit close together and share the warmth of the blanket and each other. But she didn't offer to share, and he didn't ask.

It was nearing seven o'clock, but there was still time for one more trip down memory lane, if Lydia would agree.

The old oak tree.

CHAPTER 14

Lydia was tempted by Daniel's offer. Stars twinkled in thick clusters overhead, and she knew it would be a magical night under the old tree, but she wasn't ready for that yet. She was still working on being friends with him, getting to know him again, and truly forgiving him. She was praying hard about it, and it was all coming together nicely, but friendship was all she had to offer him at this point, and the old oak tree would spark things within herself that she wasn't ready to face.

"It's been a *gut* night, Daniel, but I think you best take me home."

Lydia could see the disappointment in his eyes, but he nodded.

She tried to imagine what it must have been like for him eighteen years ago. A conviction that carried jail time, and then the start of a new and unfamiliar life. If he'd only trusted their love more, he'd have known that there was nothing they couldn't have endured together.

She recalled the way Daniel spoke of his past, with remorse over the choices he'd made. But she'd also watched his face light up when he spoke about the old woman, Margaret, who showed him the way back to the Lord. And he'd spoken fondly of a woman named Jenny, and Lydia could tell how much her death pained him. It was strange to hear him talk about caring for another woman in that way. But even with all the years gone by, she could still see her Daniel in every word he spoke, his movements, and even the way he scrunched his nose when he was trying not to laugh.

Elam's words in her dream echoed in her head. *God blessed me so by allowing me to be in the first half of your life. Consider letting Daniel into your heart for the second half. Forgive Daniel too, Lydia. He's hurting.*

Daniel turned his head her way and caught her eyes on him. "Are you all right?" he asked with such tenderness it caused her heart to flutter.

"*Ya,*" she whispered. She pulled her eyes away from his and sat quietly, lost in the moment. She couldn't help but wonder. *What if . . .*

. . .

Daniel pulled the buggy to a stop in front of Lydia's house. "Whoa, boy."

His pulse quickened as he helped her from the buggy, unsure what the proper protocol was. In his previous world, a simple kiss good night would solidify that the night went well and suggest that another date might be in order. But he was home, and this was Lydia. Doing things right had never been more important to him, and he felt his future hanging on this moment. He didn't want to scare her, but he'd never longed to take another woman into his arms the way he did right now.

At the door, she turned to face him. "*Danki* for supper, Daniel."

He searched her face and tried to read her expression. For a long moment, she gazed back. His heart pounded viciously against his chest, and he knew that he was going to kiss Lydia good night, the way he'd dreamed of for many years. He took a deep breath and leaned forward toward her.

In less time than it took for him to uproot his feet from their position, Lydia turned, opened the door, stepped through the threshold, and turned to face him. "Good night," she said abruptly. And the door slammed shut.

Daniel smiled. She might have closed the door on his intent to kiss her good night, but just the fact that she considered kissing him was enough to ensure he'd get a good night's sleep.

. . .

For a moment, Lydia stared at the wooden door. He'd almost kissed her good night, and she'd almost allowed it. She drew in a deep breath, then turned to see Anna Marie standing behind her like a mother hen waiting for her little chick to return.

"Well?" Her daughter raised questioning brows. "How did it go?"

Lydia untied the strings on her bonnet and refused to make eye contact with Anna Marie. She was fearful her daughter might see into her heart, into the secret chamber where a woman stores her most intimate thoughts. But the corner of her mouth tweaked upward unconciously.

"*Ach*, it must have been *gut*," Anna Marie said smugly.

Lydia hung her bonnet on the rack by the door and untied the strings on her cape. "I am not discussing this with you, Anna Marie," she said firmly. Although she couldn't seem to control the grin that kept threatening to form on her face.

"Did he kiss you good night?" Her daughter's eyes widened with anticipation.

"Anna Marie!" She hung up her cape, then turned to face her daughter with her hands on her hips. "It's not appropriate for you to ask me such a question." She pulled off her gloves and walked to the fireplace.

Anna Marie was on her heels.

"He did, didn't he?" Anna Marie stood beside her in front of the hearth as Lydia warmed her palms. "He kissed you good night."

"As a matter of fact, no, he did not." Lydia narrowed her eyes in Anna Marie's direction. "Anna Marie, I'm glad that you are not harboring dislike toward your *onkel* anymore, but you need not be getting any silly notions in your head."

Much to Lydia's surprise, Anna Marie turned to face her, and her eyes were serious, her voice steady. "I just want you to be happy, *Mamm*."

Lydia sighed and grabbed Anna Marie's hands. "I know, Anna Marie."

"Pop is gone. And I know that you have a history, a past with Daniel." Anna Marie's forehead crinkled. "I didn't care for him much in the beginning because I feared he would try to take *Daed*'s place, and I wasn't sure if I was ready for that. But I will be marrying Amos next year, and Jacob and John need a father." Anna Marie looked hesitant to go on. "Daniel told Amos what happened the night he left you on Christmas Eve."

"What?" *That wasn't Daniel's place to do that*, Lydia thought as she waited for Anna Marie to go on.

"Oh, he changed the names, and he probably didn't tell him everything, but it wasn't hard for Amos to figure out that Daniel was talking about himself in the story. And he told Amos enough to keep Amos from making the same mistake he did."

Now Lydia understood why Anna Marie had changed her mind about Daniel.

"*Mamm*?"

"*Ya*?"

Anna Marie gazed lovingly into Lydia's eyes. "I'd really like to hear—to hear about you and Daniel, when you were young." Anna Marie looked toward her shoes.

Lydia thought hard for a moment. Wonderful memories floated to the surface of her mind. She lifted her daughter's chin and smiled. "You go brew us some *kaffi*. I want to go check on Jacob and John." She paused and studied Anna Marie for a moment, trying to really see her daughter as the woman she was becoming. "Then I will tell you about Daniel and me."

Anna Marie's expression lifted, and she bit her lip, then headed to the kitchen. Lydia went to check on her sons.

For the next two hours, Lydia and Anna Marie cuddled under a quilt on the couch in front of a toasty fire on the cold December night, and Lydia told her daughter all about her first true love. After all these years, she could still vividly recall every detail of the times she'd spent with Daniel—times that, until now, she'd kept secretly stored away in her heart, refusing to unlock her memories for fear of the pain that loomed there.

But as she shared these precious reflections with Anna Marie, Lydia realized that instead of fear and pain—something else was forming in its place and was growing with every word she spoke.

Hope.

CHAPTER 15

Following a quiet day of rest and devotion on Sunday, Lydia awoke on Monday with a burst of energy she didn't remember having for a long time. She ran the broom along the wooden floor in the kitchen and recalled the conversation she'd had with her daughter on Saturday night, her spirit invigorated as she drew on memories from her past. And Anna Marie, a true romantic at heart, had hung on Lydia's every word with a sparkle in her eyes, often comparing her relationship with Amos to Lydia and Daniel's.

After the boys left for school, Miriam picked up Anna Marie for sisters day, a monthly affair that all the women in the community looked forward to. It was a time for sewing, quilting, baking, and any other project of the women's choosing. Mostly, it was a time for chatter—who was courting whom, upcoming baptisms, weddings being planned, etc.

Lydia declined the invitation this morning, but encouraged Anna Marie to attend. Lydia told her daughter she would take care of the Monday laundry chore. She preferred to be alone with her thoughts, which inevitably drifted to Daniel. She could still recall the way his eyes clung to hers last night, familiar and full of desire. He would have kissed her if she hadn't forced herself to turn away. She'd wanted nothing more than to press her lips to his and recapture a tiny bit of their youth, if only for a moment.

Lydia knew her walls of defense against Daniel were crumbling, leaving her heart exposed. She couldn't help but wonder if there was enough love in her heart to forgive Daniel. Again, she heard Elam's voice in her head. *You must forgive him, Lydia. Only then will you find the peace you need to move forward.*

During her morning devotions, she'd prayed extra hard for guidance. Perhaps the quiet voice in her head wasn't Elam.

Lydia cleared the last of the breakfast dishes. She was drying her hands on a kitchen towel when she heard a knock at the door.

"I'm looking for Mr. Smucker," a woman said when Lydia opened the door.

The *Englischer*, in a fancy brown coat and matching knee-length boots, towered over Lydia. "I'm—I'm sorry," Lydia stuttered, "but Mr. Smucker passed away about two years ago."

"Oh no." The woman hung her head. "I didn't know that. I was told I could find him here."

The woman's teeth were chattering, and Lydia wondered if she should invite her in. She didn't look like an *Englischer* from Lancaster County. Her sophisticated attire distinguished her somewhat from folks in the area; she looked like she was from a big city. Golden blonde hair fell loosely on top of her head, and loose tendrils blew against high cheekbones. Her eyes were heavily painted, but not in an unbecoming way. Diamond rings adorned both her hands, and her nails were long and manicured.

Lydia wasn't sure if it was the kindness in the woman's sapphire-colored eyes or blatant curiosity that compelled her to invite the *Englischer* in, but she eased to one side of the door. "Please come in out of the cold," she offered.

The woman bit down on her trembling lip and narrowed her eyes in deliberation. Then she slowly walked inside.

"Is there something I can help you with?" Lydia asked as she pushed the front door closed. "I am Mr. Smucker's wife." She sighed. "I mean, widow."

"I'm so sorry for your loss," the woman said. "He was a good man." Her eyes clouded with tears, and Lydia couldn't imagine how her husband knew this woman.

"But no, you can't help me," she went on. "I wanted to resolve some issues with Daniel, and now that's not possible."

"Daniel?" Lydia's eyes widened in surprise. "Daniel Smucker isn't dead."

"What?"

"I was married to *Elam* Smucker, who passed two years ago." Lydia wasn't sure if she felt relief or alarm at this new information. "You are looking for Elam's brother, Daniel, who lives down the way." She pointed to her north. "At the old Kauffman place."

"Thank you so much!" The *Englisch* woman wasted no time heading toward the door. "I'm so glad Daniel

Smucker is alive. I've come a long way to find him, and—"
With her hand on the doorknob, she turned around.

Again Lydia saw kindness in her eyes.

"I'm sorry about your husband, Elam." Her bright red
lips formed into a tender smile. "But I am very thankful
to have found Daniel. I just hope that he'll see me after
all this time. I pray that he will."

She gave a quick wave and was gone.

Lydia's mind spun with bewilderment, and the zest
in her spirit plummeted. How naive she'd been. Daniel
had lived among the *Englisch* for nearly two decades. It
stood to reason that he would have ties from his past—
beautiful ties. If that was the type of woman Daniel
associated with in his former life, why in the world
would he want anything to do with her?

She walked briskly to the bathroom and studied her
plain face in the mirror. Tiny lines feathered from the
corners of tired eyes, and her light brown lashes were
sparse. The circles under her eyes were a shade darker
this morning from staying up too late the night before.
She leaned in closer to inspect lips that had lost their
pinkish pucker and skin that no longer glowed with the
benefit of youth.

She stood straight again and ran her hands along
hips that had aided in the delivery of three children,
and then she held her hands in front of her and spread
her fingers wide. Short fingernails rounded out long
fingers, which wrinkled slightly beneath her knuckles
as she stretched them to capacity, giving way to more
creases across the top of her hand.

What am I doing? She lowered her chin. Vanity was

wrong in the eyes of God. Lydia knew in her heart that such pride was a sin and that her appearance in no way represented the person beneath her plain look. And yet she couldn't help but compare herself to the beautiful woman who'd resurfaced from Daniel's past. Lydia felt her stomach sink. *Why would he choose me?*

. . .

Daniel slowed his horse as he eased under the covered bridge in Ronks and enjoyed a brief reprieve from the flurry of snowflakes that had started earlier this morning. But even the bitter cold couldn't dampen his spirit. His heart was warm and his mind filled with thoughts of Lydia. Beautiful Lydia.

But for all her outer beauty, it was the woman inside with whom Daniel was in love. His Lydia. He was so happy knowing she hadn't changed a bit.

He headed up the Old Philadelphia Pike and made his way to the farmers' market in Bird-in-Hand. It was a shopping stop mostly for tourists, but Daniel wanted to pick up something special for Lydia. When they were kids, she'd said the bakery inside the market made the best molasses crinkle cookies. She had joked that she could never get her cookies to taste like the ones from the market.

Daniel suspected she had perfected the recipe after all these years, but he was going to buy her some of the cookies just the same.

. . .

Carol Stewart carried her red suitcase up to the second floor at Beiler's Bed and Breakfast—to the Rose Room, which lived up to its name with four walls painted a dusty pink color. She plopped her suitcase, coat, and purse onto the queen-sized bed, which was topped with a lovely white bedspread. Then she eased into one of the floral high-back chairs in the sitting area and pulled off her boots. She stretched her toes, leaned back, and blew out a sigh.

She'd stopped by Daniel Smucker's farm, but he wasn't home. She even waited for almost an hour to see if he would return. Her desperateness to see him was all consuming, and she was determined to somehow make things right. Perhaps after a short catnap, she'd try again. She was sleepy from her three-hour drive from New York City.

She thought back to the last time she saw Daniel, and the expression on his face when she left. He'd probably thought he would see her again. But she had run, the way she always ran when she couldn't face her troubles. She was through running now—from the memories of Daniel that haunted her, and mostly from herself. Her father was dead now, so nothing would prevent her from finding Daniel. She prayed that he could somehow forgive her.

CHAPTER 16

Daniel passed by Lydia's house on his way home and was surprised to see her in the front yard, toting firewood. He stopped his buggy. Snow was falling and starting to accumulate. It was colder than cold outside. He jumped from the seat to give her a hand.

"Why aren't you at sisters day?" he asked as he crossed the front yard.

She shrugged and kept walking, bundled up in her heavy coat and gloves.

"Here, let me." Daniel caught up with her and scooped the two logs from her arms. She allowed it, but she looked more irritated than appreciative. He followed her into the house and set the wood on the rack near the fireplace.

"*Danki*," she said. She hung up her coat and took off her gloves, never once looking in his direction. This wasn't the same woman he'd said good-bye to on Saturday night.

"Lydia?"

"*Ya*?" She walked to the fireplace where Daniel was standing and suspended her gloves from two nails sticking out of the mantel. She placed her palms in front of the fire.

"Is everything all right? Why aren't you at sisters day?" he repeated.

"I just didn't feel like going," she said, then shrugged.

Daniel remembered the cookies he bought for her at market. "I'll be right back. I have something for you."

He returned a few moments later with a brown bag. "These are for you."

She opened the brown sack and pulled out one of the individually wrapped cookies, studied it, and put it back in the bag. The hint of a smile flickered across her face, but faded when she briefly glanced up at him. "*Danki*. I'll just go put these in the kitchen."

Maybe she didn't care for the cookies anymore. Daniel followed her.

"I remember how much you used to like these when we were kids. You said the best ones came from the farmers' market in Bird-in-Hand, so I picked you up some this morning."

She stowed the bag on the counter, not acknowledging what he'd just said. "There was a woman here looking for you this morning."

"Who was she?"

Lydia briskly moved past him, grabbed the broom, and began to sweep her kitchen floor. "I have no idea," she said sharply.

"An Amish woman?"

"No. *Englisch*. A very beautiful *Englisch* woman. She looked very big-city." She raked the broom harder across the floor.

Daniel crinkled his forehead and thought for a

moment. "I can't imagine any *Englisch* woman looking for me here. What did she look like?"

"I told you. Very pretty."

Her voice was edgy, and it took him a moment to catch on.

"Hmm—" He rubbed his chin and watched the broom whipping across the wooden slats. "I know so many pretty women. I wonder which one it was."

"I'm sure I wouldn't know." Her face reddened.

Daniel stifled a grin. "Lydia, I'm playing with you. I don't know any pretty women who'd be looking for me. The only beautiful woman I'm interested in is standing in this kitchen."

She stopped sweeping and rattled off something in Pennsylvania *Deitsch*, so fast he couldn't understand what she said.

"Whoa, slow down."

"Daniel, it isn't proper for you to be here right now. I have chores to tend to." She started to run the broom over the floor again.

"Lydia, can you stop for a minute, please?" He cautiously moved toward her, and she propped the broom in the corner. She faced him, folded her arms across her chest, and bit her bottom lip.

"Are you mad at me because this woman showed up here, looking for me? I can't imagine who it is. Really."

"No, of course I'm not mad," she said. "I'm just very busy right now."

Daniel knew they'd taken a step backward. He didn't want to worsen things, but this hot and cold she played was irritating. He tipped his straw hat in her direction. "Then I'll let you get back to work." He didn't try to hide the cynicism in his voice.

Lydia walked him to the door. "*Danki* again for the cookies."

"You're welcome."

• • •

She closed the door, embarrassed by her childish behavior. But in addition to her struggle to forgive Daniel and move forward in their relationship, she needed to trust him. She'd done that once, and it hadn't served her well. She walked to the window and watched him walk to his buggy, feeling silly that she'd overreacted. He'd just opened the door to climb inside when a sleek, tan car pulled up behind his buggy.

Daniel closed the door and walked to the driver's window and leaned down. Lydia couldn't see who was in the car, since Daniel's body was blocking her view. She edged to her left, then to her right. Then she remembered seeing that same car earlier. Her recollection came about the time Daniel walked to the passenger side and climbed inside—with the elegant blonde-haired woman in the driver seat.

• • •

"Thank you for agreeing to have coffee with me," Carol said as Daniel fastened his seat belt.

He pushed back his straw hat, glanced briefly in her

direction, and offered her the best half smile he could muster up. So many times he'd thought about what he might say to her if he had the chance.

"I'm going to Europe in a few days. When I heard you were back in Lancaster County, I felt compelled to find you before I leave."

Daniel could see why Lydia would think this woman was beautiful. Carol had delicate features and full lips. Her hair was golden, like a field of grain, and her blue eyes shone with a warmth Daniel hadn't expected. But in his mind she didn't compare to Lydia, whose beauty ran from the inside out.

Lydia's reaction flattered him, but it was worrisome. He knew she was already struggling to find a place for him in her life, and he didn't want this to cause a permanent setback. His attitude when he left probably didn't help things, but she didn't need to be so snippy. The fact that Carol was in Lancaster County shocked Daniel as much as it had Lydia. He had never expected to lay eyes on the woman again.

"Is this place okay?" Carol pointed to the Dutch bakery on the right.

"*Ya*. That's fine."

Daniel fought the resentment that he felt toward Carol and told himself that he would listen to her with an open mind and heart. He'd prayed for her, despite the pain she'd caused.

Although, looking at her now, she didn't seem to be the monster he'd made her out to be. Maybe she'd changed. As she pulled her car into the parking lot of the bakery, Daniel reckoned he was about to find out.

. . .

It was later in the afternoon when Lydia took the buggy to Lena and Gideon's to pick up Anna Marie. Her daughter told her this morning that, after sisters day, she was going to go back to her grandparents' house for a while to work on a special quilt that she and Lena were making as a Christmas present for Sarah. It wasn't a full-sized quilt, but more of a lap cover. Lydia had seen the work in progress, and it was beautiful.

Everyone in the community adored Sarah and her husband, David, and the women also knew that Sarah was having a difficult time as the anniversary of her miscarriage approached. Lydia thought it was a lovely gesture for Anna Marie to want to make her something so special for Christmas.

"You've come a long way on this, Anna Marie." Lydia inspected the finely quilted squares bursting with every color in the rainbow. "And you've done a fine job."

"*Mammi* helped a lot, too," Anna Marie said as she tucked her chin.

Lena waved her off. "No, I reckon I just supervised." She pulled a pan from the oven. "Plain ol' sugar cookies, if anyone is interested." She placed the tray on her cooling rack.

"Your cookies are always *wunderbaar*, Lena." Lydia sat down at the kitchen table while Anna Marie stored the quilt back in Lena's sewing room upstairs. "How was sisters day?"

"It was a *gut* day." Lena put the last cookie on the

rack and then joined Lydia at the table. "Why didn't you go?"

Lydia shrugged. "*Ach*, I don't know. I just had a lot to do around the house." She recalled her zesty spirit and how wonderful she'd felt this morning—before the *Englischer* showed up.

"You should have gone," Lena said. She winked at Lydia. "You know how chatty everyone gets. Maybe they wouldn't have talked so much about you if you'd have been there."

Lydia's eyes widened. "What? Why would the ladies be talking about me?"

"There was much speculation about you and Daniel." Lena's voice was hopeful, and Lydia hated to disappoint her.

"We went to supper. There's nothing to speculate about. Was my daughter listening to everyone chat about me?"

Lena folded her hands on the table and sat up a little taller. "Actually, it was Anna Marie who started the conversation. She's glad you and Daniel seemed to be getting along so well, and I think she's hoping—"

"It was just supper, Lena." Lydia knew who was doing most of the hoping. But she regretted her own snappy tone. "Sorry," she said, then bit her bottom lip.

A few awkward moments of silence ensued until Anna Marie came bouncing back into the kitchen, about the same time Lydia heard a buggy pulling up in the driveway.

"Gideon will want some hot cocoa," Lena said. She stood up, walked to the stove, and lit the gas burner. "He's comin' back from Leroy Blank's place. Leroy wanted him to see a woodworking project he has going on." Lena shook her head. "It's too cold to be goin' anywhere."

"Yum. Sugar cookies." Anna Marie snatched a cookie and leaned against the counter.

Lydia heard the front door close and footsteps nearing from the den. But it was Daniel who rounded the corner, not Gideon.

"Hi," he said. He took off his hat and coat, hung them on the rack. "This is a nice surprise."

Daniel and Lydia's eyes met, but she quickly looked away. There was an edge to Daniel's voice, and she wasn't sure he found her presence a nice surprise at all.

Lydia bolted up from the table. "Anna Marie, we must go home and start supper. Jacob and John will be getting hungry soon." She retrieved her heavy coat, gloves, and bonnet from the rack where she'd hung them when she first arrived.

"Hi, *Onkel* Daniel." Anna Marie smiled at Daniel.

"Come along, Anna Marie. Get your coat on." Lydia tied her bonnet. She kissed Lena quickly on the cheek. "See you soon."

"Lydia, can I talk with you for a minute before you go?" Daniel asked.

"Anna Marie, come with me." Lena practically dragged Anna Marie by the arm through the kitchen. "I have something upstairs to show you while your *mamm* and *Onkel* Daniel talk."

"No, Anna Marie, we have to go," Lydia said firmly.

Anna Marie frowned playfully, and then mouthed the word *Sorry* to her *mamm* as her *mammi* pulled her toward the stairs.

"What is it, Daniel?" Lydia asked. She was all bundled up and ready to go, and he was just standing there staring at her. "Hmm?"

"I wanted to explain about that woman. You seemed upset about her coming here. She came to talk to me about something that happened a long—"

"Stop." Lydia held her palm up. "Please, Daniel. There is no need for you to explain. I'm sure there are many women from your past."

"And apparently that bothers you a great deal." He looped his thumbs through his suspenders.

"*Ach!* It most certainly does not." *How dare he?* "You and I agreed to be friends, nothing more. I don't care about your romantic past, nor should you feel the need to tell me about it. It's most inappropriate."

Daniel was quickly on her heels. "You know that I want to be more than your friend, Lydia, but I'm willing to accept your terms. But you have the wrong idea about Carol. My relationship with her—"

"I don't want to hear." Lydia covered her ears with her hands and shook her head.

"Can you please quit interrupting me?" Daniel thrust his hands on his hips. "That's an irritating habit you have when you don't want to hear something."

Lydia wanted to be mad at him and show anger, but instead her eyes began to instantly fill with tears. "If I'm so *irritating*, then why don't you just leave me alone?"

Daniel sighed, then reached for her arm. She jerked away from him.

"I didn't mean to hurt your feelings, Lydia. That's the last thing I'd want to do."

She stormed across the den and yelled upstairs. "Anna Marie. Let's go!"

When Anna Marie hit the bottom stair, Lydia grabbed her daughter's hand and pulled her toward the front door.

"Why does everyone keep dragging me around?" Anna Marie asked. She glanced back and forth between Lydia and Lena.

Lydia didn't answer. As the door closed behind them, one thing was for sure. Lydia had used bad judgment when she'd decided to let her guard down with Daniel, and now she needed to force some distance between them and patch the tiny cracks in her heart.

CHAPTER 17

Daniel knew that by forgiving Carol, he'd made peace with some of his past as well. She'd wept openly and said she couldn't move forward without knowing that Daniel forgave her. He knew the agony of seeking exoneration from someone. He didn't want to leave Carol in that lonely place where past regrets gnaw away at your soul, where peace is within your grasp but yanked away by your own guilt. Daniel was familiar with that place.

He'd like to think that he'd forgiven himself for the decision he'd made Christmas Eve, but occasionally he revisited that dark place where Carol had been. Maybe now she could find the kind of happiness that had evidently eluded them both.

Perhaps Lydia would find a way to open her heart to him. He'd settle for just her friendship, if that's all she could give him, but after their last conversation, he realized that even being friends was a challenge.

It was quiet in his house. Too quiet. Too much time to think. He carried the lantern upstairs and got into bed knowing sleep wouldn't be coming for a while. He knew of something he could do in the meantime. He tried to clear his thoughts so he could truly commune with God.

God's will is not to be questioned. It was a belief he'd carried with him into the *Englisch* world. Even though he'd lost his way for a while, in his heart he'd always known that to be true. If he hadn't made the decision to leave, there'd be no Anna Marie, Jacob, or John. Elam might not have shared his life with someone as wonderful as Lydia.

He recalled the way Lydia's eyes iced over at the sight of him this afternoon. She'd just started to warm up to him when Carol showed up and put a glitch in things. If Lydia only knew. His heart had always belonged to her, even when she wasn't there to accept his love. He couldn't help but wonder if she'd thought about him over the years. Guilt washed over him for having such thoughts about another man's wife, particularly when that man was his own brother.

"I'm sorry, Elam," he whispered. "She was your wife."

He turned off the lantern, closed his eyes, and prayed for God to lead his thoughts in the right direction.

. . .

Over a week went by without Daniel and Lydia resolving their troubles, and Lena knew her son was suffering. She didn't know how to ease his pain, or Lydia's, for that matter. She served Daniel dippy eggs, buttermilk pancakes, bacon, and scrapple for breakfast on this cold December morning. His favorites, and it was worth her small effort to brighten his day.

"It will take time, Daniel," she said after Gideon went to tend to the animals. "Lydia needs time to adjust to you being here."

"I know, *Mamm*." Daniel moved his eggs around on the plate. "But it's been over a week now. Did you see how she avoided me at church service on Sunday?"

Lena sat down at the table across from her son. "Daniel." She chose her words carefully. "You know how much your *daed* and me love you, no?"

He nodded.

"But your coming home after all these years took some time for us to get used to. I reckon we'd buried you, so to speak. Eighteen years is a mighty long time, Daniel. And it took many years for us to heal after you left." She paused as her forehead creased with concern. "I tell you this, son, not to hurt you, but to make you realize that Lydia is dealing with things the best way she can. These are strange circumstances.

"Nothing would please your pop and me more than for you and Lydia to court. The children need a father, and I think it is what Elam would want. But such issues can't be forced. God has his own time frame, and he will guide your way. Just be patient."

. . .

Lydia spread out the children's Christmas gifts on the floor in the den. With the boys at school and Anna Marie at market with Miriam, she wanted to take advantage of this time alone to wrap some gifts. She set Lena and Gideon's gifts to her right, in a pile next to the presents for her side of the family. None of the items she'd made or purchased were extravagant, but she had a little something for everyone—everyone except Daniel.

She picked up the battery-operated hand mixer she'd purchased for Lena and wondered if her mother-in-law would use it. It would make things so much easier on her, particularly since the natural doctor in town said she'd developed some arthritis in her hands. The herbs the doctor suggested weren't helping, and Lydia thought the ease of the portable food mixer might help her. For Gideon, she'd purchased a special blend of herbal tea that he enjoyed, and she planned to make him a batch of raisin puffs.

Lydia picked up the pink diary she'd purchased for Miriam, since she felt like her younger sister tended to keep her feelings inside. Inside the diary, she'd written Miriam a special inscription.

For her other two sisters, Hannah and Rachel, she'd selected simple black sweaters. Each of her brothers, John Jr. and Melvin, was receiving a fine pair of leather work gloves. And for her parents she'd bought a battery-operated weather warning system, like the one she kept in her kitchen. She thumbed through the rest of the presents and made sure she had small tokens for all of her nieces and nephews.

For her son John, Lydia had purchased a new winter coat and warm gloves. Her bookworm, Jacob, was getting a collection of books from an author he enjoyed. She'd struggled with what to get Anna Marie, but in the end she'd chosen the set of china she'd received from

Lena and Gideon when she and Elam were married. It would mean more to Anna Marie than anything Lydia could have bought her, especially now that she was planning to start her life with Amos.

Yes. There was something for everyone but Daniel. What could she possibly get for Elam's brother, the children's *onkel*, the man for whom she harbored such mixed feelings? She recalled his interaction with the *Englisch* woman, the way he'd hopped into her car and left. *Where did they go? What did they talk about?* She couldn't help but wonder if Daniel regretted his decision to get rebaptized. Maybe the woman hoped to reunite with him.

She tried to push Daniel from her mind, but she could still see the glow in his eyes when he handed her the molasses crinkle cookies. She'd shown little appreciation.

Lydia spread a roll of shiny red paper in front of her. She could feel the warmth of the fire behind her and wished some of that warmth would spill over into her heart and cast out the cold spots that lingered there.

Only ten days until Christmas. Lydia placed Miriam's boxed diary on the wrapping paper and folded it inward as she thought about what she could give Daniel for Christmas.

. . .

Daniel knew that Christmastime would be difficult for Lydia, so he'd stayed away from her for over a week. But tomorrow was Christmas Eve, and the entire family would be together. He took special care on this day to wrap Lydia's present. After he attached the bright red bow, he moved the gift to the far wall in his den. He glanced around the room at all the wrapped packages, and he knew he'd gone overboard. It just seemed there was so much to make up for.

Lydia's parents were hosting the worship service on Christmas Eve, and the community would have lots of time for visiting on Christmas Day and on Second Christmas, which was celebrated on the day following Christmas. Daniel knew that he and Lydia would be thrown together a lot over the holidays. He planned to give her all the space she needed, but he would continue to hope and pray that she would give him a chance. And hopefully he would find an opportunity to explain why Carol was here. It wasn't a subject he cared to talk about, with Lydia or anyone else, but Lydia had clearly gotten the wrong idea about her.

The weather forecast in the newspaper was calling for a foot of snow and blizzardlike conditions, starting the day after tomorrow, on Christmas Day. He pulled on his heavy black boots and prepared to ready his house for a storm. He worried how that would affect the community celebrations. Sarah and David Fisher were hosting a First Christmas celebration, along with several others in the district.

Surely Lydia would make sure any loose objects outside her house were secured, that shutters were fastened, and that food was in full supply in case they were shut in for a few days. How awful it would be if the weather kept everyone from enjoying the holidays with friends and family. He longed to go to her house to make sure she was prepared, but he knew she had the three children to help her.

Daniel pulled himself from his chair at the head of his kitchen table and headed outside to secure his belongings and tend to his animals. Tomorrow was Christmas Eve, and it would be a busy day.

. . .

Anna Marie snuggled into the brown blanket Amos gave her before they left on this buggy ride through the winding back roads of Paradise. A light snow was falling, and it was much too cold to be joyriding, but Anna Marie feared she might not see Amos over the holidays. He and his family would be spending Christmas Eve with relatives in another district, and she would be with her family at her grandparents' house. Then on Christmas Day, no one was sure how bad the weather would be and if it would be fit for travel. She and her family were planning to attend Sarah and David's gathering.

"I heard *mei daed* talkin' with *mei mamm*, and he said no one knows for sure when the storm is coming," Amos said.

"I hope it's not too bad to get out on Christmas Day," Anna Marie said as her house came into view. "It would be *baremlich* not to see you on Christmas." She smiled at her future husband. "Just think, we'll be married by this time next year. I'll be your *fraa*, Anna Marie Zook." A warm glow flowed through her, despite the chatter of her teeth.

"We best get you inside and warm," Amos said. He turned the buggy into her driveway.

"*Ach*, wait. Can you stop a minute? I want to grab the mail from the mailbox."

Amos pulled the buggy to a stop at the end of the long driveway, close enough to the mailbox that Anna Marie didn't even have to get out.

"I love being the first one to read the Christmas cards," she said. She thumbed through the stack of cards. "*Ach*, here's one from my cousin in Ohio!"

Three other cards were postmarked in Lancaster County, and she recognized all the names. But one piece of mail had unusual postage markings Lydia had never seen before. She held the letter-sized envelope up to show Amos. "What's this?"

Amos leaned toward her to get a better look. "That's a letter from overseas." He pointed to the postmark. "All the way from Europe. From France."

"It's addressed to *Mamm*." Anna Marie eyed the return address curiously. "I wonder who Carol Stewart is?"

CHAPTER 18

Lydia kissed her boys good night and forced a smile. "I love you both very much." She closed the bedroom door and headed down the hallway. She could hear Anna Marie bathing.

During the short buggy ride home from worship service at her parents' house, Lydia and the children had sung songs, but she was having a terrible time getting into the spirit of the season. A permanent sorrow seemed to be weighing her down. Twice she'd caught Daniel staring at her from across the room during worship, his expression forlorn and pleading for some sort of response. She'd merely looked away.

She hadn't seen him in over a week, and she'd felt a hodgepodge of emotion when she saw him this evening. Glorious visions of past Christmases with Elam and the children danced in her mind. But those good memories were invaded by recollections of a Christmas Eve eighteen years ago.

Grief, despair, and an unquenchable longing mixed with hopelessness. She plopped herself down on the couch in front of the fireplace and hoped the warmth in the flames would thaw the ice surrounding her heart. She closed her eyes.

Please, God, help me release the bitterness in my heart and truly forgive Daniel. Help me to welcome this prodigal son back into my heart with forgiveness and love—the same way you so unconditionally welcome back your children. I pray that Daniel and I will find a good place to dwell, a peaceful place, in friendship or whatever it is that you see fit for us. Help me to listen to the inner voice that is you.

Lydia rested her head against the back of the couch, kept her eyes closed, and tried to push aside all her other thoughts to make room for the one voice she needed to hear. But when no revelation came, she sighed, opened her eyes, and decided to thumb through the Christmas cards Anna Marie brought in yesterday.

She smiled when she saw that her daughter had already opened the cards. Anna Marie loved to be the first one to read good tidings from friends and family. Her cousin Mary had written a lovely note inside her card, and Lydia tried to stay focused on the blessed time of year as she read two more cards from friends in the area. At the bottom of the pile was an unopened envelope. Lydia's mouth dropped in dismay when she saw the return address.

Why would Daniel's old girlfriend be writing a letter to me all the way from France?

She twisted the envelope nervously in her hand. *This is the last thing I need right now.* But she slid her finger along the seam and unfolded the crisp white sheets of paper.

Dear Lydia,

My name is Carol Stewart. I am the woman who showed up at your house looking for Daniel. I'm so glad to have found him and feel particularly blessed that he spent several hours talking with me.

Lydia took a deep breath and considered not reading any further, but curiosity pushed her to continue.

We weren't far into the conversation before I realized that my actions many years ago greatly affected you. If I had done things differently, it certainly would have altered the course of your life.

Daniel tells me that you were married to his brother for many years and that you have three beautiful children. I am so sorry about the death of your husband. That must have been incredibly hard. I can't imagine.

Daniel and I talked a lot about God's will, in regard to everything that has happened, and it is through prayer and guidance that I decided to write you this letter. I suspect that Daniel has told you by now who I am, but on the off-chance he hasn't, I am a woman who has grown up with a lot of regret in her heart—regret that I ran from a crime scene eighteen years ago and allowed an innocent man to be convicted. Daniel went against all his beliefs to keep that horrible boy from hurting me more than he already had. But instead of going to court and explaining that to the judge, I disappeared and left Daniel to be prosecuted for a crime that Chad Witherspoon lied about. Chad's father hired a powerful attorney with a grudge against the Amish, and Daniel didn't stand a chance. And because of all this, I understand that Daniel felt like he could never return to his community—or to you.

I am so very sorry for my part in all of this. I have carried around the guilt over what I did for so long, and I prayed hard that Daniel would forgive me. It wasn't until Daniel and I talked that I realized my cowardly actions affected your life as well. It basically came down to Daniel's word against Chad's, without me there to tell the police what really happened.

You see, I knew Chad well. We had been dating, and I was trying to break up with him when he savagely attacked me. He told me he'd kill me before he let me leave him. I was afraid of him, his family, and their power. And the one thing Chad didn't know, and still doesn't know: I was pregnant. So I too ran from everything I knew to protect myself and my child.

When Daniel told me that he has spent his entire life loving you and unable to be with you, I knew I had to write you this letter. He said that you are struggling to forgive him for leaving on that Christmas Eve. I can understand that. But I hope that in some way this letter will inspire you to forgive Daniel the way he so unselfishly forgave me. His forgiveness freed my soul in a way that I couldn't comprehend. I was finally released from the guilt I'd felt for my entire adult life.

It is clear to me that Daniel loves you, has always loved you, and longs for a place in your heart. I think that he may be the best man that I have ever known, and any woman would be lucky to have him in her life.

May you have peace and be blessed this Christmas season.

In His name,
Carol Stewart

Lydia tried to control the tears streaming down her face, but through blurred eyes she watched the blue ink on the paper beginning to smudge. She swiped at her cheeks, dabbed the wet spots on Carol's letter, and placed the note back in the envelope. She could hear Anna Marie coming downstairs following her bath. Lydia quickly sat up taller and took a deep, cleansing breath.

Anna Marie strolled to the kitchen in her robe and slippers, then came back through the den carrying a glass of water. As she headed back to the stairs, she said, "Good night, *Mamm*."

She looked at Lydia and smiled—a smile that quickly faded. "*Mamm!* What's wrong? What happened?"

"I'm fine, I'm fine." Lydia sniffled, held her head high, and lifted herself off the couch. "I have to go somewhere. I won't be long."

"*Mamm*, it's late, dark, and cold. Can't it wait till morning?"

"*Ach!* I'll be right back." Lydia ran past her daughter, up the stairs to her bedroom. Suddenly, the package of socks she'd gotten Daniel for Christmas seemed incredibly wrong. She reached into her dresser and grabbed something she thought he might like much more. Clasping it within her palm, she ran back downstairs, found a small gift bag, and shoved the item inside before Anna Marie could see.

"I'm not going far." Lydia took her bonnet and heavy coat from the rack by the front door. "Daniel's house is right down the road." She smiled at her daughter, kissed her on the cheek, and walked out the door.

. . .

Daniel couldn't imagine who would be venturing out this time of night in the cold, but he was certain he heard a buggy turning into his driveway. He closed the book he was reading, placed it on the table by his couch, and picked up the lantern. He walked to the front window and watched the buggy come to a stop and a woman run toward the door. *Lydia?*

He flung the door wide, grabbed her by the arm, and pulled her into the house. "Are you crazy? What are you doing out this late by yourself? It's freezing outside."

He gently pulled her toward the fireplace. Her teeth were clicking together as she pulled off her gloves and warmed her hands in front of the hearth. She was holding a small, red gift bag in one hand. Her clothing was dusted with snow.

"Let me take your coat and bonnet." Daniel held out a hand and waited for her to shed the coat. With one hand she clung to the bag. With the other hand, shaky fingers fumbled with the strings on her bonnet. Daniel hung her wraps on a hook by the door, then turned to face her. "What is it, Lydia? Is it one of the children? Is something wrong?"

"Everything is fine. I just needed—" Her lids slipped

down over big, brown eyes for a moment. Then she slowly looked back up and blinked her eyes into focus, eyes glassy with tears. She sniffled. "I just needed to give you your Christmas present." She pushed the bag toward him.

"What?" Daniel accepted the gift with one hand and rubbed his forehead with his other hand. "You came over this late to give me my Christmas present?"

She shrugged, but a smile lit up her face, and Daniel realized—something had changed again. This time, for the better.

"I hope you like it."

Daniel opened the bag, looked inside, and then worked to control his emotions. He pulled out the red heart he'd given her the day he asked her to marry him. The small token fit in the palm of his hand, and Daniel gazed at the inscription. *My heart belongs to you.*

"Lydia . . . does this mean—"

She stepped forward, stared into his eyes, and said, "It means I love you. I've always loved you." She paused. "And I forgive you."

Daniel's legs threatened to give way beneath him. But as Lydia wrapped her arms around his waist and burrowed her head into his chest, he steadied himself and embraced her. "Oh, Lydia. My love. I've missed you."

"I've missed you too, Daniel."

He held her, and it took a lot to gently push her away, but he had a gift for her as well. "Lydia, I have a present for you too." He pointed to the large, oddly wrapped present to his right.

"Daniel—" she breathed. "Is that what I think it is?"

He was delighted when she walked to the present, squatted down, and pressed her hands against the massive structure. She twisted her head around and looked at him with eyes wide with excitement. "It is, isn't it?"

"Open it and see." Daniel walked to her side and squatted down beside her.

Lydia ripped the paper from the sides of the cedar chest and then stroked the wood gingerly. "Is it the same one?"

"I refinished the stain, but *ya*, it is."

She opened the chest. And there was the inscription. *To Lydia, from Daniel . . . I will love you forever.*

Always His Providence

Ruth Reid

CHAPTER 1

Rosa Hostetler rolled to the other side of the mattress and gazed out the window next to her bed. In the clear October sky, a faint halo of light surrounded the full moon and cast a soft glow over the rolling pasture.

Since Uriah's death two years ago, and more recently, since discovering he had let the property taxes default, sleep came intermittently at best. Tonight was no exception. She couldn't stop thinking about the future, about the looming threat of the tax sale.

Rosa yanked the wool blanket over her head. She missed Uriah's comfort, the reassuring warmth of him beside her. Now whenever her foot drifted over to his side of the bed, she felt only the chill of loneliness.

But tossing all night accomplished nothing. Rosa pushed the covers aside and crawled out of bed. She padded barefoot down the squeaky wooden stairs and into the kitchen, and struck a match against the cast-iron stove. She lit the lamp, and a soft yellow glow filled the empty kitchen.

Sometime during the night, the fire in the stove had gone out. Rosa wadded a few pages of newspaper, laid on the kindling, and touched a match to the crumpled paper. Occasionally she wished she had one of the fancy propane ovens like her friend Hope had. But as it was, Rosa had only herself to cook for, and it seemed pointless to want something so extravagant.

Coveting material items wasn't a problem for Rosa. She struggled with more basic issues: the battle she had fought throughout five years of marriage to accept her childless state and, more recently, the loss of her husband. Now widowed at age thirty, it seemed she would never experience the fulfillment of motherhood.

Rosa set the glass jar of cookies on the table, plopped down on one of the ten empty chairs, and waited for the water in the kettle to boil. The *tick-tick-tick* of the clock on the wall broke the silence. One a.m. Gorging on cookies in the middle of the night had become a routine.

Propped against the saltshaker, the latest letter from the Tax Claim Bureau caught her attention. Marked DELINQUENT in a bold red stamp, the property taxes listed not only the current tax lien but the amount due from unpaid taxes and accrued late fees from the previous years.

She scanned the document. *Notice is hereby given that the Lancaster County Tax Claim Bureau will hold a continued tax upset sale on* . . . The November date and time blurred as tears welled. She had less than a month to settle the lien. On her egg money that would be impossible.

Boiling water erupted from the kettle's spout and sizzled on the cast-iron stovetop. She dropped the letter on the table, grabbed the hissing kettle with a potholder, and poured water over the herbal tea bag. The wafting lemony scent soothed her senses.

Somewhere outside a dog barked, then others joined the chorus. She lowered the kettle and leaned over the sink to peer out the window. But even with a full moon, she couldn't see into the darkness.

The barking grew louder. Rosa jerked her cape from the hook and opened the door. The hens had gone wild, clucking and flapping frantically. She bolted back inside and grabbed her husband's shotgun.

. . .

Adam Bontrager slowly opened his eyes. His mind vaguely registered the sound of dogs barking, but he closed his eyes and slid back toward sleep.

Moments later the racket roused him again. This time he shot out of bed and went to the window that faced the Hostetler house. Light illuminated the kitchen window. The same disturbance must have awakened Rosa too.

A small shadowy figure stepped onto Rosa's porch. He couldn't understand the muffled words, but the angry tone carried through the night.

Adam pulled on his clothes and rushed out of the house without tying his boots or grabbing his hat. On his way across the yard, he snagged the heavy metal rake leaning against the utility shed. Above the panic of flapping wings and the fierce growl of an animal, he could hear Rosa shouting—something about leaving her chickens alone.

"Rosa?" he called. He didn't mean to startle her, but he also didn't want to be clubbed in the head with whatever it was she had in her hand.

"It's after *mei* chickens!" He heard a mechanism click and a half sentence about hoping the shell was loaded right.

"Don't shoot!" he yelled.

She lowered the gun. He crossed in front of her and struck the large dog with the rake. A hen thudded to the ground, and the yelping dog bolted for the corral, where it crawled under the fence and slipped into darkness.

He bent a knee next to the motionless chicken.

Rosa leaned over his shoulder. "Is she dead?"

Probably, Adam thought. It was difficult to tell if the bird was dead or in shock because of the large oak blocking the moonlight. "I don't know. I can't see."

"I'll get a lantern." She turned and sprinted toward the house.

"Hey." Adam waited for her to look his way. "Don't run with a loaded gun in your hand."

Rosa slowed.

Once she disappeared behind the door, he resumed his inspection of the chicken. If it wasn't already dead, he had a notion to put it out of its misery before she returned with the light. The other hens kept their distance yet continued to cluck.

The screen door snapped. Unarmed, she trotted back with the lantern.

Rosa dangled the lamplight over the lifeless bird. "That rotten dog killed her."

Adam reached down and picked up the chicken by its neck. "I guess you'll be making dumplings to go with this."

"That's *nett* funny. That was Penny." Her voice cracked.

He wasn't sure why, but it surprised him that she named her chickens. He cleared his throat. "At the risk of sounding insensitive, where do you want . . . Penny?"

She sighed. "In the *haus*."

At least she wouldn't let the meat go bad. Carrying the mangled chicken, he followed her up the porch steps and into the house. He'd barely crossed the threshold when he heard a loud gasp.

"What's wrong?" Adam thought he might have trailed chicken blood on her floor. Then his eyes met hers, and he understood immediately.

She stood before him clutching the woolen cape closed at her neck. Adam's gaze traveled downward, over the hem of her nightdress, to her bare ankles and curled-under toes. Without waiting for direction from Rosa, he took the hen into the kitchen, crossed the room to the sink, and plunked it into the basin.

She snatched a folded paper from the table and shoved it into a nearby drawer.

"I'm sorry to get you out of bed at this hour," she said.

"That's all right. I wanted to make sure you were safe." He turned the tap on and rinsed his hands. "I didn't realize you knew how to shoot a gun."

She shrugged slightly, reached under the sink, and handed him a bar of soap. "I'm *nett* so sure I do. I've never shot one."

The woman was more dangerous than he thought.

"*Danki*," he said, accepting the towel she offered. "Maybe I better unload the gun so you don't try to shoot something else in the middle of the night." He finished drying his hands and handed her back the towel. "Where is it?"

She led the way to the sitting room.

He spotted the shotgun propped up against the wall and groaned under his breath. She hadn't set the safety either. Clearly she had a lot to learn about firearms.

"It's best to unload it outside." If she joined him, he would demonstrate the proper technique, but she didn't. It was probably just as well; she didn't need a lecture tonight. One dead chicken to pluck was enough to deal with at this late hour. He opened the 12-gauge barrel and dislodged the shell. Adam flipped the safety lever to the locked position even though the gun was no longer loaded.

She wasn't in the sitting room when he reentered the house. He placed the gun on the rack and slipped the shell into his pocket. Pots and pans clanged in the kitchen. Adam ducked his head into the room. "Hopefully the dog won't bother your chickens again."

She looked up from filling a large pot with water. "I hope you hit him with the prongs of that rake."

He frowned. He had overheard her plenty of times talking lovingly to her animals. "Rosa, you don't mean that."

"*Ya*, I do." She placed the oversized pot on the stove to boil. "That dog's attacked *mei* chickens before. Penny laid the most eggs—the biggest too. I found several double yolks from her box. I can't afford to lose any egg sales."

"Don't worry about tomorrow, for—"

"For tomorrow will worry about its own things." She opened a drawer and removed a butcher knife. "It's after midnight. This *is* tomorrow—and I am worried."

She nudged the drawer closed with her hip. "And I will shoot that dog."

CHAPTER 2

Rosa's eyes burned from lack of sleep. She hadn't slept much before the commotion last night, and once she had plucked the feathers, cooked the chicken, and mourned over the loss of her best egg layer, sleep was a lost cause altogether.

Perhaps she could nap after she returned from her morning egg deliveries. But that wouldn't happen if she didn't get started. On a normal day, she would have already been to the bakery by this time. She donned her barn-mucking boots and grabbed the empty basket to collect the eggs.

Outside, she drew in a deep breath of the crisp morning air. Fall was always her favorite time of year.

"*Guder mariye*, girls," Rosa greeted the clucking hens. The flock clustered around her and followed her to the barn as they did every morning.

Rosa entered the barn humming "Das Loblied," one of her favorite praise hymns from the *Ausbund*. She crossed the concrete floor of the old milk parlor that now served as a storage room for the different drums of livestock feed. As she removed the lid and retrieved the coffee can at the bottom, she noticed with dismay how the melody echoed in the empty drum.

There wasn't much feed to collect. Certainly not enough to feed over forty chickens.

At least it hadn't snowed early this year. The chickens still had a few weeks to forage bugs, plants, and anything they could scratch up as their primary source of food. But in the morning, she liked to scatter corn for them to eat while she collected the eggs from the nesting boxes.

She leaned into the barrel and scooped up feed, unaware she had company until she heard someone singing along. She jerked upright, coffee can in hand, and turned toward the doorway of the milking parlor.

"Please continue," Adam said. "I've never heard you sing before."

She hadn't heard him sing before either, but it didn't mean she wanted to harmonize with him now, bent over a barrel with her backside facing him. "I usually just hum."

Why did she feel the need to explain herself to him? Next she'd be telling him how singing helped keep her mind focused on God instead of her looming tax problems.

"I see you're in a better mood this morning. You didn't shoot any dogs after I left, did you?"

"You ask, but I know you took the shell." What he didn't know was that she had more.

He smiled. "I wanted to get a *gut nacht's* sleep. I wouldn't have slept a wink if I thought you were out there trying to shoot something."

Rosa looked down at the meager amount of corn she'd collected in the can. "At least someone was able to sleep," she muttered.

She rarely ran into Adam in the mornings. Usually he tended the horses he kept in her barn while she was out making deliveries. "I'm sorry. Am I in your way?" She stepped away from the barrels. The oat bin for the horses was next to the chicken feed.

"*Nee.* I was heading to the tack room to get tools to mend the fence."

"Did the horses get out?"

"*Nee.* It's the part I sectioned off to do training."

She hadn't paid much attention to the changes he'd made to accommodate his horse-training business. After a fire destroyed Adam's barn, he needed a temporary place to keep his horses, and she agreed. It's what her late husband would have wanted. Uriah thought of Adam as his little brother and looked out for him—enough to lose his life to save Adam's.

"You have a nice voice."

Rosa wasn't sure how to respond. Since Uriah's death, Adam had pushed his way into her life like a sibling with his finger in the cake batter. In the beginning, he treated her as if it was his duty to look out for Uriah's widow. Adam's way of working out his guilt. And probably God's way of forcing her to face the bitter resentment she harbored.

"*Danki.* You're *nett* too off-key yourself," she said.

His sheepish grin gave him a youthful appearance. So did his shaven face, his long, dark lashes, and his cobalt-blue eyes. Rosa recalled what his mother, Eunice, had said at the widows' luncheon: "I don't understand why *mei sohn* hasn't proposed to Claire Milner yet. I don't even know if they've seen much of each other since the fire."

Eunice seemed to think it had something to do with the third-degree burns on Adam's neck, arm, and left hand. He'd also lost part of his earlobe. But his scars were not such an eyesore that they should chase away someone as sweet as Claire.

He looked around the building. "Ever thought about getting a few milk cows?"

"*Nee.*"

"I know you had that bovine respiratory disease run through here, but I thought—"

She shook her head. "More than half our stock died." The cattle loss trickled down to the mess she was in today. The taxes wouldn't be two years past due if they hadn't had to pay vet bills and hire a company to sanitize the place according to commercial milking standards.

Rosa recalled the defeat in Uriah's eyes. The quarantine hadn't worked. Their dreams went up in smoke with the burnt carcasses.

She shook the grain can. "*Mei* girls are waiting for me."

Once outside, Rosa resumed singing. Her clucking hens met her at the barn door and chased after the corn she spread over the ground.

She fell silent as she approached the coop. Last night it had been too dark to see the damage the dog had done. The chicken yard was filled with feathers.

Perhaps now would be a good time to have a word with the *Englischer* about his dog. Two summers ago he had moved in next door, not the friendliest *Englischer* she'd known, but at least not some nosy neighbor who thought nothing of disrupting the Amish way of life by chasing them around with a camera.

She looked toward the *Englisch* neighbor's house, a hundred yards away. There seemed to be no activity. The man's truck wasn't in his driveway either.

Rosa entered the coop and gathered the few eggs from the nesting boxes. The count was down. Way down compared to yesterday. Chickens laid fewer eggs in the colder season, but this wasn't about the weather. It was the stress and fright of the dog attack. Another reason she needed to have a talk with the neighbor about controlling his animals.

Rosa took the eggs into the house and washed them. She separated them according to the delivery route, grateful she had enough to fill the existing orders. Then she took the basket out to the barn and prepared to harness Blossom to the buggy.

She had just removed the harness from the nail stud when the stall door creaked open behind her and Adam stepped out.

"I'll do that for you." He reached for the equipment in her hand.

"That isn't necessary. I'm more than capable."

He smiled. "I know."

After a brief hesitation, she released the harness and followed him to Blossom's stall. "I appreciate that you came over to check on me last *nacht*, but . . . well, eventually you're going to have to move on with your life." She held her tongue from adding that he could never make up for her losing Uriah.

Adam's jaw tightened, but he said nothing.

Rosa sighed. Lack of sleep had sparked these emotions. He'd only offered to harness her mare.

"I suppose I should share the chicken supper since you were kind enough to chase that dog away."

"That would be nice." He guided the straps through the proper metal rings. "What time should I *kumm* over?"

Ach! She hadn't meant for it to sound like an invitation to eat at her house. He must think she was forward, suggesting such an idea. "I'll bring it over to your *mudder's haus*."

He paused in buckling the girth belt.

"It's a *gut* size chicken," she said. "There will be plenty."

Adam continued to fasten the harness.

"What do you like, white meat or dark?" She fiddled with her apron. "Of course, I could bring over a helping of both."

Stop, she told herself. *Just stop talking.* Next she would be rambling on about vegetable side dishes and dessert.

"Dark." He led Blossom by her halter out to where the buggy sat under the lean-to.

Rosa followed.

He made the final attachments, and after she climbed up on the bench seat, he handed her the reins. "Drive safe."

"Danki." She clicked her tongue and Blossom lurched forward. Once off the gravel drive and onto the road, the mare perked up her ears and trotted faster. Blossom liked the cooler temperatures of fall too. Rosa didn't discourage the pace. She was already late.

It wasn't long before the bakery came into view. The enticing scent of cinnamon rolls filled her nostrils as

Rosa entered the cozy storefront. She smiled at Becky Byler, the owner's daughter, who was busy arranging pastries in the glass display counter.

"*Guder mariye*, Becky." Rosa set the egg basket on the counter and unfolded the cloth covering.

"*Hiya*, Mrs. Hostetler." The girl wiped her hands, leaving a spot of what appeared to be strawberry filling on the front of her apron.

Rosa tried not to stare for fear that Becky would think she was passing judgment on her figure. At eighteen, Becky Byler was the largest girl in the district. She seemed to take things in stride, but Rosa suspected that the girl's size was what kept her from smiling more.

Becky carefully transferred the eggs from Rosa's basket into one of the bakery's storage bins. The girl opened the cash register and counted out the payment for the eggs, then handed the cash to Rosa. She said little and appeared particularly dejected today.

"Did your *mamm* leave a note as to how many eggs she wants tomorrow?"

"I think so." Becky rifled through a stack of papers on a nearby counter, then handed Rosa the slip.

"*Danki*. I'll see you tomorrow?" Rosa gave her a beaming smile in hopes that Becky might return the favor.

She didn't. "I'll be here," she said. "I'm always here."

Rosa continued her route and completed the remaining deliveries before she reached Stephen and Hope Bowman's farm. She wanted to spend some time with Hope and of course dote on little Faith, who always brightened Rosa's spirit.

Hope opened the door and welcomed her into the house. "I figured you were too busy to stop for *kaffi* today."

"Running late is all." Rosa followed her into the kitchen. "Where are the *kinner*?" Even though she doted on the fifteen-month-old Faith, Rosa was close to Hope's other children too.

"Faith is napping. Josie, Emily, and Greta are in *schul*, and James is outside with Stephen." Hope looked at Rosa and frowned. "You're *nett* sleeping, are you?"

"I had problems with the neighbor's dog last *nacht*. He attacked *mei* chickens. Killed *mei* best laying hen."

"That's awful."

"I plucked feathers until two in the morning." She yawned.

"*Kumm* sit." Hope tapped the wooden chair. "The *kaffi* is hot. I'll pour you a cup."

Rosa desperately needed a nap, but she also wanted to visit with her friend. So much had changed over the past several months. "James is doing well, *ya*?"

"He's adapting more and more every day to our ways." Hope set the cup before Rosa. "So tell me, was it Adam's dog that killed your chicken?"

Rosa shook her head. "Adam doesn't have a dog. He heard the vicious attack and came over to help me." She decided not to mention being outside, barefoot and in her nightdress, when he arrived. Still, Hope lifted her brows as though she suspected Rosa had left out important details. Rosa sipped her coffee before continuing. "It was the *Englischer's* dog. The man who bought the *haus* on the other side of me."

"What did the man say?" Hope offered a cookie from the jar.

Rosa shook her head. "Nothing yet. I plan to talk with him later today."

"Once a dog kills, it's difficult to change him."

Rosa set her cup on the table. "That's what I was thinking too. It might start nipping at the horses next and agitate them. That reminds me, is Stephen interested in buying *mei* plow team? Bolt and Thunder are only going to get fat and lazy. I need to sell them."

"I don't know, but I'll ask him."

"If I can't sell them in a week or so, I think I'll make arrangements for them to go to auction."

"You're in that kind of a rush?"

Rosa avoided her friend's eyes by looking into her cup. "I don't want to feed them all winter just to sell them in the spring." That should be understandable. She lifted her head and smiled. "Tell me about your *sohn*. Are he and your *daed* still getting along?"

Hope smiled. "I'm still in awe of the miracle. God has been so *gut* to me."

"*Ya,*" Rosa said with a sigh.

Dare she pray for a miracle too?

CHAPTER 3

Rosa drew a deep breath and knocked on the back door of the *Englischer's* house. Maybe she should have written a note this morning and dropped it into his mailbox. She knocked again, this time harder. No answer. She glanced over her shoulder toward the barn-style shed and debated if she should check there for him. The last owner worked on cars in the building. She wished an Amish family had bought the property when it went up for sale. But real estate prices in Paradise were such that even a small place with minimal acreage was overpriced.

The door opened, and a man in a navy T-shirt and faded jeans stepped onto the threshold. He looked to be in his thirties, maybe, with broad shoulders and longish brown hair. When he combed his fingers through his hair, she noticed a flash of silver at his temples. "Can I help you?"

"I hope so." She cleared her throat. "I'm Rosa Hostetler. I live next door." She pointed to her place on the right.

"It's nice to meet you. I'm Tate Wade." His smile was warm enough to melt a slab of butter straight from the *icehaus*, but she wondered briefly if it was completely genuine.

"Mr. Wade, I'm not sure if you're aware of it, but your dog killed one of *mei* chickens." His expression went blank. She wanted to give him the benefit of doubt, but how could he have missed the commotion? Frown lines stretched across his forehead as she continued. "The ruckus late last night." She hesitated. "You do own a large dog, don't you?" She made a hand gesture a few inches above her knee to indicate the approximate size.

"I own several, but I don't allow them to roam free."

Was he implying her chickens shouldn't be allowed to roam? It would be different if her chickens had been on his property when the attack took place. She cleared her throat again. "One of your dogs attacked my chickens. In my barnyard."

He crossed his arms over his chest.

If only she had left a note in his mailbox instead of confronting him. "I'm not asking you to pay for the chicken," she said in a calm tone. "Only that you keep your dog out of my yard—out of my chicken coop."

"I told you. My dogs are in the kennels." He pointed toward the barn. "Even if they escaped the kennel, they wouldn't have escaped the barn. And on the off chance that one did, it's unlikely that he would break into a chicken coop. All of my dogs are highly trained."

"I leave the door to my coop open so my chickens can come and go."

"I wouldn't advise that or you'll have more trouble with wild animals."

She shook her head. "It wasn't a wild animal. It was a dog. I saw it with the chicken in it's mouth."

"Then it's probably a stray." He made a slight nod as

if trying to coax her into agreeing. When she didn't, he shrugged. "I don't know what else to say."

"I've heard that once a dog has a taste for blood its disposition often changes. I just wanted to make you aware of the situation. Good day, Mr. Wade."

She turned and stepped off the porch. There was nothing more to do. No doubt he'd deny unleashing the dogs last weekend when they went off in the direction of the woods. Sure, the dogs responded to the man's whistle, but that didn't mean one wouldn't chase her chickens if its master wasn't around.

What would she have to do now, stand watch day and night?

. . .

Adam washed up and changed into his Sunday clothes before supper. He wet the comb with tap water, then slid it through his hair. But every time he flattened his hair down, the curls flipped back up, exposing his missing earlobe. He touched the grafted area on his neck where he'd been burned. Without a collar on his shirt, he couldn't even pull the material up to cover the scars. This was one time when he wished the *Ordung* didn't have such strict rules about the way they dressed.

He didn't consider it vanity, the wish to hide the scar from Rosa. Looking at him had to be a raw reminder of her losses. He foolishly went inside the blazing barn to free the horses, and there hadn't been a day since that Adam wasn't painfully aware of what that decision had cost. His best friend, Uriah Hostetler, died to save

Adam. Guilt tore through him when he looked into Rosa's eyes and found restrained animosity. He didn't blame her. But Adam begged God to give her the desire to forgive.

He tossed the comb aside. Nothing he did could shield the scars. Nothing could hide the past. It would have to do.

Rosa hadn't arrived yet when he entered the kitchen.

His mother paused from pouring coffee, tilted her face up, and sniffed at the air. "What's that smell?"

"Soap. The same stuff I use every day."

"You must *nett* have rinsed it off." She continued filling the cups, then shot him a sideways glance as he reached into the cabinet for a water glass. "I'm glad you changed your clothes. We're having company."

Adam cocked his head sideways, but before he could remind his mother that he was the one who told her about Rosa planning to bring chicken tonight, someone knocked on the back door.

He opened the door expecting Rosa, but instead Claire Milner stood on the stoop. "Claire," was all he could muster for a greeting. They had only seen each other once outside of church meetings since the fire.

She smiled nervously. "I brought an apple pie."

He looked beyond her at the buggy leaving.

"*Mei bruder* dropped me off," she said.

Mamm darted around the corner. "I'm so glad you were able to *kumm* for supper." She took the pie so Claire could remove her cape. Then after nudging Adam to take the cloak from their guest, *Mamm* led Claire to the kitchen.

Just as Adam hung the garment on the hook, some-one else knocked on the door. This time it was Rosa. "Hello." He swung the door open wider and stepped aside, but she didn't move from the threshold.

"I just wanted to drop this off." She extended the dish toward him.

"You're *nett* staying?"

His mother bounded out of the kitchen. "Is that Rosa?" She reached in front of him for Rosa's hand and led her inside. "I hope you don't mind. I had already invited Claire Milner for supper before Adam said you were bringing over a chicken."

"*Nee.* There's plenty of food. But—"

"I have the *kaffi* already poured," *Mamm* said, helping Rosa out of her cape. "I missed you at the last widows' get-together."

Rosa's jaw twitched.

His mother didn't seem to notice. She directed Rosa to the kitchen.

Adam followed behind them carrying the warm meal. He set the dish in the center of the table next to the bowl of pickled beets and plate of sliced bread.

"*Hiya*, Rosa," Claire said. "Do you take cream or sugar in your *kaffi*?"

"Just cream, please."

Adam craned his neck toward the dish. "So what did you make out of—?" *Penny*, he remembered. *The hen's name was Penny.* He stopped himself before finishing the sentence. *Don't be an insensitive fool*, he thought. "Did you make dumplings?"

"Chicken casserole with acorn squash."

Claire set a steaming mug of coffee in front of Adam as *Mamm* set one with cream in front of Rosa.

"Adam told me about the neighbor's dog," *Mamm* said once they were all seated and grace was given.

"The neighbor won't admit his dog did any harm."

"You talked with him?" Adam's jaw went slack.

Rosa nodded. "It didn't do any good."

The dog had only killed one chicken. Adam found it odd that Rosa didn't just let it go. Then again, she named her chickens. And last night she was angry enough to consider shooting the dog.

"Hopefully the dog won't bother you anymore," he said. "Then it won't matter if the neighbor admits to owning the dog or *nett*, right?" He spooned a large helping of casserole onto his plate and passed it to Claire.

"This was very kind of you to share with us tonight." *Mamm* sampled the food and smiled. "It's very tasty."

"It's a recipe passed down from *mei grossmammi* to *mei mamm*, and then down to me." Rosa's voice faded.

Mamm was too busy adding pickled beets to her plate to notice how Rosa's expression changed. Adam suspected it had nothing to do with the actual family recipes, and everything to do with not having children to pass them down to.

"I have a book saved with recipes to pass on to *mei kinskind* one day." *Mamm* shot an obvious glance at Claire and smiled.

Adam coughed and cleared his throat. After the fire, he and Claire had put their courtship on hold. He didn't want to get married until things were back on course with his horse-training business. That, and he had promised Uriah that he would look after Rosa. Claire seemed to take the postponement well enough, although neither of them thought it would be this long.

"Did you hear about the get-together tomorrow at Katherine's *haus*?" *Mamm* asked Rosa.

Rosa shook her head.

"A few of us widows are getting together to sew." His mother droned on about the planned frolic, unaware she had lost her audience, except for Claire who must have felt it her duty to follow along.

Mamm seemed oblivious, but Adam noticed how Rosa winced every time the word *widow* was used.

"Why don't you plan on joining us, Rosa?"

"Oh, I don't think I can. I have plans." Rosa fiddled with the corner of her napkin.

His mother stared at Rosa for a moment, then gently shook her head and forked the casserole on her plate. "Did you put garlic in this?"

The conversation shifted to spices and cooking, with Claire chiming in about her favorite dishes. Adam ate silently but observed closely. Until today he hadn't compared Rosa with Claire. But watching them now, he could see that Rosa was reserved, while Claire giggled and shared lofty plans of cooking for a large family one day.

He supposed that was a normal dream for most women. Still, he wished Claire wouldn't talk so much. Didn't she see Rosa's downturned mouth? Couldn't she tell that Rosa was torn up?

"A slice of your pie sounds *gut*," he said to Claire.

Mamm stood. "I'll pour us more *kaffi* while Claire serves dessert."

It was late by the time they were finished. Rosa stood. "I'll help with dishes, Eunice."

"*Nee*, I need something to do."

Adam glanced at Claire. "I'll hitch up the buggy so I can take you home."

Rosa scooted to the door, slipped on her cape, and reached for the doorknob.

He snagged his hat from the hook, grabbed his coat, and followed her outside. "Would you like me to walk you home?"

"I'll be all right." She disappeared into the darkness before he could thank her for the meal.

Adam quickly readied the buggy and drove Claire home. Neither spoke on the ride other than to agree how chilly it had turned since the sun went down. He stopped the buggy next to her house, and Claire reached for his arm.

"You didn't know your *mamm* invited me tonight, did you?"

"*Nee*."

"When do you think you'll be ready to . . . ?" Her voice quivered.

"Claire, I told you before. I gave Uriah *mei* word that I would watch over Rosa."

"What does that mean exactly? It's been two years. Surely you're ready to move—" She paused a moment before continuing. "I don't want to wait any longer, Adam. *Mei* friends are all getting married, and I'm watching *mei* life pass me by."

"I'm sorry."

"You don't share the same feelings for me anymore, do you?"

He wanted to be truthful. The fire had changed him. It seemed more and more he wanted Rosa's approval. He wanted her forgiveness.

"I don't know how I feel." He reached for Claire's hand and gave it a gentle squeeze. "But I don't want you to feel like your life is passing you by either."

"Mark Raber has asked me to go for a ride in his buggy next Sunday afternoon."

"He's a *gut* man."

"Then you think I should say yes?"

He understood the ultimatum. "I want you to be happy. If I hear someone else is courting you, I'll understand."

"I see." Claire opened the buggy door. "*Gut*-bye, Adam." She hurried into the house before Adam had time to set the brake. He turned the horse for home. Without fully understanding why, relief washed over him.

A light shone in Rosa's kitchen window as he pulled into the drive. He took care of his horse, rolled the buggy under the lean-to, then meandered across the yard and knocked on her door.

"Is something wrong?" she asked.

"I didn't want you to be alarmed when a strange truck pulls up to your barn. I have a potential buyer who wants to look at *mei* horses tomorrow."

"I know you've worked hard to train them. I'm glad you've found a buyer."

"*Ya*, well, I won't know that until tomorrow."

"Would you wait a minute? I have something I'd like

you to take home." She disappeared behind the door and a moment later returned with a small basket. "Ask your *mamm* if she will give these eggs to the widows tomorrow at their get-together."

"That's very kind, but why don't you join them?"

"Adam, it's late. I need to go to bed now." She said good night and closed the door.

He trekked over the leaf-covered lawn and stomped the dirt and debris from the bottom of his boots before entering the house.

"You weren't gone long." His mother eyed the basket as he set it on the counter.

"Rosa sent some eggs for your get-together tomorrow." He grabbed *The Budget* to scan the newspaper for upcoming horse auctions. He expected his mother to quiz him about Claire but she didn't.

"Rosa is such a thoughtful dear." *Mamm* lifted the cloth covering the eggs. "She needs a husband."

He stared at the newspaper's typed words but hadn't read a line.

"I was thinking Peter Zook would be a *gut* husband for Rosa."

Peter? Had his mother gone *narrisch*? He cleared his throat. "Peter Zook is almost twice her age."

"Exactly."

Mamm wasn't usually this far removed from reality. Peter had married and buried three wives and fathered fourteen children. He certainly didn't need to add Rosa to his lot.

"She's barren," his mother said. "No young man would knowingly marry her. She needs a husband who is beyond child-rearing days. A widower like Peter is perfect."

"*Perfect?*" He folded the paper and stood. One thing he'd learned since watching over his friend's widow, she was stubbornly independent. She wouldn't marry someone who didn't measure up to Uriah—and nobody could.

"Claire made a *wunderbaar* pie, *ya?*"

"I have an early day tomorrow."

Adam left the kitchen. Before going to bed, he stood at his bedroom window and looked toward Rosa's house. He rubbed the leathery area of his neck where he'd been burned.

So much had changed.

Too much.

CHAPTER 4

Rosa swiped the steamy kitchen window with the dish towel to get a clear view of the truck and horse trailer. She watched as Adam greeted the driver with a handshake and led the man into the barn.

The glass fogged again. She turned away from the window and removed the hissing kettle from the stove, then filled her cup with boiling water and let the lemony tea bag steep while she buttered a slice of bread.

After the barn fire, Adam had spent several months recovering from his burns, and afterward the horses needed retraining. He had put his heart and soul into those horses—a form of therapy for himself, no doubt. At first Rose regretted the decision to let him keep his horses in her barn. The horses had nothing to do with lightning setting the barn on fire, and yet she despised the creatures. But the arrival of the truck and trailer this morning made her realize that she would miss the activity once he sold the stock.

Rosa blew gently over the surface of her tea, then took a sip. She opened the journal where she kept a record of the egg sales, scanned halfway down the list, then stopped. Why did she constantly feel the need to review the list and count her expected earnings? She knew the weekly delivery schedule by heart. Her orders never changed, except when the bakery requested extra eggs over the holidays.

She slapped the journal closed. When had she become so obsessed with tracking money?

Rosa knew the answer. But she couldn't allow the looming taxes to consume her mind. Constantly worrying didn't help the situation.

It wasn't like she had no place to go. *Aenti* Lilly had offered her a place to stay after Uriah died. At that time, Rosa had respectfully declined. Paradise was her home and starting over again in Ohio wasn't something she wanted to consider. But now . . .

She ran her hand over the journal. She needed to sell more eggs in order to keep her house. Or come up with something else to sell.

A horse whinnied, and she rose from the chair and looked out the window. Adam's hard work had paid off. He led the horse up the trailer ramp, then went back inside the barn and came out with another one. By the time the men shook hands, all four of Adam's horses had been loaded into the trailer.

Rosa filled the kettle with more water and set it on the stove. She had enough time to share a cup with Adam before retrieving the eggs.

She smiled at the slight bounce in Adam's step as the truck and trailer pulled away. But instead of coming to share the news, he was heading home.

A heaviness filled her chest. Loneliness was normal—understandable—when it came to missing Uriah. But . . . was she really having that response to Adam?

Rosa rubbed her eyes. She wasn't thinking straight. Probably the lack of sleep or worry over the taxes. Clearly, Adam was moving forward, and by the furtive glances Claire made toward him at supper last night, there probably was more to the horse sale than met the eye. Now he would have money to put a down payment on a place of his own.

Rosa just needed to trust God's provision. He would provide the means to save her farm. Nothing was too difficult for God.

"Nothing," she said, snatching the egg basket from the counter.

She left the house with renewed hope. But when she spotted another dead chicken inside the coop, everything changed.

The lifeless hen made Rosa's stomach clench. She couldn't tell how long the chicken had been dead. Better bury it, just to be safe. She ducked into the barn and retrieved the shovel, then went out back and began to dig. What she really wanted to do was not bury the bird but deposit it on her neighbor's stoop. He should see what his dog did.

She dug faster. She had to get the dead carcass in the ground before she allowed bitterness to take root.

She heard the crunch of gravel and turned to see Hope Bowman climbing out of her buggy. "I'm out here in the garden," Rosa called.

Hope lifted Faith off the bench and strolled over to the edge of the dried cornstalks. "I thought you might stop by after your deliveries."

"I'm running behind. I haven't even collected the

eggs." She motioned to the bloody chicken at the bottom of the hole. "Look what I found this morning."

Hope's eyes widened. "You lost another one?"

She drove the shovel hard into the mound of dirt and left it standing. "I still can't believe I slept through the ruckus. The first full *nacht* of sleep I had in weeks, and this happens." Rosa shook her head. "That dog won't kill another one. Even if it means camping outside in the henhouse with a shotgun."

Hope shifted Faith to her opposite hip and bent closer to the chicken. "Are you sure a dog got it?" She stepped back. "I've seen an injured chicken pecked to death by other chickens."

Rosa hadn't considered that possibility. But the other chickens wouldn't have attacked if they hadn't seen blood on her. "I suppose when I finish here I should check all the chickens closer." She grabbed the shovel and scooped a load of dirt. Tossing it into the hole, the dirt landed on the dead carcass with a *thud*.

"I can make some of your deliveries if you want," Hope said. "I told *Mamm* I would *kumm* over and make apple cider, but that can wait until the girls are out of *schul*."

"Could you deliver to Byler's Bakery? Their recipes are dependent on eggs. I don't like to keep them waiting." Rosa finished filling the hole, then patted the top of the grave with the backside of the shovel.

"Sure." Hope bounced Faith to her other hip. "I wanted to ask Becky about babysitting anyway."

Rosa smiled at chubby-cheeked Faith. "I would hold you," she told the infant in *Deutsch*, "but I'm all dirty."

She held up her smudged hands and wiggled her fingers, which triggered a drooling smile from Faith. Rosa chuckled. "She's certainly a *gut*-natured *boppli*."

Hope kissed her child's cheek. "I'm blessed."

"*Ya*, you are, Hope Bowman."

Her friend frowned. "I'm sorry."

"Don't apologize. God had a different plan for *mei* life." Rosa couldn't remember how many times she had recited those words. She and Uriah had wanted children. He'd even built a kitchen table large enough to seat ten. But her body rejected every baby she conceived. Four miscarriages left her heartbroken, and she had shared the depth of those pains only with Hope.

Rosa motioned toward the henhouse. "I suppose people are waiting for their eggs. I better get them gathered and washed so I can get on the road."

Hope gasped when Rosa swung the door open to the coop. "It's a wonder the chickens have any feathers on them at all." She scanned the floor.

"Thanks to the dog." Rosa reached into the nesting box and pulled out a brown egg. Hope added the one she collected to the basket and moved to the next nest. It didn't take them long, since there weren't many eggs to gather. Rosa rechecked each box for any missed but found none. She didn't have to count them to know she wouldn't have enough to fill all the orders.

Hope elbowed Rosa's side on their way to the house. "You're awfully quiet. Is something wrong?"

"I don't have enough."

"You can use eggs left over from yesterday to fill the orders, *ya*?"

Rosa shook her head. "I sent them with Eunice Bontrager to take to the widows."

"You'll just have to short someone. At least it isn't the holiday season where everyone is baking more. I'm sure it won't be an issue."

The issue was the lack of income, but Rosa wasn't ready to confess her tax problems to anyone, including her best friend. She twisted the doorknob and bumped her hip against the back door. She placed the basket on the counter and turned on the tap water as Hope lowered Faith to the floor.

After the eggs were washed, they packed them around a piece of muslin to prevent breakage during transport. Rosa walked Hope to her buggy. "*Danki* for taking these to the bakery." She handed the basket to Hope once she and Faith were seated on the bench.

"Are you sure you don't want me to make any other stops?"

"*Nee*. I'm still not sure who I'm going to short."

Rosa watched Hope drive away, turning over the problem in her mind. She didn't want to inconvenience anyone, but it would certainly be easier for one of her *Englisch* customers to drive into town. The Amish seldom went into town—some only once a month.

She finally decided on the Thompsons, who lived closest to town. At least that was the best reason she could find to short their order. Rosa went into the vacant barn and glanced around. It seemed odd not to run into Adam. He spent most of his day either outside in the fenced area training horses or inside the barn cleaning stalls. But it was probably for the best that he sold his horses so quickly. He would no longer need her barn. Unless she could figure out a way to come up with the money to satisfy the tax lien in time, she might not have a barn to share.

She had already considered selling her plow team. But most buyers waited until spring to purchase livestock to avoid the costly winter feed bill.

And she didn't have until spring.

Her barn should already be stocked with enough hay to last the winter, and it wasn't. The supply in the barn belonged to Adam. He probably sold it along with the horses and it just hadn't been hauled away yet.

Rosa tried not to dwell on dead chickens and revenue loss as she headed down the country road to make her deliveries. She loved Paradise for its towering, leaf-covered canopies along the road and the rich hues of the rolling fields during the different seasons. She drew in a lungful of crisp fall air as Blossom picked up her trotting pace.

Spending a few moments at each stop for a cup of coffee made the morning pass quickly. By the time she knocked on the Thompsons' door to make her last delivery, her heart raced from caffeine jitters.

Camille Thompson sniffled as she answered the door.

"Is everything all right?" Rosa didn't normally pry, but her *Englisch* friend was obviously upset.

Her friend dabbed a tissue against her puffy eyes. "I know I owe you for the last two weeks, but I don't have the money to pay you."

"We can settle up another time." She lifted up the

basket. "I only had enough to fill half the order anyway. I'll bring the other half tomorrow."

Camille's eyes watered more. "Rosa, I won't be able to pay you tomorrow either."

Out of all her customers, the Thompsons probably needed the eggs more than anyone. Rosa smiled. "Like I said, we'll settle up another time."

"Thank you," Camille said. "You don't know what a blessing this is."

"I'll see you tomorrow." Rosa returned to her buggy. It was satisfying to know she was a blessing to someone else. It put her hard times in perspective. At least she didn't have to worry about having food to eat. Had Uriah left her broke and with a houseful of children, it could have been so much worse. As it was, she only had herself.

She clucked to Blossom and pulled out of the driveway. "Lord, forgive me," she whispered, "but I don't want to move in with *Aenti* Lilly."

Rosa scanned the countryside, and her mind scrambled to formulate a plan. If she was going to stay in Paradise, she had to pay the back taxes and buy enough feed for her livestock to get through the winter. She had no intention of telling any of the members in the district about her delinquent taxes. She didn't want anyone to think Uriah hadn't supported her well. Had they not lost their dairy cows, things wouldn't be so grim. "Please, God," she prayed, "show me a way to save *mei* farm."

But when Rosa pulled into the barnyard, the sight that greeted her made her physically sick. One. Two. She scanned the ground and eyed the third dead chicken.

Rosa stopped Blossom at the hitching post and jumped out of the buggy. Feathers littered the lawn. Dog prints. More slaughtered chickens near the corral. Another one next to the *icehaus*.

Rosa searched the cloudy sky. "Why?" she cried out—to God, to herself, to no one in particular. She turned a circle, staring upward. "What *nau*?"

· · ·

Adam paid the cashier at the auction house for the horses he purchased. Unlike the horses he'd just trained and sold, this stock was much younger and would take longer to train. But once they were buggy broken, they would fetch a good profit.

"Can you give me an idea of how long it will be before they're delivered?" he asked the woman behind the counter.

"Mack said to give him a couple of hours."

"That's fine." It would take him more than an hour to get home by buggy.

She picked up her pen. "Do you have a contact number you wish to leave for him?"

Adam shook his head. "I don't have a phone. But I'm less than ten miles up the road. If he has problems following the directions, tell him to stop at any Amish farm and someone will direct him to my place."

"I'm sure he won't have a problem." She set the pen on the paper and pushed it aside. "Next," she hollered as Adam moved away from the pay window.

If he'd only bought one or two horses he would have

tied them behind the buggy, but hauling eight would require too many trips. Besides, the three fillies barely weaned were not halter broken. He had no choice but to transport them by trailer.

Adam looked forward to seeing Rosa's expression when she saw the fillies. Since she named all of her chickens, he thought she might like to name the yearlings too. He crossed the vehicle parking and headed toward the grassy area sectioned off for buggies.

"Adam," a man's voice called.

He glanced over his shoulder. Stephen Bowman and his teenage lad, James, headed his way. "Bought up all the horses, *ya*?"

"I left a few old hags."

Stephen nodded at his *sohn*. "See, it's a *gut* thing we didn't bid on any of them." He turned back to Adam. "I told James we would start looking for a buggy horse for him."

A horse was important to a young man, especially once they reached the age to attend the singings. Adam remembered how long it took him to pick out his first horse. He bought a fast horse, but it didn't help him win the *maedel's* attention. Rosa only had eyes for Uriah.

Heat had already started to crawl up his neck. He pushed aside the thought. He'd rather not rekindle that old attraction. As if he could avoid it.

"I might have one for sale in a few months." It wouldn't take long to determine which horse of the eight had the best disposition. Someone as inexperienced as James would need a fully trained driver. Boys his age often raced their buggies.

"How many horses do you own *nau*?"

"Eight, but I hope to have twenty within a year or two."

Stephen nodded. "Is that why Rosa told Hope she's selling her draft team? To make room for your new herd?"

"What?" He hadn't heard anything about her selling the team.

"*Ach*, I thought you were still using Rosa's barn."

"*Ya*, I am."

"*Mei fraa* said Rosa was looking for a buyer. I passed the information along, but you and I both know this isn't the time of year to buy a draft team."

Adam agreed.

"You should tell her if she waits until spring, she'll fetch more money."

"*Ya*, I'll be sure to."

Not that Rosa would listen to him. He'd trained stallions less stubborn.

. . .

Rosa knocked hard on the neighbor's door. She would have taken care of this earlier, but she had to clean and pluck the chickens. She hung them in the *icehaus* long enough to speak with the neighbor, and afterward she would cook and can them.

She knocked again.

No answer.

Rosa muttered under her breath and knocked again, this time rattling the aluminum screen door with her fist. She planted her hands on her hips and turned, surveying the area. Determination stiffened her spine. She had no intention of leaving without speaking to the owner.

Rosa marched across the yard toward the barn.

By the sound of vicious barking, his dogs didn't like visitors. Large cages were anchored to the back of the barn. She stopped abruptly as several liver-spotted brown-and-white dogs charged the caged run. The fence clattered as the dogs jumped against it.

Rosa backed away, but not before noticing that one of the dog runs was empty. The missing dog must be the one that attacked her chickens. Tate Wade denied his dog's involvement the last time. This time she would show him the empty cage.

The dogs settled down once she was out of sight. She strode around to the front of the barn where she had seen the man working before. She knocked on the door, then eased it open.

A dim overhead light illuminated the small workspace. Tools lined a pegboard on the wall and the bench held an assortment of electrical drills and saws.

The dogs' barking erupted once more. Only this time, instead of vicious protective barking, the yipping sounded excited.

A voice rose over the din. "Can I help you?"

She spun to face Tate Wade.

"You're the neighbor lady." He cocked his head to one side. "What are you doing in here?"

She eyed the double-barrel shotgun in his hand.

"You didn't answer my question—why are you in my barn?"

Panic washed over her as the dogs barked behind her and Tate moved closer. She motioned in the direction of the kennel. "Did you know you have an empty cage? I think one of your dogs is missing."

He crossed the room with a few long strides and opened the door leading to the kennel.

"The last cage on the left," Rosa shouted over the shrill barking. She lifted to her toes and peered around his side.

"They're all there." He closed the door, muffling the sound. "Now, will you tell me what you're doing in here?"

"Maybe you should put the gun down first."

He shifted the shotgun to his other hand. "Let's go outside."

She followed, grateful to leave the barn. The bishop wouldn't be pleased if he heard she spent any amount of time in a closed barn with an *Englischer*.

Tate stopped near the door, squatted, and grabbed two dead pheasants by their feet.

"You shot those?"

He nodded and grinned proudly at the birds dangling from his hand.

That explained the gun, the orange hat, and the whistle around his neck. It also explained why his dogs went after her chickens. Her Rhode Island Reds probably reminded them of game birds. Rosa straightened her shoulders. "Your dogs attacked my chickens, *again*."

"Not my dogs. The two you said were missing from the cage were with me." He turned toward the house and started walking.

She stormed behind him. "That makes eight they've killed."

He continued walking.

"Mr. Wade, my chickens were mangled. What are you going to do about—"

He pivoted to face her. "Two years ago I made your husband a fair offer to buy your property. That offer still stands."

"What are you talking about?" She shook her head. "My farm is not for sale."

He shrugged. "You would be smart to accept my offer now, but I can wait."

"You'll wait a long time."

"Isn't the auction less than a month away?" He grinned. "Twenty days, if I'm not mistaken."

A flash of heat traveled up the back of her neck. "You read my mail?"

"Back taxes are public record." He fixed her with a steady gaze. "All sales are final. You are aware of that, right?"

CHAPTER 5

Rosa suppressed her tears until she reached her house. Once inside, her knees buckled and she collapsed onto a kitchen chair in sobs.

The heartless man wanted to take her farm. No wonder he wasn't concerned that his dogs were killing her chickens.

"God, do You see what I'm up against? He wants my land." She brushed the tears away with the back of her hand. "Is this Your will?"

It was the same question she asked when the dairy cows caught the respiratory disease. But she'd had Uriah then. Now she had no one.

Anger flared toward her late husband. Had he really considered selling their home without telling her? At one time she would have believed it unthinkable. But he had let the taxes go unpaid without telling her. He had left her unprepared. And alone.

An image of *Aenti* Lilly flashed in her mind. Rosa didn't have to be alone. All she had to do was leave everything she knew behind.

She pushed away from the table and got to her feet. She wasn't going to sit around feeling sorry for herself.

If she lost the farm, it wouldn't be because she hadn't done everything in her power to prevent it. There were six chickens out in the *icehaus* that still needed to be cooked and canned.

Rosa slipped on her cape and headed outside. The *icehaus* worked well in the middle of winter or when packed full with frozen foods. Otherwise, the insulated walls were not sealed tight and didn't keep a consistent temperature.

She opened the door and stepped inside, leaving the door propped open for light. Her teeth chattered as a chill passed through her. She snatched the stiff chickens, turned, and bumped into Adam who stood in the doorway.

"*Ach!* You startled me."

"Sorry. I thought you saw me."

"I'm a little preoccupied."

"I see that." He reached for the lifeless hens. "When did this happen?"

"While I was out delivering eggs." She glared at the neighbor's house. "Do you know how many dogs he owns over there?"

"*Nee*, and if you do, I'm *nett* so sure I want to know how you found out."

"Eight."

"It's *nett* illegal." He continued toward the house.

"Do you know what he does with his dogs?" She didn't wait for him to guess. "He hunts *birds*."

Adam climbed the porch steps and paused at the door. "Did you see the dog attack the chickens?"

"*Nee.*" She pointed to the muddy paw prints on her

porch. "But there's the proof." She nudged the door open with her hip, waited for him to enter, then closed the door and followed him into the kitchen. "You can put them in the sink."

Before going to Tate Wade's house, Rosa had removed the gizzards and plucked the majority of feathers, but the chickens still needed to be washed more thoroughly and cut before she cooked the meat.

Adam set them inside the basin. "Chicken for supper tonight?" He wiggled his brows.

Despite her best intentions, she cracked a smile. "Are you inviting yourself?"

He nodded.

"*Hmm.*"

He smiled. "I'll help you clean them."

"They're plucked. I've already done the hard part."

"I know."

The twinkle in his blue eyes dispatched a jolting current. It was no brotherly look. Goose bumps ran up Rosa's arms, as bumpy as the naked chickens. She forced herself to look away. If she wasn't careful she would fall for his caring and sweet nature.

Rosa turned on the tap and pretended to inspect the chickens. "I suppose I might have missed some feathers."

He edged up next to her at the sink, his shoulder touching hers as he rolled up his cuffs. "I've never prepared a chicken. You'll have to tell me what to do."

Working this close was awkward. Even Uriah hadn't helped her prepare a meal. "You can start by pulling any feathers I missed." She pushed up the sleeves of her dress.

He inspected the first hen, then flipped it over.

"Do you think your *mamm* would want a chicken? I could send it with you."

"*Nee,*" he was quick to reply. "She's already made meat loaf. Besides, she's *nett* that fond of chicken."

She crinkled her brows. "I suppose chicken more than once a week does get old."

"*Nett* to me. I'd rather eat chicken with you than meat loaf any day."

With you. Rosa swallowed hard. He didn't have to work very hard to lift her spirits. "Maybe supper isn't such a *gut* idea."

"There isn't anything wrong." He peered into her eyes. "Friends can spend time together."

Her neck hairs bristled. "I don't want to keep you from spending time with Claire Milner."

"You're *nett.*" He held up the chicken. "This one is ready."

Gut. She needed a distraction. Rosa tapped the cutting board, and he lowered the chicken onto the wooden block. Distracted, she rummaged through the utensil drawer for a knife.

He leaned closer. "So how did I do? Did I miss any feathers?"

She pretended to look it over. "I think you could be a cook's helper."

"*Danki,* but I'll stick with horse training."

"Apparently you're a *gut* trainer. You sold all of your horses." She concentrated on cutting off the drumstick. The lighthearted banter between them faded as her thoughts shifted to the bleak situation with the neighbor. "I'm glad you found a buyer for them all."

After a moment he nudged her arm with his elbow. "Something bothering you?"

Baited words. She was vulnerable enough to spill it all: The years of unpaid taxes, the endless hours of fretting over losing her farm, the prospect of moving to Ohio. Even, if she wasn't careful, the pain of being childless. A red truck pulled into the driveway. Adam lowered the chicken back into the sink and washed his hands. "This won't take long." He wiped his wet hands on the side of his pants as he hurried out of the kitchen.

· · ·

"Sorry I'm late." The driver climbed out of his truck.

"That's no problem. I was helping a friend with her chickens." Adam went to the opposite side of the trailer as the driver unlatched the ramp. Now that the horses had arrived, he was anxious to get them unloaded so he could show Rosa the fillies.

Adam eased the heavy ramp down as the driver guided the other side. He made a makeshift halter from a piece of rope and led the sorrel gelding into the corral. The fillies were last to leave the trailer and jumpy. One nipped and another one lifted her front hooves and pawed at the air.

"Easy, girls." Adam tightened the hold on the ropes. They were too young and high strung to release into the ring, so he placed them in the larger stall and removed the rope halters. Adam filled the trough with fresh water and tossed them some hay. Pleased with the new stock, he jogged to the house.

"Rosa," Adam called from the back door. "Will you *kumm* out to the barn for a minute?"

She came around the corner, wiping her hands on a dish towel. "It's *nett* another dead chicken, is it?"

"*Nee*, nothing like that. I want to show you something."

Midway to the barn, her eyes locked on the corral and she froze. "You bought more horses?"

"*Ya*. That's what trainers do. Buy, train, sell . . . then buy more. What's wrong?"

She didn't move.

"*Kumm* on. I want to show you the ones inside the barn."

"There's more?" She cringed. "*Ach*, Adam."

He reached for her elbow and gave it a slight tug. This wasn't the reaction he had expected. "You'll love the ones inside."

He directed her to the large stall at the far side of the barn. "What do you think?"

She stared for a moment, then reached between the fence rails. The chestnut-colored filly nuzzled her outstretched hand. "They're beautiful."

"*Nau* I have *mei* girls in the barn, and you have your girls in the coop." He chuckled, but stifled it when it came out sounding nervous. "I thought maybe you would like to name them."

She shook her head, retracting her hand from inside the pen.

"Why *nett*? You name your chickens."

She pushed away from the stall. "I wish you had said something before you bought them."

"This upsets you?"

"I, ah . . ." She brushed past him and headed out the door.

"Rosa?" He followed across the lawn. "Tell me why you're upset."

She walked faster.

He reached for her arm and stopped her before she started up the porch steps. "This isn't like you. Why are you running off?"

"Things changed when the dog attacked *mei* chickens again. You can't keep the horses here."

"What are you talking about?"

"You have to move them." She lowered her head, and he had to bend to look into her eyes.

"That isn't going to be easy. I just bought eight horses."

Her shoulders straightened as she drew in a breath. "You have twenty days to find another place to keep them."

CHAPTER 6

Adam tried to recall Rosa's exact words. Something about the dog and another chicken attack. But what did that have to do with him keeping his horses? And twenty days. What kind of a notice was that? He couldn't find a place to keep eight horses in that short time.

She turned toward the house and Adam waited, stifling the urge to question her. He had to find out what was going on with her. He wanted to *understand* her. But she said nothing, just disappeared inside without so much as a glance in his direction.

If he remembered correctly, Uriah would drive her to town for ice cream whenever she was upset about something. But Adam doubted she would be willing to go into town with him. Besides, ice cream might make matters worse if it reminded her of Uriah.

Maybe he frightened her by admitting he wanted to have supper alone with her. She had turned somber only moments before the truck arrived.

"Lord, I'm *nett* any *gut* at figuring out women," he muttered. As he plodded toward the barn, he looked back once. But she wasn't standing at the window.

Adam grabbed the pitchfork and stabbed at a mound of hay. He filled the wheelbarrow and carted the feed outside to the horses. He took his time tossing the hay over the fence, talking to the horses, returning the wheelbarrow to the barn. He still had plenty of time before supper. If he arrived too early, Rosa might cancel. He wouldn't risk it.

A handful of clucking hens met him near the barn door and followed him to the coop. The chickens triggered an idea far better than ice cream. If he left now, he might have enough time to get to town before the feed store closed.

He jogged home.

Entering the house, his mother called out from the kitchen, "I'm making meat loaf."

"I was invited to supper," he called back. "I'm heading into town *nau*."

Adam went directly to his room, washed up, and changed his clothes. It was the second time this week he wore his Sunday clothes, and it wasn't even Sunday.

• • •

The last canning jar lid popped. The chicken safely sealed, Rosa twisted the ring into place and pushed the hot jars to the back of the counter. After telling Adam he needed to find a new place for his horses, she didn't expect him for supper. And she wasn't hungry either, but the raw chicken wouldn't keep.

Earlier in the day she had gone down to the cellar, brought up carrots and red potatoes, and left them soaking in a pot of salted water. It was more than she could eat, but they wouldn't save for another day. She put the vegetables on to boil, then heated the skillet to fry the chicken.

Someone knocked on the door just as she added the last piece of chicken to the pan.

Adam smiled warmly from the other side of the screen door, as though their earlier conversation had never taken place. "I hope I'm *nett* late."

"*Nee.*" She eyed his white shirt, dark pants, and black hat. He only wore those clothes on Sundays. She looked beyond him to his tied horse. "You drove your buggy from next door?"

"I had an errand to do in town."

"In your Sunday clothes?"

He arched an eyebrow. "I hope we're *nett* going to talk all *nacht* with the screen door between us."

Rosa pushed open the door. "I didn't mean to put you on the spot about your clothes. It was merely an observation."

He stepped inside and leaned closer. "You sound like *mei mudder.*"

True, Rosa was older than he was, but only by two years. It wasn't as if—

She sniffed. "*Mei* carrots!"

Rosa turned toward the stove to see dark smoke curling toward the ceiling. The pot had boiled dry. She grabbed a couple of potholders and carried the hot pan to the sink. "*Nee* carrots for supper."

"That's okay." He sidled up beside her. "Close your eyes."

She turned off the tap water and shut her eyes. Beside her she heard a strange chirping sound and opened her eyes to see a tiny chick cupped in his hands.

"For you," he said.

She shook her head and frowned. *No more animals.*

"What? You don't like *mei* gift?"

The little bird chirped. She wasn't sure which looked more out of sorts, the bird or Adam.

He extended his cupped hands. "I think she's calling you."

She hesitated. Then, unable to resist the baby chick, she tossed the potholders on the counter and reached out for it. "It's cute." She had almost forgotten what it was like to hold a fuzzy peeping chick.

Adam blew out an exaggerated breath. "You had me worried for a minute."

"*Danki*, but I can't keep it." She went to give it back, but he threw his hands up in the air. "Adam!"

He backed up. "You love your chickens."

She stepped toward him.

"Are you really turning it down?" He sighed and took the baby chick from her hands. "I should've brought you ice cream."

"Ice cream?"

He looked down at the floor. "You were upset over losing your chickens . . ."

"What does that have to do with ice cream?"

He shrugged one shoulder. "Uriah used to take you into town for a treat when you were upset over something."

She and Uriah had eaten a lot of ice cream. Every

time she suffered a miscarriage. Rosa sighed. "I can't believe he told you about that."

"We were like *bruders*."

Rosa fell silent. She had been so caught up in her own losses that she hadn't given much thought to Adam losing his best friend. "You meant a great deal to him." She cleared her throat. "And you're like a *bruder* to me."

It obviously wasn't the right thing to say. He stared at her, his eyes glazed with sorrow.

She motioned to the chick. "So it was between ice cream and a chick." She sighed. "Ice cream would have been simpler."

He smiled. "But this darling won't melt."

"Where am I going to keep it? It's too young to go out to the coop with the other chickens."

"Hold that thought." He handed her the chick and rushed to the door.

. . .

Adam hoisted the oversized wooden crate containing the baby chicks from the back end of the buggy. Now that Rosa had accepted the one, it shouldn't be too difficult to convince her to keep them all.

As he reentered the house with the crate, she stepped cautiously toward him, her head tilted slightly. "Is that more peeps I'm hearing?"

"You wouldn't want to break up the family." He spotted an area out of the way, yet close to the heat of the woodstove, and lowered the crate to the floor.

"Just how large is the family?"

"A dozen."

She gasped.

"You were upset over losing your chickens. I thought you would want to replace them."

"I need laying hens. *Nett* some straight-run batch of chicks from a hatchery. They're probably cockerels, and I certainly don't need more roosters." She rubbed her temple. "I can't afford them."

"I bought feed already." At the time, he thought this was a good idea. Especially since he'd never known anyone to cry so hard over losing a few chickens. But something was wrong. She seemed even more troubled than earlier today, when she told him to find a new place for his horses.

He crossed the distance between them. "I'll build a brooder box."

"It's more than that," she muttered, turning away from him.

"Should I have bought the gallon of ice cream?"

She cracked a smile.

"What flavor do you like? Chocolate? Vanilla? I'll even buy you the fancy stuff with chunks of brownies or cookie dough."

She shook her head. "You're a *gut* friend, Adam."

Friend. Well, he supposed it could be worse. Especially since she had just said he was like a brother.

"I hope this means you'll reconsider allowing me to keep my horses here."

Her smile vanished and she lowered her head.

"Rosa, please." He shifted his feet. "Eight horses are going to be hard to place."

"That's why I gave you almost three weeks."

He groaned.

A barking dog broke the tension.

Her eyes widened. She thrust the baby chick at his chest, rushed past him, and removed the gun from the rack on the wall. Rosa stormed outside as he juggled to keep from dropping the chick.

Adam lowered it to the floor. He would put it in the box with the others later. First, he needed to get the gun away from Rosa.

Before he took his first step, a shot rang out.

CHAPTER 7

Have you lost your mind?" Adam snatched the shotgun from Rosa as the dog's yelp faded into the distance. He set the gun's safety lock.

Rosa covered her face with her hands. "I hit him, didn't I?"

How did she want him to respond? Be pleased for her?

"The dog's *nett* dead, if that's what you're asking." He stormed to his buggy, set the gun inside, then grabbed the lantern he kept in the back and lit it.

"Are you going to look for the dog?"

"*Nee,*" he snapped. "I'm going to check on *mei* horses."

"I'll get another lantern." She whirled toward the house.

"Rosa, just go inside." His horses hadn't calmed down yet, and he didn't want her making matters worse. At times the woman lacked any sort of judgment. "Please," he said. "Wait in the *haus.*"

The startled horses had vaulted to the opposite end of the corral. He lifted the lantern higher and counted, then counted again. None appeared harmed, but they were visibly distressed, and might trample him if he were to crawl through the fence to get a closer view.

Inside the barn, the three fillies greeted him at the stall gate. He checked Bolt and Thunder next. Rosa's draft team was fine, as was her buggy mare. He blew out a breath. The dog's fate might be another issue, but the horses weren't injured.

Adam leaned against the stall. "God, I think the stress of losing Uriah has finally caused her to crack."

He hung his head. Uriah died in the barn fire to save him, but he couldn't save his friend's wife from herself. How could losing a few chickens trigger that type of erratic reaction?

The door creaked on its hinges and lantern light flickered from the opposite side of the barn. He groaned under his breath as Rosa approached.

She stopped a few feet from him. "Is everything all right?"

"The horses are fine." Her sudden timid stance tore at his heart. He stepped closer. "We should leave them alone."

"I'm going to look for the dog," she said, looking off into the field.

"*Nee*, you're *nett*." His tone was firm.

She snapped up her head. "Adam, I have to. The dog yelped, that means it's injured."

"Did you see the dog? Do you even know if it was your neighbor's?"

"You sound like Tate Wade. He refused to admit his dog killed *mei* chickens. *Nau* look what happened."

"And I suppose if you killed his dog, you're even. Are you pleased?"

"*Nee!*" Her glassy eyes flickered with lantern light.

A stretch of silence passed between them. He cleared his throat. "I don't want you searching for an injured animal. They tend to attack."

"*Ya, mei* chickens," she muttered under her breath.

"What's done is done." He placed his hand on her shoulder and turned her toward the house. "Go back inside."

She lowered her head and shuffled away.

"Rosa?"

She turned. "*Ya?*"

"Do you have any more guns in the *haus*?"

She shook her head.

She wasn't getting this one back either. Not until he was certain she wouldn't shoot at something else. As she slipped into the house, he removed the twenty-pound bag of chick feed from his buggy and left it on her porch next to the door.

He had so looked forward to eating supper with her. Now he just wanted to go home.

. . .

Rosa sipped her coffee as she waited for sunrise. Adam was right. She had lost her mind. She'd spent most of her sleepless night praying for the dog, its yelping cry replaying in her mind. How could she have let anger take control of her actions? She was ashamed of her lack of self-control. She hadn't intended to shoot the dog, only to fire into the air. The gun went off accidently while she was loading it.

Still, if the dog died . . .

Rosa glanced out the kitchen window. The sky was

turning a lighter shade of blue. She pulled her cape off the hook next to the door, pushed her feet into a pair of shin-high mud boots, and headed outside. No matter what Adam said, she was going to search for that dog.

The cool morning air frosted her breath as she walked. She slipped under the pasture fence and plodded over the furrowed ground. Birds chirped as she entered the woods. She hiked the winding, red-and yellow-leaf-covered path and stopped at the creek. The dog wasn't anywhere in sight.

Perhaps it didn't run off to the woods to die. Maybe it was all right. Even so, she had to keep searching. She chose a different path home, weaving around the towering oaks and maples with no success.

Finally, she tromped out of the woods, but instead of coming out on her property, she found herself on her neighbor's land. She had already cut halfway across the field when she decided to double back. Since Tate Wade's dog pens were on the backside of his barn, it wouldn't be too difficult to count the number of dogs in the kennels.

As she neared the cages, the dogs charged and she jumped back, clutching her chest. This wasn't a good idea. The noisy commotion was bound to draw attention. She took a quick count. One missing.

Behind her, a man cleared his throat.

She turned toward him, smoothing out the wrinkles on the front of her dress with her hands. "Good morning, Mr. Wade."

"Mrs. Hostetler." His tone was as cold as his unblinking, dark eyes. "What do you plan to do, destroy my other dogs?"

"I, ah . . ."

He crossed his arms over his chest. "I had no idea how cruel you were. I thought Amish people didn't believe in violence."

She flinched. No one had ever described her that way. Then again, she'd never taken a shot at someone's dog. She lowered her head.

"My prized German shorthaired pointer's leg was shot."

"I'm sorry. It was an accident."

"For your sake, he'd better recover. His champion bloodline will cost a great deal to replace." Rosa watched, alarmed, as his face flushed a dark red.

For your sake? Was that a threat?

"I do hope your dog makes a full recovery," she said. "But I'd like him to *live* on your side of the property line, not mine."

"I don't want to see you near my kennels again."

Rosa nodded. "Again, I'm sorry." She circled to leave. The quicker she could get home, the sooner her heart would stop pounding so hard.

"I'll let you know when I receive the final bill from the vet."

She turned and traipsed across the pasture that separated their properties and came up on the backside of her barn. He expected *her* to pay? She had suffered losses too.

"The dog might be a champion, but he's also a killer," she muttered under her breath. "The man doesn't care about the chickens I lost."

Rosa stomped closer to the fence talking to herself. Even as she fumed, she realized that this wasn't about evening the score. The gun might have misfired, but that didn't erase the fact that she shot the dog.

Adam looked up from cleaning a horse's hoof. "What do you do, go to bed mad and wake up even madder?" He lowered the mare's front leg and straightened his back, hoof pick in hand. His stare followed her as she closed the gap between them.

Last night he was too upset to eat supper, or to even let her know he'd left the chicken feed on the porch. She didn't want him upset with her today. *"Guder mariye,"* she said, keeping her voice calm.

He stepped closer. "Were you out looking for that dog?" She nodded.

"Rosa . . ." He shook his head.

She winced at his tone. "I felt awful. The gun went off accidently." Her throat tightened as her mind reeled with what could have happened.

"That's a *gut* reason for you *nett* to have a gun in the *haus*. You don't know how to use it."

He was right. Rosa had never shot a gun before last night. She didn't want to admit that she nearly dropped the gun when it kicked.

"I've never seen you like this." He softened his tone. "I'm worried."

She forced a smile and pulled her emotions back. "I'm going to put a pot of *kaffi* on after I feed the chickens. Would you like a cup?" She fully expected him to decline.

"Sure."

"Oh . . . okay." Rosa motioned to the barn as she started walking in that direction. "I have to feed the chickens first."

Inside the barn, she leaned into the barrel and scooped up the last remnants of corn. In a pinch, she could use some of the chick feed, but it contained additives that she didn't like to feed to her egg-producing chickens.

The feed barrel was a metaphor of her life—empty. She was at the bottom of the barrel, both figuratively and literally. Financially and emotionally, she was barely scraping by.

She stepped outside and shook the can. Several hens flocked around her as she rattled the grain. One of her noisiest hens, Gabby, was missing. So were Chuckles and Chops. She tossed the remaining grain and hurried into the coop. Gabby was on the ground dead.

Rosa gritted her teeth and turned her eyes to the heavens. "Why, God?"

She felt a tug on her arm and turned to see Adam at her side. *"Kumm* on."

"I have to . . . gather the eggs . . . and . . ." All her reserve failed her, and the tears came.

"Shh." As though she belonged in his arms, he steadied her against him and guided her head to his shoulder. "I'll bring the eggs inside."

She closed her eyes and breathed in the scent of soap. For a moment she just rested there, comforted by the feeling of his arms around her. Then she opened her eyes and caught a glimpse of his mother staring in their direction as she hung laundry on the line.

Rosa pushed away from him and ran to the house. The only man to have enfolded her in his arms was Uriah. She never believed another man would hold her.

A few moments later Adam knocked on the back door and came into the kitchen. "Had you already gathered some eggs?"

"*Nee*, why?" She got up and prepared the teapot. Anything to calm the jitters.

"I only found six." He extended his hands, each holding three brown eggs.

"What?"

"I looked through all the roosting boxes."

"How can that be?"

He shrugged. "Maybe the dog traumatized them. I wouldn't worry about it. You'll have eggs tomorrow."

"I *am* worried. I have deliveries scheduled. People are relying on those eggs." As it was, the six he collected were the ones she had promised to the Thompsons to make up what they'd been shorted.

"Folks will understand."

She shook her head.

The lines on his forehead crinkled. "Do you want me to look again?"

"I'll do it." Without putting on her cape, she went outside.

Adam followed her into the coop. She searched each nesting box, but he was right. All forty-some chickens had stopped laying.

. . .

Adam washed down the last bite of peanut butter sandwich with a drink of milk. His mother had paced the kitchen since serving him lunch. He wasn't sure if he should ask her why or pretend she wasn't fretting about something.

"What did Claire and her *mamm* prepare for supper last *nacht*?"

"I didn't have supper with the Milners."

His mother didn't look too surprised. Perhaps she'd heard the gunshot and the commotion in Rosa's yard. She wrung her hands together, busied herself at the counter for a moment, then turned to face him. "You're spending a great deal of time at Widow Hostetler's *haus*."

The widow reference wasn't lost on him. His mother liked Rosa, or he thought she did. The only negative comment he'd ever heard was about Rosa's inability to have children. Perhaps his mother viewed barrenness as a curse.

"I wish you wouldn't spend so much time with her."

Adam pushed his chair away from the table. "I promised Uriah I would look after Rosa."

"Isn't it asking a lot for Claire to wait for Rosa's time of mourning to pass? I'm sure Uriah didn't expect you to spend so much time—"

"Before you finish, you might want to look again at this." Adam jerked the hem of his collarless shirt down and pointed to the burn scars on his neck. "Uriah died trying to save me."

"And I'm grateful. It's just that . . ."

He glanced out the window at the empty lot where the barn once was. "Rosa's life wouldn't have been turned upside down if I had died in that fire instead of Uriah."

Mamm bowed her head.

Adam swiped his hat from the table. "I'm going into town."

He needed to buy a roll of chicken wire. Something he should have done after the dog attacked Rosa's chickens the first time. Erecting a fence was the only way to keep the flock safe, and even that wasn't a guarantee.

Tomorrow was Sunday. Rosa needed to get away from the farm, to spend time in fellowship. Lately, she'd become so consumed with her chickens that she'd almost lost sight of the people who cared about her. If he didn't put up some fencing, she'd spend Sunday services at home watching over those hens.

He wanted to blame sleep deprivation for her odd behavior, but it had to be something more. She had pulled away when he held her. He could only conclude that she was repulsed by his scars. Thank goodness he hadn't tried to kiss her.

Still, the memories of holding her lingered. It felt right to have her in his arms. Her head nestled on his shoulder, her warm breath driving fire to his core.

He shook his head.

She didn't share the same feelings. She would never fall in love with him, not the man who was to blame for her husband's death.

CHAPTER 8

After another sleepless night, staying attentive during the three-hour church service proved challenging. Rosa shifted on the wooden bench. The same thoughts of Adam that had assailed her mind last night continued to vie for her attention today. But every time she recalled the warmth of his embrace or the thumping of his heartbeat against her ear, she thought about Eunice, standing at the clothesline gaping at them.

She could only guess what Eunice thought of her now, after seeing that public display of affection. Rosa had wilted against him as if she belonged in his arms.

But Adam was just a kind man, that was all. A man who would offer a comforting gesture to anyone in distress.

Rosa felt a poke in her ribs and glanced sideways at Hope. The service had ended and the members were starting to stand. Rosa stood and stretched. Hope thrust Faith into her arms.

"Will you hold her while I get *mei* potato casserole out of the buggy?"

"Of course."

Rosa cradled the sleeping infant and fought against

a rising tide of jealousy. It was hard not to be envious of her best friend. Four beautiful daughters and a fine son, not to mention a loving husband. Everything Rosa wanted, Hope had.

Becky Byler appeared with her arms outstretched. "Do you want me to take her?"

"Don't you want to join your friends?"

Becky shrugged. "It doesn't matter." But her downcast expression and slumped shoulders didn't match her words. It did matter.

Most of the unmarried girls congregated together during the fellowship hours. Even as they helped with the meal preparations, they stayed tight-knit, whispering among themselves. Becky Byler didn't fit in with that bunch.

Rosa released Faith into Becky's arms. If the girl needed something to do instead of interacting with the other young folks, Rosa wouldn't monopolize time with the infant. Besides, she hadn't planned on staying for the meal. She didn't want to leave the chickens unattended for too long.

Rosa spotted Hope coming from the house and walked across the lawn to meet her.

"I'm going to head home," Rosa said. "Becky Byler is watching Faith."

"Home already? Are you *nett* feeling well?" Hope eyed Rosa suspiciously.

"I feel fine." She leaned closer. "I don't trust the neighbor to keep his dogs in the kennel, and I don't want to lose any more chickens."

"Oh, Rosa, listen to yourself. You're willing to sacrifice

Sunday fellowship to watch your chickens? Don't let a dog control your life."

"It isn't just *mei* laying hens. I have to feed *mei* chicks."

"When did you get new chicks?"

"A gift from Adam."

Hope's brows lifted.

"Don't read anything into it," Rosa warned. "He felt bad that I had lost so many chickens."

Hope smiled. "Adam's sweet, *ya*?"

Rosa had already said too much. This wasn't the time or place to talk about Adam. "We can chat one day next week after I make *mei* deliveries."

"*Ya*, it sounds like we have some catching up to do."

"Don't be mapping out a spot in *mei* garden for a celery crop," Rosa said. "It isn't like that."

The reference to celery, traditionally served at their weddings, made Hope laugh.

Rosa turned toward the row of parked buggies. "I'll see you soon."

"You need to consider building a fence for your chickens."

"Adam already built one." She kept walking, ignoring Hope, who was demanding to hear more.

Halfway to her buggy, Rosa heard someone call her name. She turned. "*Hiya*, Peter."

He ambled closer. "I heard you wanted to sell your plow team."

"*Ya*, are you interested?" Normally buying and selling were not discussed on Sunday, but she took it as a sign from God to keep hope that she could raise the money she needed.

"Maybe. I'd like to look at them. Say tomorrow?"

"Sure. I get back from *mei* egg deliveries around ten."

"I'll see you then." He turned back toward the crowd.

Danki, God. The money from the draft horses plus her savings would more than cover her taxes. She caught a glimpse of Adam in the distance, carrying a bean crock in one arm and guiding Widow Esther by the elbow with his other. Since her stroke, Esther wasn't too steady. Adam showed great patience walking beside her, matching his stride to her short, shuffling steps. The other unmarried men were hanging around near the unmarried women, Claire Milner among the group.

Rosa continued toward the parked buggies. She had reached Blossom when she heard footsteps behind her.

"You're *nett* leaving already, are you?" Adam asked.

"*Ya.*" She untied the reins from the post.

"I saw you talking with Peter Zook . . ." His voice trailed and he looked down at the ground and toed a stone.

"He's interested in buying *mei* plow team."

"I heard you might be selling them." He looked up at her. "I don't think it's wise. You'll get a better price if you wait until spring."

Spring was too late. "I have to sell them *nau*. I can't afford to feed them this winter if I don't have eggs to sell."

The womenfolk were busy taking food into the barn while the men loitered in a circle by a piece of farm equipment. They were not within earshot, but she still didn't want to continue discussing the sale of her horses. It wouldn't take much to figure out she was broke and selling the team was a necessity.

"How did your new girls do in the brooder *haus* I built?"

Rosa smiled. "Fine, but I still think there are a lot of roosters in that flock."

"Maybe so." A grin split his face. "I like chicken dinner."

Looking past him, she caught sight of Claire and Mark Raber talking next to the barn. Rosa must not have disguised her shocked expression, because Adam turned to see what she was looking at.

He stared silently.

"You better get back to the group." It hadn't been that long ago that whispers had spread of Adam sitting with Claire on her parents' porch swing.

He faced her. "I'd rather talk with you."

"I have to check on *mei* chickens."

"Your chickens are safe. Besides, if you leave *nau*, what will you eat?"

"Probably chicken."

"Rosa." He frowned.

"I also want to see if they laid any eggs," she said. "You said that the fence would give them a sense of security and they'd start producing again."

"You hover over those boxes like you expect them to lay a golden egg." He unearthed another stone with the tip of his boot. "Do you remember the *nacht* a bunch of us stood under that old oak?" He motioned to the large tree on the far corner of the property.

As children, they had played under most every tree in the district at one time or another.

"It was raining." He shoved his hands into his pockets.

"I asked to drive you home from the singing. You don't remember?"

"You were joking."

"*Nee*, I was serious." Adam leaned toward her ear. "If we walked over to that tree and I asked you today, what would you say?"

She looked at him. Her heart began to race as if she were nineteen again. "We're too old to attend the youth singings," she said, and climbed into the buggy.

. . .

Adam watched as Rosa's buggy rolled away. He couldn't have made his intentions any more direct, and she rejected him, just as she had so many years ago. He understood the past. Later that same night she accepted Uriah's invitation. But now . . .

Adam sighed. She hadn't been interested in him then, and she wasn't attracted to him now. He rejoined the others for the meal, but his appetite was gone. There was only one thing on his mind: how could he fulfill his promise to Uriah to look after Rosa, while keeping his heart at a distance?

CHAPTER 9

The next morning Rosa received another delinquent tax notice in the mail. She opened the kitchen drawer and added the latest reminder to the stack with the others. "I'm running out of time, God. I need a miracle." She had said those same words earlier when she found the nesting boxes empty again.

Maybe she should go ahead and write her aunt a letter, just in case. It was a last resort, but she was almost there, and she didn't think she should show up on *Aenti* Lilly's doorstep unannounced.

Rosa reached for a pen and notebook from the drawer, but instead picked up her ledger book and began flipping through the list of her egg customers "God," she said, "this isn't just about me. What about the widows? I've never charged them for eggs, so it's an unexpected expense for them. This is the middle of October. Soon it'll be Thanksgiving and Christmas. Everyone bakes more during the holidays." She paused. "But I guess I don't have to tell You about the widows' needs. You have provided for them, and You will continue even without *mei* eggs."

Rosa scanned the income log. With nothing to

record, the tally hadn't changed. She'd never be able to pay the taxes before the auction day. She closed the book and slipped it back into the drawer. Unless she sold Bolt and Thunder . . .

Did she dare hope that was part of God's plan? It would make sense. If she sold the horses, not only would she be able to pay her taxes, but she wouldn't have winter feed to buy.

God would provide. He often worked in mysterious ways.

A buggy pulled into the yard. Rosa craned her neck at the kitchen window and saw Peter Zook climbing out of his buggy. She opened the door before the man knocked. *"Hiya."*

"Wie geht's?"

"Fine, *danki*." Now with the formalities accomplished, she wanted to whisk him out to the barn and show him the horses. "Let me get *mei* cape, and I'll take you out to see Bolt and Thunder." She yanked her wool cape from the peg and slipped it on as she left the house. "They're a *gut* team. I want to sell them together."

"How old are they?" She had to think. Uriah bought them the year after they married, and they were three at the time. "Nine."

He opened the barn door, waited for her to enter, and followed her to the stalls. "I didn't realize you had so many horses."

"These aren't mine. Adam Bontrager is using *mei* barn." She stopped in front of Bolt's stall. "This one is Bolt and the next stall over is Thunder."

While he inspected the draft horses, Rosa checked

on the fillies in the nearby stall. She ran her hand over one filly's silky coat. The smaller of the three nuzzled her cape while the one with the white star on its forehead nipped at her elbow. Under different circumstances, she would love to spend more time with them.

Maybe those circumstances would change today. Selling the team would improve everything. She wouldn't lose her farm. Adam wouldn't be forced to relocate his horses.

Peter came outside of Bolt's stall and entered Thunder's. "They packed on some extra weight, *ya*?"

"They gained a little." A lot. They were fat and borderline lazy. Sometimes when a horse wasn't worked it lost its stamina, and often its value as well. "The only planting I've done is in the garden. So they haven't been worked in two years. But they're a strong team."

"*Ya*, so I see."

She breathed easier.

Peter closed the stall gate. "I'm interested if I can pay on time."

"How much time do you need?"

"I would have all the money by spring. Maybe early summer."

The air left her lungs, her hope along with it. "I wanted to sell them this winter."

He looked into the stall as if recalculating their worth. "You could take them to the auction, but you'll get pennies on the dollar for them. It'd be a shame."

Exactly what Adam had told her too. *Lord, this wasn't how I thought You would answer* mei *prayers.*

"I could give you a down payment at the beginning of next month."

That wouldn't help either. The tax sale was in eighteen days.

"I'll be honest with you." She fought to control the quiver in her voice. "I don't have the money to buy hay. I can't wait until spring to sell them."

He nodded. "If it helps, I'll take them *nau* so you're *nett* out the winter's feed bill. And I'll pay your asking price on payments."

One way or the other she had to sell the team. She couldn't move them to her aunt's place in Ohio. She wasn't even sure when the next livestock auction was scheduled.

She swallowed down the lump in her throat. "*Ya*," she said, "I'll accept your offer."

But all the while she was wondering, *Where is God?*

. . .

Adam stood next to the barn and directed Stephen Bowman as he backed up the hay wagon. The load wouldn't fill the loft, but it should carry both his and Rosa's horses through the winter. At least now she could wait until spring to sell the team.

Adam held out his hand to signal Stephen to stop. "That's far enough."

Stephen set the wagon brake and jumped down from the seat. His son, James, followed.

Adam slipped his hands into a pair of worn leather gloves. With Stephen and his son helping to unload the wagon, the hayloft would be loaded in no time.

And none too soon, if the storm clouds on the horizon were any indication. This late in October, any rain could turn into sleet. Rosa's buggy was missing from the yard. He worried she might get caught in bad weather.

Stephen cranked the engine on the gas-powered conveyor belt. "We should get started, or we might *nett* get this hay undercover before it rains."

Adam went into the barn and climbed the wooden ladder into the loft. He stood at the opening and waited for the bale to reach him. With both Stephen and James tossing bales on the belt, Adam wasn't able to keep up with the volume reaching him. Every other bale fell off the belt while he carried another one by the twine over to the stack. It didn't matter so much that they weren't piled nicely, what mattered was getting them under cover.

From his elevated view, Adam spotted Rosa's buggy a quarter mile down the road. The wagon was half unloaded when she pulled into the yard. She looped Blossom's reins around the post and nodded a greeting to Stephen and James. Then her gaze carried up to the loft, and her smile quickly turned to a frown. She shook her head as she went into the house.

An hour later they unloaded the final bale just as the drizzle turned to sleet. Adam leaned out of the loft opening. "*Danki* for helping."

"What about stacking? Should we *kumm* up?"

Adam shook his head. "I'll be fine. You two should be on your way. It's getting *kalt*." He shot them a quick wave, then wrapped his fingers around the twine and hoisted the bale on top of the pile.

Stephen's wagon had barely rattled out to the end of the drive when Rosa's screen door slammed. Adam glanced out as she marched toward the barn. A few moments later she stood at the bottom of the ladder, arms crossed, calling his name.

He shimmied down the ladder. His foot landed with a *thud,* and when he turned, he met her glare. "Something wrong?"

"What are you doing putting hay *in* the barn? You should be taking it out."

He wiped his shirtsleeve across his sweaty forehead. "You said you were worried about getting through the winter." He picked loose hay off his shirt.

"I told you. You have to find another place for your horses. All the hay too."

"Rosa, be reasonable."

"I don't have that option," she said. "And neither do you."

He followed her outside. "There's enough hay to last the winter for all of our horses. You don't have to sell the team either."

"They're already sold. Peter is picking them up later this week."

"I don't understand the problem." Unless it had something to do with him wanting to court her. "I've used your barn for a couple of years *nau.*"

"And it was supposed to be temporary."

He groaned and followed her into the house. "We need to talk about this."

"It's too late." She stressed the words. "I didn't have any eggs again today." Her eyes brimmed with tears. She whirled away and darted into the kitchen.

"I told you, it takes time."

She turned on him with fire in her eyes. "I don't have time. I have sixteen days to pay *mei* delinquent taxes or I'm going to lose this farm." She bowed her head. "When the cows got sick, Uriah let the taxes lapse. When they came due, I wrote a letter to the county clerk explaining that *mei* husband was deceased, but it didn't matter. They said the taxes were too far behind."

He pulled a handkerchief from his back pocket and handed it to her. "How long have you known?"

"Since the beginning of the year." She swiped at the tears. "If *mei* chickens hadn't stopped laying . . ."

"I wish you had told me sooner. I spent the last money I had on hay. I won't have an income until the horses are trained."

"I won't ask anyone for money. You included." Rosa crossed her arms and turned her back on him. "I don't want anyone to think Uriah wasn't a *gut* provider."

"He would never have wanted you to go through this alone," Adam said. He felt his stomach twist into a knot. He'd made a promise to Uriah to take care of Rosa, and he'd fallen short of fulfilling his vow. "There's a widow's fund. Maybe you should speak with one of the elders—"

She spun to face him, her eyes narrowed. "I would never ask for money from that fund. It's for the widows."

"*Ya.* You fall into that group."

She shook her head. "There are women in much greater need." She locked eyes with him. "And don't you say anything about this—to anyone."

He buried a groan under his breath. Pride would devour her if she continued on this path. "Rosa—"

"I mean it. I won't ever speak to you again."

"Things will work out. God has a plan."

"*Ya.* Apparently His plan is for me to go live in Ohio with *mei aenti.*"

He shook his head. "I can't let you go there. How would I watch over you?" He inched closer and touched the wet streak on her cheek. "Have faith. God will see you through."

Her shoulders slumped and she sniffed.

"He will, Rosa. Trust me. Trust God."

Adam believed what he said. But he knew he had to figure out some way to help, or her eyes would haunt him forever.

. . .

Rosa poured *kaffi* into two cups as Adam leaned against her kitchen counter. She wanted to break the silence between them, but her thoughts were a jumbled mess.

He rubbed his jaw. "So how much money do you need yet?"

"A lot." She set the pot on the stove.

"Even after selling Bolt and Thunder?"

She cringed. "Peter didn't have the money." Rosa handed him a cup of coffee. "He's going to make payments." Right or wrong, she'd already agreed to the terms. These past two years without Uriah had proven unbearable, and battling the delinquent taxes left her weary and questioning God's will more than ever.

"How does that help you? I wish you had talked to me first."

"I couldn't afford to feed them all winter, so taking payments was the only choice I had."

"Why don't we sit down and go over what you owe? Maybe we can figure something out." He pulled out a chair and tapped the seat.

Rosa hesitated.

"You can't do this alone. Please let me help."

She opened the kitchen drawer and removed the stack of notices from the County Tax Bureau, along with the book she used to record her income. She handed the information to him, then sat in the chair next to his. "The top envelope is the most recent."

He unfolded the letter, and as he scanned the page, his expression turned hopeful. He set the paper down. "It says you only have to pay twenty-five percent by the auction date."

"I'm aware of that."

He pointed to the clerk's letter. "That's the amount you're trying to raise?"

"*Ya,*" she said. She opened the log book and pointed to the first column. "This is how much I have saved. In this row I've listed what I had counted on from egg sales."

He blew out a short breath.

"It's hopeless, isn't it?"

"Nothing is beyond God's help." He reached for her hand and gave it a gentle squeeze. "I'm glad you shared this with me."

She was too. Even knowing he lacked the financial means to help, it still comforted her to know she wasn't alone.

He sipped his *kaffi* and set down the cup. "I guess we have some work to do."

"*Ya.* I need to pack, and you need to find a new home for your horses."

He shook his head. "I meant horse training. I'll pick the one that shows the most promise. Lord willing, there's a chance I can find a quick buyer once he's trained."

"Really?"

"Don't you think that would be God's will?" He shrugged. "I do."

She found a ray of hope in his faith and smiled. "I'm blessed to have a friend like you." She patted his hand. "I mean that."

He placed his other hand over hers, opened his mouth as if he wanted to say something, then closed it again. Adam released her hand and pushed away from the table. "I'm going to pick out a horse."

"You really want me to help train?"

"Of course I do." He winked. "I like your company. Besides, you'll find working with horses will get your mind off your problems. Make sure to wear old clothes."

When Adam left the house, Rosa dashed upstairs to change. She hadn't felt excitement like this since Uriah had convinced her they could make a go of dairy farming.

She changed into the old charcoal gray dress she saved to wear for spring cleaning. It was spotted white where bleach had splattered, with the hem tattered beyond repair. The dress should have gone into the rag pile long ago. Rosa hurried down the stairs to the door where she kept her work boots. She had one boot on when someone knocked on the door.

Rosa opened the door. "Mr. Wade! What—what can I do for you?" She hopped on one foot, trying to get the other boot on.

He thrust a piece of paper toward her. "Here's the vet bill."

She glanced at the charges, and her heart plummeted.

"Had the dog not lived, the amount would've been higher. As it looks now, the vet says he'll eventually be able to compete in hunting competitions. So I guess you're lucky."

Lucky? She'd paid less for Blossom than the price of this vet bill. She extended the paper toward him.

"Keep it. That's your copy." He made to leave but turned back. "If I have to file a lawsuit, you'll have court costs tacked on to the vet bill."

Rosa closed the door and stared at the long list of charges. Fifty dollars for bandages. Three hundred for each night at the animal hospital. Over two hundred for medications and IVs alone. She flipped to the second page as the itemized costs continued.

Paying this would leave her destitute.

CHAPTER 10

Rosa lagged behind Adam as he headed toward the corral. He had said working with the horse would take her mind off her problems, but he failed to warn her how achy she'd be at the end of the day. She was stiff and sore from sitting on the fence, and even a thick application of arnica ointment didn't alleviate her soreness.

Every night she dropped into bed exhausted. But as worn out as she was physically, she still wrestled with the empty nesting boxes and the neighbor's vet bill.

She hadn't slept in three days. Not since Mr. Wade had given her a copy of the bill. Last night she got down on her knees and prayed for wisdom . . . and forgiveness. Every time she thought about taking up that shotgun, she wondered how she could have exercised such poor judgment. She could have killed the dog—or one of the horses—or even worse, a person.

It was true that the dog was on her property and had attacked her chickens, but that was rationalization. She felt prompted by God to hold her tongue, make amends with the neighbor, and pay the vet charges.

But even with that strong conviction and sleepless

nights, she couldn't bring herself to deplete her savings. She prayed that God would show her another way. So far, she hadn't received an answer. Not even a hint.

Rosa climbed up the fence rail as Adam adjusted the harness on the sorrel gelding. He hitched Flapjack to the open buggy and took a seat on the bench. Adam clicked his tongue and ordered the gelding forward. Flapjack sidestepped but quickly calmed down under Adam's tone of voice and steady actions.

Adam steered the horse around the corral, the first lap walking, then trotting. Rosa marveled at the level of skill Adam demonstrated. After making several laps of stopping and going, walking and trotting, and changing directions, Adam pulled up next to the fence railing. "Would you like to take him around a lap or two?"

"Sure." She climbed off the fence too quickly. The horse jerked his head up. "Sorry." She reached her hand to his neck and the horse flinched again. "Maybe this isn't a *gut* idea. I don't think he likes me."

"He's a little nervous yet." Adam slid over on the bench, making space on the driver's side.

"Are you sure I can hold him?"

"I'll be right beside you." He extended the reins.

She eased onto the bench.

"Give him a tap and tell him to go," Adam said.

The horse's ears perked at the sound of Adam's voice. Rosa only had to click her tongue for Flapjack to move forward. Except for the young gelding stretching his neck to gain more reins, his gait was smooth. They completed the lap and she pulled back on the reins. "I think you've done an amazing job training him so fast."

Adam smiled. "You can take him around again."

She wasn't sure if the ripple in her stomach was from the thrill of driving a newly trained horse or simply sitting shoulder to shoulder next to Adam. She clicked her tongue and lightly tapped the horse's rump. Taking the first bend, the horse pulled on its lead and at the same time increased his pace.

"Slow him down," Adam said calmly.

Flapjack ignored her command and didn't respond to her yanking on the reins. Rounding the corner, the buggy tipped. Her body slammed against Adam.

He reached over her and took control of the reins. "Whoa." His arm muscles tightened as he held the reins taut. Flapjack obeyed.

"I guess he got away from me," Rosa said once she caught her breath.

"He's a little cantankerous. I was premature letting another driver take him."

Flapjack pawed at the ground. He was lathered in sweat and foaming around the bit. He jerked his head up, but Adam kept him in check.

"It isn't good to end the lesson after a horse gets away," Adam said. "If you want to get out, I'll take him for a few more laps, then we can give him a break."

She climbed down from the bench and crawled between the fence railings to get out of the training area. "I'll go make lunch."

Eating lunch together had become part of their daily routine. The long hours they spent together was stirring up feelings Rosa didn't want to admit. Adam was a pillar of strength, a reservoir of support. But respect and admiration for someone wasn't the same as love. She couldn't allow her heart to be fooled.

Adam Bontrager was a good man. He needed a wife and family.

She kicked her boots off beside the door. Her house cleaning had suffered over the last few days of working with him. The women would be appalled at her floors. Even with Adam stomping his boots on the outdoor mat, it would take a hard bristle brush and scrubbing on hands and knees to clean all the dirt tracked in.

Rosa had a fresh pot of coffee and sandwiches prepared by the time he tapped on the door.

"It's open." She set the sandwich plates on the table as he entered the kitchen. He washed his hands while she set the table. Then he sat in the chair opposite hers. After spending this time with him, it was going to be difficult to go back to eating every meal alone.

She caught a glimpse of Flapjack tied to the fence post. "You didn't remove his tackle?"

"*Nee*, he needs to get used to standing for long periods with it on."

That made sense. She'd often wondered how horses tolerated the long Sunday services and the extended mealtime afterward. "How do you think his training is going?"

Adam shrugged. "He's *nett* ready to go on the road yet." He must have seen the disappointment in her expression because he quickly added, "We'll know more by the end of the week."

She smiled but doubted it masked all her worry. There weren't many days left. Less than two weeks didn't seem like enough time to train a horse, let alone find a buyer.

"Don't worry," he said.

She traced the rim of the mug with her finger. "You know me too well."

"You spend too much time worrying about things you need to give to God. All of this is in God's plan. His provisions will meet your need."

"I know." She was thankful for his faith. Even Uriah had never stood so boldly. When the cows became ill with the bovine disease and it looked as though they would lose their dairy herd, Uriah had told her not to worry, but his voice shook and the wrinkles across his forehead indicated otherwise. Adam's faith was stronger than anyone she knew, and it reassured her.

"What else are you fretting over?" Adam took a bite of the sandwich.

The answer leaped to her mind immediately: she was worried about falling in love with him. But to that, she couldn't admit.

He pressed on. "Ever since the neighbor stopped over the other day, you've been acting strange."

Rosa sighed. "I might as well tell you. He showed me his vet bill. It's more than I paid for Blossom and her harness."

"It would have been cheaper to build a pen his dog wouldn't escape from."

"It was foolish to take the gun off the rack. I should have chased the dog off with a broom."

Rosa knew her impulsive actions weren't pleasing to God. The scripture she had read that morning played in her mind: *Forgive those who trespass against you.* God's Word was clear. She prayed the neighbor would forgive her for shooting his dog.

"What's done is done. You can't do anything about it now."

"He expects me to pay the expenses. He called me cruel."

Her neighbor wasn't interested in a mere apology. He wanted payment. Payment that would deplete her savings, cement the loss of her farm, and force her to move to Ohio.

"His dog was on your property." Adam pushed his empty plate aside and moved his *kaffi* cup forward. "Should I wait for you to offer me a cookie or just help myself?"

She retrieved the jar from the counter and handed it to him. "Since the chickens haven't laid any more eggs, I haven't been able to make another batch."

"I need to go to town later. I'll pick up a dozen eggs for you."

"*Nee*. I can't pay you."

He dug his hand down to the bottom of the jar and pulled out a broken cookie. "You just did."

She smiled. If her chickens started laying again, she planned to make him a double batch to take home.

He stood. "Flapjack is waiting. Are you going to *kumm* back out?"

"You don't need *mei* help."

"But I enjoy your company."

Warmth spread over her face.

"Pink is a *gut* shade for your cheeks," he said. "It brightens your eyes."

She had warned herself not to pry, but she couldn't keep from doing it. Adam had to have seen Mark Raber and Claire talking after the Sunday services last week.

"Aren't you a little concerned about *nett* spending enough time with Claire?"

Adam strode to the kitchen entry and stopped. "Don't lose sleep over me and Claire. She and Mark Raber are courting *nau.*"

. . .

Adam untied Flapjack from the post as Rosa took her place on the rail. He wanted to take the gelding around the corral a few times before letting Rosa drive again. So far, the training had gone better than expected. He had pushed Flapjack harder than normal, but he had to. He couldn't let Rosa lose her house without doing everything he could to help.

It bothered him that she made him promise not to tell anyone in the community. She had spent her life helping others; if anyone deserved help from the widows' fund, it was Rosa. But he couldn't bring himself to breach her trust either.

Adam clicked his tongue, encouraging Flapjack into a faster trot. If all went well, he would take the horse out on the road tomorrow and try some country roads to avoid heavy traffic. Maybe even show him to a few people he knew were looking to buy a buggy horse.

An engine revved next door. Flapjack shied. It took a great deal of strength for Adam to regain control.

In the distance he saw Wade working on his truck. How could he expect Rosa to pay the vet bill when his dog killed her chickens? Perhaps if he talked with the neighbor, he could convince him to let the matter drop.

. . .

"Here you are," Eunice said to Rosa. "I knocked on your door, but there was no answer."

Rosa jumped off the fence. "I was helping Adam."

"*Mei* son has an assistant *nau*, has he?"

"I just watch usually."

"I wanted to return your dish." She held up an empty dish in her hand, the one Rosa had used for the chicken casserole.

"*Danki*." Rosa motioned to the house. "I could use a cup of *kaffi*. How about you?"

"Maybe a half a cup. I can't stay long. I'm meeting some of the other widows in town at the fabric store. You know we like to get together."

Rosa smiled.

"Did you want to join us? We could ride together."

"*Nee*—I couldn't." The answer sounded unnecessarily abrupt, so Rosa tried to temper her response. "I have some things already planned for this afternoon." She had promised Hope she would babysit if Becky Byler wasn't able.

"Our group is very supportive," Eunice said. She stepped into the house, her eyes roaming the sitting room. "I don't have to tell you how lonely—"

The peeping chicks caught her attention. She spotted the crate across the room and lifted her brows.

Rosa kicked off her boots. "*Boppli* chicks," she said. "A gift from Adam. He built that brooder box too. They'll soon be old enough to go outside."

Surely this wasn't the first time she'd seen chicks in the house. It wasn't as though they were running around loose. "Here, let me take that." Rosa reached for the dish.

When she saw the state of the kitchen, she cringed. She should have taken a few minutes to clean up after lunch.

Rosa set the casserole dish on the counter, then hurried to clear the table. Bread crumbs on the counter, dirt on the floor, deplorable to someone like Eunice. Her house was always in order.

"I wish you would reconsider going into town with me. It isn't about picking out material as much as enjoying fellowship. And you must be lonely living here alone."

"I'm sure it's a *wunderbaar* gathering." Rosa placed the coffee-pot on the stove and willed it to boil. Truth be told, she despised participating in the widows' gatherings. They were a loving group of women and had welcomed her after Uriah's death, but Rosa couldn't manage to feel comfortable among them. As it was, it had taken her two years just to get beyond cooking for two and not jumping out of her skin every time the century-old farmhouse creaked. Despite the widows' certainty that she would adapt to living alone, she hadn't.

Besides, all of the other widows had children or grandchildren to help pass the long hours of silence. She had neither.

"I just think if you had group activities, you wouldn't depend so much on Adam," his mother said.

Rosa moved the pot to a hotter spot and avoided looking at Eunice.

"I know he feels it's his duty to look after you." She sighed. "Please don't take this the wrong way. Adam is a thoughtful *sohn*, and I'm very pleased he has such a giving heart. But I worry he is missing the opportunity to find a *fraa*. And I so want *kinskinner*."

Rosa had dreamed of having a houseful of children and grandchildren too. She pushed down the pain, plastered on a smile, and faced Eunice. "I understand completely."

"*Ach* dear, I wasn't thinking." Eunice covered her mouth. "I'm so sorry."

"You didn't say anything wrong," Rosa said. "Did I tell you *mei* chickens still haven't laid any eggs? Please tell everyone I hope to be able to bring them some soon." She shifted her attention back to the stove. More kindling would heat the pot faster. She opened the side compartment and peered in at the dying embers. "I'm afraid the fire is almost out."

Eunice glanced at the wall clock. "If you don't mind," she said, "could we have *kaffi* another time? I don't want to be late to the frolic."

"I don't mind at all." Rosa hoped the relief in her tone wasn't too obvious.

Once Eunice left, Rosa washed the dishes, scrubbed the counters, and mopped the floor. She added oil to every lamp in the house, rearranged the canned goods in the pantry, and still she couldn't erase the conversation with Adam's mother.

She was filling the chicks' pan with fresh water when someone knocked on her door.

"Did you walk off the job?" Adam stomped the dirt from his boots on the mat before entering the house. "I waited for you."

She wiped her hands on her apron. "I needed to clean the house."

"I'm done for the day. Would you like to go to town with me?"

"I can't." She disappeared into the kitchen long enough to grab the watering pan.

Adam went over to the box and lifted the wire lid. "What did *mei mamm* want?"

Rosa eased the pan inside. "She invited me to the widows' gathering."

"So you're going?" He smiled.

"*Nee.*"

His smile faded. "Are you upset about something?"

"Do you think the neighbor revved his engine purposely to spook Flapjack?" That wasn't the only thing upsetting her, but it was the only thing she was willing to share with him.

"Don't let him upset you. Anger's a sin."

"I thought you were going into town." She walked to the door, knowing he would follow. "I think we might be spending too much time together."

He closed the distance between them. "I don't."

"I really appreciate everything you're doing for me, but—"

"Don't say it."

"Adam, I don't want *mei* problems to interfere with your life."

He opened the door. "Get some sleep tonight, and don't fret over the neighbor."

Don't fret over the neighbor.

There was only one way she was going to stop fretting over the neighbor: she had to make amends with Tate.

CHAPTER 11

Rosa counted out the money down to the last penny for the vet charges. After wrestling all night with what she felt God was directing her to do, she had to obey. She closed the lid on the canning jar filled with coins. *God, I don't know where the money will* kumm *from for the taxes, but I can't live with the animosity either.* She slipped on her cape and headed across the yard. *If there's another way, stop me, please.*

Tate answered the door after the second knock.

Before he said anything, she pressed the coin jar against his chest.

"It's all there," she said. "I'm sorry your dog was injured."

"Thank you. Do you want the jar back?"

"No. That's yours to keep."

He stared at her. She couldn't breathe. She needed air. Without a word, she pivoted on her heel and fled.

A gust of wind and a sudden pelting of hail sent a chill through her bones. She cut through the garden. The moment she stepped inside the house, a blast of heat from the woodstove hit her. She kicked off her shoes and padded into the kitchen to make a cup of tea.

As the kettle heated, she looked out the window. Hail

pinged against the brown lawn. Freezing rain mixed with snow would come next. Through the window she caught a glimpse of Adam as he traipsed from his property over to hers. He must have seen her, because he waved on his way to the barn.

Shouldn't she feel better? She had done the right thing, so why wasn't there some sort of relief?

Well, whether she felt better or not, it was over. No matter what happened now, she wouldn't be able to pay the taxes. One way or the other, she was going to lose the farm.

She opened the drawer and pulled out the letter she had started to *Aenti* Lilly. Everything she had saved was gone. It was time to make other plans.

She jotted a couple of sentences about the change in weather, then put the pen down. Her mind reeled in all directions. Traveling by bus would limit how much stuff she could bring. She would have to sell most of her belongings and ship the rest to Ohio.

Rosa left the kitchen and roamed through the house, trying to inventory what would have to be left behind. Parting with the rocking chair her father had made would be difficult. The bed Uriah had crafted so lovingly by hand wouldn't ship either.

She wandered back downstairs. The dishes held no sentimental value; she would find someone in need of them. The table for ten only mocked her with lost dreams. She ran her hand along the fine wood grain. She had wanted a large, noisy, happy family. What God had given her instead was grief and solitude.

Rosa started pulling jars off the shelves. Living

alone, she hadn't eaten much in the past two years, yet she'd put in an oversized garden and canned as if she had a huge family to feed. Even if by some miracle she didn't lose the house, she wouldn't eat this much food in twenty years. Someone else could use it.

She had a good portion of the pantry unloaded before Adam tapped on the door and entered.

"It's too dangerous to work the horse today," he said. "I'm sorry. I tried, but Flapjack kept slipping."

That didn't surprise her. Judging by the amount of mud on his boots, the rain had softened the ground. "You look *kalt*."

"I could use a cup of *kaffi*." He took one step in, then looked down at his boots.

"Don't worry; mopping gives me something to do." She shrugged. "I mopped at three this morning when I couldn't sleep. The floors weren't even dirty."

He followed her into the kitchen. "Rosa, you can't keep losing sleep."

"I couldn't get the dog out of *mei* mind," she said. "I really feel terrible about how quickly I lost *mei* temper." Her lips quivered. "I don't know what happened to me. I'm *nett* a violent person."

"I know you're *nett*."

"The neighbor doesn't. Do you know what he said to me? He said he had always heard that the Amish were nonviolent. Until he met me." She shook her head. "What kind of a life have I portrayed? *Nett* one that resembles Jesus."

"You don't need the neighbor's approval."

"It's God's approval I want." Her vision blurred. None

of her actions lately exemplified Christ. Worry, fear, and anxiety ruled over her.

"Jesus said, 'In Me you have peace.' He tells us plainly to expect tribulation."

She nodded. "I know. Jesus overcame the world."

"And you will overcome this." He reached out and took her hand. His fingers were frigid. "Things will work out if we put our trust in God."

Adam's soft voice had a way of touching her soul with reassurance. She didn't want to spoil his hope by telling him the vet charges emptied her savings. The kettle hissed. Rosa removed two mugs from the cabinet.

He glanced at the table. "Were you unloading your cupboards in the middle of the *nacht* too?"

"I made that mess a few minutes ago." She filled the mugs with *kaffi*. "Do you think the weather will clear so we can work with Flapjack later this afternoon?"

"I suppose it's possible." He moved in front of the window and stared outside. He rubbed the back of his neck and sighed.

She handed him a cup. "The horse isn't going to be trained in time, is he?"

"I wish you would let me talk with the bishop. The widows' fund is intended to—"

"Nee." She shook her head.

"I know you've given to that fund."

"Sure, we've all added to the offering. But that doesn't mean I'm entitled to draw from it."

He groaned under his breath. "You *are* a widow."

Her eyes welled with tears. She set her cup on the table and fled the room.

"Rosa!" He followed her to the foot of the stairway. "You're *nett* thinking straight. You haven't slept in days."

She ran up the steps and into her bedroom and slammed the door. Dropping onto the mattress, she buried her face in her pillow.

Adam tapped on the door. "Can we talk?"

"Later." What was there to talk about? She wasn't going to ask for money without having a way to repay the fund. This mess was created while her husband was alive. He should have told her he didn't pay the back taxes. He had to have known the county would auction the farm.

She punched the pillow. *Why did Uriah die and leave me in this jam?*

But no answer came. Only the sound of Adam's footsteps retreating down the stairs.

CHAPTER 12

Adam spent a restless night petitioning God on Rosa's behalf. He climbed out of bed in the morning not sure what he would say to Rosa's neighbor to change the man's outlandish payment demands but believing God would provide the right words.

Adam crossed the neighbor's property line just as Wade pulled up in his pickup truck. He waited while the man shut off the engine and opened the door.

"Can I talk with you a minute?" Adam said.

The man got out of the truck and turned to face Adam. "Who are you?"

"I'm Adam Bontrager. I live on the other side of Rosa Hostetler. I wanted to talk with you about your dog."

He smiled. "Nice of you to ask about him. He'll probably be in the cast a few more weeks, but—"

"I'm more concerned about Rosa's chickens. Your dog killed several and traumatized the others."

Tate narrowed his eyes. "Now that she's put up a fence around her coop, it's no longer an issue."

"I hope that's true." Adam shifted his feet. "Rosa is a widow. She sells eggs to make a living, and because of everything that's gone on recently, her chickens have stopped producing."

The man stared without blinking.

"I heard you've asked her to pay the vet bill." He continued without giving Tate time to acknowledge. "I don't believe it's her responsibility. If you had kept your dog on your property, he wouldn't have killed her chickens, and he wouldn't have been injured. She's not a cruel person."

"She admitted to shooting my dog."

"The gun went off accidently. But your dog was on her property attacking her chickens." To his credit, Tate Wade didn't try to deny or rationalize this. Adam figured he'd better get the rest of it in while he had the chance. "As a widow, she needs to keep her expenses to a bare minimum. She doesn't have money to pay vet bills, *especially* since she hasn't had any eggs to sell."

Tate reached for the doorknob. "I'll be back in just a minute." He disappeared inside his house and a moment later stepped back outside. "She already settled the vet costs." He handed Adam an empty, gallon-size pickle jar. "She told me to keep the jar, but I don't need it."

He stepped back into the house and shut the door in Adam's face.

Adam's mind reeled. *I don't understand, God. I thought You sent me to talk with him.* He plodded back across the field clutching the empty jar. *I thought You would have prepared his heart to see reasonably. Was that only wishful thinking?*

He reached Rosa's steps, drew a deep breath, and knocked.

The door opened. *"Guder mariye,"* she said.

"Is it really?" He brushed past her and went into

the kitchen. Setting the empty jar on the counter, he turned to her. "We need to talk."

"Where did you get that?"

Adam ignored her question. He opened the drawer where she kept her records, removed the logbook, and flipped it open. A quick scan to the bottom entry on the page explained everything. She was broke.

Rosa snatched the book from his hand. "This isn't your business." She jammed the book back into the drawer and slammed it closed. "I didn't designate you as my keeper."

"*Nee*, but Uriah did."

She glared at him.

"Rosa, why didn't you talk to me—to anyone—before paying him a dime?"

"I didn't know any other way to make amends." She began to sniffle, and he pulled a handkerchief from his pocket and gave it to her. She blew her nose and wadded the handkerchief up in her hand. "I didn't want to disappoint God by being bitter and angry, and I was. I was so upset with Tate Wade that I couldn't sleep."

Adam sighed. "I should have talked with him earlier. I could've made some sort of arrangement with him."

"Adam," she said softly. "I'm all right with *mei* decision."

"Well, I'm not."

"I sent a note to *mei aenti* in Ohio about living with her."

He couldn't bear the thought of her moving so far away. "Rosa, let me talk with the bishop. This can all be taken—"

"I've decided to butcher the hens. If they're not going to lay eggs, I might as well." She headed to the door, darted outside, and marched toward the shed.

Her stubbornness had stretched his patience thin. Adam trailed her to the woodshed and stopped her as she grabbed the ax. "Why are you doing this?"

"I told you they're *nett* laying eggs. I won't be able to take them with me to Ohio . . . and people are hungry. Earlier I took some canned goods over to one of *mei Englisch* egg customers whose husband is out of work, and she really appreciated the food." She paused. "Helping others is the right thing to do, and these chickens will go a long way."

Adam swallowed back tears. In the midst of all her struggles, she was thinking of ways to help other people. *Lord*, he thought, *I don't want her to move to Ohio. Isn't there a way?*

"Let me do it." He reached for the ax. "You can get the water boiling."

. . .

Rosa added a pinch of salt to the pot of water simmering on the stove. She was adding wood to the stove when the back door opened and Adam called, "Rosa, *kumm* quick."

She wiped her hands on her apron and rushed to the door.

"You have to see this." He took hold of her elbow and guided her outside.

The gusty wind made her shiver. She wanted to

double back for her winter bonnet and cloak, but his eagerness piqued her interest. "What's this all about?"

Adam unhooked the fence around the henhouse. "They're laying again."

She followed him into the coop. Adam pointed first to one nesting box, then another, and another. She'd never seen so many eggs. "It's a miracle!" She spun around and flung herself into Adam's arms.

Stirred up by the commotion, the chickens flapped and clucked around them. His eyes bored into hers and he leaned closer.

She pulled away just before his lips touched hers. "I should get a basket." She ran to the house, her heart hammering.

When she returned, he gently lowered the ones he had collected into the basket. Rosa focused on gathering eggs from another nesting box. The basket quickly filled, almost overflowing.

"I've never had this many eggs," she said as they entered the house.

"A miracle like you said, *ya*?"

She smiled. "*Ya*, so it is."

Rosa set the basket on the counter next to the sink. "Once I get these washed, I'm going to make *mei* deliveries." She chuckled. "Won't they be surprised to see me so late in the afternoon?"

"Do you want me to drive you?"

Unbidden, an image rose up in her mind—Adam leaning toward her in the coop with those piercing eyes. But his mother made it clear she disapproved of Rosa. She didn't want to upset Eunice more.

"*Nee.*" An expression of utter disappointment filled his face, and she tried to explain without using his mother's name. "*Danki* for the offer, but I don't know what people would say."

He motioned to the door. "It stopped raining. I think I'll work with Flapjack."

She laid a hand on his arm to stop him from turning away. "Adam," she said, "I don't normally . . ." She lowered her head. "I've never thrown myself into a man's arms like that before."

"Maybe that's another miracle," he said.

CHAPTER 13

A dam coaxed the gelding around the ring one more time, but his heart wasn't into training today. He'd kept a safe distance from Rosa since she pitched herself into his arms and then gave him a gibberish apology for her impulsive behavior. He'd been just as excited to see eggs in the nesting boxes. It meant God had answered his prayer—one part. He was still praying for someone to buy Flapjack.

If he hadn't tried to kiss her yesterday, maybe he wouldn't feel so awkward today. It was plain that she didn't share the same feelings for him. He needed to accept that they would only be friends.

Rosa left the henhouse toting two baskets and a wide smile. The count must be even higher today.

Danki, God, for providing another abundance of eggs. Please show me how I can help her. She's going to need more customers.

. . .

Rosa hoisted the oversized egg basket into the buggy seat and climbed in beside it. "Lord, You provided the eggs," she murmured, "*nau* please provide the buyers."

The blue sky was a welcoming sight. So was seeing Adam in the corral working with Flapjack. She shot him a quick wave, but he was preoccupied with the horse and didn't see her.

Byler's Bakery was first on the list. Becky was busy sorting pastries at the back counter when Rosa entered. She swiped her hands on the front of her apron and stepped to the register.

"What can I help you with, Rosa?"

"*Mei* chickens surprised me with an overabundance again today. I was hoping the bakery could use more."

Becky peered into the basket. "Wow, that is a lot." She smiled. "I've been wanting to try some new recipes. I suppose we could use another dozen or two." Becky disappeared into the kitchen area and returned with a container.

"I really appreciate you helping me out." Rosa counted out two dozen. Her basket was still full. "So what new recipes are you planning to try?"

"I have one for an apple turnover, and I need to use up the pumpkins from the garden, so I thought I would make some muffins."

"Sounds delicious. Let me know how they turn out." Rosa didn't have as much success selling to her other customers. She landed at Hope's house with more than half her basket unsold.

"I'll buy a dozen," Hope offered after hearing Rosa's dilemma.

"You raise your own eggs. You don't need to buy

mine." Rosa plopped down on her friend's kitchen chair. "But I suppose I am desperate to sell them."

Hope poured two mugs of *kaffi* and set them on the table. "That's exactly what Adam said last *nacht* when he stopped over to talk with Stephen about buying his gelding."

"He did?" Rosa toned down her excitement when Hope's brow arched. "He's a *gut* trainer."

"And . . ."

"And Flapjack will make a fine buggy horse."

"You have feelings for Adam, don't you?"

Rosa's cheeks warmed and she shifted on her chair.

"You can't hide it from me." Hope reached across the table and patted Rosa's hand. "I'm glad you're ready to move forward."

If she didn't find a way to pay her taxes in the next few days, Rosa would be moving, all right. But she didn't exactly consider Ohio as moving forward.

Hope smiled. "He gave you the chicks and put up a fence around your coop."

"Adam has . . . become a *gut* friend since Uriah died. It was hard at first, but through prayer, God helped me put aside *mei* anger about the fire. I don't blame Adam for Uriah's death. But I don't see us as more than friends either."

"Uriah would want you to be happy. And from what I've heard, you and Adam have spent a lot of time training that horse together."

"Did Adam say something about us working together?" *About my taxes?*

Hope shrugged. "If you started attending the sewing frolics, they would talk about someone else. Probably Becky Byler. You know how every woman in the settlement has something to say about her size."

Rosa wanted to ask if the sewing circle gossip was Eunice, but she resisted. Instead, she asked about Becky. "Do you think that might be why she's withdrawn?"

"I've been praying for her to feel accepted."

Rosa nodded. "I find it's easier to pray than to risk giving the wrong advice. I think she's tried every diet, and working around all those sweets must be difficult."

Hope wouldn't be distracted. "It's difficult for you to accept you're falling in love again, isn't it?"

"It wouldn't work. I can't have children. I already lived through seeing the disappointment in Uriah's eyes every time I miscarried. I couldn't bear it again."

Faith's cry rang out from the other room and pulled Hope's attention away. Just as well. The inability to have children was the least of Rosa's worries. She needed to sell eggs and find a way to pay her taxes, and that was as far into the future as she was willing to go.

"I better get moving." Rosa reached into her basket and removed a dozen eggs. "If you hear of anyone who needs eggs, please send them over."

. . .

Adam met Rosa outside the henhouse and helped her carry the eggs into the house.

"Have you ever seen so many eggs from so few chickens? It takes two of us to carry them all." Rosa beamed.

"What am I going to do with them all? I practically had to beg everyone to buy extra yesterday."

"God answers prayers, all right," Adam said. "And He never gives us more than we can eat." He grinned. "I like egg salad sandwiches."

"I'm serious. What am I going to do with all of these?"

He set the basket on the table. "Let's get this straight. You pray for a miracle, get it, and then question what you're going to do with it? Do you think God made a mistake? Or maybe He forgot to tell the chickens they could stop laying eggs?"

She bowed her head sheepishly.

"Remember how God brought quail to the Israelites? So much quail it came out of their nostrils. This was after they complained of only having manna to eat."

"I complain too much, don't I?"

"*Nee.*" He winked, then held up his index finger and said, "I'll be right back." He jogged out to the barn and grabbed the Eggs For Sale board he had painted earlier.

Rosa's eyes lit up. "What a great idea. But we don't live on a busy road. Do you think I'll get many customers?"

"I think the only reason the chickens laid so many eggs is because God has buyers already lined up. You'll see." He tapped the board. "I'll get this put up."

Adam carried the sign out to the mailbox, and even before he finished nailing it to the post, a vehicle entered Rosa's driveway. As that car pulled out, another one pulled in.

Rosa should be pleased. For a road without much traffic, God seemed to be sending people to buy her eggs.

Adam had another idea for increasing the sales, but

it involved his mother. He hiked home while Rosa was busy with customers.

"If you're hungry there is stew to warm up," *Mamm* said as he entered the kitchen.

"Okay, maybe later. Rosa's chickens laid a bunch more eggs today."

"That's *gut*. I know for a while they haven't been laying anything."

"I was hoping you could spread the word that she needs to sell them." He paused, debating how much to tell her without breaking his vow to Rosa. "Maybe the women in your group will buy them this week."

Mamm studied him silently for a moment. "Is she hurting for money?"

He looked down at his boots. Maybe saying something wasn't a good idea. "Like everyone, she has expenses. She's always been so *gut* about giving eggs to the widows . . ." He shrugged. "She's also a widow and not with much income."

"I know how it is, *sohn*."

"But don't most of the widows have adult *kinner* who help pay expenses? Rosa has no one."

Mamm sighed. "*Ya*, it's a shame." Her brows rose. "I'll suggest a bake sale. That will give everyone a reason to buy plenty of eggs."

Adam hoped he wouldn't regret getting his mother involved.

CHAPTER 14

Rosa's customer list grew daily—and so did the number of eggs her chickens laid. Since Adam put up the road sign, she had sold out every day before noon. Days away from the tax deadline, she'd begun to believe Adam was right. God would provide the tax money.

Rosa carried a quart of water out to the training ring for Adam. She perched on the fence rail as Adam removed his coat and draped it over the horse's head.

"He needs to trust me completely," Adam said. He boarded the buggy and clicked his tongue, but Flapjack hesitated. With some verbal coaxing from Adam, the horse lurched forward. They made one complete circle before the horse's gait smoothed out. Several starts, stops, and turning repetitions later, Adam halted the buggy. He kept the head covering in place, tied Flapjack to the post, then strode over to the fence.

"I thought you could use some water." She handed him the quart jar.

"*Danki.*" He leaned against the fence and took a drink. "Why did you cover Flapjack's head?"

"Blind trust," he said. "It trains him to listen to his

master's call." He took another drink, then handed her the empty jar. "Like God wants us to trust Him."

"So I've discovered."

"Have you counted your money again?"

She shook her head. "*Nett* since your suggestion." Adam had pointed out that she fretted more when she constantly tallied her sales. He challenged her to wait to count it again until the morning of the auction. It took restraint, but she followed his advice. She didn't even keep a mental tally.

Behind them, the Bowmans' horse whinnied as their buggy entered the driveway. Rosa jumped off the fence and waved as she and Adam crossed the drive.

"*Hiya,*" Rosa said.

Adam greeted Stephen as he climbed off the bench.

"Stephen and James wanted to check out Adam's horses." The girls clambered out from the back and the women meandered to the house. Adam, Stephen, and James headed toward the corral.

Once inside, Rosa gave the girls some paper to draw on while she and Hope chatted over tea. Rosa hadn't seen her friend since Hope's mother took ill. "Is your *mamm* better?"

"She isn't coughing as much."

"That's *gut* to hear."

"And I hear your chickens are still laying a lot of eggs." Hope sipped her tea.

"More every day. I've been able to sell them all too. *Danki* for passing the news."

Hope shook her head. "I've been so busy with *mei mamm*, I haven't spoken to anyone but Becky Byler when she came over to babysit."

"That's odd. Lately everyone in the district has needed extra eggs."

"Probably for the bake sale."

"When is the sale?" Rosa had been preoccupied, but she would certainly find time to bake for the sale. Most of the sales benefited a family who had health care burdens or who had lost their home in a fire. She hadn't heard about any families that had fallen on hard times.

"The sale was today. I dropped off some pumpkin pies on the way to *mei mamm's*." Hope reached across the table for Rosa's hand. "I'm sorry I've been tied up so much with *Mamm* and we haven't had much time to talk. Is there anything I can do for you?"

The men entered the kitchen. Stephen smiled at Hope. "James *nau* owns his first buggy horse, *fraa*."

Rosa's heart skipped. "Flapjack?"

Adam nodded. "He still needs several more weeks of training to get him road ready, but James wants to help me work with him."

"We should head home, *fraa*," Stephen said.

Hope nodded and walked her cup to the sink. "I'll talk with you soon," she said to Rosa before leaving.

Adam waited until the Bowmans left before showing Rosa the wad of cash. "It isn't the entire amount you need, but it should help." He added the money to the jar. "I told you I didn't want to move *mei* horses."

She didn't want him to find a new place for his horses either. "I don't know what to say."

"Just praise God."

"Praise God, indeed." Rosa peered at the jar. "Should we count it *nau*?"

Adam shook his head. "You only have a few more days to wait. God will provide." He motioned to the door. "I need to tend the stock, but maybe afterward we can have *kaffi* and a cookie?"

She nodded. "I'll make a fresh batch."

Rosa mixed up Adam's favorite peanut butter cookies. The first batch was cooling on the counter and another pan was in the oven when someone tapped on the door. Eunice and two women from the widows' group stood on the stoop.

"We wanted to give you this," said Mrs. Lehman, the shortest of the three. She extended an envelope toward her.

Rosa peeled open the flap and removed the cash contents. "I don't understand."

Eunice stepped forward. "You know how the widows' group enjoys working together on a project. These are the funds we raised from our bake sale."

"From your eggs," Enos Mast's widow said.

Rosa caught a glimpse of Adam as he came out from the barn. The moment their eyes connected, he ducked back inside. Rosa looked at Eunice. "Did Adam say something to you?"

"He mentioned you had too many eggs and sort of suggested that we buy them."

"That's why none of you would accept them for free? You felt obligated to pay for them?" Adam's good intentions settled in Rosa's stomach like a rock at the bottom of a pond. "Did he suggest you have a bake sale too?"

"*Nee,*" the women said in unison. "That was our idea."

Rosa stared at the money.

Dorothy Lehman patted her hand. "You've been so *gut* to all of us, giving us eggs when you could have sold them. We wanted to help you."

"We don't have husbands to look out for us, but we have each other." Adam's mother squeezed Rosa's arm. "You're a member of our group."

Rosa smiled, and suddenly her skewed view of being a widow shifted. It wasn't a life sentence of loneliness. Loneliness was not sharing herself with others. Perhaps God was leading her to embrace being one of them.

"Maybe you could *kumm* to our next get-together," Eunice said.

"*Ya*," Rosa said without reservation. "I'd like that."

CHAPTER 15

On the morning of the tax deadline, Rosa emptied the jar onto the table and sorted the money. Adam counted bills and she counted the change. Once they finished, she tallied the amount.

Twice.

Adam slid his chair back. "Money must have dropped on the floor."

It hadn't, but she didn't stop him from searching.

"Let's count it again," he said.

Numbness settled into her core. She had fully expected that the needed amount would miraculously be there. Just as he had. "We already recounted."

Adam rechecked the count, then slumped farther down in his chair. He rubbed his eyes. "I can't believe it."

Neither could she.

Like a hammer driving a nail, Adam had repeated over and over: *Have faith. Just have faith.*

But faith had failed her.

She got up and went to the sink—not because she was thirsty, but because she needed space around her. She needed to find a way to silence the voices in her head.

"Rosa." Adam crossed the room and gathered her into his arms.

She twisted away from him. "Take the money you gave me from selling the horse."

"We can worry about that later."

"*Later?*" She stared at him. "Don't you understand? There is no *later*. Time is up." She sighed. "I should have been packing all along."

"There's a chance no one will bid on the property. We can always hope—"

"Hope?" she said. "I'm fresh out of hope." She couldn't even bring herself to apologize for her lack of faith.

"All I'm saying is, it wouldn't be unlike God to—"

"Adam, I'd like to be alone."

He stared at her a moment "It's *nett* over, Rosa. You're still working your way up the mountain."

"What's that supposed to mean?"

"Remember when God commanded Abraham to sacrifice his son Isaac? God provided a ram as a substitute for the boy. But it was on the top of the mountain. Not at the bottom."

Adam left, and Rosa sank down at the table to give over to her despair. She cried until she had no tears left. She didn't know how long she sat there, or whether she dozed, only that when she sat up and looked around again, the day seemed half gone.

She was alone. The house was quiet. But Adam's final words still echoed in her ears. Abraham. Isaac. The mountain. The ram.

She reached for her Bible and turned to the story in Genesis.

Isaac spoke up and said to his father Abraham, "Father?"

"Yes, my son?" Abraham replied.

"The fire and wood are here, but where is the lamb for the burnt offering?"

Abraham answered, "God himself will provide the lamb."

. . .

Three days later, Adam was dumping a wheelbarrow full of horse manure on the compost pile when he spotted the mail truck pull up to Rosa's house. Why was the driver hand-delivering the mail?

He watched from a distance. Rosa ripped open the letter and turned away from the door as the mail truck drove off.

Adam wasn't sure she would welcome him inside. Since the day of the auction, she had kept her distance. But he decided to risk it. He left the wheelbarrow upended and headed for the house.

Adam tapped on the door. No answer. He knocked harder this time. When she still didn't answer, he let himself inside. His stomach knotted. Obviously she'd been busy. Boxes lined the walls of the sitting room.

He found her sitting at the kitchen table with her face buried in her hands and a letter open before her. "Are you okay?"

She didn't look up or even answer.

He caught a glimpse of the letterhead on the official-looking form: *County Tax Claim Bureau: notice to vacate.* He didn't need to read any more.

"Rosa?" he said.

No response.

"I, um . . ." He cleared his throat, but words wouldn't come.

She lifted her head and stared at him with bloodshot eyes. "You need to unload the hay in the barn and move your horses." She stood, reached for the jar of money on her counter, and thrust it at him. "Take out what's yours. Apparently it's God's will for me to move to Ohio and live with *mei aenti*."

"This isn't how—" He wiped his clammy hands against his pant legs. "You don't have to."

She waved the eviction notice in his face. "What choice do I have?"

He swallowed hard. "You can stay and . . . marry me."

Her eyes closed and she shook her head slowly. Then she pushed her chair away from the table and stood.

Adam followed her out of the kitchen. She stopped at the door, opened it, and motioned for him to exit. He paused in the threshold. "I don't want you to move to Ohio."

"Your loyalty to Uriah is commendable," she said. "To think you would feel such indebtedness."

He rubbed the burned side of his neck. Indebtedness? Is that how she saw it? A debt that needed to be settled, the price Uriah had paid to save Adam's life?

She shut the door behind him and left him standing alone on the stoop. He felt empty, hollowed out. His legs trembled under him, and he sat down on the top step.

"God," he said, "I don't understand any of this. I assumed You were providing the money to pay her taxes when the chickens over produced. Like a fool, I even assured Rosa that was Your plan. Please forgive me." He got up and stalked toward the barn, kicking at a stone in his path. "I messed up *mei* proposal too. She thinks I'm doing it out of obligation. God, You know that isn't the truth. Can You somehow talk to her for me?"

. . .

A raw November wind chapped Rosa's face as Blossom trotted along the road. But she didn't care; maybe the drive and the cold and the damp would help clear her head.

"Lord, please forgive me," she prayed out loud as she drove along. "I trusted and relied on Adam's faith instead of standing on *mei* own faith in You. He wasn't wrong to believe—but I was wrong to believe in his word rather than seeking Yours. I accept Your will for my life and I will move to Ohio. I only ask that You help me make amends with Adam before I leave."

The road in front of her blurred as tears welled in her eyes. "I never realized just how attached I had become to him." She wiped her face with the back of her hand. "I've—well, I might as well admit it—I've fallen in love with him. But, Lord, how could I marry him when I know I can't have children? I would only disappoint Adam."

Rosa took the long way home and returned to find a note stuck in her doorjamb. When she unfolded the paper, money fluttered to her feet. She bent down to pick it up. The note said that the money was to buy eggs for another upcoming bake sale the widows had planned.

She glanced next door. Eunice's buggy was parked in its usual spot. This was as good a time as any to take the eggs next door and return the money. Rosa packed more eggs than requested into a container and headed to Adam's house.

Eunice opened the door. "I see Adam gave you *mei* note." She waved her in. "Have a cup of tea with me. I'd like to talk with you about a few things."

Rosa hesitated.

"Adam's not here, if that's what's concerning you."

"All right. Maybe a half a cup." She followed Eunice into the kitchen. "I just thought of it *nau*, but I have extra flour and sugar I'd like to donate to the bake sale."

"That would be great." Eunice dunked a tea bag in one cup, then transferred the bag over to the next one. She set the cups on the table. "I would like to apologize," she said. "I was selfish when I talked so adamantly about wanting *kinskind*." She paused for a moment. "I thought you and Adam were growing close and, well, I know you've had miscarriages in the past."

"Four," Rosa clarified. It wasn't a secret, nor did it matter now.

Eunice sighed. "I thought if I discouraged you from becoming involved, *mei sohn* would—"

"You don't have to worry any longer." Rosa set her cup down and stood. "I'm moving to Ohio."

"Rosa, I was wrong to interfere."

"I have to finish packing." Rosa got up and rushed blindly to the door—and bumped directly into Adam.

He kept her from falling but said nothing.

"*Danki.*" She rushed across the yard and into the

house, gasping for air. Surely this would all be over soon. Surely the feelings she had for Adam would subside once she had moved.

Minutes later Adam stood on her stoop. Hands deep in his pockets, he shuffled his feet. "*Mei mamm* sent me. She said something about flour and sugar."

Rosa opened the door wider and stepped aside. "Come in." She took a few long strides to the kitchen with him trailing behind her and opened the pantry. Almost all the canning jars were gone, but some of the staples still lined the shelves. "Flour," she mumbled, grabbing the ten-pound bag.

"Rosa."

His husky voice caught her off guard and she turned.

"After Uriah pulled that burning rafter off me in the fire, he made me promise him that I would take care of you. But that isn't why I asked you to marry me." He reached for her hand. "I love you, Rosa."

"Adam . . ." Her voice shook. *I love you too*, she wanted to say, but the words wouldn't come.

"I thought you shared the same feelings for me." He rubbed his neck. "*Mei* scar reminds you that I'm the reason you lost Uriah. He should've survived, *nett* me."

At last she found her voice. "I don't blame you for Uriah's death. Please believe that." Rosa lowered her head. "I have fallen in love with you too."

"Then marry me."

Her heart screamed yes, but she shook her head no. "I've had four miscarriages. That's why Uriah took me into town for ice cream all those times, to try to cheer me up. But you need to know. I can't carry a *boppli*."

She swallowed hard. "I saw the pain it caused Uriah. I won't put you through that."

He inched closer. "If you want children, we can adopt."

"You say that, but—"

"I mean what I say." He cupped her face in his hands. "Last year you did all that research about foster families for Hope. Why can't we be a foster family?"

She opened her mouth to respond, but his kiss hushed her words.

"I love you," he said, his warm breath feathering against her cheek.

"I love you too."

Adam trailed kisses across her cheek to her ear. "Will you marry me?"

She pulled back. "Your mother wouldn't approve. She wants—"

"She wants what's best for me. And that's marrying you." He swept his hand over her cheek. "Rosa, say that you'll marry me."

"Yes." Tears clouded her vision. "Yes, I will marry you."

He twirled her around the kitchen, then kissed her again.

They were interrupted by a knock on the door. Rosa pulled away. "I better see who it is." She adjusted her dress as she walked to the door.

Adam followed.

Tate Wade stood on the other side of the screen door.

"Can I help you?" she said.

"I wanted to talk to you about your house," Tate said. "I'm the one who bought it."

Rosa motioned to the boxes stacked against the far wall. "As you can see, I'm packing. I'll be out in—"

"Wait." He held up his hand. "Please hear what I have to say. I'm willing to sell it back to you. For the same price as I paid."

Rosa glanced at Adam.

"Mr. Bontrager," Tate said, "I couldn't get it out of my mind, what you told me about Rosa being a widow and the eggs being her only support. Growing up, I watched my mother struggle after my father died. There were days we had very little to eat." His focus returned to Rosa. "I'm sorry for the pain I've caused you. I hope you can forgive me."

Rosa stared at him for a minute or two. "Apology accepted."

"Good. The guilt was eating me up." He exhaled a pent-up breath. "So, do you want to buy the place or not?"

"Yes! I want it." She glanced at Adam, then back to Tate. "I mean, we want it."

"Fine." He nodded. "I buy houses at auction all the time. I'm a real estate developer, so we can work out the paperwork later. I've reinforced the kennel so my dogs won't get out again. And I'll reimburse you for your chickens. I hope from now on we don't have any neighborly issues."

He turned to leave, then stopped and faced her. "One more thing. The property is currently zoned commercial. Apparently at one time it was a dairy business. If you petition to have it rezoned, you'll cut your taxes to a fraction of the cost. Buy some cattle and have it zoned under agriculture, and you'll save even more."

He nodded. "Well, I'll be off. I hope you both have a good day."

. . .

When Tate was gone, Rosa closed the door and turned to Adam. "Can you believe what just happened?"

"It's a miracle." Adam pulled her into his arms. A glint of light danced in his eyes. "Tate said guilt changed his mind, but what really happened is that God softened his heart."

She swiped at her eyes. "And God provided a way to keep the *haus*, even after *mei* faith failed."

"I thought I had it all figured out," Adam said. "But God didn't pay much attention to my plans."

Rosa laughed. "From *nau* on we will be patient and trust completely in His providence."

"Always," Adam said.

She closed her eyes as his lips brushed against her forehead. In that moment she knew that no matter how much she had lost, her life was full and complete. Everything she needed had been provided.

Joy instead of mourning. An end to grief. The beginning of a new life.

Light. Love. Home. A place to belong.

"Always," she repeated. "We will trust God's providence. Always."

A GIFT FOR ANNE MARIE

KATHLEEN FULLER

CHAPTER 1

Anne Marie Smucker pulled back the light-blue curtains and peered outside into the darkness. On her rural street, the only available light was the tall streetlamp a few houses down. She tapped her fingers against the window frame and squinted. *Where is he?* Her best friend Nathaniel was never late for game night.

She let the curtains fall and breathed in the scent of wintergreen and cinnamon. The spirit of the holiday was in the air. Her mother had started decorating for the season—placing pine boughs, cinnamon sticks tied with winter-white ribbon, and dried orange slices in a small arrangement on an end table near the front window in the living room. Like all her decorating, she kept it simple, yet lovely.

A few minutes later she went into the kitchen. Her mother stood by the stove, peeling off the foil from a pie plate. "What's that?" Anne Marie asked.

"A new pumpkin pie recipe I tried yesterday. I'm hoping it will be *gut* enough for this year's Christmas cookbook." Her mother looked at her. "Would you like to try some?"

Anne Marie frowned. "Pumpkin? *Nee.*"

"I thought you liked pumpkin."

"That must be your other *dochder.*"

"I only have one *dochder*, and she's handful enough."

Anne Marie chuckled as she moved closer to her mother and peeked at the pie. Flawless, as usual, with a golden, high-edged crust. It looked appetizing—to someone who liked pumpkin.

Mamm picked up a knife and sliced a small wedge. She put the piece on a nearby saucer. "Nathaniel's not here yet?"

"*Nee.*" She frowned.

She heard a light tapping sound on the window of the back door. She turned and saw her friend Ruth Troyer waving a mitten-covered hand.

Anne Marie opened the door and let Ruth inside. "This is a surprise."

Ruth smiled, the tip of her nose red from the cold air. "I hope you don't mind me dropping by for a minute." She looked at Anne Marie's mother. "*Frau* Smucker."

"*Hallo*, Ruth. Would you like a piece of pie?" *Mamm* asked.

"*Nee.* I just need to speak with Anne Marie for a minute." Ruth came closer to her and leaned in, her honey-colored eyes wide with curiosity. "Is Nathaniel here?"

Anne Marie shook her head. "He's a little late tonight."

Ruth let out a breath. "*Gut.*" She lowered her voice. "Is there somewhere we can talk?"

"We can *geh* into the living room."

Once they entered the room, Ruth walked to the coffee table where Anne Marie had laid out the Scrabble board and tiles. "I see you're ready for your game night." She looked at Anne Marie. "I wish you'd come to the singing with me and Hannah tonight. You used to like them."

"I did when I was younger. I don't really see a reason to *geh* anymore."

Ruth frowned. "Because you're busy with Nathaniel?"

It seemed like the temperature in the room dropped twenty degrees. Anne Marie blinked. "Is something wrong, Ruth?"

Her friend paused. "Not really. It's just . . ." Ruth clasped her hands together, her mittens making a soft clapping sound as they met. "I need your help."

"Of course."

"But I need to know something first."

Anne Marie nodded. "What's that?"

"Are you and Nathaniel together?"

That was the last thing she expected Ruth to say. "What? Of course not."

Ruth blew out a breath. "*Gut.* Then you can help me get Nathaniel's attention."

"Attention? Why?"

Ruth cocked her head and rolled her eyes. "I have to explain it to you?"

Anne Marie paused. Then her eyes widened. "You like Nathaniel?"

She rolled her eyes. "You're just as oblivious as he is."

"What?"

Ruth put her hands on the back of the chair near the coffee table. "I don't know what to do to get him to notice me. I've dropped so many hints on him the past

couple of weeks, I'm surprised he doesn't have a head-
ache. I even asked him to tonight's singing. But then
he reminded me about Sunday game night, which *of
course* he couldn't miss."

Was that a touch of bitterness in Ruth's tone? "I didn't
know you felt that way about him," Anne Marie said.

"Now you do. So, will you help me?"

Anne Marie turned up the damper on the woodstove
in the corner of the room. "I'm not sure what I can do."

"You can give us your blessing."

She whirled around, confused. "Ruth, I'm not Nathaniel's
keeper. He's free to court anyone he wants to."

Ruth dug her hands into her coat pockets. "You
know how shy he is, so if you'll just give him a nudge
in *mei* direction. A small one. Then I'll take care of the
rest." Before Anne Marie could respond, Ruth added,
"I have to *geh* or Hannah will have a fit." She touched
Anne Marie on the arm. "*Danki.*"

"You're wel—"

But Ruth had disappeared before the words left Anne
Marie's mouth.

She stood there in the living room, feeling the
warmth of the woodstove and looking at the Scrabble
board, trying to absorb what her friend had told her.
Ruth liked Nathaniel. She hadn't seen that coming. She
also hadn't thought her friend would be so forward
about it. And she wouldn't consider Nathaniel shy.
Reserved, sometimes. But not shy. As she walked back
to the kitchen, she tried to picture Ruth and Nathaniel
as a couple. But she couldn't see him with Ruth. She
thought about other young women in the district. Who

would she pair up with Nathaniel? For some reason, she couldn't imagine him with anyone.

"Ruth blew out of here in a hurry." *Mamm* wiped down the counter to the left of the white cast-iron sink. "Is everything all right?"

"*Ya.* I guess."

Mamm lifted a questioning brow. "What does that mean?"

"Sorry I'm late." Nathaniel appeared in the kitchen doorway. "Jonah let me in." He'd already removed his jacket and hat, his thick, dark-brown hair popping up in hanks all over his head. He tried smoothing it down, but it was no use. He'd always had trouble taming his hair. When they were sixteen he had come over to help her spread sawdust on the floor of the barn. Before they started, he'd tripped into the huge pile. She remembered how the small chips of wood and dust had stuck in his hair, how she'd run her fingers through the thick strands to help him get it out . . .

"Something smells *gut.*" He lifted his nose as he stepped into the kitchen.

Anne Marie shook her head, clearing her mind of the memory, and the tingly sensation suddenly coursing through her.

"What are you making, Lydia?" Nathaniel asked.

"Pumpkin pie." *Mamm* cast a sharp look at Anne Marie. "Keep your comments to yourself."

Anne Marie held up her palms. "I wasn't going to say a word."

"Are there samples?" Nathaniel asked.

"Of course." Her mother cut another slice. "I'm glad *someone* appreciates my cooking."

"Now that's not fair," Anne Marie said. "You know I like everything you make. Everything that doesn't contain pumpkin, that is. Plus, your cookbooks are in such high demand, we can barely keep up production. Clearly, many people in Paradise love your recipes." She moved away from the counter. "That reminds me, I can help you bind the rest of the cookbooks and fill the Christmas orders. It's just a couple weeks away."

"I think you have enough to do with your candle orders," *Mamm* said.

"I can handle both."

"Always thinking about work." *Mamm* shook her head. "We have time." She looked at Nathaniel, then at Anne Marie. "Now *geh* play your game."

When they entered the living room, he moved one of the chairs closer to the coffee table and sat down. He leaned over and started selecting tiles. But Anne Marie's mind wasn't on Scrabble. She was still thinking about Ruth's request. How should she tell him that Ruth liked him? Just blurt it out? Hint at it? She had no idea what Ruth meant by nudging Nathaniel in her direction. She'd never played matchmaker before.

He glanced up. "You going to sit down?"

She looked at him. Saw the competitive gleam in his eye. Ruth could wait—they had a game to play. She grinned and sat down.

He wiggled his dark brows. "Ready to lose?"

"Um, *nee*. When was the last time you beat me at Scrabble?"

"A month ago."

"I let you win."

He smiled and clasped his hands behind his head. "Keep telling yourself that."

Determined to prove him wrong, they began to play . . . and she forgot all about Ruth.

. . .

Nearly two hours later, the game was almost tied. Nathaniel didn't know how she did it. But with stealthy play and a lot of thought—sometimes so much thought he had to prod her to take her turn—she'd racked up the points. She twisted the end of one of her *kapp* strings as she surveyed the board. Her thin finger traced a line across the top of one of her tiles leaning against the holder, her blond eyebrows forming a *V* above her pale-blue eyes. He tapped his foot, glancing at the clock hanging on the wall. "Anytime now."

"Don't rush me. I'm thinking."

"Think a little faster. I have to get home."

"Ready for more pie?" Nathaniel looked up to see Lydia walk into the living room carrying a tray with one piece of pie and two glasses of tea. Anne Marie took the glass. She sipped, her attention still on the board. Nathaniel accepted the pie and tea. "*Danki.*" He took a huge bite, the taste of cinnamon and pumpkin exploding in his mouth. There was a good reason Lydia Smucker's holiday cookbooks sold out every year right before Christmas. He scooped a smaller portion with his fork and held it out to Anne Marie. "Sure you don't want a little taste?"

She smirked at his offering. "*Ya.* I'm sure."

"You don't know what you're missing." He waved it in front of her. "It's the best pumpkin pie I've ever had."

"That's kind of you to say, Nathaniel," Lydia said.

He moved his fork closer to Anne Marie. "I know why you won't try this."

She folded her arms. "Why?"

"Because you're afraid you might like it. Then you'll have to admit you were wrong."

"Fine." She grabbed the fork and stuck the tip of her tongue to the pie. She closed her mouth and smacked her lips. "I tasted it. I still don't like it."

"More for me, then." He finished off the bite, looking up at Lydia. He paused at her puzzled look, the fork still in his mouth. "What?"

Anne Marie's mother looked at him, then at her daughter. "*Nix.* Just . . . *nix.*" She turned and left the room.

"What was that about?" Nathaniel asked after he polished off the bite.

Anne Marie shrugged, still focused on the game board. With a swift movement she grabbed the rest of the tiles on her stand and placed them on the board. *T A S T Y.* She gave him a triumphant smile.

"More like ironic." He set down the empty dish. "Congratulations. You won."

Her smile widened, the tiny scar at the corner of her mouth disappearing. He remembered the day she'd gotten it. They were both seven, and he'd pushed her a little too hard in the swing at school. She face planted on the ground and the ragged edge of a stone had sliced her lip. Thirteen years later, he still felt bad about it.

After cleaning up the game, he and Anne Marie walked

to his buggy. "Same time next week?" He grabbed the horse's reins. "Although I'm picking the game this time."

"Life on the Farm?"

"Of course." He unwrapped the reins from the hitching post underneath the barn awning and took the blanket off his horse. He folded it and tossed it in the buggy.

"Before you *geh* . . ." She moved nearer, rubbing her arms through the thin long sleeves of her dress. "I have something to tell you."

"Okay." He faced her.

"Um . . ." She looked away.

Nathaniel frowned. "Is something wrong?" She had never been hesitant to talk to him before.

"*Nee*." She faced him again, drawing in a breath. "Ruth Troyer likes you." The words flew out of her mouth like a caged bird being set free.

He leaned against the buggy, his cheeks heating against his will. Ruth was one of the prettiest girls in their district, but he had never thought about her romantically.

"Well?" Anne Marie drew her arms closer to her chest.

"Well what?"

"What are you going to do about it?"

"I don't know. Give me a minute to think."

"You should probably ask her out." Her eyes narrowed in the faint yellow light from the lamppost down the street.

He didn't respond. He'd gone out with a couple of *maed* in the past two years. Yet he wouldn't have called the dates successful. More like awkward. And forgettable.

"Don't be so gun-shy." Anne Marie rubbed his horse's nose.

"Don't be so bossy."

She glanced at him. "Sorry." She faced him. "Nathaniel, if you don't ask her out, you'll never know if you're well suited. Maybe ask her to next week's singing."

"What about our game night?"

"We can miss it for one week. Especially for a *gut* reason."

Nathaniel climbed into the buggy. "I'll think about it." He looked at her. "Why are you so eager for me and Ruth to *geh* out?"

She took a step back and looked at the ground. "Because . . ."

"Because?"

She finally met his gaze. "I just think you two would be a *gut* couple. That's all." She turned and hurried toward her house.

"*Gut nacht*," he called after her.

She gave him a half wave and ran inside, like she couldn't get away from him fast enough.

Huh. He frowned, wondering why she was acting strange all of a sudden. Things were fine all evening until she brought up Ruth. Was something else going on? Maybe, but knowing Anne Marie he'd have to pry it out of her. Or wait until she was ready to tell him.

He tapped on the horse's flank with the reins and headed home, his mind on Anne Marie, not Ruth Troyer.

CHAPTER 2

After Nathaniel drove off, Anne Marie walked into the living room, rubbing her hands together to warm her cold fingers. She'd done her duty where Ruth was concerned. Yet something didn't feel right. Ruth was one of Anne Marie's closest friends. She was kind to everyone, one of the more intelligent people she knew, and of course, extremely pretty. Yet despite all of Ruth's wonderful qualities, one question kept nagging at her.

Was she good enough for Nathaniel?

She snatched up the half-empty tea glasses off the coffee table, feeling guilty for even thinking such a thing. Who was she to judge Ruth? Still, she had to wonder. Nathaniel deserved someone special. Someone who could appreciate his quiet nature, his almost obsessive attention to small details, his ability to make sure everyone around him felt comfortable, his—

"*Yer* boyfriend gone already?" Her younger brother Christopher walked into the room.

Anne Marie grimaced. Fifteen-year-old brothers were a thorn. The tea glasses clanked together in her hand. "That joke is getting old."

"Not as old as you." Christopher laughed and left the room.

Anne Marie sighed. Christopher never missed a chance to tease her about Nathaniel. At least her other brother, Jonah, left their friendship alone. She entered the empty kitchen. *"Mamm?"* No answer. Odd, since the pie remained uncovered on the counter and her mother never left food sitting out. Anne Marie placed the foil over the pie plate and crimped the edges. Then she started on the dishes. She had just finished washing the last tea glass when her mother scurried into the room.

"*Danki* for cleaning up, Anne Marie. I meant to do that. I went upstairs for a moment and got distracted." A small smile formed on her mother's face as she grabbed a rag and started wiping down the table.

Anne Marie put the glasses away. "You seem happy tonight. Any particular reason?"

"I'm excited about Christmas," *Mamm* said quickly. She looked at Anne Marie. "Aren't you?"

"I will be once all the candles are made."

Her mother patted her on the shoulder. "I'm so glad you've taken over that part of our business. I just couldn't do both anymore."

"I'm happy to do it. And remember, I can help with the cookbooks too."

Her mother shook out the rag over the sink. "I don't want you to spend all your time working. You need to *geh* out and socialize more."

"I plan to visit *Aenti* Miriam before she has her *boppli.*"

Her mother lifted her brow. "Anyone else?"

"If I have time."

"We make time for the people who are important to us."

"Which is why I'm going to visit *Aenti* Miriam." At her mother's sigh, Anne Marie held up her hands. "What?"

"Never mind. *Gut nacht*, Anne Marie."

Anne Marie shrugged and completed the finishing touches in the kitchen before heading to her room. She unpinned her *kapp*, giving one last thought to what her mother said. Lately *Mamm* had been making comments about Anne Marie spending more time with her friends. Anne Marie was satisfied with her life—she loved her candle business, and she saw her friends more than her mother realized. Just because she didn't go to singings or date didn't mean she didn't have a social life, or that she wasn't happy.

Yes, things were fine the way they were.

Anne Marie turned off the battery-powered lamp on her bedside table and snuggled under several thick quilts her aunt Miriam had made over the years. She thanked God for all the blessings in her life before closing her eyes and drifting to sleep.

After what seemed like only seconds later, the door to her room flew open. Her mother rushed to the bed. "Anne Marie! Seth is here."

She sat up, bleary eyed. "What?"

"It's Miriam. She's having the *boppli*."

"But it's early yet—"

"Get dressed. We must hurry."

Anne Marie scrambled out of bed, the sense of peace she'd felt before falling asleep replaced by alarm over her aunt going into early labor. She said a short, heartfelt prayer for her *aenti* Miriam's safety, and for the health of the unborn child.

• • •

Anne Marie bit at her nails as she paced the length of Miriam and Seth's small living room. Her mother had taken their son, Seth Junior, back to their house. Anne Marie thought it a wise decision. She flinched as Miriam's screams pierced the air.

She glanced at *Onkel* Seth standing by the window. He leaned against his cane. He and her aunt were only a few years older than she was. His handsome face and strong body bore the scars of a reckless youth. Now he was a responsible *mann* and father who deeply loved his family.

"Miriam will be all right," she said, crossing the room to stand next to him. She looked outside the window at the pink-and-lavender-tinged clouds streaking across the horizon, signaling the rising sun.

Another scream. Seth's knuckles turned white. "It wasn't this bad with Junior," he whispered. "I feel so helpless."

She grabbed his hand. "Then let's pray for God's help."

They both stood in front of the window, holding hands, each of them saying their own silent prayer for Miriam. When Miriam screamed again, Seth gripped Anne Marie's hand. She winced. As his wife's cries subsided, he loosened his grip.

"Sorry." He pulled out of her grasp.

"It's okay." She put her hand behind her and flexed her sore fingers.

At the sound of a newborn's cry, they both turned around. Seth's shoulders slumped. "Thank God."

A few moments later, Nathaniel's mother, Mary,

entered the living room, a huge smile on her face. A midwife for years, Mary had delivered Seth and Miriam's son. "A girl, Seth. You have a *maedel*."

"Can I . . . ?" He glanced at Anne Marie. "I mean, we, *geh* see her?"

Mary nodded, her smile widening. "*Ya*. She's beautiful, Seth. Both *mudder* and *boppli*."

Anne Marie followed Seth into the bedroom. Her aunt Miriam was propped up in bed with several pillows behind her, her hair still damp from the strain of childbirth. She smiled wearily.

Seth hobbled to the bed and sat next to her. He brushed back a lock of Miriam's hair and glanced down at the newborn. "She's amazing," he murmured. "And *schee*." He looked back at Miriam, gazing into her eyes. "Just like her *mudder*."

Anne Marie swallowed. For years her aunt had been insecure about her appearance, which was considered plain, even among a plain people. Yet Seth never hesitated to tell her how pretty she was.

Miriam and Seth looked at their new daughter. She was perfect, with fair skin and a dusting of dark hair on top of her head.

"We should let them be," Mary whispered to Anne Marie.

Anne Marie nodded and they both slipped quietly from the room.

In the living room, Mary sat down on the hickory rocker near the window, her plump hips wedged between the chair's curved arms. At the same time, Anne Marie's mother walked through the front door.

"*Gut* timing," Anne Marie said.

"Then she's had the *boppli*?"

"*Ya,*" Anne Marie said. "A beautiful girl."

Mamm knelt next to two-year-old Junior and removed his tiny jacket. "Let's meet *yer* new *schwester.*"

The little boy nodded, letting *Mamm* take his hand.

Golden sunlight streamed through the front window. Anne Marie pulled the shade halfway. "Looks like a pretty *daag.*"

"Which is needed after such a long night." Mary took a white handkerchief out of her apron pocket and dabbed her broad forehead. "But Miriam handled it well." She sighed, smiling at Anne Marie. "The women in *yer familye* have little trouble birthing *boppli*. Which is fortunate for you. Whenever you have *kinner*, that is."

Anne Marie glanced away. Mary never hesitated to speak plainly or, in some instances, boldly.

"Miriam and the *kinn* are doing fine," *Maam* said as she walked into the room. "And of course, Seth is relieved."

"He has a wonderful little *familye*." Mary rocked in the chair, scrutinizing Anne Marie. "I've spent years helping women have *boppli*. I wonder when I'll help *mei* future daughter-in-law have one of her own?" She turned to *Mamm*. "It's in the Lord's hands, I know. But *mei* Nathaniel isn't getting any younger. Neither is your Anne Marie."

"I'm standing right here," Anne Marie said, a bit irritated.

Both women looked at Anne Marie. Mary leaned forward. "Do you have something to tell us? Maybe about your Sunday evening 'game nights'?"

"What? *Nee.*"

Mary leaned back in the chair and sighed. "Oh. Well, *nee* harm in hoping, is there?"

Anne Marie looked to her mother. She remained silent but had a sly grin on her face. Why wasn't she saying anything? This wasn't the first time Mary had hinted about Anne Marie and Nathaniel dating, and her mother knew that they weren't. She wished she could tell Mary that Nathaniel had an admirer so his mother would leave her alone. But he wouldn't appreciate it. "I think we could all use some *kaffee,*" she said, scrambling out of the room before Mary could say anything else.

CHAPTER 3

Nathaniel sat at his bench and repositioned the gas lamp on his worktable, brightening the light and shining it on the watch mechanism he was repairing. As he adjusted the jewels in the pocket watch, he sensed someone looking over his shoulder.

"*Sehr gut*, Nathaniel." His father nodded, peering down at the watch. "That was not an easy repair."

Nathaniel snapped the back on the pocket watch and wound it. He brought it to his ear and listened to the steady ticking. It had been dead when the owner brought it into his father's clock shop earlier last week. "I need to polish it up a bit—"

"Not too much." His father straightened, the tip of his iron-gray beard touching the middle of his barrel chest. "We don't want it too fancy."

Nathaniel nodded. "*Ya.*"

Daed clapped him on the shoulder. "You'll make a fine repairman, *mei sohn*. Like your *grossvatter* and *mei grossvatter* before him." He walked back to his desk in the small repair shop.

Nathaniel smiled, looking around at all the clocks on the walls. His favorite was the century-old cuckoo clock from the Black Forest of Germany. The mechanism had been dismantled because, as his father said, it drove him cuckoo. But it was a fine piece of craftsmanship, like so many of the clocks and watches in the shop.

He pulled out a soft cloth and lightly buffed the outside of the pocket watch. He enjoyed working in the shop, repairing the watches, even trying his hand at carving some of the wood casings containing the clocks. He'd been born into this job, and his father had mentioned how thankful he was for it, Nathaniel being his only child. The business would pass on through the family for one more generation at least.

Just before five that evening, he and his father began closing up the workshop. While he was putting all the tools away in their specific compartments in his toolboxes, his father walked up beside him. He took off his glasses and wiped the lenses with his handkerchief. "You were at the Smuckers' the other day, *ya*?"

Nathaniel nodded. "Game night with Anne Marie."

"How did their wood supply look? I know Lydia's got those two *buwe* to help out, but it won't do for them to run out of fuel during the cold months." As a deacon of the church, his father's responsibility was to make sure the widows of the district were taken care of. Lydia and her family had always been self-sufficient, but his father never took his responsibility lightly.

"They have a *gut* pile laid in, enough to last a couple of weeks. I'll help Jonah and Christopher chop more on Friday after work."

"Take that afternoon off. Don't want you chopping

wood in the dark." He put his glasses back on. *"Danki, sohn."*

"Glad to do it." He checked the clock on the wall.

"Mamm probably has supper ready. You know how she gets if we're late."

"Last time I checked she was taking a nap. Spent all night delivering Miriam's *boppli.*"

Nathaniel smiled. "That's right. Anne Marie has a new little cousin, Leah. Lydia was finishing up a quilt a couple weeks ago when I was visiting. A gift for the *boppli.*"

"That reminds me. Wait here." His father went to the back room. Nathaniel straightened his chair, wondering why a baby quilt would remind his father of anything. A few moments later, he returned carrying a small, old-fashioned clock. He placed it on Nathaniel's workbench.

"What's this?"

"A *familye* heirloom. *Mei* great-grandfather made it. Gave it to his *frau* for a wedding gift, and *mei grossvatter* gave it to *mei grossmutter* when they got engaged. Then she passed it down to me."

Nathaniel picked it up. It was fairly ornate for an Amish piece. The elaborate silver overlay on the corners of the slate-blue box containing the clock had tarnished over the years. "How old is it?"

"A hundred years, at least. It came from Switzerland. Has been in our family a long time."

"Needs some restoring," Nathaniel said.

"I thought you could handle the job."

Nathaniel set the clock down. "Who's it for?"

"You."

"Me?"

"*Yer* mother said it was past time I gave it to you."

Nathaniel looked at the clock again. "It's not that I don't appreciate it, but I don't need a fancy clock like this."

"Eventually you'll give it to someone special. I'd better check on *yer mamm*. Maybe heat up some leftover soup for her so she doesn't have to worry about supper." He left the workshop, a small bell tinkling as the door shut behind him.

Nathaniel looked at the clock again. Picked it up. Ran his fingers over the slate body, the tarnished embellishments. It was a fine clock, and with a little elbow grease, he could make it as beautiful as it originally had been.

He set the clock down, his hand lingering on the smooth case. It would be a great gift for someone . . . someday. But not anytime soon.

. . .

That Friday, Anne Marie sat at the kitchen table and cut candle wicking. She measured each strand at nine and a half inches, cut it with sharp scissors, then tied a small metal washer at one end to weight it. These would be used for simple white taper candles, which she would dip this afternoon in her candle workshop behind the house. She had three dozen to make today if she was to stay on track with her Christmas orders.

After she weighted the last wick, she went to the kitchen sink for a glass of water. She looked out the window as she drank. Dried, crunchy, brown leaves, the remnants of fall, swirled around the gravel driveway. Although it was December, it still hadn't snowed yet. But each day snow threatened, bringing with it dense, overcast skies and brittle wind.

Anne Marie watched her mother stroll across the yard, the strings of her white *kapp* flying out behind her as she made her way to the mailbox. *Mamm* pulled out a few pieces of mail. She thumbed through them quickly, then stopped. Pulled one out. And smiled.

Anne Marie set her glass on the counter and watched as *Mamm* pocketed the letter in her dark-blue jacket and headed for the house. At the same time, Nathaniel's buggy pulled into the driveway. He paused next to her mother, who said a few words to him before he drove toward the barn.

The kitchen door creaked open and her mother walked into the room. "Nathaniel stopped by to help the *buwe* chop firewood."

The gesture didn't surprise her. He was always thoughtful. But Anne Marie was more curious about what her mother had in her pocket. "Anything interesting in the mail?" she asked, leaning against the counter.

Mamm dropped a stack of letters on the table. "Just the usual. A couple of bills. Those never seem to stop coming." But instead of frowning, her mother seemed happy. She looked past Anne Marie for a moment before she started to leave. She made a sudden stop at the doorway and turned around. "Anne Marie, could you do me a favor?" *Mamm* reached into her pocket.

Anne Marie leaned forward, dying to know what was in the letter. "Sure."

Her mother pulled out an index card and handed it to her. "This is a new recipe I planned to try today. Would you mind preparing it for me?"

Anne Marie took the card, trying to mask her disappointment. Chicken and corn soup. "I've never made this before."

"It's a simple recipe. I have all the ingredients in the pantry and the stewing hen is in the cooler on the back porch."

"All right, but—"

"*Danki*, Anne Marie." Before she could say anything else, her mother left.

Anne Marie frowned. What did her mother have to do that was so important she couldn't test a recipe? Anne Marie had always helped her mother cook, but she wasn't as skilled in the kitchen, which was why she took over the candlemaking part of the business.

Anne Marie picked up the pile of mail, shuffled through it, and cast it aside. Why had her mother lied to her? Well, not lied, exactly, but she wasn't being completely truthful either. Something was going on . . . something her mother didn't want her to know.

CHAPTER 4

After spending a couple of hours outside with Jonah and Christopher chopping, splitting, and stacking wood, Nathaniel was dripping with sweat, despite the cold temperature. "I think we have enough wood laid to last until next Christmas."

Jonah dropped his stack on top of a neat, towering pile. "We need more. Just to be sure."

"Aw, Jonah. Nathaniel's right," Christopher said. "We got enough."

"I think Jonah's the wise one, Christopher." Nathaniel leaned his axe against the woodpile. "Nothing wrong with laying in a little extra. How about I *geh* inside and get some drinks?"

"I'll *geh* with you." Christopher started toward the house.

Jonah reached out and grabbed his brother by the arm of his jacket. "*Nee*, you're not getting out of work that easy."

Nathaniel headed toward the house, chuckling at Christopher's grumbling. He neared the kitchen, recognizing the scent of chicken and onions stewing. Lydia must be trying a new recipe.

But when he walked in, he saw Anne Marie standing

over the stove. She was staring at the pot, absently stirring the contents.

"Anne Marie?" He walked toward her, then tapped her on the shoulder.

She jumped, turning toward him. The wooden spoon flipped out of her hand, hit her forearm, and landed on the floor.

"I'm sorry." Nathaniel grabbed the spoon and set it near the sink. "I didn't mean to startle you."

Anne Marie snatched a dish towel off the counter and wiped the hot food from her arm. "It's all right. I wasn't paying attention."

He watched as a welt formed on her arm. "Here," he said, taking the rag from her and running it under cold water. He pressed it against her arm.

"Really, Nathaniel, I'm okay."

"Just making sure." He pulled the rag away. The redness had calmed. Without thinking, he blew a breath lightly across the burn. He froze, still holding her hand. What made him do that?

Her eyes widened and she pulled away from him. "Uh, see? I'm fine."

She yanked open the drawer and retrieved a clean spoon. "My fault for not paying attention." She focused on stirring what was in the pot. "Did you need something?"

If she could ignore the weird moment between them, he could too. And it really wasn't that strange. He'd tried to cool off the burn, that's all. He forced a casual tone. "I came in to get some water for me and your *bruders*."

"You know where the glasses are." She glanced at him and smiled.

Now things were back to normal. Relieved, he opened the cabinet door. "I'm surprised to see you cooking," he said, turning on the tap. "Smells *gut*."

She shrugged. "I suppose. It's a new recipe, so it will probably taste awful."

"Let me try it." He took the spoon and scooped out a small bite of what looked like a thick soup. After he'd tasted it, he said, "Not bad. Needs a little salt."

She grabbed the saltshaker and shook it vigorously. He took it from her. "Not that much."

Anne Marie sighed. "*Mamm* should be making this, not me. But *nee*, she's too busy."

"Doing what?"

"I don't know." She went back to stirring the soup.

Nathaniel knew better than to pry, especially when Anne Marie was in one of her moods. He retrieved two more glasses and filled them with water. "Better get back to chopping."

She didn't respond. He resumed his work, but his thoughts were still on Anne Marie, wondering why she was irritated with her mother.

He had finished stacking another batch of logs when Jonah approached and said, "Nathaniel, can I talk to you for a minute?" Jonah took off his hat and wiped the sweat from his damp bangs. "I wanted you to know how much I appreciate your help with the wood."

"Anytime your *familye* needs something, just let me or *mei daed* know and we'll take care of it."

"I know." Jonah shoved his hat back on his head. "It's just . . ."

"What?"

Jonah looked into the distance. "I'm seventeen, ya know. Christopher is fifteen. We're not *kinner* anymore."

Nathaniel rubbed his cold hands together, seeing where this conversation was going. Jonah had always been serious-minded and mature for his age. "*Yer* doing a *gut* job taking care of *yer familye*, Jonah."

He looked at Nathaniel, his mouth twitching slightly. "You think so?"

"*Ya*. But it doesn't make you any less of a *mann* to accept help."

Jonah nodded. "When we need it."

"Right. And I trust you'll let me know if you do."

"I will. I just didn't want you to think we were helpless."

"I've never thought that." He picked up his axe. "But *mei mamm* says many hands make quick work, so let's get this done already."

Jonah nodded, the sharp wind lifting up the ends of his dark-blond hair. "*Danki*. For understanding."

Nathaniel tipped his head in Jonah's direction. He was glad to see him taking responsibility for his mother, sister, and younger brother. But it also proved that he wouldn't need Nathaniel's help as much.

Even as he continued splitting the wood, Nathaniel's thoughts drifted back to Anne Marie. He hadn't thought about it much before, but eventually she'd find a boyfriend and a husband. She was already encouraging him to date Ruth. What would happen when they didn't need each other anymore? It was something he couldn't—and didn't—want to imagine.

• • •

An hour later Anne Marie finished making the soup. Her mother was right—it hadn't been that hard to make. The most difficult part had been the most tedious—picking the meat off the chicken bones. She took a taste and thought it was decent, but nowhere near her mother's standard.

She let the soup simmer on the stove so it would still be warm when her mother came home, whenever that would be. She'd left a few minutes ago without an explanation—and without giving Anne Marie a chance to ask her about the pocketed letter.

She looked down at the red mark on her arm. A shiver ran through her as she remembered Nathaniel's gentle breath on the welt. He was being nice, of course. But that didn't keep goose bumps from forming on her skin at the memory.

Anne Marie entered her mother's bedroom looking for some salve to put on the burn. Her bed was neatly made with her grandmother's quilt and one of Aunt Miriam's beautiful lap quilts folded across the end. The faded fabric of the old quilt contrasted with the sharper colors of Miriam's quilt. But both were beautiful.

She went to her mother's side table and opened the drawer. *Mamm* kept everything from adhesive bandages to sewing needles to ink pens in the messy drawer, the only untidy place in their house.

Anne Marie searched through the deep drawer, lifting objects and looking for the small cylinder that held the homemade salve. She spied it in the far back of the drawer. As she moved the random contents aside to reach for the jar, she touched a stack of papers held together with a rubber band. She pulled it out. Letters.

Unable to help herself, she looked at the return address. Thomas Nissley, Walnut Creek, Ohio. Her brow scrunched. As far as she knew, her family didn't know anyone in Walnut Creek.

She should put the letters back. But curiosity won over indecision and she slipped one of the envelopes out of the pack and lifted the already opened seal. She began to read, ignoring her guilt.

. . .

"Anne Marie?" Nathaniel walked into the kitchen. He'd left Jonah and Christopher to stack the rest of the fire-wood before sundown. Before he went home he wanted to check on Anne Marie's arm. It was a small burn, but he couldn't leave without making sure she was okay.

He faced the empty kitchen and looked at the pot of soup on the stove. His stomach rumbled. He fetched a spoon from the drawer and took another taste. Now it was perfect. Even though she always denied it, Anne Marie was just as good of a cook as her mother. "Anne Marie, do you care if I have some more of this soup?" he called out.

She didn't answer. He headed into the living room. Not finding her there, he started walking through the house, calling her name. When he was midway down the hall, he spied a light peeking through the crack at the bottom of Lydia's bedroom door. He frowned. He had seen Anne Marie's mother leave earlier in the day, so why was the light on in her room?

Nathaniel pushed open the door a little farther and saw Anne Marie sitting on the bed, reading a letter. Next to her, more letters were littered on the pastel quilt covering Lydia's bed. The lines on Anne Marie's forehead deepened. "Anne Marie?"

Her head shot up, and he saw the fury in her eyes. She stood, holding out one of the letters in her hand. "How could she do this?" she said, thrusting the letter at Nathaniel.

"Do what?"

She whirled around, her cheeks as red as holly berries. She started to pace. "I can't believe this."

"Anne Marie—"

"It's one thing to keep a secret. I mean, I've kept my fair share of secrets." She glanced at him. "But to do this?" She held up the letter.

He walked over to her and thought about putting his hand on her shoulder, but quickly changed his mind. "Anne Marie, calm down. It can't be that bad."

"*Ach*, it's bad. *Sehr* bad." She opened the letter. "'My dearest Lydia,'" she read aloud. "'I never thought I would feel this way about a woman again. It gives my heart wings to know you feel the same way.'" She pursed her lips in a sour expression. "Gives his heart wings? What kind of romantic nonsense is that?"

Nathaniel didn't think it was too bad. But he did feel like an intruder.

Anne Marie plopped on the bed, her shoulders slumping. "She's been writing to him for months. Apparently she's in love with him." She looked up. "Oh, and he's coming for Christmas. When was she going to tell us?

When he landed on our doorstep? 'Oh, by the way, this is Thomas, my secret beau that I didn't bother telling anyone about. Merry Christmas!'"

Nathaniel bit his lip to keep from chuckling. Anne Marie in a snit was entertaining. But he didn't want her anger directed at him. He cleared his throat and sat down next to her. "I'm sure your mother had her reasons for not telling you."

"They better be *gut* ones."

"What's going on here?"

Nathaniel froze at the sound of Lydia's sharp voice. He glanced at her standing in the doorway, her nostrils flaring much in the same way Anne Marie's had moments ago.

Lydia crossed her arms over her chest. "What are you two doing in my bedroom?"

CHAPTER 5

Anne Marie jumped from the bed and faced her mother. "Don't be upset with him. He was only checking on me."

Her mother uncrossed her arms, lowering them to her sides. "Nathaniel, I think you should leave."

Nathaniel rose. He glanced at Anne Marie, concern in his eyes. She looked away. He slipped out the door, not saying anything to either of them.

Lydia shut the door behind him. She looked at the letters on the bed. "I see you've been snooping."

"I wasn't snoop—"

"Don't lie." Lydia scooped up the letters.

"I was looking for salve for my burn—the one I got making your recipe, by the way." She lifted her chin. She sounded childish, but she didn't care.

Lydia folded the letters carefully and began putting them in the envelopes. "How did the soup turn out?"

"Soup? Don't you think we have something more important to talk about?"

Her mom turned to Anne Marie, her eyes starting to blaze. "I'm trying not to lose my temper. I'm very disappointed in you."

"Disappointed in me? You're the one keeping secrets."

She averted her eyes. "I was going to tell you and the *buwe* about Thomas."

"Before or after the wedding?"

Lydia froze, keeping her gaze from Anne Marie.

Dread pooled inside Anne Marie. "*Nee* . . . you're not . . ."

Her mother sat down on the bed. She moved the letters to the side and patted the empty space beside her. "Anne Marie, sit down."

"I'm fine standing."

Lydia sighed. "All right. As I said, I was waiting until the time was right. You've been busy with your candle-making, and I've been trying to get things ready for the cookbook."

It sounded like a list of excuses to Anne Marie. "Who is Thomas?"

"He's a *mann* I knew from my childhood. He used to live in Paradise. When he was twelve, he moved to Walnut Creek. Like me, he married and had children, although now they are grown and have their own families. He's lived alone for several years."

Anne Marie refused to feel sorry for him. But she couldn't help but soften her stance a little. "How did you start talking to him again?"

"He came to Paradise six months ago, to visit his *bruder's familye*. I was delivering some soaps and candles, and when I saw him . . ." Her eyes grew wistful. "He recognized me right away."

"How *romantic*." Anne Marie nibbled on her finger, unable to keep the bitterness out of her tone. "Love at first sight."

"*Nee*, it wasn't like that. You have to understand, Anne

Marie. I loved your *daed* very much. I never thought I'd fall in love with someone else. But something changed these past few months. Thomas started writing me first. Friendly letters, reminiscing about childhood. Then the letters became more personal."

"So I read."

Her mother scowled. "You're not making this easy, *dochder.*"

"You should have said something to me. To all of us."

Mamm raised her voice. "I'm not allowed to have anything of *mei* own? Any privacy?"

Anne Marie opened her mouth, then shut it. She looked at the letters. Her mother was right. But that didn't change anything.

"Thomas is visiting his *bruder* for Christmas. He'll be coming here to meet you and Jonah and Christopher." Her mother stood, squaring her shoulders as she faced Anne Marie. "You will treat him better than you've treated me today."

Anne Marie pressed her lips to keep from saying something she'd regret.

"Since you want to know everything," *Mamm* continued, "I went to see Miriam today. I needed her advice about Thomas."

"And?"

The hardness in *Mamm's* eyes softened. "He asked me to marry him." She smiled. "And when he comes here for Christmas, I'm going to tell him *ya.*"

Although the words made Anne Marie take a step back, she couldn't deny the look of love in her mother's eyes. She looked away, guilt gnawing at her. She'd been unfair to her mother. And immature.

"Say something, Anne Marie. Please."

Anne Marie finally looked up, the glistening tears in her mother's eyes melting away the betrayal. "I want you to be happy, *Mamm*." She took a deep breath, forcing out the words. "If Thomas makes you happy, then that's what counts."

Her mother hugged her. "*Danki*, Anne Marie." She stepped back, wiping her eyes. "I understand why you were upset. It's a lot to take in, especially when we start packing for the move—"

"What move?"

Her mother paused. "The move to Ohio."

Anne Marie's chest felt like a load of baled hay landed on it. "Moving? We're *moving*?"

"Thomas's home is in Walnut Cre—"

"Our home is *here*."

"And his business is there. I can produce my cookbooks anywhere. Although I probably won't anymore. I want to focus on making a *gut* home for our *familye*."

"We have a *gut* home." She spread her arms, gesturing to the space around them. "We always have."

"And we will have one in Walnut Creek."

"What about Miriam? *Grossmutter* and *Grossvatter* have already moved away. You'll leave her here alone?"

"I talked to her about that too. She'll miss us, but she understands. And Seth's family is here. She'll hardly be alone." *Mamm* took Anne Marie's hand. "I know it will be a big adjustment for everyone."

She pulled her hand from her mother's. "I won't leave. I can live with Miriam and Seth."

"You can't. You know how small their *haus* is."

"I'll sleep on the couch."

Mamm rubbed her fingers across her forehead. "Miriam and Seth would take you in if you asked, but you know it would be a hardship. And unnecessary, since you would have a home with me and Thomas."

Anne Marie blinked away the tears. Her mother and Thomas. It sounded strange. Unnatural. But her mother spoke of her future husband as if he'd always been a part of her life. She spoke of Thomas with love.

Her heart constricted. What about her life? Her friends, her candlemaking business? She had to start everything over because her mother fell in love?

"Now that you know," *Mamm* said, sounding more cheerful than she had in a long time, "we can start packing. The wedding will be in early January. We'll move right after that."

Anne Marie fisted her hands together. She couldn't do this. She couldn't leave everything she knew. Everyone she loved.

"*Mamm?*" Jonah's voice sounded from the opposite end of the house. "Anne Marie?"

Her mother sighed. "I guess it's time to tell the *buwe*." She looked at Anne Marie, hope in her eyes. "It would help if you could be supportive and an example for your *bruders*. You're not the only one having to sacrifice."

Anger bubbled up inside her. Unable to speak, she rushed past her mother, past Jonah and Christopher in the living room.

"Hey!" Jonah said, spinning around. "Where are you going?"

"Out." She opened the front door and ran into the cold evening, the screen door slamming behind her.

. . .

Nathaniel guided his buggy down the road, tucking his chin into his coat to ward off the chill. Good thing his horse knew the way home, as he wasn't as focused on driving as he should be. Anne Marie consumed his thoughts.

She was overreacting, but he sympathized with her. He couldn't put himself in her place, since his parents had been married for years. Just thinking about one of them being with someone else was impossible. But Lydia deserved to be happy. So did Anne Marie.

A car behind him honked its horn, pulling his attention back to the road. As the vehicle zoomed past, Nathaniel looked in his side mirror. He squinted in the pale light of dusk. Someone was walking behind him. As he slowed his buggy, he could see it was Anne Marie.

He pulled the buggy to a stop, holding the reins as he came to a halt on the shoulder of the road. Although her street wasn't busy, it was best to be cautious. As she neared, he could see her rubbing her hands over her arms.

"Anne Marie," he said, moving toward her but keeping a grip on the horse. If he let go, his horse would head straight home. Anne Marie stopped a few feet away. "What are you doing out here?" he asked. When she didn't say anything, he tilted his head toward the buggy. "Get in."

She shook her head but walked toward the buggy.

"Wait." He slipped off his jacket and handed it to her. "You're freezing. Put this on."

"Then you'll freeze."

"I'll be all right."

She looked at the coat for a moment, then took it. The edge of the sleeves reached past her fingertips. Then she climbed into the buggy. When they were on their way, he said, "Want to talk about it?"

"*Nee.*" Her voice sounded thick.

His heart lurched. Anne Marie was several things: a bit excitable, a little melodramatic, and occasionally annoying. She was also tough. During their long friendship, he'd only seen her cry once, and that was when they were talking after her father's funeral. Whatever happened between her and Lydia after he left was serious.

Without thinking twice, he reached for her hand. She gripped it. Her fingers were cold, but they soon warmed in his palm. Neither of them spoke as he drove to his house. When he pulled into his driveway, he stopped in front of the clock shop. "Are you ready to talk now? We can *geh* into the workshop. *Nee* one will bother us there."

She nodded. Looked at him with tears in her eyes.

And his heart melted.

CHAPTER 6

"Here. This will warm you a little more."
Anne Marie took the mug of coffee from Nathaniel. "I never knew you had a coffeepot in here."

"It's in the back. We use a camping stove to percolate it. *Daed* can't *geh* more than a couple of hours without his *kaffee*."

She took a sip of the hot, strong brew as she sat on Nathaniel's workbench. He pulled a chair over and sat across from her, holding his own mug. "Now are you ready to tell me what's going on?"

Anne Marie paused. She didn't want to say the words out loud. But Nathaniel would find out soon enough, as would the rest of the district. She wanted him to hear it from her. "We're moving."

He frowned. "Who's moving?"

"My *mamm, mei bruders* . . . me." She explained everything to Nathaniel.

He became very still, as he usually did when he was deep in thought. But his expression remained unreadable. Finally he leaned forward. "I know you're upset, Anne Marie, but this isn't the end of the world."

The warmth she'd felt from the coffee and his coat

dissipated. "That's easy for you to say." Her eyes narrowed. "Your world hasn't been turned upside down."

"Look, I don't like the idea of you moving either." He stared at his coffee. "I really don't like it," he mumbled.

"What?"

He looked at her again, a muscle twitching in his left cheek. "At least you're not moving too far."

"Nathaniel, it's Ohio. That's a day's ride on a bus."

"*Ya.* Just a day's ride. It could be worse. You could be going to Florida."

"It doesn't make any difference." She set the mug on his spotless workbench, next to an old clock. "What if I lose touch with everyone here?"

"That won't happen. There are letters—"

"You know I don't like writing letters. I don't even mail out cards."

"Then you'll have to come back to visit. And I'll come visit you."

She looked at him, trying to judge if he was serious. He glanced down at his mug so she couldn't read his expression. Then he looked up, smiling. "And until you move, I promise we'll spend as much time together as we can."

She shot up from the bench. "But what if it isn't enough?" she said, shoving her hands into the pockets of his coat. She wasn't cold anymore, but for some reason she didn't want to take it off. "I feel like I'm losing everything. My home. My friends . . ." She looked at him. "You."

He stood and faced her, his deep brown eyes meeting hers. "That won't happen. I promise."

The words were easy to say with only a few inches between them. With a few months and several hundred miles separating them, there was no guarantee they would stay close. "I want to believe you."

"Then do."

She kept her gaze locked on his, and for the first time since her world had been flipped over, her pulse slowed. His steady presence had that effect on her. She forced a small smile. "I should *geh*. I don't want to worry *Mamm*."

"I thought you were mad at her."

"I am."

He half-smiled. "You know how contradictory you sound?"

She shrugged. "That's me, one big contradiction."

"*Nee*, you're not." He moved toward her. "I'll take you home. You'll feel better tomorrow."

She shook her head. "I'll walk. I need to clear *mei* head before I get home."

He pulled open a drawer underneath his worktable and gave her a flashlight. "Then at least take this. And keep *mei* coat. I'll get it from you later."

She nodded and took the flashlight. She spied the clock again. "This is unusual," she said, examining the tarnished silver. She loved old things. Every scratch, dent, and imperfection carried a memory. "It's very *schee*."

"You think?" He picked it up. "Looks neglected to me."

"Not neglected. Full of history." She glanced at him. "Are you restoring it?"

He nodded and placed the clock back on the bench.

"Then it will be even more beautiful when you're finished." Able to genuinely smile now, she ran her hand down his arm and linked her pinkie with his. "Thanks again, Nathaniel. You're always here when I need you."

"It's what friends are for, *ya*?"

"*Ya*." Her smile dimmed as she released his finger. A thick lump formed in her throat. She couldn't believe that in less than a month they would be saying good-bye. Before the tears started and she embarrassed herself, she turned to leave.

"Anne Marie?"

The softness in his voice stopped her. When she saw his outstretched arms, she didn't hesitate to walk into them. How did he know she needed this? *Because he knows me better than anyone.*

"We'll figure this out." He rubbed his hand over her back. "Promise."

She closed her eyes and leaned against him, hearing the beat of his heart through his home-knitted sweater, waiting for the steady rhythm to comfort her. But despite his promises and the comfort of his strong embrace, she couldn't be hopeful. After tonight, nothing would ever be the same—including their friendship.

• • •

Almost an hour later, chilled to the inside of her bones, Anne Marie walked into her house. Through the darkness, a pale yellow gaslight shone from the kitchen.

She paused, weary but steeling herself for the scolding. But when she entered the kitchen, *Mamm* jumped up and ran to her. "I was just about to send Jonah and Christopher to find you." Her mom hugged her. "Please, Anne Marie. Don't do that again."

Anne Marie plopped down in the chair and nodded,

snuggling into Nathaniel's coat, relieved that her mother wasn't angry, even though she deserved to be. Anne Marie inhaled, breathing in his scent that infused the wool and remembering the hug they'd shared.

"Do you want *kaffee*?" *Mamm* asked. "Maybe some chamomile tea?"

"You're not mad at me?"

Mamm joined her at the table, shaking her head. "I understand why you left."

"I shouldn't have been gone so long."

"You were at Nathaniel's, *ya*?"

She nodded.

"That's why I wasn't that worried." Her mother laid her hands in her lap and looked down at the table. "I told Jonah and Christopher about Thomas."

Anne Marie fingered an empty peppermint candy wrapper in Nathaniel's coat, not saying anything.

"Christopher seems okay with it, but you know him. He's always been easygoing. Jonah, on the other hand . . ." She looked up at Anne Marie and sighed.

Anne Marie didn't know what to say. Had she expected all of them to be happy to leave the only home they ever knew? "Where's Jonah?"

"In the barn. He needs some time, just like you." Her mother looked tired. "I know you all are upset. But I really want you to give Thomas a chance. You don't understand what it's been like . . . I've been lonely since your *daed* died. Thomas has brought a light to *mei* life that I thought was snuffed out long ago. He's an answer to prayer. Not the way I expected because I never thought I'd leave Paradise. But God doesn't work according to our plans."

What about my plans? Why do I have to give up every-thing? Guilt stabbed at her again for being so selfish. Yet she couldn't help it. She stood. "I'm going to bed."

Her mother gave her one last look, then nodded.

Anne Marie went upstairs to her room and lay down on the bed, not bothering to take off her *kapp* or Nathaniel's coat. She fingered the wool lapels, drawing them closer to her face. Her mother was right about so many things. Anne Marie could have her candle business in Walnut Creek. She could come back and visit her aunt Miriam and her other friends. Her life wouldn't end if she left Paradise. She knew that to be true.

So then why did it feel that way?

. . .

Nathaniel tried to concentrate on repairing the simple alarm clock in front of him, but he couldn't focus. He kept remembering the way Anne Marie felt in his arms—fragile, vulnerable, yet comforting. He gripped a small screwdriver. He had tried to cheer her up by talking about letters and visits. But he'd lied. The idea of her leaving, of her not being a part of his life . . . how was he supposed to accept that?

The alarm clock went off in his hands, the shrill noise making him jump. He searched for the switch to turn it off. When that didn't work, he pried the batteries out—something he should have done beforehand.

"Nathaniel? Are you all right?"

He glanced over his shoulder at his father and forced a nod.

"You seem distracted."

"I'm fine."

"Does it have something to do with Anne Marie being here last night?"

Nathaniel turned to face his dad. "How did you know she was here?"

"*Yer mamm* told me. Somehow she manages to know everything." His father stood, slowly straightening his back. He slid a thumb underneath one of his suspender straps. "Why didn't you invite her inside?"

Nathaniel turned his attention back to the alarm clock. "We needed to talk."

"How about you? Do you need to talk?"

Nathaniel stared at the alarm clock. What good would it do to talk about it? Anne Marie was leaving. Nothing he could say would change that. And nothing could fill the emptiness that started to grow inside him the moment Anne Marie told him she was moving.

"Let me know if you do." The tread of his father's work boots thumped on the floor as he left the workshop.

Nathaniel went back to fixing the clock. After the third time the screwdriver slipped off the screw, he gave up and shoved the alarm clock away.

CHAPTER 7

I'm sorry," *Aenti* Miriam said over her daughter's squalling. "The *boppli* is always hungry. Junior's appetite was never so big." She lifted the corner of her mouth. "Nor was his cry."

"She has a strong pair of lungs." Anne Marie faced Junior in his high chair and tried to get him to eat a piece of cubed ham.

Miriam sat in a chair in her kitchen and settled into feeding the baby. When Junior finally started eating and the baby stopped crying, Anne Marie glanced at her aunt.

"You didn't come over here to feed *mei sohn*," Miriam said.

"I need to spend as much time with him as possible. And with you." She looked at her tiny cousin. "I don't even know her," she whispered.

"Anne Marie." Miriam touched her hand. "It will be all right."

"That's what everyone tells me." She sighed. "Did you know about Thomas?"

"*Nee*. Lydia has always been a private person. We didn't know she was dating your *daed* until they had announced their engagement."

Anne Marie nudged the sippy cup toward Junior. Keeping an engagement secret wasn't all that unusual in their community. The reminder made her mother's secretive behavior make more sense. But it didn't make the situation any easier to accept. Junior picked up the sippy cup full of milk and started to drink. "*Mamm* says you're fine with us moving," Anne Marie said.

Her aunt frowned. "I wouldn't say *fine*. I understand, though." She looked at Anne Marie, her expression sympathetic. "I'll miss all of you. But we can write to each other—"

"And visit. I know." She turned to her cousin and touched the brown hair that flipped up from Junior's bangs. He shoved a cheese-flavored cracker in his mouth. "It won't be the same."

"True, it won't. But I haven't seen your *mamm* this happy in a long time."

Neither had Anne Marie. Since telling them about Thomas, her mother was more productive and chattier than ever, even humming while she was putting the bindings on her cookbooks.

Anne Marie couldn't say the same thing for herself. She had stacks of Christmas candle orders to fill, a few for specialty carved candles that took extra time to make. Yet instead of working on them, she was here with her aunt. She had to cherish every minute she had left in Paradise.

She had thought she would have seen Nathaniel over the past couple of days, but he hadn't been able to come to their usual Sunday game night and he hadn't stopped by. She still had his coat, although she knew he had another one. Still, she should have dropped it off at his house but she'd taken to snuggling with it at night. Part of her felt foolish for doing something so sentimental. Yet she couldn't bear not to have something of his with her as she tried to sort out her feelings.

She would miss Aunt Miriam and her family. She would miss Ruth and her other friends. But the ache in her heart that appeared every time she thought of leaving Nathaniel . . . that was new, and more painful than anything else.

"Anne Marie?"

She turned to look at her aunt again. "Sorry."

"Are you okay?"

"Just distracted, thinking about everything."

"There's a lot to think about." She removed the blanket covering the baby. Little Leah was sound asleep, her pink, heart-shaped mouth still puckered in a tiny *O* shape. "Your grandparents are happy living in Indiana. They say it's a new chapter in their lives."

"I don't want a new chapter." She sighed. One look from Aunt Miriam confirmed what Anne Marie already felt—she was being immature. "I do want *Mamm* to be happy. I just don't want to leave Paradise."

"I understand."

Everyone kept saying that, but Anne Marie had her doubts. She started to bite her fingernail, caught herself, and put her hands in her lap. "If you had moved away, you wouldn't have married Seth."

She adjusted the baby in her arms. "*Ya.* But I would have trusted that God had someone else for me."

"So it's that simple?"

Miriam paused. "*Nee*," she said softly. "I would be lying if I said it was." Her aunt's eyes grew wistful. "I wasn't sure I'd ever get married. I never thought I would be with someone as wonderful as Seth."

"But why? You and *Onkel* Seth are perfect for each other."

"I know that now, but at the time I didn't think so." She glanced down at her infant daughter. "I didn't think I deserved him, or anyone else." She looked back at Anne Marie. "But that was *mei* own insecurity, *mei* own lack of trust and belief. So, *nee*, I wouldn't have trusted God. Not that easily, not at that time."

Anne Marie wiped the crumbs off Junior's face, feeling touched by Miriam's admission. At least her aunt was being honest.

"Are you upset about leaving Nathaniel?" Aunt Miriam asked.

"Nathaniel?" Anne Marie lifted Junior out of the high chair. For some strange reason heat crept up her neck. "Why would you bring him up?"

"We were talking about Seth and I just assumed . . ." She shook her head. "Never mind." Aunt Miriam smiled. "I know you can't see it now, but this might be part of God's plan. I'm sure He has *gut* things in store for you in Ohio. Maybe you'll meet your future husband there."

Anne Marie frowned. "I'm not looking for a husband."

Miriam leaned closer, her gaze intense. "Maybe because Nathaniel's in the way?"

Anne Marie settled Junior in her lap, not looking at her aunt. "What do you mean?"

"It's one thing that you were friends with Nathaniel when you were children. But you're adults now. And if there's nothing romantic between you, then it's time to let each other *geh*."

She smoothed a wrinkle out of Junior's shirt. "It's not like I have a choice anymore."

"That could be God's point."

Anne Marie's head snapped up. "He wants to break up a lifelong friendship? How is that *gut* for me?"

"To make you move from childhood to adulthood. You need to put childish things behind you. Nathaniel, nice *mann* that he is, is part of that. It's time to grow up, Anne Marie."

Anne Marie rested her chin on Junior's head. Was her aunt right? No one could argue she'd been acting like a child about the move, and she was ashamed of that. She was twenty years old. An adult. Yet she couldn't see how sacrificing her friendship with Nathaniel was in God's plan. How could she give up the most important person in her life?

That evening, Anne Marie helped *Mamm* with supper. Neither one spoke as they prepared the pork chops, creamy noodles, and sweet potatoes. When the pork chops were almost done, her mother finally said, "Did you have a nice visit with Miriam?" She began to slice a half loaf of bread.

Anne Marie tensed, her mind still filled with her aunt's advice. "*Ya.*"

"Leah is doing well?"

"Everyone is fine." She continued scrubbing the bowl she'd mashed the sweet potatoes in.

"Anne Marie." Her mother put her hand on her daughter's shoulder. "You're going to clean the finish right off that bowl."

"What? Oh, sorry." She rinsed it and put it in the drainer to dry.

Mamm stepped to the side, picked up the bowl, and ran a dry towel over the outside. "Christmas is in less than a week. Could you at least pretend to enjoy the holiday? I can't have both you and Jonah moping around."

A heavy weight pressed against her chest. Miriam and *Mamm* were right. She had to accept the wedding, the move, everything. She handed her mother a large metal spoon. "Don't worry. I won't put a damper on Christmas." She managed a smile. "You know it's my favorite holiday."

Her mother set down the dish and hugged her. She stepped back and wiped the tears from her eyes.

"Why are you crying?"

"I'm happy, Anne Marie. It tore *mei* heart out that you were so upset."

Anne Marie was surprised. Her mother hadn't seemed upset the past couple of days. Then again, lately she'd hidden her feelings well. A lot better than Anne Marie had.

"I'm so glad to have your support. And I know Jonah will come around." *Mamm* smiled through her tears. "You'll come to love Thomas. He's a wonderful *mann.*"

Anne Marie hugged her *mamm.* "If you love him, he must be."

• • •

Later that night, Anne Marie entered her room to prepare for bed. She removed her *kapp,* unclipped her hair, and let her braid fall over her shoulder. She turned and saw Nathaniel's coat lying on her bed. She'd slept with it for the past couple of nights, drawing warmth and comfort from it. She picked up the garment and ran her fingers over the stitching. She noticed the small dark stain on the edge of one cuff, and realized the elbows were starting to wear a little thin. She squeezed the fabric one more time before taking a breath, then hung the coat up in her closet and shut the door. Tomorrow she would make sure Nathaniel got it back.

It was time to move on.

CHAPTER 8

The next morning, Anne Marie had just finished cleaning up the breakfast dishes when she heard a knock on the back kitchen door. She opened it to see Nathaniel standing there. "Can I come in?" he asked.

Her body tensed. What was wrong with her? She'd prayed last night for God to help her let go of the past, her close friendship with Nathaniel at the top of the list. She asked Him to help her see the move as a fresh start. An adventure, like *Aenti* Miriam said. She thought she'd succeeded. But seeing him after they'd been apart for a couple of days brought unexpected feelings—both old and new—flooding over her.

There was no denying he was attractive. He always had been, even as a little boy. And he'd grown into a cute—no, make that handsome—*mann*. Yet Nathaniel's looks were the last thing she noticed about him—until now. Her heart fluttered as she looked at his lips. She glanced away, her face heating.

"I, uh, came to get *mei* coat," he said. He shifted from one foot to the other, not looking at her.

He was acting as awkward as she felt. So this was how it was going to be between them? She already missed their closeness, and she hadn't even moved away yet. "I'm sorry. I shouldn't have kept it so long."

"It's okay. I have this one." He tugged on his jacket, which was a thinner version of the one she was borrowing. "You know the real cold weather doesn't set in around here until January anyway."

She wouldn't be here in January. The frown on his face showed that he was thinking the same thing.

"Anne Marie, I'm sorry—"

"I'll get your coat." She fled the kitchen and ran to her room, opening the closet door where she'd left the coat last night. She didn't linger over it. She grabbed it off the hanger and dashed back to the kitchen.

"Here," she said, thrusting the garment at him.

"Danki." He took it from her but didn't move. A moment later he sat down at the kitchen table. She threaded her fingers together and rocked back and forth on her heels.

"Can we talk for a minute?" he asked.

She sat down across from him. "What about?"

He leaned forward. "I didn't come here just to get *mei* coat. I wanted to see how you were doing."

"I'm fine." She straightened and forced a smile. "I'm seeing this move as an adventure." She gritted out the last word.

"Oh. *Gut.*" He rubbed the palm of his hand back and forth on the table. "I'm glad you're okay with it."

"Ya."

"And like I said, our friendship isn't going to change."

But it already had, and they both knew it.

"I'll write to you, even if you don't write back," he added. "And I promise I'll visit."

Until he forgot about her. She nearly choked on the bitter thought.

"I'm also serious about spending more time together. I took the *daag* off from work."

Her eyes widened. "Your *daed* let you do that?"

"When I told him I was coming to see you, he didn't have a problem with it."

Anne Marie's heart tripped a beat. She'd never known him to put anything ahead of work. That he would set it aside to spend time with her . . .

But she had vowed to let him go. She grabbed a dishrag from the sink and started rubbing down the already clean counter. "I'm really behind on work. I have a lot of candles to make."

"I can help you."

She glanced over her shoulder at him. "It's pretty boring work."

"You don't seem to think so. You love it."

True. She paused. What would it hurt for them to make a few candles together? It wasn't like she could refuse the help. "All right. As long as you don't mind."

"I never mind being with you, Anne Marie."

She turned and put her hand over her quickening heart. Letting him slip out of her life wasn't going to be easy.

. . .

"Nathaniel, you're a terrible candlemaker."

Anne Marie thought she'd given him the simplest job, dipping red tapers, but he dipped them either too fast or too slow. The last ten he made were lopsided and had drips down the sides. She glanced at him, his brow furrowed in concentration. At least his terrible candle-making had made her finally relax around him. "For all the delicate work you do on watches and clocks, I'm surprised."

"Watches and clocks are easier to deal with, trust me." He smirked as he looked at her, holding a hoop of candles over the wax-dipping can. "You should give me a break. This is *mei* first time, remember?"

Anne Marie took the warped candles from him and set them on the counter. Two years ago when she'd taken over the candlemaking business from her mother, she converted a small garden shed into her own workshop. A gas-powered heater kept the workshop warm, along with several metal tubs of colored, melted wax warming over three camping stoves. She'd recycle the wax later and make proper candles, but right now she needed to give Nathaniel a different job.

She looked up at the two fancy carved candles on a shelf by the door. She used them as samples of her more intricate work, which she made for *Englisch* customers. She'd just made a red-and-white-layered cylinder candle. It was warm and pliable and ready to be carved. With his skilled hands, maybe he'd do better with a more complex job.

She picked up the sample candle and set it on the small round table in the middle of the workshop. Then she pulled out the chair. "Have a seat."

"For what?"

"To carve this." She put the freshly dipped candle

next to the sample and handed him three carving tools. "Make this plain one look like the fancy one."

"You're kidding." He eyed the sample. "I can't do this. I messed up your simple candles."

"Nathaniel, I know how well you draw. I've also seen the nice work you do on those wooden clock cases. I think you can handle carving the candle. It doesn't have to look exactly like that one. Just make it pretty."

"Pretty." He sat down, still looking dubious.

"All right, then. Make it nice."

"Nice I can do." He studied the sample, picked up a round-tipped tool, and started to carve.

"You have to work quickly," she said, watching him cut and pull down thin strips of the candle, revealing the stacked red and white layers beneath. "If the candle cools it will be hard to work with."

"That won't be a problem." He wiped beads of perspiration from his forehead with the back of his hand.

"If it is, tell me, and I'll warm it—" But she could see he had already tuned her out. She should have had him do this to begin with. The candle was already looking better than pretty, with curlicues that surpassed her sample.

She turned to the pots of wax and started working on more red tapers.

"This is a nice workshop," he said from behind her. "I should have come in here before."

"Uncle Seth helped me fix it up. It was easier to work out here while *Mamm* perfected her recipes in the kitchen."

"Smells pretty *gut* too. Like . . ."

"Vanilla and cinnamon?"

"*Ya.*"

"Those are the most popular scents for Christmas." She forced the wicks out of the candles he'd ruined and folded the soft wax in her hand. "I make scented ones for the candle jars. They're already finished, thank goodness, or I'd be really behind." She dropped the ball of wax in the red wax can.

When he didn't say anything, she turned and checked his progress. Her eyes widened. The candle was beautiful, better than she could have ever made, even with years of practice. Nathaniel had put his own design on the candle. The base was a solid red, which would be shiny after she dipped it in the final setting wax. The strips of wax were curled over and under each other, with some rolled at the top to resemble tiny candy canes. The top of the candle was pure white, with small hearts carved in a wavy pattern a few inches from the rim.

"Oh, Nathaniel." She sat perched on the edge of his chair. "It's so *schee.*" She carefully touched one of the delicate candy canes. The wax was still warm, but hard enough that it didn't give under the light pressure of her finger.

"You think so?" He peered at the candle, turning his head to look at it from different angles. "I think the hearts are crooked."

"The hearts are stunning. Mrs. Potter will love this candle."

He looked at her, his chin nearly touching her shoulder. They were so close she could see the light shadow of dark-brown stubble on his face. "We make a pretty *gut* team, *ya*?" he said, smiling.

But she couldn't speak. All she could do was stare at him, taking in his golden eyes. Why had she never noticed they were the color of honey before? Or that his breath smelled sweet, like the peppermints he was fond of chewing when the weather turned cold? They reminded him of Christmas, he always said.

And why hadn't she ever noticed how badly she wanted to kiss him?

"Anne Marie—"

"Nathaniel—"

They both stopped speaking. She thought his mouth was moving closer to hers. Or maybe she was hoping it was. It didn't matter, because her heart was certain that in a few seconds, she would know for sure.

. . .

A moment ago, Nathaniel wanted to bite off his tongue. He shouldn't have told Anne Marie what a good team they made. Just like he shouldn't be sitting this close to her.

But when she sat down on his same chair, he couldn't bear to move. It didn't matter that there was only one chair in the room and she had nowhere else to sit. He liked it. He liked everything about her—the way her lips pursed, the rosy color appearing on her cheeks, her pale-blue eyes that were so clear and vulnerable, his pulse thrummed. His heart ached at the thought of her leaving. He knew letters and visits wouldn't be enough for him.

Things had changed between them. He could feel it, and he didn't want to resist. Unable to stop himself, he leaned forward, closer . . . closer . . .

"Knock, knock!" said a female voice.

His head jerked from Anne Marie's. He looked over her shoulder and swallowed. Ruth Troyer walked inside.

CHAPTER 9

"There you are!"

Anne Marie shot up from the chair and turned around, almost knocking over Nathaniel's perfect candle. "Ruth?" She struggled to catch her breath. "What are you doing here?"

"Trying to find you." She walked farther inside and pulled a piece of paper out of the pocket of her coat. "I know it's late notice, but *Grossmutter* decided she needed more candles to put in the windows for Christmas. I told her it might be better if she got them at the store, but she wouldn't think of it."

Anne Marie took the paper from Ruth, hoping her friend didn't see the flames of embarrassment rising in her cheeks. "She's always been a loyal customer."

"*Ya.*" But Ruth wasn't looking at Anne Marie. Her gaze was planted on Nathaniel, who was putting finishing touches on the carved candle, his hand as steady as ever, while Anne Marie's insides were quaking.

Maybe she'd imagined the whole thing. And the thought of kissing Nathaniel never should have entered her mind. But now she couldn't think about anything else.

Ruth leaned close to Anne Marie. "What's Nathaniel doing here?" she whispered.

"Helping me. I'm behind on my orders."

"Oh." She kept staring at Nathaniel, but he didn't seem to notice. "Did you tell him?"

"What?"

"About . . . you know." Ruth tilted her head in his direction.

"I think I'm done." Nathaniel put down the tool and leaned back.

"My goodness!" Ruth clasped her hands together and walked over to the table. "Nathaniel, I had no idea you were so talented. It's the most *perfekt* candle I've ever seen."

Anne Marie rolled her eyes. Then she realized she had said almost the same thing. But hearing it from Ruth irritated her.

Nathaniel looked at Ruth. "I'm glad it turned out all right."

"It's better than all right." She bent down, as if she was inspecting the candle with great concentration. She leaned over a bit too far and put her hand on Nathaniel's shoulder.

"Sorry. Lost *mei* balance." But she didn't remove her hand.

"It's fine." He glanced at her, and didn't move either.

Anne Marie crumpled the piece of paper in her hand.

"Is this candle for sale?" Ruth asked Nathaniel. "I'd like to buy it."

"*Nee.*" Anne Marie swooped up the candle and put it on her workbench. "It's already spoken for."

"Oh. Well, maybe I can order another one. As long as Nathaniel carves it."

He shrugged. "I don't know, I'm just helping Anne Marie out for a little while."

"Actually, I don't need any more help." She glared at him. He seemed to be enjoying Ruth's touch a little more than necessary. Just a few days ago she was encouraging him to ask Ruth out. Now the thought of them together made her sick.

But it was for the best, wasn't it? Hadn't she come to that conclusion herself last night?

"I don't know about you, but I'm hungry," Ruth said. "We should have some lunch." She looked at Anne Marie. "Don't you think so?"

Anne Marie didn't miss the pleading message in her friend's eyes. She couldn't be mad at Ruth, who didn't know about the turmoil going on inside of Anne Marie. "I'm not really hungry. But you and Nathaniel can get something to eat."

He finally moved from underneath Ruth's grasp. "That's okay, Anne Marie," Nathaniel said. "I can stay and help."

"Like I said, I don't need any help." She stared at him, crossing her arms.

"But I thought you were behind on your orders."

"I just got caught up."

Ruth moved in between them. "She said she wasn't hungry, Nathaniel. But I'm starving. Do you mind sharing lunch with me?"

• • •

Bewildered, Nathaniel looked at Ruth, her light-brown eyes practically begging him to say yes, and Anne Marie, whose pale-blue eyes seemed colder than chipped ice. What was wrong with her? She'd gone from being her usual happy self to being snappish. No, not just snappy. She was angry. Was she mad that he tried to kiss her? Or did he do something else wrong?

"Going to lunch with Ruth is a great idea," Anne Marie said, unfolding her arms and going to the door. When she opened it, a welcome blast of cool air swept through the small workshop. Sweat rolled down his back as Anne Marie's cold gaze landed on him. "You two *geh* have lunch."

His brows pulled in. Usually he could figure out what she was thinking. Anne Marie wasn't exactly a closed book. But she'd shut herself off from him, and he didn't like it.

"Come on, Nathaniel," Ruth said. "We'll *geh* to *mei haus*. I'll make you the most *appeldicht* roast beef sandwich you've ever had. Plus apple pie for dessert."

"You don't have to *geh* to so much trouble." He kept his gaze on Anne Marie. She looked away, then finally turned her back on him and started dipping candles, as if both he and Ruth were invisible.

Fine. If she wanted to play games, so be it. She could be so childish it drove him *ab im kopp*.

But she was also funny. Talented. Intelligent. Beautiful.

"Nathaniel?" Ruth was already halfway out the door.

He paused, then turned. "Coming." He walked out the door with Ruth, but his mind was still on Anne Marie.

• • •

"Ouch!" Anne Marie peeled off a small splash of melted wax from the back of her hand. She'd been careless since Nathaniel and Ruth left a short while ago. Her last batch of tapers looked worse than his. She put her hands against the edge of the counter and closed her eyes, praying for focus and patience.

The door opened, and for a second, her heart flipped over, thinking Nathaniel had returned. But it was only her brother. "What do you want, Jonah?"

He held up his hands. "What are you snapping at me for?"

"Sorry." She squeezed the bridge of her nose with her fingertips. "I shouldn't have done that."

"It's okay." Jonah came over to her workstation. "The candles look great."

"Liar." She picked up the warped tapers and held them in front of him.

"I didn't mean those." He pointed to Nathaniel's candle. "That's the best one you've done."

"It's not mine. It's Nathaniel's."

"Ah."

She looked at him. "Okay, Jonah. Why are you here? You never come in the workshop." He'd always complained it was too hot, smelly, and cramped.

"Just checking on you. We haven't had much time to talk about . . . you know."

She sat down. Jonah was rarely in a talking mood, and she could see he needed her undivided attention. "How do you feel about it?"

He shrugged. "I think I'm okay with it now."

"You sure?"

"*Ya. Mamm's* happy. That's what I want." He picked at the bumpy dots of hardened wax on her worktable. "How about you?"

She tossed the useless candles to the side, not in the mood to fix them. "I've already told *Mamm* I'm happy for her. The rest will work itself out."

"Ah."

"Would you stop that!" She faced him. "Jonah, I'm okay with *Mamm* getting married, I'm okay with moving to Ohio. Everything is absolutely fantastic. Couldn't be better."

"Now look who's lying."

She hunched her shoulders. When did her brother suddenly grow up? He was acting like an older brother, not a younger one. "Okay, maybe not fantastic. But it's well enough." She picked up a candle rack. "If you're done drilling me with questions, I have to get back to work."

"Your sour mood wouldn't have anything to do with Nathaniel leaving with Ruth Troyer?"

She kept her head down. "Why would I care if Nathaniel is with Ruth?"

"I don't know. Do you?"

This sibling chitchat was making her head pound. "Jonah, I'm the one who suggested he *geh* out with her. It was a coincidence that they were both here at the same time, and she invited him for lunch. End of story."

"Okay. As long as you're not upset or anything."

"I'm not! Now get out of here so I can finish these candles!"

Jonah backed away. Then he paused, as if wanting to say something.

Her patience was paper-thin. "What now?"

"*Nix.*" He shook his head and hurried out the door.

She put her head into her hands, frustrated. She'd been rude to her brother, she was upset with Ruth, and she resented Nathaniel. "*Ya*, everything is just perfect," she muttered.

She lifted her head and took in a deep breath. Her face heated, and not because of the hot wax in the pots on the camper stoves. How could she have been so foolish to think Nathaniel would want to kiss her? And why, after all these years of friendship, was the thought of him being with Ruth almost unbearable? So much had changed between them in such a short time. She'd never been so confused.

She stepped away from her workbench and closed her eyes. *Lord, help me.*

• • •

"I hope you like the pie." Ruth set a plate in front of Nathaniel, filled with the largest piece of pie he'd ever seen. She must have given him almost half of it. But after a huge lunch of an open roast beef sandwich smothered in gravy, pickled eggs, and cabbage slaw, he wasn't sure he could eat another bite. For sure, Ruth could cook.

She could also talk. And talk and talk and talk. Sitting in front of her, he could see her mouth moving but had no idea what she was saying. He'd tuned her out halfway through the meal. Apparently she'd never heard the old saying that silence was golden.

He and Anne Marie could spend hours together. Fishing, playing checkers, sitting on the grass at the edge of a pond—it didn't matter where they were. Neither of them ever felt the need to fill the silence between them.

He frowned. If Ruth hadn't walked in, he would have kissed Anne Marie. The thought of kissing his best friend should unnerve him. Instead, he was irritated he didn't get the chance.

But clearly she had a different idea. She couldn't wait to shove him out the door with Ruth.

"Is there something wrong with the pie?" Ruth asked.

He blinked, her face coming into focus. "*Nee*. Why?"

"You haven't tried it yet." She folded her hands on the table and smiled, her posture as straight as a fence post. "I picked the apples myself, from the Bakers' orchard. I know they're an *Englisch familye*, but they grow the best apples in the area. Do you like their apples?"

"I guess." He took a bite of the pie. The flaky crust dissolved in his mouth. Wow. He could probably choke this down, even with his full stomach.

"Are you going to the singing at the Keims' on Sunday? It's the last one before Christmas."

"*Nee*. I'll be at Anne Marie's."

Her bottom lip poked out slightly. "Why?"

"I always *geh* over there on Sundays."

"Don't you think it's time you stopped?"

He put down his fork and looked at her, dumbfounded.

She unclasped her hands. "Nathaniel, she's leaving."

"Which is why I'm going over there on Sunday." He ran his hand across the back of his neck. They wouldn't have too many Sundays left.

Ruth tapped her fingernail against the edge of her plate. "You're spending too much time with her. You always have."

He clenched his hand. "You're not one to judge how I spend *mei* time. Or who I spend it with."

"I don't mean it that way." She sighed softly and reached for his hand. He wanted to pull away, but she held onto it with a tight grip. "I care about you, Nathaniel. A lot." She smiled and squeezed his hand.

He leaned back. When Anne Marie had encouraged him to ask Ruth out, he'd briefly considered it. But so much had changed in a few short days.

"I know you and Anne Marie are *gut* friends," she continued, her voice sticky sweet, like the pie he couldn't finish. "But you have to be realistic. Your relationship with Anne Marie can't last forever. You can't spend your Sundays playing games, pretending you're still *kinner*. You're a *mann* now." She leaned forward and licked her bottom lip. "You need to be thinking about the future. Maybe one with me."

He squirmed, finally able to pull his hand away from hers. "Ruth—"

"If you're worried about Anne Marie, she told me she doesn't think about you that way."

"You don't know that." The words flew out of his mouth.

Ruth folded her hands in her lap, her smile tightening. "I see."

"See what?"

"That you have feelings for her." She shook her head, as if she felt sorry for him. "I can't say I'm surprised. You wouldn't be with her so much if you didn't."

Her superior tone irritated him. "You don't know what you're talking about."

She tilted her head. "It's okay. I've talked to Anne Marie about us." Ruth stood and walked around the table. She moved close to him, then leaned against the table edge. "She's already given us her blessing." She touched his shoulder, then bent over and whispered in his ear. "I can help you get over her, Nathaniel. What you feel for her will fade in time."

He looked up at Ruth but didn't move beneath her touch. He didn't appreciate the way she acted like she knew him. She was too pushy, and bolder than he was comfortable with. Yet he could see she was genuine.

And she was right. Anne Marie would always think of him as part of her childhood. Not part of her future.

Ruth reached out her hand. Nathaniel looked at it. Paused. Then hesitantly put his hand in hers.

CHAPTER 10

On Sunday evening, Anne Marie paced the living room. She kept peeking out the window looking for Nathaniel. An hour after his usual arrival time, she decided he wasn't coming.

She turned to the coffee table in the living room. She'd already set up the game. Life on the Farm, his favorite. She knelt down and started gathering up the pieces, trying to stem the despair welling up inside. She hadn't seen him since he'd left with Ruth a few days ago. Today they didn't have church, so she hadn't expected to see him until tonight. Hadn't he promised they'd spend as much time together as possible?

But that was before she'd pushed him and Ruth together. Before she decided to let him go. Before she realized her feelings for him ran deeper than friendship.

Still, she had hoped he would come. Even though she pushed him away, tried to get him out of her mind and heart, she had wanted to see him tonight.

"Why are you putting up the game?" Her mother walked into the living room, holding several white taper candles in plain brass candleholders. She went to the window and placed one on the sill. "Where's Nathaniel?"

"He's not coming."

"Oh?" She turned around. "Did something happen?"

"I guess he couldn't make it tonight."

"That's strange. He never misses game night." She crossed over to the other window in the living room and put a candle in it. Tomorrow she would tie back the curtains, and in the evening, she and Anne Marie would light the candles for the few nights leading up to Christmas.

"I'm going to Miriam's tomorrow to talk about wedding preparations." Her mother smiled, her eyes sparkling. "Would you like to join us?"

Anne Marie fiddled with the lid of the board game. She had promised to be supportive. And she wanted to be. But she couldn't take discussing wedding plans, especially right now. "I'll let you know."

"Oh. Okay." Her mother's smile faded a bit.

Anne Marie stood, chastising herself for being selfish. "I'm sorry. Of course I'll *geh*."

"Miriam and I can take care of it."

"I know, but I want to help. I wasn't thinking straight when I answered the first time."

Her mother touched her arm. "*Danki,* Anne Marie. I'm glad you want to be a part of this." She started to leave the room.

"*Mamm?*"

She turned around. "*Ya?*"

"How did you know you were in love with Thomas?" The question wrested free from her thoughts, like a bird escaping its cage. She hadn't meant to voice the words or to pry. But suddenly she really wanted an answer.

Her mother sat down on the couch. "I'm not sure how it happened. I can't really pinpoint a moment when I realized I loved him."

Anne Marie sat on the floor at her mother's feet. She wrapped her arms around her knees, the skirt of her dress touching the tops of her stocking-covered feet. "What if you change your mind?"

"What do you mean?"

"When he gets here. What if you regret saying you'll marry him?"

Mamm crossed her legs at the ankles. "Anne Marie, even though this is sudden to you, it's not to me and Thomas. We've prayed about this. I've never been more sure about anything in my life . . . except when I married your *daed*." She touched her knees and leaned forward. "Remember, Thomas and I were friends when we were younger. We rekindled that friendship when we started writing each other. One thing I've learned is that friends are life's treasures. But sometimes when you least expect it, a friendship blossoms into love." Her mother stood. "I hope that eases your mind."

Anne Marie nodded. It did about *Mamm* and Thomas, but confused her further about Nathaniel.

"I still have a couple of cookbooks to finish binding. Nothing like doing things at the last minute."

Popping up to her feet, Anne Marie said, "I'll help you."

"I can do them." She looked at the game on the table. "You shouldn't put that on the shelf just yet. Nathaniel is sure to come."

She nodded, but didn't agree.

After her mother left, Anne Marie sat down on the

couch and stared at the game, willing Nathaniel to
come as the minutes ticked away. Half an hour later
she gave up and put the board game away.

Her mother's friendship with Thomas started a
new beginning, but it appeared that Anne Marie and
Nathaniel's friendship was coming to an end.

. . .

Nathaniel stood outside Anne Marie's house on the
edge of the yard by the road. Instead of driving, he
had walked, hoping the cold air and exercise would
straighten his thoughts. They didn't, and the closer he
got, the more confused and nervous he became. When
he arrived, he couldn't bring himself to go inside.

For the first time in his life, he had no idea what to
say to Anne Marie. Should he tell her about his changing feelings toward her? Or follow Ruth's advice and
end their friendship? The thought pained him. Still, he
couldn't deny they both needed to be free of each other
in order to move on.

The problem was, he wasn't sure he wanted to move on.

The light in the window disappeared. Nathaniel
exhaled, his breath hanging in cloudy puffs in front of
him. A full moon filled the clear sky. He pushed his hat
lower on his head, shoved his hands in the pockets of
his coat, and headed for home.

"Nathaniel."

He turned at the sound of Jonah's voice. The kid was
walking toward him from the barn. He didn't stop until
he was a few feet away, close enough that Nathaniel

could see the spark of anger in his eyes. "What are you doing?" Jonah asked.

"Leaving." He hated the dejection in his voice. "Anne Marie's gone to bed already."

"Because you didn't show up for your game." Jonah put his hands on his hips. He wasn't wearing a coat, and his stance emphasized his broad shoulders. "I don't know what's going on with you two," Jonah said. "Normally I stay out of things. But when *mei schwester* is upset, then it becomes *mei* business."

Nathaniel faced him. "She's upset?"

"Of course she is. You left with Ruth Troyer the other day. Then you don't show up for your weekly game night that's been going on forever." He frowned. "Except you did, but you didn't tell her you were here. I don't get that at all."

"It's complicated."

"I don't care." He stepped forward and looked Nathaniel in the eye, the straight, serious line of his brow illuminated by the silvery moonlight. "If you have something to say to Anne Marie, you need to say it. If not, stop wasting her time." Jonah turned and started to walk away. "Don't be a coward, Nathaniel. You're better than that."

His ego stinging, Nathaniel opened his mouth to rebuke him. He didn't have to take advice from Anne Marie's little brother. Or from Ruth Troyer, for that matter. He could make his own decisions. And it was time he did just that.

CHAPTER 11

"Anne Marie, did you polish the furniture in the living room?"

Anne Marie stilled the broom she was holding and rolled her eyes at the sound of her mother's frantic voice from the other end of the house. She'd been like this for the past two days, fluttering around, making sure everything was ideal for Thomas's first supper with them tonight. "*Ya, Mamm.* I polished it."

"All of it?"

"*Ya.*" She went back to sweeping the kitchen as her mother rushed in. Anne Marie looked up and saw the gleam in her eyes, the rosy tint of her cheeks. She put her hand on her mother's arm. "Everything is fine, *Mamm.* Don't worry."

"I'm not worried." *Mamm* hurried to the stove, wiping her hands on her clean apron. She opened the oven, releasing the scent of garlic and peppercorns in the air. "Almost done," she said, closing the door.

"*Gut.*" Christopher looked out the kitchen window. "Because he's coming up the driveway."

"He's what?" Her mother turned to Anne Marie. "But supper's not ready, the table isn't set—"

"Christopher can set the table," Anne Marie said.

His jaw slacked. "What? That's a *frau's* job."

Anne Marie shot him a glare before turning back to her mother. "*Geh* ahead and let Thomas in. Once you're settled in the living room, I'll bring you both a glass of tea."

"Okay." Her mother nodded, but seemed anything but okay. Anne Marie smiled. She wasn't used to seeing her *mamm* this flustered. She turned her mother by the shoulders and shooed her out of the kitchen.

"Jonah doesn't have to set the table," Christopher grumbled.

"I'm sure he's helping Thomas with his horse." Anne Marie tasted the mashed potatoes, which were warming on top of the stove. Scrumptious, as usual. She hoped Thomas knew how lucky he was to be marrying a good cook. If he didn't know, he was about to find out.

A plate landed on the table with a clatter. Anne Marie left the stove and took the rest of the dishes from her brother. "Never mind, I'll do it."

Christopher grinned and retreated from the kitchen.

She tried to focus on setting a pretty table, not on the nerve-wracking fact that her mother was in the living room with her future stepfather. As she placed the last plate on the table, she guided her mind elsewhere. It immediately went to Nathaniel, as it had done since Sunday, despite trying to keep herself busy making her candles.

She gripped the edge of the table at the image of Nathaniel and Ruth. Jealousy twisted inside her like an ugly weed winding around her heart. She'd never had a reason to be jealous, and she didn't like the feeling. For the first time she was looking forward to the move. She couldn't bear the thought of seeing Nathaniel and Ruth together.

She finished setting the table, calming her frayed nerves with a silent prayer. She set the candle Nathaniel had carved in the middle of the table. Her customer had canceled her order, and Anne Marie decided to keep the beautiful wax creation. Just then her mother walked in the kitchen.

"That's lovely." She put her hand on Anne Marie's shoulder, her face glowing. "Your skills have improved."

"*Danki*." She didn't bother to explain the truth. It didn't matter anymore. "Where is Thomas?"

"Talking to Jonah outside. That *bu* is giving him a thorough questioning."

"I'm not surprised." She felt a little sorry for Thomas.

The distant thud of heels against wood sounded right outside the kitchen. "They're coming. Are you sure everything is okay, Anne Marie?"

She nodded and gave her mother a quick hug. "It is. I promise."

Jonah and Christopher walked in the kitchen first, followed by a stocky man with a mop of ginger-red hair threaded with gray. His blue eyes were wide set, and he held onto his hat, gripping it by the brim as if it were his lifeline. He looked nothing like her father, who had been taller, thinner, and darker. But he was handsome in his own way.

She glanced at her mother, who couldn't keep her eyes off him. They both seemed frozen in their own moment.

Watching them, Anne Marie realized how deeply her mother loved him, and that he truly loved her.

She relaxed and gave Thomas a genuine smile, beckoning him into the kitchen. "I hope you're hungry," she said, pulling out the chair at the head of the table. "*Mamm* made a feast."

· · ·

Anne Marie put away the last clean pot, then drained the dirty dishwater from the sink. Her mother and Thomas had disappeared into the living room after eating. Jonah and Christopher went to the barn, leaving her to clean the kitchen alone.

She wiped down the counter, then turned to the table. The candle was still in the center, unlit. She walked to it, touching one of the delicate white and red curls. The empty kitchen instantly felt too small. She grabbed her coat off the peg by the back door and went outside.

The light of a lantern shone from the barn, where her brothers were probably taking care of the animals for the night. She breathed in the cold air, crossing her arms over her chest. It still hadn't snowed, unusual for this time of year.

"You're not too cold out here?"

She turned to see Thomas approach. He had his hat on but wasn't wearing his coat. "Sure you're not?" she asked as he arrived at her side.

"I'm a human heater." He smiled. She could see his slightly crooked teeth gleaming in the darkness. "That's what my late wife told me." He paused. "She would have liked you."

Anne Marie tilted her head and looked at him. *"Ya?"*

"She appreciated hardworking people. Lydia told me about your candlemaking business. How successful it is. You don't have success without hard work."

A knot formed in her throat. It felt good to have someone acknowledge her efforts.

"I know the move will be tough, Anne Marie. I wish it could be different."

"It's as God wills." She turned to him, a sense of peace slipping over her. "I never thought I'd leave Paradise. But that seems to be what God wants of me. Of our family."

Thomas's shoulders relaxed. "There's a busy tourist business in Holmes County," he said, his deep voice sounding less tentative. "You won't have any problem finding customers for your candles."

"That's *gut*." She turned to him and gave him her warmest smile. "We should *geh* back inside. I'm sure *Mamm* is waiting for you."

He faced her and swallowed. "Your *Mamm* said you were something special. She was right."

"She was right about you too."

As they walked back inside, Anne Marie realized everything would be okay. While she was still unsure about Nathaniel and the part he would play in her life in the future, she was sure about one thing. Thomas Nissley was a *gut* man who made her mother happy. She couldn't ask for more.

CHAPTER 12

While Christmas Day was a time of contemplation and quiet celebration of Christ's birth, the day after Christmas was anything but.

The Smucker house was filled to bursting with people. Jonah and Christopher were playing Dutch Blitz against Seth and Thomas, who in a few short days had fit seamlessly into the family. *Mamm* was holding a sleeping Leah while *Aenti* Miriam played blocks with Junior on the floor. Anne Marie watched her mom and Thomas sneaking sweet glances at each other when they thought no one was looking.

Anne Marie stood to the side, breathing in the scent of fresh popped corn, buttered and seasoned to mouthwatering perfection. Flames flickered on several of her vanilla and cinnamon candles, their sweetly spiced aroma mixing with the mugs of warm apple cider. She heard the laughter, saw the smiles. And wished she could share in their happiness, instead of being on the sidelines.

She hadn't forgotten that Nathaniel had a standing invitation for Second Christmas, but apparently he had. He was probably with Ruth and her family today. Or maybe with his own.

She went in the kitchen to fix herself a cup of hot cocoa. Her mind wandered back in time, to all the memories she held close over the years. She thought about when she and Nathaniel were eight and they'd lie in the grass, counting the stars, only to end up covered in mosquito bites. When she was twelve and he and her brothers had hidden in the loft of the barn and dumped a bucket of cold water on her head when she walked in. But she had gotten him back when she stuck a frog in his coat pocket before he went home.

She peered out the kitchen window. Large, fluffy flakes of snow floated down from the dark sky. A white Christmas after all. She took her hot chocolate and stepped out on the back porch. Stuck her tongue out and caught a snowflake. Another memory with Nathaniel. She'd never realized until now that most of her sweetest memories included him.

She didn't know how long she stood outside, sipping lukewarm hot chocolate, wrapped in a cloak of the past, until she noticed her own shivering and the snow that had blanketed the ground.

When she went back into the kitchen, her aunt was putting two mugs in the sink. She looked up at Anne Marie. "I wondered where you went off to." She grimaced. "Have you been outside long? You must be freezing."

Anne Marie set the half-full mug in the sink. "I just needed some fresh air."

"I'm pleased with how you're handling this, Anne Marie. I know you were troubled at first, but I'm glad you've come to terms with everything."

Not everything. She exhaled. "I'm sorry for the way I

acted when I first found out. I should have been more supportive."

"You don't need to apologize. Everyone understands, especially *yer mamm*." Aunt Miriam walked toward the mudroom off the kitchen. "Seth and I are heading home before the snow gets too deep." She disappeared for a moment and returned with coats, hats, and her black bonnet. "Merry Christmas, Anne Marie."

She hugged her aunt. "Merry Christmas."

Thomas left shortly afterward, also not wanting to get stuck in the snow. Her brothers were already upstairs and her *mamm* had started tidying up the living room. "I'll get that," Anne Marie said.

"You sure?" Although her mother looked happy, she also seemed tired.

"I'm sure. Get some rest. *Gut nacht, Mamm.*"

Moments later Anne Marie put the card game in the drawer of the side table. She cleaned out the popcorn bowl and the corn popper and put them away. Folded the green-and-red quilt Aunt Miriam had given them for Christmas ten years earlier and laid it over the back of the couch. And tried not to cry.

She looked around the living room. The wedding was planned for two weeks from today, and a couple of days later she would be on her way to Ohio. *God, help me. One minute I think I'm okay with moving, and the next I'm not. I think I'm okay with Nathaniel not being in my life, and then I'm not. I can't get through this without Your help, Lord.*

She blew out the candles in the windows, then walked to Nathaniel's candle, the flame dancing and illuminating his exquisite carving. Her mother had wanted to light it, still not knowing Anne Marie hadn't carved it. She watched red wax drip down the side, altering the curves and curlicues, changing it forever. The candle, like her life and her relationship with Nathaniel, would never be the same.

She leaned over to blow it out when she heard a knock at the back door. Who would be coming over this late and with heavy snow falling? When she answered the door, she froze. "Nathaniel?"

"I . . ." Snow covered his black hat, the shoulders of his coat. The coat she'd slept with for several nights. She leaned against the doorjamb, weary of being confused, upset, hurt. She was tired of it all.

"It's late, Nathaniel. Christmas is over." She started to close the door when he stopped her.

"Don't." He locked his gaze on hers. "Don't send me away . . . even though I deserve it."

. . .

Nathaniel's knees buckled at the pain in Anne Marie's eyes. Pain he'd caused. He shouldn't have stayed away so long. He shouldn't have waited until now to see her. To let her know how he felt.

Before she could push him away, he walked inside. He set down the paper bag he was carrying and put his arms around her. He heard her gasp as he pressed her against him, burying his face in her neck.

Yes, he should have done this a long time ago.

When she relaxed against him, he closed his eyes.

When he heard her sob, he looked at her. "I'm sorry," he whispered.

She pulled away and wiped the tears from her face. "We need to talk."

He nodded as she turned on the gas lamp near the window. He followed her to the couch and sat down. She rubbed her hand over her eyes one more time before looking away.

He'd practiced the words all the way over here, hurrying his horse through the newly fallen snow that had turned to slush on the roads. But now that he was here, the words wouldn't come. He couldn't tell her how he'd spent the past few days in prayer, had talked to his father, and had told Ruth that they were over before they'd even started. He didn't doubt his decision. But he did doubt his ability to convince Anne Marie.

"I'm glad you're here," she finally said. "I have something to tell you." She took a deep breath. "Nathaniel, it's time we both moved on."

His breath hitched. "What?"

"I know we talked about writing letters and visiting, but that won't last."

"Anne Marie—"

"And I'm glad you and Ruth found each other." Tears pooled in her eyes again. "You'll both be very happy together."

He couldn't stand to listen to this anymore.

"Maybe I can come for the wedd—"

He took her face in his hands and kissed her.

. . .

Anne Marie couldn't stop Nathaniel from kissing her, and she didn't want to. The kiss was sweet and gentle and he parted from her too fast. When he drew away, she fought for words. "What about Ruth?" she asked when she was able to catch her breath.

He shook his head. "There's nothing between me and Ruth." He took her hand.

Her palm tingled in his. Then she came to her senses. "Wait a minute." She pulled out of his grasp. "You stood me up on Sunday."

He rubbed his right temple. "About that—"

"And then you're late tonight." She crossed her arms over her white apron. "Now you're kissing me. What's going on, Nathaniel?"

"I'm sorry about last Sunday and about being late tonight. But I needed time."

"Away from me?"

He cupped her chin in his hand. "I had to sort things out. Most important, I had to pray about us. I've always cared about you, Anne Marie. You're *mei* best friend. I didn't want to do anything to ruin that. But I knew things couldn't stay the same between us."

"Because I'm moving." She looked away.

He tilted her face toward him. "*Nee.* Because I love you."

She stilled, letting his words wash over her in a warm wave. "You do?"

He chuckled and let his hand drop to his side. "That shouldn't be a surprise. Everyone else has known. Even before I did. And I think from the way you kissed me back, you do too."

She couldn't deny it. "So? We love each other." It felt

strange and right at the same time to say the words out loud. "There's not much we can do about it now."

"We could get married."

Her eyes widened. "Are you serious?"

"Very. I don't want you to leave. I don't want to be separated from you. I know I said letters and visits would be enough." He drew her to him. She laid her cheek against his chest, feeling him rest his chin on top of her head. "But we both know it won't."

He was right. Being in his arms, feeling his heart beating in time with hers . . . how could she be apart from him? "*Ya.*"

"Does that mean . . . ?"

She looked up at him. "It means I'll marry you."

He pulled her to him and held her. A moment later, he sat back. He grinned, his expression holding a mixture of happiness and relief. He stood, went to the door, and picked up the brown paper bag. He opened it and pulled out the antique mantel clock she'd admired in his workshop. "Merry Christmas."

She took it from him, touching the polished silver decorations, every trace of tarnish removed. The smooth blue box that encased the simple clock looked fresh, but still showed its age. "It's beautiful."

He sat down next to her. "I'm glad you like it."

She looked at him. "And all I did was make a plate of your favorite brownies."

"Can't wait to eat them." He grinned.

She looked at the clock again. "I can't believe you're giving this to me. Doesn't your *daed* want to sell it in the shop?"

"He gave it to me, to give to someone special." He took the clock from her and turned it around. A small brass plate was attached to the back. She read the engraved words: *Out of friendship grew love. Nathaniel and Anne Marie.*

Tears came to her eyes. Goodness, she'd never been this weepy in her life. But they were tears of joy. "You were that sure I would say *ya*?"

"I was pretty sure." He rubbed his thumb over her knuckle. "Okay, I was praying. Really hard."

She leaned over and kissed his cheek.

"It's about time."

Anne Marie pulled away from Nathaniel and found Jonah standing on the steps. "How long have you been there?" she asked, cutting her eyes at him.

He waved her off and continued down the stairs. "Don't mind me, I'm just getting a brownie."

"Those are Nathaniel's."

"Okay, some pie, then." He headed toward the kitchen. "So when's the wedding?" he asked over his shoulder.

Her mouth dropped open. "How did you know?"

He gave her a wily grin. "Like I said, it's about time."

CHAPTER 13

I wish I wasn't so nervous."

Anne Marie smiled at her mother. She straightened the shoulders of *Mamm's* wedding dress, the dark-blue fabric complementing her deep brown eyes. "You look *schee*, *Mamm*. And happy."

"So do you." She hooked her arm through Anne Marie's. They turned and looked in the mirror above the dresser. "Are we ready for this?"

Anne Marie studied the two of them in the mirror. In a few minutes their lives would be altered forever. Several weeks ago she'd fought against change. Wondered about God's plan. And along the way, fell in love with her best friend. She placed her hand over her mother's. "*Ya*. We're ready."

They walked out of *Mamm's* bedroom and into the living room. Anne Marie instantly locked eyes with Nathaniel. He grinned, and the butterflies dancing in her stomach calmed. Her mother moved to stand next to Thomas. Anne Marie took her place next to Nathaniel. Between them, the bishop started the double wedding ceremony.

As he spoke, Anne Marie glanced around a room filled with family and close friends. Her grandparents, her aunt Miriam and uncle Seth, her brothers. Then she saw Nathaniel's mother wipe a tear. She'd been the most overjoyed of all when she heard the news. Like Jonah, she had simply said, "It's about time."

She glanced at her mother and Thomas. Soon enough she'd have to say good-bye to them and her brothers. While they started a new life in Ohio, she would start her new life as Mrs. Nathaniel Mast. The thought added a touch of bittersweetness to her heart.

But she didn't have to think about good-byes right now. Today was her wedding day, and she was rejoicing over the greatest gift she'd ever received—friendship that turned into love.

Acknowledgments

Beth Wiseman

Thank you to my friends and family who continue to support me on this incredible journey. With each new book, I am learning to balance my time a little better, and your patience with my tight deadlines is much appreciated. My friendships and personal relationships are important to me, and I will always find the time to nourish them.

Patrick, thank you for providing me with an environment that affords me this grand opportunity to live my dreams—dreams of writing full-time and of living the rest of my life with you, my forever love.

Eric and Cory, dreams do come true. Work hard, strive to be the best you can be, and maintain a relationship with God. Talk to Him as you would a dear friend. He listens. He blessed me with the two of you.

To Natalie Hanemann—I'm so blessed to have you in my life, as both editor and friend. You push me to hit my writing potential, and I always end up with a better book after your input. Equally important is the friendship we share. God puts people in our lives for a reason, and I feel sure He was smiling when He introduced the two of us. Thank you for everything.

My entire fiction family at Thomas Nelson is awesome. I am so honored to be a part of this group. I thank God for each and every one of you.

Thank you to LB Norton for your editorial assistance. It was a pleasure to work with you.

A sincere thanks to my dear friend Barbie Beiler. As always, your Amish and Mennonite background helps me to keep the books authentic. You always make time amid your busy schedule to read the manuscripts prior to publication, and I am so grateful to you. You are a blessing in my life, my friend.

To Anna B. King, thank you so much for the time you spent on the phone with me, making sure that I understood the details of Christmas as celebrated in an Old Order Amish community. By the time this book goes to print, I will have met you in person in Pennsylvania, and I am really looking forward to that—to meeting Barbie's mom!

Thank you to my agent, Mary Sue Seymour. You are a special person, and I value our professional relationship as well as our friendship. Thank you for everything.

Special thanks to those "first responders" who read behind me as I write—Reneé Bissmeyer, Rene Simpson, and my wonderful mother, Pat Isley. You all keep me on my toes and push me forward to completion. Rene, thank you for reading behind me on this particular novella and for all your input.

To my friends and "sistas" who constantly promote the books, thank you so much. Just to name a few—Laurie, Dawn, Melody, Valarie, Pat, Carol, Amy, Bethany, and Gayle. You gals are great!

And always, my most heartfelt thanks goes to God for providing me with this wonderful opportunity to spread His Word through inspirational stories about faith, hope, and love.

RUTH REID

I praise God for His providence! God has blessed me with a wonderful supportive family. Dan, Lexie, Danny, and Sarah, I love you all so very much. God has also blessed me with many prayer warriors who lift me up in prayer and with trustful friends who help critique my books. I especially appreciate Kathy Droste, who bravely reads and red-inks my first drafts. I'll forever be thankful for my outstanding editorial team: Becky Philpott, Natalie Hanemann, and line editor, Penny Stokes.

May God bless the reader in miraculous ways!

KATHLEEN FULLER

Thank you to my family—my husband James, my children Mathew, Sydney, and Zoie, and my parents Jim and Eleanora Daly. I love you all so much!

DISCUSSION QUESTIONS

A CHOICE TO FORGIVE

1. Throughout the book, Lydia struggles with forgiveness. First she must find it in her heart to forgive Daniel, and later she must forgive her deceased husband. Have you ever found yourself in a situation where you needed to forgive someone who has passed on? Did forgiveness give you a sense of peace or resolve, even though you were not able to voice your feelings directly to that person?

2. Anna Marie is experiencing her running-around period (*rumschpringe*). Is her behavior different from that of *Englisch* teenagers at this age? If so, how? Is Lydia more trusting about her daughter's actions than *Englisch* parents might be, or is this simply reflective of a generational shift across both cultures? For example, Lydia states that her parents would have been much stricter with her if they'd caught her sneaking out of the house. Are you less strict with your children than your parents were with you?

3. The Amish believe that all things that happen are of God's will. Is Lydia being true to her faith by questioning the way things happened, harboring ill will, and struggling to forgive—or is she just

human? Have you ever questioned God's will in a situation where a different outcome would have affected far more people than just you?

4. Daniel and Lydia were each other's first loves, yet they went on to live separate lives. Do you know anyone who has reunited with his or her first love? Did it work out?

ALWAYS HIS PROVIDENCE

1. Rosa prays about her finances but continues to fret about what might happen. How is this taking it out of God's hands? Has there been a time when you've continued to stress over a situation you've already prayed about?

2. How did the neighbor's attitude about Rosa's chickens influence her actions? Have you ever thought God might be waiting for your heart to change over a matter so that He can pour out His blessing on you?

3. Even though Rosa had given throughout the years to her district's widows' fund, she didn't want to ask for help when she was in a time of need. Why do you think her pride stood in her way?

A GIFT FOR ANN MARIE

1. Anne Marie knew she shouldn't have read her mother's letters. What would you have done in the same situation?

2. Do you think Nathaniel was fair to Ruth? Why or why not?

3. Anne Marie questioned God's plan when she found out she was moving. Have you ever wondered why God has led you down a certain path, especially if it caused disappointment or discomfort? How did you deal with it?

4. Do you think Anne Marie and Nathaniel would have fallen in love without the threat of her moving away?

ABOUT THE AUTHORS

BETH WISEMAN

BETH WISEMAN is the award-winning and bestselling author of the Daughters of the Promise, Land of Canaan, and Amish Secrets series, as well as novellas that have been included in many bestselling collections such as *An Amish Year* and *An Amish Garden*.

RUTH REID

RUTH REID is a CBA and ECPA bestselling author of the Heaven on Earth, the Amish Wonders, and the Amish Mercies series. She's a full-time pharmacist who lives in Florida with her husband and three children. When attending Ferris State University School of Pharmacy in Big Rapids, Michigan, she lived on the outskirts of an Amish community and had several occasions to visit the Amish farms. Her interest grew into love as she saw the beauty in living a simple life.

KATHLEEN FULLER

KATHLEEN FULLER is the author of several bestselling novels, including the Hearts of Middlefield novels, the Middlefield Family novels, the Amish of Birch Creek series, and the Amish Letters series as well as a middle-grade Amish series, the Mysteries of Middlefield.